David G. Hogarth

Philip and Alexander of Macedon

two essays in biography

David G. Hogarth

Philip and Alexander of Macedon
two essays in biography

ISBN/EAN: 9783337235345

Printed in Europe, USA, Canada, Australia, Japan

Cover: Foto ©Raphael Reischuk / pixelio.de

More available books at **www.hansebooks.com**

PHILIP AND ALEXANDER

OF MACEDON

TWO ESSAYS IN BIOGRAPHY

BY

DAVID G. HOGARTH

M.A., FELLOW OF MAGDALEN COLLEGE, OXFORD, F.S.A., F.R.G.S.

WITH MAP AND ILLUSTRATIONS

NEW YORK
CHARLES SCRIBNER'S SONS
1897

University Press
JOHN WILSON AND SON, CAMBRIDGE, U.S.A.

Clarissimo et Carissimo

Collegio

Beatae Mariae Magdalenae

Apud Oxonienses

PREFACE.

THE heroes of these essays need no introduction, and I have no excuse for making them my theme if this book supplies none. I treat the two Makers of Macedon, not in proportion to their respective bulk in history, but to the number of books written already about them. Philip, so far as I know, supplies the central figure to no extant biography; Alexander has inspired a whole literature.

My debts to previous students are obvious enough, even when not indicated in footnotes. I believe I have left very few works bearing on the subject unread, and my unconscious obligations must be many. I thank the authorities of the Departments of Coins and Medals and of Classical Antiquities at the British Museum, and also of the *Cabinet des Médailles* at Paris, for material supplied for my illustrations. To those who have criticised my book while in the press — Mr. R. W. Macan, Reader in Ancient History in the University of Oxford, and

Mr. C. H. Turner, Fellow of Magdalen — I can offer, by a mere expression of thanks in a Preface, no return in the least commensurate with the acute and learned labour which they have bestowed. They have emended many things; and if still many shortcomings remain, I can plead only the interruptions which are inseparable from the life of an exploring scholar.

D. G. H.

London,
December 14, 1896.

TABLE OF CONTENTS.

LIST OF ILLUSTRATIONS.

PHILIP

T   L/ Thi—Cabinet de France

PHILIP

THE Man of an Age is judged least justly by those who have lived in the Age; for historical vision can adjust its focus to the nearest objects no better than the natural eye. Posterity, therefore, while taking contemporary evidence for fact, must reserve the verdict to itself, and most jealously in an epoch of great change. While an old order is passing into a new, the destruction of the one obscures the construction of the other; and those who watch the great man to his grave seldom attain to more than a dim suspicion that he has been neither wholly dreamer nor wholly devil. Thus, although Theopompus condemned Philip of Macedon with utter condemnation, none the less his chronicle of the king's deeds, so far as preserved, makes it clear that, had we it all, we should say of the hostile historian, as has been said even of Demosthenes, " personne mieux n'a fait ressortir les grandes qualités du fondateur de la puissance Macédonienne." [1]

[1] Weil: introduction to his *Plaidoyers de Démosthène*, p. 18.

Every cloud that can gather about a great man has darkened the fame of Philip. No work of a contemporary historian has come down to us except in fragments; and until some Egyptian grave gives up the *Philippica* of Theopompus, or the *Macedonica* of Anaximenes, we must be content to glean the facts of Philip's life from late epitomes of late historians, from scanty narratives of universal chroniclers, and from gossips and retailers of anecdote; while for first-hand evidence we have only the partial utterances of the Athenian orators, his enemies or his hirelings. The eyes of posterity, both in ancient and modern times, have been dazzled by Alexander, and hardly have remarked the great figure which stands behind him; and enthusiasm for Hellas in a cultivated modern age has begotten bitter hatred for the name which is associated with the fall of Greek autonomy. Grote, for example, insensible to the fact that he himself has described with masterly skill the process of inevitable decay, at the end, not the beginning, of which stands Macedonian supremacy, seconds the champions of a shadow of liberty as though they were fighting still for a Periclean Athens. Even Thirlwall, most judicious historian of the last age of free Greece, feels constrained to deny personal merit to Philip, "great, not for what he was, but for what it was given him to do!" What is this distinction between a man and his acts? Philip is the great individual, who stands in the gap between two stages of human progress and is himself the link. He recognized entirely neither what was passing away

nor what was coming to pass, but he was not therefore
more a blind tool of Heaven than all human agents of
destruction and construction have been and must be.
Few men have seen so surely as he the faults of a
dying order, and set themselves so consciously to
create a new. The defects of the city-state, its
premature senility, resultant on too intense political
life, its incapacity for growth and combination, and
its weakness in the face of wider unions — these
things Philip discerned, and history warrants us in
crediting him with a reasoned conviction that the
city was to pass away before the nation ; that division
of labour and mutual assistance must take the place of
the direct fulfilment of all functions by all ; and that
spasmodic individual effort would be superseded by
permanent organization. Reading the lesson of his
times, and marking the proved inferiority of citizen
militia to standing forces, and of the capricious rule
of the many to an imperial system under a single
head, he evolved the first European Power in the
modern sense of the word — an armed nation with a
common national ideal. This, his own conception,
he understood clearly and pursued consistently
through twenty-three years. Surely such a man
may be called great for what he was.

PHILIP was born in the year 382 before our era.
The baby's prospect in life was not brilliant. He was
third son of Amyntas of Macedonia, a petty king
of no account in the world as it was then, who had
been chased once to the last hold in his kingdom
and compelled to see a rival sit on his throne;
who had been restored by foreign swords, and was
still in direst danger from barbarians on the north
and Greeks on the south, but most of all from his
own subjects. To understand both the position of
this man's son, and his conduct when, twenty-three
years later, he succeeded to a throne whose occupants
hardly ever had died in their beds, it is necessary
that we examine briefly the conditions under which
Macedonian monarchy existed.

The origin of the peoples who in the dawn of
history inhabited the part of south-eastern Europe
since called Macedonia,[1] is a question singularly
obscure and perhaps insoluble. Fortunately the
point really important for later history is neither
insoluble nor obscure, namely, the belief held and

---

[1] I use the name in its ordinary, not its Roman, sense, to
include only the country between the mouth of the Nestus,
Olympus, the Cambunian range, and the vague northern frontier
of Paeonia.

acted upon in ancient times. Tradition asserted that the population of "Macedonia" had neither one source nor one history; for one element in it was (as Hellenes said) "barbarian," another Hellene. The first element it pleased antiquarians to call "Pelasgic,"[1] but that name, meaning, in the first instance, probably no more than "the old folk," had come to be used of any early people of doubtful origin who had lived where in later times Hellenes were found. It is certain now that the element in question was largely composed of that race, to which the Bryges and many other European tribes pertained, together with their myths[2] of Gordius and Midas, whose final home is Phrygia. Its progress across Europe and its overflow into Asia have been traced by ethnologists, and the wanderings of its groups at various epochs account perhaps for those traces of "Thracian" and "Carian" occupation in Hellas and the isles which have puzzled antiquarians in all ages.[3] This race was Aryan, but in the eyes of the Hellenes "barbarian."

Tradition held the other element to be Hellenic, and no one in the fourth century seriously questioned its belief.[4] We meet with it in legends of the

[1] *Vide e. g.* Justin, vii. 1.

[2] We have the early authority of Herodotus for these myths (viii. 138) ; cf. Justin, vii. 1, etc.

[3] Strabo (p. 445) quotes Aristotle for "Thracians" in Euboea and Phocis. The "Carian question" is well known. The best views on the whole matter are Professor W. M. Ramsay's, in "A Study of Phrygian Art" (*Journ. Hell. Studies*, vols. ix. and x.).

[4] The taunts of a hostile orator levelled against Philip are no evidence at all of popular incredulity on the point (Demosth., *Phil.* i. 10; *Olynth.* iii. 24; *F. L.* 327, etc.). The fact that Philip

migrations of "Macedonian" peoples out of Hellas, such as Bottiaeans from Crete,[1] or Athens, and Dorians from Histiaeotis of Thessaly,[2] or Argos. The evidence that the latter city was believed to be the earliest home of the Macedonian kings and their immediate followers (for kings do not establish them- selves on thrones without strong battalions behind them) is overwhelming;[3] on the strength of that belief the Macedonian kings obtained admission to the common festivals of Hellas, and consistently acted in the government of their realm.

To the second element it was believed that the dominant race, the Macedonians properly so-called, belonged. They were (in Greek opinion) an immigrant people from the south, whose leader "conquered land for his subjects and became king;"[4] they settled in the fertile plains about the mouths and lower

ruled over many barbarians would give those taunts quite point enough for the occasion. Herodotus (v. 22) tells us that Alexander I. was called βάρβαρος when he tried to enter the stadium at Olympia early in the fifth century, but triumphantly refuted the libel.

[1] A view strongly supported by place-names like Gortynia, Idomenaea, etc., found in historical times in the Vardar valley. See Strabo, pp. 330, 279, 282; Plut., *Thes.* 16 (quoting Aristotle), and Qu. Gr. 35, etc.

[2] Hdt. (i. 56) calls this race Μακεδνόν. Abel thinks that the root Μακ is also that of Μάγ-νητες.

[3] See, *e. g.*, Hdt., v. 22; viii. 137; Thuc., ii. 99; Isocr., *Phil.* 32; Theopomp. fr. 30; Justin, vii. 1; Strabo, p. 329; Paus., vii. 8, 9; Appian, *Syr.* 63; Diod., xvii. 1; Plut., *Alex.* 2, etc. Abel's ingenious theory that another Argos in Lyncestis was the real source, even if proved, makes no difference to Greek *belief*, which unquestionably looked to the Peloponnesian city.

[4] Cf. Thuc., ii. 99.

courses of the Kara Su and the Vardar, which were called in ancient times Pieria and Emathia (or earlier Bottiaea),[1] and they pushed the older peoples into the western and northern highlands, where they continued to subsist under many titles — Orestians, Lyncestians, Elimiotes, Paeonians, and so forth. So far as we can tell, the belief that the " Macedonians " of the coast-plains and the men of the hills were distinct peoples with distinct traditions and claims was held not only in Greece but in Macedonia as well. The clearest distinction is always drawn between " Macedonians " and all other components of the national phalanx in the Asiatic army of Alexander.[2]

I have said already that we are not concerned with the truth or falsehood of these opinions. In this matter, as so often in history, it imports infinitely less that an event did not happen than that it was believed to have happened. We even need not have definite views as to the exclusively Hellenic character of one element,[3] or the exclusively barbarian character of the other; probably much intermixture took place.[4]

[1] Strabo, p. 330 ; cf. also Justin, vii. 1.

[2] Cf., e.g., Arr., iii. 18, 20, 23, with vii. 4; and Plut., Eum. 4.

[3] It is beyond the scope of this essay to attempt any inquiry into the real ethnic affinities of the Macedonian people, based on philological or archæological evidence. In point of fact, there is not nearly enough evidence available to lead to any useful result; in proof of which I will only refer the curious to such inquiries as that in Parts I., II., of Abel's Makedonien vor König Philip, and Fick, in Kuhn's Zeitschrift, xxiii. p. 193.

[4] Thucydides, indeed, includes the Lyncestians and Elimiotes among " Macedonians," at the same time insisting on their separate political status (ii. 99) ; and we know the Lyncestian princely

Our cardinal point is this — that between the "Macedonians" of the coast-plain and the free men of the hills before the time of Philip the Second there was not that community of tradition and hope, which alone consummates the identity of a nation. There were hostile elements in the political whole, one element having been conquered by another but not completely enough to lose its independent constitution and to become absorbed or enslaved, as was the case in Laconia, the second of the three monarchical realms surviving in Greece in the time of Aristotle.[1]

The key to the history of Macedonia lies in this disunion of tradition. The king was chief in the first instance of a race of plain-dwellers, who held themselves to be, like him, of Hellenic stock, and were his faithful Companions (ἑταῖροι), retained by ties of common interest and common danger. In the second place he was over-lord of a more numerous but less united body of hill-tribes, whom he had forced to acknowledge his power, but not to give up their princes.[2] There had been some kind of compromise between two not very unequal forces, with a result so near equilibrium that a little weight thrown into one scale or the other made always peace or war. The king ever and anon is struggling with hostile

house to have been Bacchiad, and to have borne Greek names like Alexander and Eurydice. Eordaea, Thucydides says, was completely conquered, like Bottiaea. Cf. Strabo, p. 326.

[1] *Pol.* v. 8. 5.

[2] There were still semi-independent kinglets in the extreme west after Philip's death. Arr., i. 5.

feudatories, who try to regain their lost autonomy or
even to establish a supremacy in place of his. All
we know of the earliest reigns is the fact of recur-
ring wars with "Illyrians."[1] Now, that nationality,
as Abel[2] has observed, to reach Emathia must pass
through the lands of the feudatory hill-tribes, with
whom we find it often allied during the fourth century.
Indeed, there is some evidence[3] to show that Greek
historians did not clearly distinguish between the
allies, and a probability that in nine out of ten cases,
when Macedonian kings went out to battle with
"Illyrians," they were at war first and foremost with
their own great feudatories of Lyncestis, Orestis,
Elimiotis, or Paeonia. Furthermore, when the succession to the Macedonian throne was interrupted —
as, for example, after the death of Archelaus — or
when "pretenders" arose, as in the reign of Amyntas
or the first year of Philip himself, then a subject
hill-people or a group of tribes was asserting itself
successfully against the hereditary foe.

The Macedonian therefore came to learn that he
must cultivate the Hellene, and identify himself and
his interest with the south. From Alexander I., who
rode to the Athenian pickets the night before Plataea
and proclaimed himself to the generals their friend
and a Greek, down to Amyntas, father of Philip, who
joined forces with Lacedaemon in 382, the kings
of Macedon bid for Greek support by being more

---

[1] Justin, vii. 2.   [2] Page 206.
[3] E. g. Eurydice, Philip's mother, a Lyncestian princess, is called
an Illyrian.

Hellenic than the Hellenes. Alexander I. contended in the stadium at Olympia, and earned, like Amasis of Egypt, the epithet "Philhellene." Archelaus patronized Athenian poets and Athenian drama,[1] and commissioned Euripides to dramatize the deeds of his Argive ancestor.[2] Even those kings who, like Perdiccas and Amyntas, were prevented by internal difficulties from cultivating the peaceful arts of Hellenism,[3] maintained alliances and friendship as consistently as their necessities or their interest would allow.

"Macedonia," therefore, throughout historical times until the accession of Philip the Second, presents the spectacle of a nation that was no nation but a group of discordant units, without community of race, religion, speech, or sentiment, resultant from half-accomplished conquest, and weak as the several sticks of the faggot in the fable. The history of its stronger kings is a history of attempts to complete the original conquest, and with Greek help to bind the faggot together ; the history of its weaker kings is a history of a series of successful reactions by the hill-men, aided by Illyrians or Thracians from beyond the border. The work done by that Aeropus, who as a child was placed in a cradle behind his army, to force it to face the "Illyrians,"[4] and as a man broke the "Illyrian" power, was continued by his successors, Amyntas and Alexand⬤ with the aid

---

[1] Agatharch. ap. Phot., s. v. 'Αρχέλαος.

[2] Archelaus also instituted a Macedonian festival of Zeus Olympius. Arr., i. 11. See Holm, *Gr. Gesch.* iii. 14, p. 230.

[3] See Isocr., *Phil.* 107.

[4] Justin, vii. 1.

of Persia, whose satraps they consented for the time
to be. When the Persian was gone, Alexander allied
himself openly to the Greek, and his son, Perdiccas,
a diplomat of the first force, played with masterly
skill a double game to gain Greek support without
risking Greek encroachment. For nearly a hundred
years the great feudatories were coerced ever more
and more boldly until Archelaus, succeeding in 413
B. C., hoped to complete the process and indissolubly
to bind the faggot together. He seems to have been
an enlightened strategist, for he instituted great works
of communication and centralization, cut direct roads
through the mountain passes to tie the tribes together
and to promote trade, laid out chains of forts, and
perhaps began to form a national army,[1] the best
unifier of all, as a greater king was to find half a century later. But, overstrung, the bow snapped ; and
Archelaus' murder[2] in 399 was the beginning of forty
years of turmoil and trouble. The feudatories warred
against their Macedonian over-lord, and either openly
seized his throne, as Argaeus did that of Amyntas
II., or forced their " guardianship " on a young king,
as Ptolemy Alorites, after murdering Amyntas' eldest
son, intruded with the queen-mother's connivance on
the independence of the second brother. The relation
of the " Steward " Aeropus in 399 to Archelaus'
son, Orestes, whom he afterwards murdered and

---

[1] See a remarkable passage of Thucydides (ii. 100).

[2] The result of conspiracy, according to the contemporary Plato
(*Alcib.* p. 141 d.), and Aristotle (*Pol.* v. 8. 11–13) : the παιδικά
who effected it was probably no more than the agent of others.

succeeded, was doubtless of the same equivocal character.

Thus Macedonia, when Philip was born, had sprung back with a rebound to the internal discord and external weakness of a century before. The "pretender" Argaeus had vanished from the throne, but Amyntas held his own merely by sufferance of Thessalians and Spartans. An Acanthian envoy at Sparta in 383 describes the Macedonian king as forced to retire from his cities and "all but fallen out of his kingdom."[1] He retained it, indeed, up to his death twelve years later, but in what jeopardy we may judge from events immediately consequent — from the conspiracy of his wife against his person, the tragic end of his eldest son and successor, the usurpation and murder of Ptolemy Alorites, the battles of the second son with the "Illyrians," and the crop of "pretenders" who greeted the accession of Philip — these the events of just ten years! A Macedonian prince in the early part of the fourth century could hope to succeed to little more than the chieftainship of a clan, imperilled by a necessity for asserting over hostile aliens an hereditary suzerainty, which, like the wolf's ears in the Greek proverb, it was equally dangerous to hold or to leave.

He was king, however, absolute as in heroic times among his peculiar people, that small dominant clan of Macedonian settlers who held themselves to be of like origin with him. Thucydides,[2] a contemporary

[1] Xen., *Hell.* v. 2, 13.   [2] ii. 99.

of Archelaus and Perdiccas, and personally acquainted to some extent with the Macedonian land, makes it clear that the original holding of the Macedonians was just that semi-circular expanse of low land which lies west and north of the Gulf of Salonica. Whoever has sailed up that sea and ridden three days north to Vodhena, and three days east to Cavalla, has seen the whole cradle of Macedonian power. The three-pronged peninsula of Chalcidice was not included, for it was in Greek hands; nor were the high valleys, lying between the first conspicuous western range and the loftier mountain chain behind, which now divides Macedonia from Albania, since those were the holdings of the Elimiote, Orestian, Lyncestian, and Pelagonian feudatories; nor, again, was the plain of Monastir on the north between Mount Scardus and the hills which close upon the Vardar at Demir Kapou included, for this was Paeonian territory. All these lands, indeed, except Chalcidice, as Thucydides bears witness, were to be called later by the common name Macedonia, and Lyncestians and Elimiotes and other upland peoples were included eventually among Macedonians, but as a result of conquest; the Athenian historian is clear that the early Temenid kings ruled, in the first instance, only over the " lower " or " maritime " Macedonia, from which they had thrust the Pierians, Eordaeans, Bottiaeans, and Edonian Thracians.

We know very little about the condition of this low tract in early days. The words put by Arrian into the mouth of Alexander, taunting his mutinous

army at Opis with base ingratitude to the son
of the man who had given them cloaks in place of
coverings of skins, brought them down from the hills
to inhabit cities in the plains, and be men of wealth
and ease instead of savages [1] — those often-quoted
sentences, if based on Ptolemy's or Aristobulus'
recollection of the conqueror's own words, were
spoken, be it remembered, not to the little Clan
of pre-Philippian days, but to the new military
Nation of Philip's making, in which Lyncestians,
Orestians and the like were one with the dwellers
in the Emathian and Pierian plains. These last
were inhabitants of rich, low-lying levels, fat corn-
land and deep grass at the present day, close to
centres of Greek civilization. To suppose that the
farmers themselves were civilized up to a Greek
standard, because Archelaus and other kings were
φιλόμουσοι, is probably as absurd as to assume
that the Scottish Highlands were civilized in the
seventeenth century because certain chieftains " had
the English" and had been in London; but we
have the evidence of an extensive coinage issued
from Pella,[2] and ranging over a long period, to
prove that the early Macedonians carried on much
trade with Greeks. They were a feudal race of
sturdy farmers,[3] not unlike the Boeotians, well-to-do
in peace, and affording admirable material for heavy

---

[1] vii. 9.

[2] The ancient χρηματιστήριον of Macedonia (Strabo, p. 330),
even when Aegae was still the capital.

[3] " Ein kräftiges Bauernvolk, eifrige Krieger und Jäger."
Holm, *Gr. Gesch.* iii. p. 232.

cavalry or infantry in war. If ever the Tombs of the Kings be found at Vodhena (Aegae or Edessa), we may learn something of this primitive Macedonian life. At present so little has the land been explored, that we know far less of its civilization than of that of far remoter parts of the classic east : no remains of early native art, either decorative or industrial, have been found; there is not an early tomb nor an archaic inscription to teach us anything at all.

Surrounding perils apart, the valleys of Haliacmon and Axius were goodly heritage enough for a king as absolute as the Macedonian. A "constitution" the Macedonians had no more than Highland clansmen. Their land seems to have been all property of the king,[1] to be granted by him in fief; Alexander distributed estates broadcast before he crossed the Hellespont,[2] and remitted by a word all imposts on the land as well as all obligations of personal service to himself[3] in favour of the families of those he delighted to honour. The king levies whom he will for military service,[4] and can depute to another in his absence functions as absolute as his own.[5] Regents

[1] See an inscription of Potidaea cited in the French edition of Droysen, *Hellenismus*, i. p. 76.

[2] Plut., *Alex.* 15.

[3] Arr., i. 16; vii. 10: οἱ κατὰ τὰς κτήσεις εἰσφοραί, and αἱ λειτουργίαι τῷ σώματι. The families of the ἑταῖροι who fell at Granicus were so honoured.

[4] Arr., i. 24; vii. 12.

[5] So Antipater, authorized by Alexander's seal, collects fleets, (Arr., ii. 2), makes war, and holds a royal court (Arr., vii. 12), supreme even over the queen-mother.

and governors he appoints and removes at will.[1]   He
can do no wrong;[2] he marries and puts away wives,
apparently as it pleases him,[3] and is the sole fountain
of honour.[4]   Seldom can the principle of absolute
submission to a monarch have been implanted deeper
than in the Macedonians.   When Eumenes, the only
Greek of pure blood among Alexander's Successors,
wished to exalt his authority over that of the Regent
and the Generals, he erected an empty tent, placed
within it the emblems of Macedonian royalty, and
commanded unquestioned obedience, as the representative of the presence within.[5]   In the words of
Demosthenes, comparing the centralized and silent
rule of Philip with the diffused and loquacious
sovereignty of Demos, the Macedonian king was, " in
his single person, lord of all things, both open and
secret, at once General and Lord Absolute and
Treasurer." [6]

He was, in short, a clan-chieftain.   The greatest of
his subjects had no rights against him, but only privileges,[7] as children may have by favour of a father.
They were proverbially free of speech [8] in his presence, and the absence of servility, which emboldened

---

[1] See esp. Arr., vi. 27 and vii. 11.

[2] Arr., iv. 9. 7.   [3] Plut., *Alex.* 9.

[4] Compare the institution of the Pages, Arr., iv. 13 ; Ael. *V. H.*
xiv. 49.

[5] Plut., *Eum.* 13.   So Eumenes also distributed royal gifts (c. 8).

[6] *De Cor.* 235.

[7] Polybius' statement (v. 27. 6.) that the Macedonian king ruled
βασιλικῶς οὐ τυραννικῶς, implies no more than this.

[8] Polyb., v. 27. 6.

them to refuse his gifts[1] or give advice unasked,
earned for them in antiquity the repute of ἐλεύθεροι
ἄνδρες. But it was no more than a "shadow of
liberty;"[2] they must follow whenever and wherever
the king might lead, and leave farm or market to
fight his battles.[3] One constitutional right, and one
only, can we trace in Macedonian history. If we are
to believe that Curtius uses good authorities, the
Macedonians, strictly so called, were summoned by
the king to general assembly if a charge were in question involving the life of one of their number : "*De
capitalibus rebus vetusto Macedonum modo inquirebat
exercitus — in pace erat vulgi — et nihil potestas regum
valebat, nisi prius valuisset auctoritas.*"[4] This statement is confirmed in the main by Arrian, who
narrates that Alexander accused Philotas "before the
Macedonians," while another suspect of conspiracy,
Amyntas, made his defence ἐν τῇ ἐκκλησίᾳ, and
obtained leave from the latter body to bring his brother
Polemon before the king to be exonerated from the
charge.[5] If condemnation ensued on such an accusation, the Assembly itself appears to have executed its

[1] So Parmenio and others refused Alexander's gift of lands,
offered before he crossed the Hellespont. Plut., *Alex.* 15.
Unasked advice is offered commonly enough by Alexander's
marshals.

[2] Lucian, *Dial. Mort.* 14.

[3] Cf. Demosthenes' descriptions of Macedonia tired of, but
helpless to protest against, Philip's many wars (*Olynth.* ii. 15 ; *Ad
Epist. Phil.* 9, 10) — tirades hardly, however, to be taken *au
pied de la lettre.*

[4] Curt., vi. 8. 32.   [5] iii. 26. 27.

own sentence — or rather that of the king, who was
the actual judge — by overwhelming the culprit with
javelins or stones.[1] These cases, however, do not
warrant us in supposing that a Popular Assembly
met for any but very special purposes in Macedonia; as, for instance, if one of the great Companions was accused of high treason in time of war.
We have no warrant for supposing (and it is highly
improbable) that in the case of meaner men such a
cumbrous court had to be constituted, nor for a less
crime than treason against the king's majesty. In
ordinary cases the king was judge alone.[2]

In all monarchical states we expect gradations of
rank, an aristocracy of birth or of honours conferred
by the king, and a lower class which tills the land.
In Macedonia there was no serf-population. The
original conquest had not been complete enough to
produce Helots or even Perioeci; and the Emathian
and Pierian farmers tilled their fields with the aid
only of such slaves as they could buy or make prize
of war.[3]

It appears that the whole body of Macedonians
(in the restricted sense of the original settlers in
Emathia and Pieria) distinguished themselves from
the semi-subjugated "Macedonians" of the hills as
the king's ἑταῖροι, or Companions; but that within this

---

[1] Arr., iii. 26. 27.; cf. also the case of Hermolaus the Page
(iv. 14).

[2] Plut., *Alex.* 42.

[3] *E. g.* the Greeks captured at Granicus were sent to till the
soil in Macedonia (Arr., ii. 16).

large class, considering itself privileged, there were narrower circles of privilege, based on property — that is to say, in the first instance, on the favour of the king, who granted lands. In ancient states the outward and visible sign of a higher class consisted often in the providing of a war-horse, and in service therewith in the cavalry. So in Macedonia we find a smaller body of ἑταῖροι, especially so-called, who are the flower of the cavalry, and a larger body of πεζέταιροι,[1] who are the flower of the infantry; and it is probable that under these two names was included (either on the active list or in the reserve) every able-bodied man among the descendants of the original settlers who followed the Temenid kings to Pieria. The superior class of horsemen in Philip's time was almost certainly identical with those eight hundred landed proprietors who, as the contemporary Theopompus[2] tells us, enjoyed estates as large as those of ten thousand Greeks; but the same authority and Anaximenes[3] state that their original numbers had been swelled somewhat before this period, not only by Philip's admission of foreigners to their ranks,[4] but by the policy of his eldest brother, Alexander II., who added also to the πεζέταιροι.

[1] I have discussed this disputed term in an article on the "Army of Alexander," in *Journal of Philology*, vol. xvii. No. 33, pp. 10 ff.; but must modify now many of my early views. See note *infra*, p. 56.

[2] Fr. 249.

[3] Fr. 7.

[4] Philip freely made such men as Callias of Chalcis (Aesch., *Ctes.* 89) Hetaeri in the later years of his life; and probably Theopompus is here reviewing his whole policy.

The latter king, however, during a reign of hardly
twelve months, could not have effected much change,
and the total of Philip's earliest body of cavalry —
six hundred[1] — is probably as near as may be to that
of the Companions.   Within even this circle was one
still more select, that of the court, the intimates — Companions in the strictest sense — of the king himself, in
war-time his staff — οἱ ἀμφ᾽ αὐτὸν ἑταῖροι, as Arrian
often calls them, — whom, to the number of something
less than a hundred, Alexander married at Susa to the
noblest of the Persian ladies.[2]   They formed a natural
council for the king to consult on great matters,[3]
and in order to qualify for this high honour, the
noblest youths were glad to become Pages of the
Body, according to Philip's institution, and perform
menial offices about the king's person.[4]   The highest
distinction of all was still one of immediate personal
service, the rank of Guard of the Person, only
attained, it appears, after some signal service rendered
directly to the king.   Of eight Guards of Alexander's
Person, two are known to have saved his life, one
to have been his ally against his father, and one his
second self.[5]

[1] Diod. xvi. 4.

[2] Arr. vii. 4.   I dare not suggest a number for the lower
class, the πεζέταιροι.   The scanty *data* we have apply only to
post-Philippian days, and, as I hope to show, to a wholly changed
national system.   Herein lies the cardinal difficulty of determining
anything whatever with regard to early Macedonia.

[3] *E. g.* the policy of marching to Issus (Arr. ii. 6).

[4] Arr. iv. 13; Curt. viii. 6.

[5] See the article quoted above (p. 19).   The qualification must
have been as stated, for the list does not include Alexander's

Thus we find privilege within privilege, ascending to the fountain of all honour, the king. The lowest Macedonian felt himself exalted above the highest Orestian, as a king's Companion : the highest in rank was the nearest to the king's person. If such a system tended to breed insolence towards the un-privileged,[1] it implied also an inherent unity which in master-hands was capable of much. The clan spirit makes for strength almost as much as the political self-subordination of the Greek city-state, but is not, like the latter, incapable of expansion. For the present, the Macedonian community had the same fault as the city-state — it was too small ; and no way had been found to increase it, and at the same time preserve its unity. It had further a fault, natural to landed aristocracies, that, while possessing a narrow territory, it did not increase its wealth by sea-going trade. Macedonia was a poor land,[2] and its clansmen a numerically insignificant unity in the midst of hordes in political disunion. How could

greatest marshals, *e. g.* Antipater, Parmenio, or Craterus, while it does include men too old to have been his "aequales." The eight were : Lysimachus and Peucestas, Ptolemy Lagus, Hephaestion, Perdiccas, Leonnatus, Aristinous, and Peithon.

[1] As proved to be the case when first Macedonians were set over subjugated races. See Arr. vi. 27.

[2] Ἡ οὐδὲ βόσκουσα ὑμᾶς καλῶς, says Alexander to the mutineers (Arr. vii. 9). The mines of Pangaeus were in Thracian or Amphi-politan hands ; the rich corn-lands, forests, and ports of Chalcidice under the Olynthian power. (See the speech of the Acanthian at Sparta in the year 383, Xen., *Hell.* v. 2. 16, and an inscription relating to a treaty between Philip's father and the Olynthians about B.C. 389, H. Sauppe, *Inscr. Mac. Quattuor*, in *Jahresbericht* etc., Weimar, 1847.)

a source of wealth and a way of expansion be found ?
It looked little likely in the year 382.

Of Philip's father, Amyntas, we know little but his
misfortunes and his death. Philip's mother, Eurydice,
belonged to the Bacchiad house of Lyncestis [1] — that
is, to the enemy — and in after years she was to betray
her husband.[2] Marriage may have been the price
paid by Amyntas for the recovery of his throne from
the pretender Argaeus, perhaps the reigning Lyncestian of the time.[3] If ever the veil be lifted from
the events of early Macedonian history, we shall
find, perhaps, that the vicissitudes of the royal house
were connected directly with changes in the balance
of power in Greece. The Athenian Aeschines [4] once
claimed, in Philip's presence, that it was Athens
that had supported his predecessors. The orator
reminded the king of the good will shown and good
deeds done by the Athenian city towards his father,
who in his turn had adopted the Athenian Iphicrates
as his son. From an Attic inscription [5] we know
that Macedonian envoys were at Athens about 382,
and a scholiast [6] alleges that Amyntas owed his recovered throne in some sense to Athens. In the

---

[1] Strabo, p. 326.   [3] Justin, vii. 4.

[2] Philip, born in 382, had two brothers, and perhaps a sister,
older than himself. The marriage of his parents must be put
back, therefore, to 386, or earlier. Amyntas regained his throne
in 360, according to Clinton's chronology (*Fasti Hell.* ii., App.
ch. 4).

[4] *F. L.* 26 ff.   [5] *C.I.A.* ii. 15*b*, and Add.
[6] On Aesch. *F. L.* 26.

turmoil which followed the murder of Philip's eldest
brother, it was Iphicrates, says the orator, who
secured the throne for the second son; and the latter,
when he had slain his "Thebizing" guardian, allied
himself with Timotheus, newly come against Amphipolis. Certainly there are notable coincidences. The
fall of Athenian power on the Thracian coasts
succeeds a long peace in Macedonia, and is followed
by the murder of Archelaus and ten years of turmoil.
Amyntas establishes his throne ever more firmly as
the second Athenian league is formed. Leuctra is
followed by the murder of Alexander II., by Pausanias' rebellion, and by the domination of the
"Thebizing" Ptolemy Alorites.

In the face of the statements of Aeschines it is
impossible to doubt that it was a maxim of Athenian
policy to support the Macedonian House,[1] and it
ceases to be wonderful that, in years to come, Philip
himself, when Athens had most provoked his vengeance and was most at his mercy, so signally stayed
his hand.

The boy was brought up at Pella [2] — a mean place
then, compared with its after-splendour, but still the

---

[1] See Schäfer, *Demosthenes*, ii. p. 6, for evidence of connection
between Athens and Macedon.

[2] Strabo, p. 330. He may have been born there; for although,
in 383, Pella was in Olynthian hands (Xen. *Hell.* v. 2, 13), the
appearance of Eudamidas with his Spartan expeditionary force in
the winter of that year (which was followed by the revolt of
Potidaea from Olynthus), most probably caused the Olynthians to
retire within their own territory, where Teleutias seemed to have
found them on his arrival in the spring of 382.

greatest of Macedonian cities.[1] It had a beach on
the Ludian lake, and an outlet to the sea—not, in those
days, the sluggish creek, lost in pestiferous marsh, which
the traveller sees now — and it was the centre of such
trade and civilization as existed in the Emathian plain.

There the young Philip learned the rudiments of
Greek letters, and grew to be, even among Hellenes,
cultured and polite. It was a time of peace and
comparative security under the shelter of Greek
supremacy. Sparta had broken the Olynthian power
when Philip was three years old, and given back to
his father the lands and cities about the Thermaic
gulf. Jason of Pherae also became Amyntas' ally
and friend.[2] Philip had reached the age of six when
the battle of Naxos was won by Athens, and Spartan
influence replaced by hers; but the royal house of
Macedon became probably only the more secure by
the change, for strong Athenian fleets, maintaining
friendly relations with Amyntas,[3] were constantly
about the coasts till 371. In that year an event,
of far graver import than the sea-fight at Naxos,
shook Greece from end to end — the battle of Leuctra.

---

[1] Cf. Strabo, l.c., with Xen. l.c., and Dem. de Cor. 68. The
old capital and royal burial-place was Aegae, or Edessa, a short day's
journey higher up the plain; but Pella had long been, it appears,
the mint and home of the court. I visited its site in 1887, but
found that the city had vanished as though it had never been.
The plateau above the marsh, on which it stood, is now plough
land, where a few fragments of marble and mouldings and many
coins have been turned up from time to time. See for description, H. F. Tozer, *Highlands of Turkey*, vol. i. p. 153, and an
article of mine in *Macmillan's Magazine*, 1889, Aug., p. 287.

[2] Diod. xv. 60.   [3] Aesch. F. L. 26.

Its wave of disturbance did not travel at once northwards. Amyntas reigned for two years more, beset with domestic trouble, but died after all in his bed, leaving his throne to Alexander, his firstborn, when Philip, his youngest, was barely thirteen years old.

The passing of a sceptre from old hands to young in a half-barbarous land seldom is effected in peace; and in Macedonia in 369 the times were ripe for trouble. The repressive influence of the old imperial cities of Hellas, whose interest it had been to maintain peace in the inner country, operated no longer, for they were overshadowed now by a new power — that of Thebes — which had no foreign empire, and a policy directly contrary to theirs. Accordingly, the old feud between suzerain and feudatory broke out again, and the more bitterly for long repression. We know almost nothing of this stormy year, 369. The young king appears to have courted southern help by rendering service to the great Larissan house of the Aleuadae,[1] and perhaps he enrolled some of their Thessalians among his "Companions;"[2] but to no good purpose. The kingdom was torn between rival forces. On the one side was a "pretender," Pausanias, backed by Greek swords, drawing half

---

[1] Diod. xv. 61, 67.

[2] Anaximenes (fr. 7) says that he increased his ἑταῖροι and πεζέταιροι. As these terms, I believe, included already all true Macedonians, Alexander must have enrolled members of other races, and was little likely to include his feudatories.

Macedonia after him; [1] on the other, stood the Lyn-cestian queen-mother, already enamoured during her husband's lifetime of her son-in-law, Ptolemy of Alorus, and now plotting against her son. Heedless of the advance of Pausanias, she and her paramour put their plot into execution. A troop of dancers was introduced to the king's presence, and in the midst of the performance of a war-dance,[2] they fell upon and slew him. The immediate result, however, was disastrous to the plotters. If we are to interpret closely Aeschines' speech to Philip, Pausanias at once advanced with giant strides, supported now by the infuriate adherents of the murdered king.[3] Anthemus, Therma, Strepsa, and other strong places opened their gates to him. But once more Athens, anxious for her remaining dependencies, interfered on behalf of the royal house. Invited by Eurydice, the famous Iphicrates, who was on the coast, went up to the court. The murderess of Amyntas' firstborn besought the Athenian, by the memory of Amyntas, to save Amyntas' children, and she bade the elder boy, Perdiccas, take the old man's hands, and the younger, Philip, embrace his knees. Thus Aeschines describes the scene, veiling the fact that the chief actress was

---

[1] Aesch. F. L. 27; cf. Justin, vii. 4.

[2] Marsyas, fr. ap. Athen., xiv. p. 629 D. The name of one assassin, Apollophanes of Pydna, is preserved by Dem., F. L. 195.

[3] This must have been the meaning of οἱ δοκοῦντες εἶναι φίλοι, who "betrayed" Eurydice after the murder (Aesch. F. L. 26). There is no means of telling whom or what this "pretender" Pausanias represented. Aeschines describes him as φυγὰς μὲν ὤν, τῷ καιρῷ δ' ἰσχύων. About the time of Perdiccas' death, in 360 or 359, he reappeared with Thracian backing.

an adulterous mother who had slain her child. The veteran general could hardly have felt much emotion, but he knew that his best policy lay in supporting the legitimate succession. He took up the quarrel, chased Pausanias beyond the border, and set Perdiccas on the throne.

In the councils of the minor the Lyncestian mother and her paramour continued to rule, and the latter, whom Aeschines calls Regent, others call King.[1] The favour of Athens was worth much, but of more worth in those days was the favour of Thebes. Pelopidas chanced to march with a Theban force into Thessaly early in 367;[2] Ptolemy opened negotiations, and invited the famous captain to Pella. Terms were agreed to, but a substantial guarantee of good faith was demanded of the slippery Regent. The young king's brother, Philip, was already a pledge in the hands of Eurydice's kinsmen, as security for certain payments, probably blackmail levied on the plainsmen, whose obedience to the Regent and the Lyncestian adulteress was far from assured. Pelopidas agreed to support the Lyncestians, and their illustrious

[1] Diodorus, xv. 71, 77, and Dexippus *ap.* Syncell., p. 263 B.

[2] It must have been in very early spring, for Pelopidas went up to Susa also in 367. If he took the usual overland route through Asia Minor, he would start not later than April, for the passes are open then. He would pass the summer in Susa and return in the cool of autumn. I cannot follow Clinton in assigning more than one year to Alexander II. Surely Aeschines implies that the interval between the deaths of father and son was of the briefest. Allow a few months for the establishment of Perdiccas and Ptolemy, and for the latter's change of policy, and we reach 367 for the year of Philip's removal to Thebes.

hostage was transferred to his custody together with twenty-nine other noble youths; and thus at the age of fifteen Philip came to spend three most momentous years of his boyhood at the house of Pammenes in Thebes.[1]

Thebes, in 368, was the most powerful state in south-eastern Europe. Her title to pre-eminence rested singly on her citizen soldiery, and she instilled into the young prince, during his sojourn within her walls, the lesson that nothing need be impossible to a worthy and confident leader of big battalions.

[1] As is well known, our authorities for the circumstances of Philip's transference to Thebes cannot be reconciled altogether. Diodorus (xvi. 2) says it was Amyntas who placed him with the "Illyrians;" Justin (vii. 5) that it was Alexander II. Diodorus says that the Illyrians passed him on to Thebes; Justin, that Alexander did so "interjecto . . . tempore;" Aeschines (*F. L.* 26, 28) that he was still with his mother when Alexander had just died; Plutarch (*Pel.* 26) that Ptolemy gave him to Pelopidas. The last two are the best authorities, and the coincidence they show with Pelopidas' well-known Thessalian expedition is strong. Philip stayed three years in Thebes, and returned therefore in 364, just when his brother had slain Ptolemy and reasserted himself in Macedonia — also a strong coincidence. A further question arises, why "Illyrians" should have sent their hostage to Thebes? I believe (with Abel, though I differ from him in one or two details) that much of the confusion is due to the common use of the name "Illyrians" for Lyncestians. The "Illyrians" here are Eurydice's kinsmen, holding Philip as hostage for the good faith of Perdiccas and Ptolemy (a Pierian of Alorus), whom they were allowing to reign on sufferance. Their interest and that of Thebes were identical: both were anti-Athenian, and wished to keep Macedonia out of Iphicrates' hands; and it is the Lyncestians who therefore hand over Philip, with Ptolemy's consent. Diodorus and Justin, finding that Philip was given to "Illyrians," and not aware that Lyncestians are meant, have to go back to the reigns of Alexander or Amyntas to find an "Illyrian" invasion.

The Theban of the fourth century (with certain brilliant exceptions) was of an animal type, common in aristocratic states. Generations of his forefathers had devoted every energy of mind and body to the pleasures of the flesh. The Boeotian plains gave the Theban citizens meat and corn, wine, women, and horses, in abundance; the nearest hills afforded them the varied excitement of the chase. They were well-grown, εὔρρωστοι τοῖς σώμασιν, [1] fond of extending exuberant muscles in the gymnasium,[2] and they fought for the love of fighting. A full-blooded, boisterous race, proud of their past,[3] they were determined to enjoy the present. Born to domineer, and bend to their purposes all who could subserve their pleasures, they became a menace to their neighbours whenever they needed space for their healthy stock, but bounded ambition by the satisfaction of appetite. For the barren glory of leading Hellas they cared not a jot. They despised commerce as men who know that their internal resources are amply sufficient to supply internal wants. Handicraft they held beneath the dignity of gentlemen, and denied a magistracy to a citizen if he had followed a trade within ten years.[4] Their capital lay near good harbours on three seas, but only once sent out a fleet, and a contemporary historian,[5] who saw Thebes at her highest and her lowest, remarks that she might have been leader of Greece, had she not

---

[1] Diod. xv. 50; Plut. *Pel.* 3. [2] Diod. *l.c.*; Nep. *Epam.* 2.
[3] Diod. *l.c.* [4] Arist. *Pol.* iii. 3. 4.
[5] Ephorus, *ap.* Strab., p. 400 (cf. Isocr. *Phil.* 93).

neglected, in the cultivation of warlike valour, the gentle arts of literature and converse with men. Even rude Sparta has its School of Sculpture; but no type of art is known to us as Theban,[1] nor do we hear of any conspicuous man of letters born actually within her walls. Even at the very zenith of her power she can base no claim to consideration by universal history on those glories which most redeem the political insignificance of other states of Hellas.

Certain qualities which the Thebans shared with the Spartans they owed to similar circumstances. They, too, were a conquering caste in an alien land. What upper Laconia and Messenia were to Sparta, the northern Boeotian plain and the Attic marches were to Thebes. Like Sparta, Thebes coveted her neighbours' lands, and only offered to be federal leader when unable to be sovereign lord. The key to Boeotian history and Theban character is to be found in the relations of the Cadmeian city to her neighbour cities. Among them she was an upstart; for tradition maintained, and recent research has supported the contention, that Minyan Orchomenus in the northern plain was the richer and greater in heroic times.[2] Subsequent to that era is the age of racial flittings: the Cadmeians appeared in Thebes, whence no one in aftertimes knew certainly, but

---

[1] There is much *Boeotian* art of course; but Theban sculptors only appear after the civilizing efforts of Epaminondas, and none attain to pre-eminence.

[2] Cf. *Iliad*, ii. 494–510; and Strabo, p. 401.

men said from the East; the northern peoples were pressed southward by some unknown cause; and Boeotia, like the Peloponnese, was overrun.[1] When the turmoil, in which the heroic civilization of the Argolid perished, has died away, we find the Minyae vanished from Orchomenus,[2] and the cities of Boeotia in unwilling dependence on Cadmeian Thebes. They would gladly have been beholden to any other lord.[3] The cities of the Asopus valley looked to Athens, the cities of the west and north were ready to rally round Orchomenus, should Thebes be weak and outside support strong. Unable to annex them, the Cadmeians pose as their federal leaders, and inscribe Βοιωτῶν on the coinage of the "League." In the last half of the fifth century, the coin-legend changes to Θηβαίων, for the Boeotian cities in 447, the disastrous year of the first battle of Coronea, lose the support of Athens. Thebes at once begins to bully and reduce the cities to mere appendages — περίοικοι — of herself,[4] and they fight under her banners, in name, but not in fact, a federal army,[5] the bolder spirits constantly intriguing with foreign powers to regain freedom.[6] Never did a "Confederacy"

---

[1] Thuc. i. 12.   [2] *Ibid.* iv. 76.

[3] *Ibid.* iii. 61.

[4] She seizes Plataea (Thuc. ii. 2) and transplants Oropus seven stades from the sea (Diod. xiv. 17).

[5] Thuc. iv. 91. The Theban Boeotarchs are in supreme command; the rest wish not to fight.

[6] Cf. for this feeling at a later time, Xen. *Hell.* iii. 5. The Orchomenians admit Lysander to Boeotia, and do not rank with the Thebans at Corinth. *Hell.* iv. 2, 17.

less merit a name associated with Liberty and Fraternity. When a foreign power at last prevailed against Thebes, the cities one and all rushed into its arms. They did, indeed, no better than change masters; but the spectacle of a Spartan garrison in the Cadmeia reconciled Orchomenus and Thespiae to Spartan men-at-arms within their own walls.

When Thebes has expelled her foreign lords and her own traitors, and made sure that neither Sparta nor Athens had power or leisure to hinder, she throws off any mask she has ever thought it worth while to assume.[1] She establishes δυναστεῖαι in all the cities;[2] she makes no secret of her suppression of αὐτονομία,[3] or her determination to organize Boeotia καθ᾽ ἕν;[4] she sweeps Plataea again from the face of the earth for past offences, and punishes Thespiae hardly less severely for having favoured Sparta; once more she lays hands on Oropus, and only spares Orchomenus for the moment after Leuctra, to destroy it root and branch three years later.[5] At the zenith of her power, Thebes was so far from leading a free confederacy that she had appropriated absolutely the lands of five of the leading cities of Boeotia — Orchomenus, Chaeronea, Thespiae, Oropus, and Plataea; and the coinage of her supremacy, which bears neither Βοιωτῶν nor Θηβαίων, but the name of a Theban magistrate, fitly commemorates the notorious character of her " League."

[1] See Paus. ix. 13. 2.   [2] *Hell.* v. 4. 46, 63; vi. 1. 1.
[3] *Ibid.* vi. 3. 19.   [4] *Ibid.* v. 2. 16; vi. 4. 3; Diod. xv. 51.
[5] Cf. Diod. xv. 57, 79.

No wonder the Theban was the "oligarchic man!" He could be no better a democrat than can the Englishman or any other member of a dominant race in modern times that stands in an imperial relation to weaker peoples. When democracy was planted in Thebes, it was but a sickly growth, and soon died.[1] There were parties indeed in the city during her supremacy; but to call them aristocratic and democratic is to use names without meaning. Within the established aristocracy there were men of liberal views like Epaminondas, and men of more conservative and generally accepted views like Pelopidas; but the disgrace of Epaminondas in 363[2] implies not a revolution, but only the temporary prevalence in a Tory state of ultra Tory politics. The constitution of Thebes has as good a claim as that of Sparta to be called changeless. From the days of Philolaus[3] to those of Sulla, there is no warrant for the existence of political division, except that caused by the presence within the walls of a "Boeotian" minority identified with the interests of the subject cities. This it was, and not a party of democratic idealists, that invited the Spartans in 382 to garrison the Cadmeia.

Like Sparta in so many of her characteristics and circumstances, how different is the history and the fame of Thebes! Sparta, by force or persuasion, welds the southern Peloponnese into a peaceful whole,

[1] Arist. *Pol.* v. 2. 7.
[2] Nep. *Epam.* 7 ; Plut. *Pel.* 28 ; Diod. xv. 71.
[3] Arist. *Pol.* ii. 9. 7.

and embarks on foreign conquest; Thebes never
really assimilates a single subject city. Sparta is
hardly more comparable to Athens in art and literature, but her name is coupled with that of the
Ionian city as fellow-bearer of the message or Hellenic
civilization; Thebes ranks with Thessaly or Epirus.
The Theban is the equivalent of the Spartan, with the
most Hellenic features in the nature of the latter left
out; reserve and sense of proportion are exchanged
for overweening pride and unmeasured exultation, and
the " Leuctric insolence "[1] of the Theban became a
byword in Greece. Of devotion to the common weal,
and anthropomorphic idealism in worship, in which
consisted the best heritage of Hellas, Spartan history
can show many evidences, Theban history none.
The Cadmeian characteristics are those of a conquering
people of the East; both in war and in peace they
foreshadow those of the Ottoman Turk. Tradition,
various in all else concerning the founders of Thebes,
agrees in this alone — that the Cadmeian was an
alien in Bœotia in a far more real sense than the
Dorian Spartan among the earlier races of the
Peloponnese. Whether he came from the East or
the North, whether he was Semite or no, we can at
least assert that most that is known of him recalls
the barbarian rather than the Hellene, Cadmus the
" Phoenician " rather than Amphion and Zethus, his
rivals in the honour of founding Thebes. The
familiar legends of Thebes are as gloomy as the
horrible nature myths of the East. Oedipus, who

---

[1] Dem. *de Cor.* 18; Diod. xvi. 58. Ch. Justin, viii. 1.

fertilizes his own mother; the man-eating Sphinx; Actaeon devoured by his hounds; Agave and her hideous orgy; Dirce tied to the wild bull's horns — all these forms of horror find parallels in Thrace Phrygia or Phoenicia rather than in Hellas. Even in 371 the Theban commanders at Leuctra could debate the propriety of offering human sacrifice to the unpropitious gods;[1] and, whatever excuses be made for the consistent "Medism" of Thebes by modern apologists, the fact that the Greeks themselves made none, but scored her crime against her when those of Argos and Thessaly were forgiven, suspected her of treachery against Hellas even in 354,[2] and formally condemned her for old sins in 335, suggests that the contemporary world believed her to incline to the barbarian of her own preference and her good will. The Theban is oriental in his sluggish fatalism, oriental in his addiction to and open avowal of sexless love,[3] oriental in his orgiastic worships and in his orgiastic feasts. The supper of the Polemarchs on the night of the Liberation in 378 might have been held in a banquet hall of Babylon!

Unintelligent fatalists of powerful build, whose ambition is limited to their bodily wants, make unequalled soldiery. The athletic gentleman of Thebes and the stolid farmer of the Teneric plain supplied as fine material as there was in the world for the solid phalanx of the days of "political" armies. Theban military strength was notorious in

---

[1] Plut. *Pel.* 21.   [2] Dem. *de Symm.* 33.
[3] Cf. on the Sacred Band, Plutarch, *Pel.* 18 ff.

Greece before the Theban "supremacy." Slow to stir, the Cadmeian city was a dangerous foe when roused, and her weight, thrown into the scale at critical moments, had changed more than once the course of history. She, not Sparta, checked the flowing tide of Athenian conquest at Coronea in 447, and she, more than Sparta, in 424 restored equilibrium during the Ten Years' War. Confessedly the third power in Greece, she showed little fear of the first or second, stood with neither one nor the other at the Peace of 421, and boldly urged her views on victorious Sparta in 404. Feeling herself wronged in the matter of the spoil of Athens, she dared to affront the conqueror,[1] and suffered only a Pyrrhic defeat at Coronea at the hands of the best general and the best army that ever fought for Sparta.

But fatalistic soldiers, to be effective in attack, must be animated by a brilliant leader; otherwise, like the best Turkish troops of the present day, they fight their best only at bay, and relapse into inaction when stress is past.[2] In the hands of a great commander, however, soldiery such as the Theban makes a finer fighting material than the quick-witted Athenian, who understood his peril, or the mechanical Spartan, who fought from sheer habit.

Therefore the simultaneous appearance of two great men at Thebes in the fourth century was fraught

---

[1] *Hell.* iii. 4. 4.

[2] Cf. the attitude of the Thebans after killing Lysander at Haliartus in 395. *Hell.* iii. 5. 21, *sq.*

with possibilities exceptional even in an age of small city-states, where a constructive individual was always a most potent force. The avalanches of eastern conquest in all ages have been set rolling by the great man, and Thebes was an eastern state. The lesson was not lost on Philip: the man who had witnessed at close quarters the careers of Epaminondas and Pelopidas, estimated later the potential danger from Thebes at a very high value. While he ignored Sparta, and courteously left Athens alone, the founder of Macedonian supremacy paid Thebes the rude compliment of garrisoning the Cadmeia with Macedonian men-at-arms; Alexander razed all but her temples to the ground.

Great men are those that use their opportunities, and the fame of Epaminondas is not less well deserved because external conditions were very favourable to the expansion of Thebes in the fourth century. The great city-states — Sparta and Athens — were suffering already from that premature exhaustion which is the penalty of too intense a political life. The sloth of the former was thrown in her teeth by her allies in 376;[1] the slackness of the latter is the monotonous theme of her orators. Athens was feeling the obliteration of her free working class, which Periclean state-socialism, based on slave labour, had brought about; Sparta was combating the steady decrease of her nobility.[2]

---

[1] *Hell.* v. 4. 60.

[2] The ὀλιγανθρωπία of Sparta in the fourth and third centuries may be seen in the diminution of the Spartiate army by one half after Leuctra — 12 λόχοι instead of 24, as of old. Cf. *Hell.* vii. 4. 20 with 5. 10. Aristotle, *Pol.* ii. 6.

Nor, again, is credit less due to Epaminondas because he was aided in the task of rousing the Thebans by the action of Agesilaus.[1] A taunt levelled at the latter by a political rival,[2] that he was teaching the Thebans the art of war, was justified enough in fact; the boldness of the Thebans, who, four years before Leuctra, gratuitously and alone attacked a superior force of Spartiatae at Tegyrae,[3] after three years of Spartan invasion, smacks of contempt, bred already by familiarity.

Without Epaminondas, the Thebans of his generation would have been as their ancestors and posterity — men abiding in their tents, eating, drinking, and lusting.[4] With Epaminondas their whole character was for a time changed; and Philip, living in close intercourse with that great man, and watching the effect of his personality upon a people singularly like that over which he hoped one day to rule, learned a lesson in the power of individual will, of which his later life was a consistent exposition.

Alas! no master-hand has drawn for us the portrait of this greatest of Philip's teachers, but his figure detaches itself from the crowd that passes over the historic stage. He is the ideal Hellene, for all the Cadmeian blood in his veins, as cultured as an Athenian, as disciplined as a Spartan, pre-eminent in all provinces of his powers. Not less brilliant and forceful a political idealist than Pericles, he far transcends the Athenian in the ruder fields of

---

[1] Plut. *Pel.* 15.   [2] Plut. *Ages.* 26.   [3] Plut. *Pel.* 16.
[4] Nepos, *Epam. ad fin.*; Diod. xv. 39.

action. Too rigorous,[1] and too complex to be wholly understood or loved by the rude Thebans, as he understood and loved them, he won their blind obedience by sheer dominance of will and their awe-struck respect by consistent subordination of self to their common good. Many of his countrymen were powerful athletes and brave soldiers, but, their equal in physical excellence, Epaminondas stands alone in intellectual eminence, a devoted student of philosophy, an orator in the first rank, a master in music.[2] Majestic and unapproachable as a Phidian god, one story only connects him with a softer passion, as Greeks understood such passions: for the rest, the private man is absorbed in the patriot, who dies happy that his soldiers have won Mantinea, and that two great victories, rather than human offspring, will perpetuate his name.

Pelopidas, his famous henchman, is better known to us than his master, although one of his biographers admits that he was " magis historicis quam vulgo notus." [3] He is a more human figure, easier to portray, a type of his nation purged of its coarsest qualities. Removed by no such gulf as Epaminondas, he was the idol of the Theban people from the night when he slew the Polemarchs to the day of his reckless death in Thessaly.[4] History credits him with neither statesmanlike ideals nor intellectual tastes, but with fiery enthusiasm, perfect courage, and

[1] Nepos, *Epam.* 4.
[2] *Id. Epam.* 3; Diod. *l. c.*, and 88.   [3] Nepos, *Pel.* i.
[4] Diod. xv. 81.

lifelong devotion.[1]　He was the fiery soul of the body
politic, the link between the brain and the members.
Liberator of the city, sole victor of Tegyrae, animating
spirit of the Leuctran charge, dauntless avenger of
the oppressed in Thessaly, Pelopidas glitters through
the short, glorious epoch of Theban history like a
knight errant of the days of chivalry. Historians
have not hesitated to set the impetuous soldier below
Epaminondas; but in turn they must maintain that
to awaken the state, the hot recklessness of the one
was not less necessary in Thebes than the cool
calculation of the other.

There were elements in the coarser but stronger
nature of Philip that recall both the great Thebans.
His union of practical genius with appreciation of the
power of culture, and his comprehensive vision of the
co-operating forces which constitute a Power, elevate
him to the same pinnacle with Epaminondas. In his
sympathy with the rudest of his soldiery and in the
rough good fellowship which so often won hearts in
spite of themselves, he resembled, consciously or not,
Pelopidas. And, did we know more of the details of
history during either the supremacy of Thebes or the
reign of Philip, it might be possible to detect often,
in the latter's words and deeds, distinct reminiscences
of the great men with whom he must have been
brought in contact, either directly or through their
chief disciples Gorgias, Pammenes (with whom the
young hostage lived in most intimate relations), or
others now unknown. Certainly Philip had had a

---

[1] Plut. *Pel.* 4; Nep. *Pel.* 4.

singular object-lesson in the power of the individual ;
certainly it had been given to him to see what a
new military idea could do ·for infantry warfare.
The last stage in the efficiency of a citizen army had
been reached, and new formations, new weapons,
and new tactics must be developed by any one who
should aspire to supremacy.

Philip was no longer in Thebes when her sun passed
its zenith.[1] He heard of the deaths of Pelopidas
and Epaminondas when once more in Macedonia,
whither he had returned in 364, after Perdiccas his
brother had slain his self-styled guardian and resumed
the reins of power. He found the head of his house
co-operating with Timotheus the Athenian against
Amphipolis. Nothing, however, came of repeated
efforts of Athens to seize the key of the mines ; and
Perdiccas, when a Theban fleet began to hover about
the Thracian seas, seems to have changed his game ;
before 361 he had taken Amphipolis into his own
possession.

For the moment the Macedonian king seemed
strong. He established his brother Philip in a semi-
independent principality, for he had by this time an
infant son to succeed to his own throne. But new
trouble was brewing. The Lyncestian Athaliah had
vowed vengeance for her leman's murder. The
death of Epaminondas, and general peace in Greece

---

[1] We do not know why the hostage was released. Perhaps those
in authority at Thebes felt that by this time they could rely upon his
admiration or his fear, and that he might exert a useful influence in
his own country.

deprived Perdiccas of the active support of Thebes,
even as his own action in the matter of Amphipolis
had shut out possible help from Athens. Eurydice
seized the moment. The fiery cross went out among
her tribesmen of Lyncestis, and a cloud of hillmen
and "Illyrians" burst on Emathia. Perdiccas faced
them and fell. His clansmen swore allegiance to the
infant son and to his uncle Philip as Regent. But
swiftly a new storm broke on the north, where the
Paeonians were out; from the east the old pretender,
Pausanias, was advancing with a Thracian host at
his back; and the angry Athenians welcomed the
opportunity to nominate also a creature of their own.
The heart of such a cyclone was no place for a baby
king. Macedonia clamoured for a man, and, persuaded at last, Philip climbed into the perilous
throne.[1]

[1] So Justin, vii. 5. His words are, "*Diu non regem sed tutorem
pupilli egit. At ubi graviora bella imminebant serumque auxilium
in exspectatione infantis erat, compulsus a populo regnum suscepit.*"
A mass meeting of the clan probably took place, similar to that
held by the army at Babylon after the death of Alexander the
Great, in which it was decided to await the birth of Roxana's
child.

THE new king could count on little but his faithful clansmen, his hopes, and his youth. He had legions of enemies, no money, no allies, and, for inheritance, the sins of his fathers. Had he boasted that he could make a nation and an empire out of nothing, he hardly had desired a more genuine opportunity.[1] But in personal capital he was rich. He had been trained in the school of the two greatest men of his age; nature had given him a frame of iron, and the Pythagorean doctors the habit to nurture it hardly; neither the many lusts of his flesh[2] nor the pride of his body held him back a moment from action, and he could sacrifice to his ambition his own person as resolutely as that of his foe. "What a man," said Demosthenes[3] after his death, "had we to fight! For the sake of power and dominion he had an eye thrust out, a shoulder broken, an arm and a leg mortified. Whichever member fortune demanded, that he cast away, so the rest might be in glory and honour." His intellectual force was of the first order, his perception as rapid

---

[1] Cf. Diod. xvi. 95.
[2] See Polybius, quoting Theopompus (viii. 11).
[3] *De Cor.* 67.

and certain as the action which followed it. The
width of his sympathies, coupled with a radical
insincerity of character, enabled him to adapt himself
to all things and all men — to talk with Aristotle, or
to drink to excess of good fellowship with boors and
bravos.[1] No obstacles of principle beset his path,
and two-thirds of the anecdotes recorded of him
illustrate his perfidy. To one thing, however, he
was never false — his personal ambition as involved
in the greatness of his own people. Self-sufficing,
masterful to all men, without scruples and without
foibles, he was a man rather to fear than to love.
Like a Napoleon, he could inspire those whom he
kept at a distance with enthusiastic admiration for
his strength and his star; but perhaps no heart of
man or woman ever beat for him with gentler passion.

Philip's character had been formed in the school of
exile and danger by the time that he was twenty-
three; and already he had proposed to go far. For
the moment, Athens was his most dangerous foe.
The Macedonian had recourse to his first weapon,
craft; he declared her long estranged colony, the
mining city Amphipolis, independent of himself.
Athens turned to the lure, let the Macedonian chase
her pretender to his ships, and ratified a peace
with the first of the many ambassadors she was to
receive from Philip. The other pretender, Pausanias, found his forces melt away; Philip knew that
he had only to give the Thracians and Paeonians gold

---

[1] Cf. Plutarch, *Dem.* 16, who calls him a "sponge," and
Theopompus, quoted above.

while he prepared his steel. The Illyrian-Lyncestian host, however, fought for a cause and a woman not to be bought; but it stayed at the sight of Philip's energy and the approach of winter, and he gained a few months' space to breathe.

His clansmen's spirits rose,[1] and their faith centred in him. Here was the nucleus of an army, but as yet too small and too little professional. Philip must train and arm this Clan like Greeks, and swell their number by the only method open to him as yet — the hiring of mercenaries. But first and foremost he had need of money. Ports and ships the Macedonian did not possess, but the mines on Pangaeus above Amphipolis, belonged as much to him as to any one. He went cautiously to work in the matter, for fear of alarming Athens. A number of Thasian miners came to the mainland, and settled at Crenides on Pangaeus, apparently as spontaneous colonists, but (beyond doubt, when we consider after events) on Philip's invitation.[2]

The winter was spent by Philip's recruiting sergeants in enlisting soldiers of fortune, and by himself in training his clansmen to be the soul of the new army. He went to work as Agesilaus had done forty years before, when he trained the army at Ephesus, which he hoped to lead to Babylon. Philip taught his Macedonians the Greek drill and tactics, constantly exercised them under arms, and made them cover as much as five and thirty miles a day in heavy marching order, each man with flour for a

---

[1] Diod. xvi. 3.   [2] Id. l.c. Cf. Strabo, p. 331.

month and full baggage.[1]   No personal effects would
the king allow any foot-soldier to place on a vehicle;[2]
and his discipline was more than Spartan.   He once
heard that a Tarentine captain had taken a hot bath.
" A Macedonian woman washes in cold water in
childbed! " exclaimed the king, and dismissed him
from his command; and at a later period, we hear
that two distinguished officers were banished their
country for introducing a prostitute into camp.[3]
Knowing Philip's discipline of self, we may say safely
that he asked his men to do nothing that he did
not do habitually.   Emulation was awakened by
the institution of contests in military gymnastics,
which Alexander copied at a later period.[4]   Philip
himself wrestled and boxed in the common arena,[5]
drank with his knights, and was prodigal of good-
fellowship and bounty.[6]   Little by little he welded
all together and to himself, taught the foot-soldiers
to stand firm as a Theban phalanx, and the knights
to manœuvre at his will, not merely to skirmish or
pursue: and by this means and that, when the
season of 358 opened, he was at the head of six
hundred knights and ten thousand infantry, the like
of which for discipline had not been seen north of
Olympus.

The Paeonians surrendered after a single engagement.   Bardylis, leader of the Lyncestian-Illyrian

---

[1] Diod. xvi. 3; Polyaen. iv. 2. 10 ; Frontin. iv. 1. 6.

[2] Frontin. l. c.   [3] Polyaen. iv. 2. 1 and 3.

[4] Diod. xvii. 2.   [5] Polyaen. iv. 2. 6.

[6] Cf. Theopomp. fragments 27 and 240; Diod. xvi. 3; Polyaen.
iv. 9.

host, proposed peace on terms *uti possidetis*. Philip demanded that the Lyncestian towns be surrendered at discretion and the Illyrian allies be sent away. The armies met, and Philip experimented for the first time in the new tactics, which were to crush Greece and conquer Asia. The foe was in solid formation; Philip opposed to them the phalanx, strengthened especially on the left by the cavalry. He led his solid centre and right to engage the whole barbarian front, keeping his left in reserve, till the foe's formation became somewhat disordered. Then the real attack was developed; the Macedonian Knights galloped forward and fell on flank and rear; the phalanx pushed into the front of the disordered mass, while the cavalry rode in from the left. The Illyrians turned and fled. Hundreds were cut down in the pursuit, and when it was over, and the barbarians came to fetch their dead under flag of truce, Philip, with callous treachery, attacked again.[1] They left more than seven thousand dead on the field; and Philip swept the lands of the feudatories as far as the Lake Ochrida and the watershed of the Adriatic.[2]

In one short campaign Philip had restored the Macedonian monarchy to a position that it had not held since the days of Archelaus. The king was once more lord undisputed over the greatest of his feudatories. It remained to secure the mines. Philip

---

[1] Diod. xvi. 4; Frontin. ii. 3. 2. I have used also Polyaenus' thoroughly characteristic story (iv. 2. 5) of the second rout.

[2] Diod. xvi. 8.

marched across his kingdom, gathered up a siege-
train prepared during the winter, and incontinently
summoned Amphipolis to surrender. The townsmen
shut their gates, and sent to apprise Athens; Philip
countermoved by courteously informing the Athenians
that he was acting on their behalf, and would hand
over the town to their representatives, and in the
meantime he brought up his engines. The Athenians
hesitated; Philip's rams broke the wall; Amphipolis
fell in the autumn of 358, and all sympathisers with
Athens were expelled from her gates.[1] The news
caused a panic among the Greek towns of Chalcidice,
and their leader, Olynthus, sent at once to Athens.
But the latter had more on her hands now than she
could deal with. Her great dependencies had declared
the Social War against her, and she was fain to
content herself with Philip's studious courtesy to her
captured citizens, and a vague understanding[2] that
in his own good time he would exchange his new
conquest against their holding of Pydna, the outlet
of Pierian trade. For the present Philip openly acknowledged as his men the Thasian miners of Crenides, and built up their settlement into a great
frontier-fortress, called after himself Philippi, which,
with Amphipolis, should command not only the
mines, but the Thracian coast from Galepsus to the
Nestus.[3] He had found at last his sinews of war.
The gold ore of Pangaeus presently brought in more

[1] Dem. *Olynth.* i. 8.
[2] The famous ἀπόρρητον, Dem. *Olynth.* ii. 6.
[3] Strabo, p. 331.

than a thousand talents yearly, a much larger revenue than was accruing at this time from external sources to any state except Persia, — and he began to strike that extensive coinage[1] of staters which penetrated to Britain, and originated the types of certain of our early coins.[2]

In the winter of 358 Philip could begin in earnest the great work which he had conceived at Thebes — the creation of a national standing army.

He cannot have been unconscious that his work would prove in the event not merely military. If his national army was to be more than an organization of his own clansmen, he must incorporate the feudatories; and whenever the army should become an accomplished fact, there would be in Macedonia no longer a disunion of tribes, but the unity of a nation. It is not to be supposed that his main object was the promotion of a political union, nor indeed that in 358 he had that end more consciously in view, than had the organizers of the Prussian military system in 1864; but neither he was not more ignorant than they of the unifying influence of common service in a great war. Salamis had consolidated the Athenian Demos, and Leuctra made Bœotia almost one in sentiment with Thebes. Community of hope passes in very short time into community of tradition.

---

[1] Diod. xvi. 8.

[2] The remarkable series, illustrating the degeneration of the type, is well known. Philip's original staters have been found in greater numbers than almost any other gold coins of antiquity.

As the Germans in 1870, so the Macedonians in 352 marched out an Alliance to return a Union. Philip's claim to rank among great creative statesmen is not that he foreknew all the ultimate results of his action, but that he seized in their inception and directed successive developments. Both his ideal, and his knowledge of the means to attain it, grew with the growth of events. If in 358 it did not rise above the consolidation of the military strength of Macedonia, and chance in the main made him the creator of Macedonian political unity, it is very certain that he had come to be possessed by a clear conception even of the unification of all Hellas,[1] when he spent his last two years in enlisting the Greeks for common service with Macedonians in a great war. Twelve years later again his son, rising to a conception of world-wide empire on the stepping-stone of his father's pan hellenic kingdom, dreamed of effacing the distinction of Macedonian, Hellene, and Asiatic, by making all march shoulder to shoulder to the conquest of Africa and Europe.

A national standing army was a new thing in those days. The world was familiar with armies, national, but not standing, levies of citizens, or the subjects of a king, called out for particular campaigns and relegated presently to private occupations. Even the most 'professional' of such armies, that of

---

[1] Holm (*Gr. Gesch.* iii. ch. xvii. p. 278) and others date this conception and Philip's Asian schemes almost to the beginning of his reign, but on no evidence. Both evidence and probability are all for later development.

Sparta, was not kept constantly under arms, and took a more soldierly than civic character only through constantly mounting guard over a disaffected population. The world was becoming familiar also with armies, standing, but not national, maintained at various epochs by kings and governors of Persia or Egypt, commercial cities like Carthage, or individual adventurers such as the elder Dionysius of Syracuse, or Jason of Pherae. Such forces as theirs were difficult to control, devoid of *esprit de corps*, liable to seduction, and withal enormously expensive. The citizen army, on the other hand, was either sheer militia, incapable of any but the simplest manœuvres, or very small in numbers, and in both cases difficult to retain in the field. Philip's new army was to combine the merits of both the civic and the mercenary; its chief constituent was to be a large force, derived from his own subjects, imbued with national spirit, and induced by rewards and prizes of war to make soldiering a profession, and remain long enough with the colours to acquire drill and discipline superior to the best mercenary armies. A professional army with a national spirit — that was the new idea; and Philip, equally great in practice and theory, intended to add later a new organization, a new weapon, and new tactics. But the introduction of those novelties' detail must depend on the successful realization of the main principle; for only an army perfect in cohesion, temper, and drill can profit by an elaborate organization, make effective use of a weapon of abnormal character, or be depended upon to execute rapid scientific evolutions in the face of an enemy.

Neither an army nor a nation is made in a day. The six years which succeeded the capture of Amphipolis and preceded the first serious attempt on Greece, probably saw in Macedonia the birth of both one and the other; but Philip was engaged all his life in completing his work. Time alone could cause the all-important tradition to grow. At the beginning of his reign, Alexander had still to face some political reaction on the part of the feudatories, and to beware a little longer of the Lyncestian; but in his army of Asia there is left hardly a trace of race hatred. Philip, in fact, had completed his military creation ere his death. In many details of organization his system was modified by both his son and his son's successors, till it became crystallized in the *corps d'armée* known as the Macedonian to the tactical writers of Roman times; but it is practically certain that the army which won Granicus, Issus, and Arbela was the army of Philip, and that we may use the authorities for the early campaigns of Alexander as evidence for the father's work. We have detailed information of the reorganization of certain *corps* at Susa, and of the whole force after Alexander's return from India, but no hint of any earlier changes. It was the opinion of antiquity that Alexander received his Asian army from his father;[1] and it must be our opinion also if we reflect on the little leisure enjoyed by Alexander from the first moment

[1] Frontin. iv. 2, 4.

he ascended his throne, and on the reputation already possessed far and wide by his Macedonian soldiery before he had met any Persian army in the field.[1]

It was the unanimous opinion of antiquity also that Philip did his work alone. No one of his marshals is ever credited with a share. Parmenio, of whom his king said that he was the only general he had ever known,[2] and Antipater, the future regent of Europe, alone among them rose above mediocrity. The rest of the elder marshals of Alexander — Perdiccas, Craterus, Leonnatus, Polysperchon, Antigonus — shone only with reflected light. The one man, whose after-career warrants the supposition that he may have helped in a great work of organization, is Eumenes, whom Philip found a boy at Cardia,[3] and made his secretary in later years.

Already, before Philip's time, there had existed the levy of the Macedonian clan, a race long inured to guerilla warfare,[4] and organized to some extent by Archelaus[5] and by Philip's eldest brother.[6] The problem was, how to incorporate with the clan the feudatories who had been regarded hitherto at best as its allies?[7] The clan-spirit lives only in the clan;

---

[1] See Memnon's advice to the Persians before Granicus, Arr. i. 12.

[2] Plut. *Apophth. Phil.* 2.   [3] *Id. Eum.* i.

[4] Justin, vii. 2.   [5] Thuc. ii. 100.

[6] Anaxim. fr. 7. *Vide supra*, p. 19.

[7] Such as Derdas of Elimia, whose excellent cavalry joined Amyntas in 382. *Hell.* v. 2, 39.

civic patriotism was exotic outside the city-states of
Hellas; national patriotism as yet did not and could
not exist. Philip knew that what he must create
was a purely military *esprit de corps*, and his army
must be induced to set up itself and himself as gods.
He began by enrolling all his subjects according to
their local and tribal divisions, and assigning them
to standing territorial regiments. Of the infantry
we can only infer the fact;[1] but the names of certain
squadrons of the cavalry are actually recorded, for
example, ἡ 'Ανθεμουσία and ἡ Λευγαία, and so are
the homes of others, "the horsemen from Upper
Macedonia," or "Bottiaea and Amphipolis."[2]

These standing regiments are known each by its
colonel's name, and quoted thus by Arrian, who
reflects the military usage of his authorities. A τάξις
of foot, whose colonel is absent, is still referred to as
his, though led by another; and Clitus' cavalry command bears his name after his death.[3]

All were called alike "Macedonians;" the only
general distinction, made hereafter, is between Macedonians and Greeks, Thracians or Illyrians.[4]

Philip knew, however, that it was not enough to
make distinct territorial regiments; he must endow

---

[1] From Arr. iii. 16, where the recruits (foot) from Macedonia
are distributed into τάξεις. Cf. Curt. v. 2. 6, where we are told that
Alexander's main innovation at Susa was the abolition of all local
and national divisions throughout the army.

[2] Arr. ii. 9; i. 2. [3] *Id.* iii. 11; vi. 6.

[4] So in Diodorus' catalogue of the army about to cross to
Asia (xvii. 17); and *passim* in Arrian, where the common phrase,
οἱ πέζοι τῶν Μακεδόνων (*e. g.* as early as i. 6), includes every one —
Lyncestian, Orestian, Elimiote, and the like.

them with common emulation. He conceived therefore for different corps a scale of honour rising towards
the person of the king. Service in the heavy cavalry
ranked above service in the foot, for the former were
more especially the ἑταῖροι, or " Companions " of the
king ; their generals have the most important commands in Alexander's army, and their troopers enjoy
treble share of prize money.[1] Philip promoted whom
he pleased to this service,[2] Macedonian or Greek, and
thus in time swelled the six hundred who accompanied him on his first campaign, to the two thousand
who followed his son to Asia.[3] The whole body of
ἑταῖροι were " Royals," but one squadron was of
greatest honour, the " Royal," or " King's Own,"
sometimes called the Ἄγημα,[4] which took the right
of the whole line at Arbela.[5]

Most honoured among the Foot was the Corps of
Guards (ὑπασπισταί), specially attached to the person
of the king. They became very famous in Alexander's
wars, and later under the name of the Silver Shields
(Ἀργυράσπιδες).[6] Like the cavalry they were all
" Royals," but there was among them a special corps
d'élite (τὸ ἄγημα τὸ βασιλικόν)[7] one thousand strong,

[1] Cf. Diod. xvii. 63,74 ; Curt. vii. 5. 23.

[2] Theopomp. fr. 249.

[3] Perhaps even more, if the fifteen hundred horse left with
Antipater be reckoned into the calculation.

[4] Arr. iii. 11.

[5] Also at the crossing of the Hydaspes (Arr. v. 13).

[6] Plut. Eum. 16 ff. For the grounds of the certain identification of the Argyraspids and Hypaspists, see " Army of Alexander,"
in Journ. of Philology, xvii. No. 33, p. 14.

[7] Cf., e. g., Arr. iii. 11 ; v. 13.

a third of the whole.   This force took the right of all
the infantry at Arbela.

As Philip had extended the honourable title of
" King's Followers " to all his native cavalry, so he
took the corresponding term πεζέταιροι, and applied
it to all the Macedonian infantry, whether of his
clan or no : thus distinguishing the new nation from
the Greeks, as the clan had once distinguished itself
from the feudatories.[1]

---

[1] This is the view to which I am compelled, on reconsideration
of the passages in which the term πεζέταιροι (already in dispute
in the days of Ulpian) occurs.   When I wrote the article on
Alexander's army, referred to above, I was inclined to regard it as
equivalent only to the one τάξις of Coenus (on the strength of
Arr. ii. 23).   In some sense a distinction is implied in the term,
or the mutineers at Opis would not have coupled it with the ἄγημα
and ἀργυράσπιδες (Arr. vii. 11).   But I now believe that Demosthenes is approximately accurate when he uses the term to express
all the constituents of Philip's Phalanx that were not ξένοι
(Olynth. ii. 17).   Such a distinction would be sufficient to account
for the phrase οἱ π. οἱ καλούμενοι, used by Arrian four times out
of seven.   One of Ulpian's explanations is that the π. were the
pick of the infantry ; but care must be taken not to include in
the term the Hypaspistae, if Arrian is to be credited with any
precision of nomenclature at all.   Droysen and Grote go wrong
on this point.

I conceive, therefore, that each of Alexander's great regiments
of foot (e. g. the six enumerated at Arbela, Arr. iii. 11) was
made up of two battalions — one of most honour, containing only
Macedonian πεζέταιροι, one of less honour, made up of allies and
mercenaries.   The second composed the δευτέρα φάλαγξ at Arbela
— the line of reserve designed to face about and meet an
attack — and also probably formed the rear of the διπλῆ φάλαγξ
before Granicus (Arr. i. 13).   Whenever Alexander, therefore,
takes οἱ πεζέταιροι οἱ καλούμενοι on special expeditions, he is
picking the first battalions of his regiments.   Not infrequently
these regiments are credited with two commanders by Arrian
(e. g. iv. 22, τὴν [τάξιν] Πολυσπέρχοντος καὶ Ἀττάλου ; iv. 24, τὴν

Here, then, is a system of honourable nomenclature — βασιλικοί, βασιλικαὶ ἴλαι, ἀγήματα, ἑταῖροι, πεζέταιροι — designed to give the army pride in itself, and to attach it to the person of the king. We cannot doubt that promotion into the distinguished corps was made possible for all Macedonians who should win the king's favour; it could even be granted to aliens. Further, there was, of course, a scale of military honour for individuals; this man takes the lead of his file and faces the foe in the front rank; that one brings up the rear, and is important as a pivot. One private receives double pay; another ten staters;[1] and so forth, up to the culminating distinction of Guard of the Person, which in Alexander's time was enjoyed by four natives of Pella, one of Orestis, and two of Eordaea.[2]

If military service is to be accepted readily as the main reason and object of existence, the soldier must be caught young. Philip, therefore, enacted that all

Κοίνου τε καὶ ᾿Αττάλου τάξιν; v. 12, τὴν Κλείτου τε καὶ Κοίνου), as are also the cavalry ἱππαρχίαι (e. g. v. 12, τὴν Περδίκκου τε καὶ Δημητρίου). Unfortunately Arrian is not exact in his use of the names of corps, especially τάξις; but still some value may be attached to these twin commands, in view of the other evidence for the dual nature of the regiments. If Diodorus' figures (xvii. 17) are accurate, the πεζέταιροι in Alexander's force, when he crossed to Asia, numbered 9000; each first battalion, therefore, at Arbela would be 1500 strong. The allies and mercenaries numbered 12000, and the second battalions may therefore have been 2000 strong, but more probably 1500 also, 3000 men being reserved to counterbalance the 3000 Hypaspistae.

[1] Arr. vii. 23.
[2] Id. vi. 28. The home of one — Peucestas, added in 324 — is unknown.

sons of the upper classes of his subjects should be
sent to the court to serve as Pages of the Body, in
peace to be Equerries or Gentlemen of the Chamber,
in war to follow the campaign as an inner Guard,
and always to study those military duties which they
would have to perform presently as officers of the
Cavalry or the Line.[1] If he made any special provision for the boys of the lower classes, we do not
know it; but we do know that the child born or bred
in barracks grows up in the military tradition, and
there must always be many such children where
there is a standing army. It is noteworthy that
Alexander, when he sent the time-expired veterans
home in 324, retained all their children born in
Asia.[2]

By such means did Philip hope to make the pride
of service in a great army the ruling passion of his
people; and he must have foreseen that, if he was
successful, the small race divisions among his subjects would fade little by little into a common
distinction of all from the rest of the world. In
the event the Macedonians became one people, and
their common military pride and exclusiveness barred
even Alexander's way when he dreamed of a wider
union. He could abolish the territorial regiments
without trouble at Susa in 330, as having become
already superfluous divisions, but his first attempts

[1] Such an institution at a court half Greek, half barbarian,
gave, of course, many occasions to scandal; but Arrian (iv. 13)
and Curtius (viii. 6) agree as to the object which Philip had in
view when he instituted it.

[2] Arr. vii. 12.

to expand the great Macedonian union provoked open mutiny.

The ancient treatise on Tactics, which has come down to our times in two recensions, to which the names of Arrian and Aelian have been attached, furnishes elaborate detail of the Macedonian military organization; but so seldom do either the names or strength of the corps agree with our authorities for Alexander's army,[1] that we must suppose them to be of later times. Furthermore, the system described in that treatise, of units ascending in arithmetical progression from the file of 16 to the full brigade of 16,384,[2] belongs to a time when the territorial battalion had ceased to be the unit. It is more probable that Philip organized his new army by regiments than by brigades; and that Alexander first began to work towards the latter system at Susa in 330.

Contemporary authority makes it clear that Philip's army was a standing force of men with arms always in their hands,[3] ready to march in summer or winter alike;[4] and that it was organized as a *corps d'armée*, the phalanx of Macedonian foot having a regular complement of all arms, light troops, cavalry, and archers, attached to it, and both siege and field artillery.[5] It was in the strictest sense a professional

---

[1] See article on "Army of Alexander," p. 20, *cit. supra*. The coincidence of names is about fifty-five per cent., that of numbers not above thirty per cent.

[2] *Tact.* 10.   [3] Dem. *De Cor.* 235.

[4] *Id. Phil.* iii. 48 ff.

[5] Cf. Diod. xvi. 8 and 74; Arr. i. 6.

army, elaborately trained to march under heavy arms and baggage,[1] highly paid and rewarded, and as capable of fortifying a camp or mining a wall as of executing every movement in the face of the enemy.

Relying on its training and discipline, Philip could introduce it to new fighting methods. He taught his Cavalry to charge, not in line, but in wedge-shaped formations,[2] a device destined to be resorted to by his son at Arbela. For the Infantry, he perfected the famous phalanx. Though in conception this phalanx was not different from the existing Greek fighting array, Philip so far developed and systematized it that he came to be regarded as its inventor. His new ideas seem to have been two : *First to render bodies of pikemen more mobile and pliable than the Theban or Spartan.* So far as we can judge, the idea of the Greek formations had been to range pikemen together in one compact mass, and win by sheer weight of man pushing on man, breast to back and shoulder to shoulder. It was hardly possible in such formation for the man-at-arms to make play with his pike, and uneven ground or any accident caused serious confusion. With highly disciplined soldiers like the Spartan, able to re-form quickly, and knowing how to use their weight, a considerable advantage might be gained ; but, nevertheless, as was proved in 394 at Coronea, training in this formation could not overcome sheer weight sturdily applied. Epaminondas saw

---

[1] *Vide supra*, p. 45.   [2] *Tact.* 16.

that the traditional deep formation[1] of the Bœotians, if practised by trained and resolute men on good ground, must break a thin line opposed to it; but only able to find enough trained men to strengthen one wing, he conceived the idea of attacking with one part of his line only, and trusting to the moral effect upon all the foe of the breaking of their formation at an important point. The Leuctrian " Wedge " marked the extreme that could be attained in the use of sheer weight. It was obvious, however, that, if opposed to a mobile and ready foe, its clumsy mass would be in grave peril, the weak part of the line might be cut off, and a very little movement over uneven ground would cause disorder. Philip, therefore, in search of a new idea, did not proceed on Theban lines, but reverting to shallow formations of eight, ten, or perhaps sixteen deep at the most, drilled his pikemen to stand in open order, in which they could ply their pikes easily and move quickly. If we can trust the *Tactica,* there were usually three feet between each man, both in rank and file interval, and in the closest order a foot and a half. Ample room therefore was left for individual and sectional movement, such as that implied in the opening of lanes in Alexander's array on the Balkans to allow passages for the Thracian waggons, or at Arbela to give the frightened horses yoked to Darius' scythed chariots a chance to bolt clear through the lines. All tacticians know that soldiers must be more thoroughly

[1] Cf. their depth of twenty-five shields as early as 424, at Delium (Thuc. iv. 93).

drilled and of better temper to preserve their formation and steadiness in open than in close order; but Philip had secured those essential first requisites, and thus could form a fighting force able to charge over bad ground and engage formations much deeper than their own.

His second idea was the "*sarissa*," or long pike, *which would enable his phalanx to strike the first blow.* To the efficient using of such a weapon, training and discipline were all essential. Macedonian armies of the third and second centuries plied a *sarissa* even twenty-four feet long,[1] and six points protected the front rank man. It is needless to credit Philip's pikeman with so monstrous a weapon as this; it belongs to the days of decline when generals, deficient in tactical ability, had reverted to solid immobile formations as more within their power to handle.[2] No allusion is made by any historian of Alexander's wars to so abnormal a weapon as the *sarissa*, which astonished Polybius and Livy. On the contrary, the mobility, which stands out as the most striking virtue of Alexander's phalanx, witnesses that its weapon was not unwieldy. His formations are never

---

[1] The coincidence of Polybius (xviii. 12) with Polyaenus (ii. 29. 2) and the second recension of the *Tactica* (13) puts this beyond doubt. Cf. also Livy's remarks on its unwieldy length (xliv. 41). The first recension of the *Tactica* reads πόδας for πήχεις, reducing the length to fourteen or sixteen feet; but either this is a manuscript error or correction, or it is a reminiscence of the earlier *sarissa*.

[2] In the same way, heavy body armour was introduced in the Middle Ages, to compensate for degeneracy in drill and tactics.

(like those which the Romans met) at the mercy of uneven ground. They even crossed the Pinarus at Issus and re-formed in the face of the enemy. The Greek weapon may be assumed not to have exceeded the greatest length assigned by the author of the *Tactica* to a practicable pike, viz. twelve feet.[1] Let a foot or two more be allowed to the phalangite of Philip and Alexander, and we save the indubitable fact that a longer weapon than the Greek was introduced, and do not render the attack at Issus a practicable impossibility.

This Phalanx, however, be it observed, did not prove instantly superior to the Greek infantry formations that it encountered; and it is a frequent error, derived from the Romans, to attach to it a supreme importance in the Macedonian fighting line. Its inventor and his son used it to play a great but subordinate part; secure of its discipline and steadiness, they could engage with it the whole front of a superior enemy, while the real attack was developed by the cavalry on the flanks. We have seen already the first outcome of these tactics against the Illyrians: they were to win Chaeronea, and be used with signal effect at Issus. The secret of the success of Philip and Alexander in their pitched battles lies in their handling of the magnificent horse, Macedonian and allied, and, in lesser affairs, of the lighter Guards[2]

---

[1] 12.

[2] The Guards (ὑπασπισταί) are often reckoned into the Phalanx, *e. g.* in Arrian's catalogue of the array at Arbela (iii. 11); but they are also distinguished clearly from the heavy phalangites whenever

and archers. In later days only, when there was
no longer a general to handle them, did these corps
sink in repute below the automatically moving
Phalanx.

The perfected military system must have been the
work of many years. For a long time Philip's
national army was supplemented largely by mercenaries,[1] and the use of such auxiliaries was not
abandoned entirely even by his son.[2] But we know
that Philip at his death left to Alexander forty
thousand seasoned men, and a system established so
firmly that Phocion was moved to warn the exultant
Athenians that the belauded poniard of Pausanias
had done no more than diminish the army of
Chaeronea by just a single man.[3]

Four years passed while Philip organized, plotted,
and planned, but made hardly a sign to the outer
world. In that obscure interval not only an army
of soldiers was created, but another army with golden
weapons sent forth to serve within the walls of every
city-state of Hellas.[4] Fraud before force, but force
at the last — such was Philip's principle of empire.
Once only he aggressed, and that, perhaps, in reply
to a hostile move. Athens, who still included in her

any occasion arises for distinction, e. g. on Alexander's rapid march to
the Cilician gates (ii. 4).

[1] Cf. Diod. xvi. 8; Dem. *Olynth.* ii. 17.

[2] There were 5000 in Alexander's Asian army (Diod. xvii. 17).
Cf. the corps of ἀρχαῖοι καλούμενοι ξένοι at Arbela (Arr. iii. 12).

[3] Plut. *Phoc.* 16.

[4] Demosthenes (*De Cor.* 19) implies that there were already paid
agents of Philip at Athens in 356.

League some of the ports round the Thermaic Gulf,
had begun a year or two before this date to intrigue
with cities and chieftains of Thrace.[1] Now, however,
she was struggling with revolt elsewhere, and the
allegiance of all her dependencies was shaken. At
such a favourable moment secret overtures were
made by certain citizens of Pydna and Potidaea.
Philip accepted their conditions, the gates were
opened, and both towns passed unresisting into his
hands. He was not, however, ready either to use
them or to fight for them, and with cool perfidy he
handed them over, together with Anthemus, to the
keeping of a local Greek confederation, which Olynthus was striving to increase at the expense of
Athens. For he knew that the gift would be
guarded gratefully, till in his own good time he might
swallow that confederation and his gift at a gulp.

For the rest, Philip lived in comparative peace,
doing no more than egg on a Thracian neighbour,
Kersobleptes, to loosen the grip of Athens on his
coasts,[2] and harry the Illyrians by deputy.[3] Visiting the isle of Samothrace, to be initiated into the
mysteries of the Cabiri, he met another royal novice,
Olympias, daughter of a dead Epirote king and
reputed of the Greek stem of Aeacus.[4] Her fierce

[1] Neopolis, *C. I. A.* ii. 66; Ketriporis and Lykkeios, ii. 66 *b.*
[2] But cf. Diod. xvi. 22. Cf. also Isocr. *De Pace*, 22 (spoken in
355) with Dem. *in Arist.* 183.
[3] Plut. *Alex.* 3.
[4] *Id. Alex.* 3. Cf. Paus. i. 9. 8. The Alexander Romance
alludes to a former marriage and an earlier offspring (Ps. Callisth.
i. 13), but there is no corroborative evidence.

fantastic nature appealed to the Macedonian in the
common excitement of the orgies, and as soon as
might be he wedded the wild woman. Men believed
that portents marked her bridal night, and visions and
strange dreams the early months of her pregnancy;
and on a stormy night of October, 356, while the
Ephesian fane of the Goddess of Asia was aflame,
she bore Philip a son.

In the spring of 353 the king was ready at last with
soldiers and plans. He came out to war with a double
purpose — to free his new-made nation from all frontier
danger once and for all, and to increase to a sufficient
degree its internal strength and wealth. He had
chastised already the Illyrians and Paeonians, and
allied himself by marriage with Epirus. Thracian
chieftains, whom he had courted hitherto to keep
them indifferent to the seductions of Athens,[1] must
be crushed now to secure the northern and eastern
marches. The Greek cities on his southern coasts
from Olympus to the Chersonese were a standing peril; while Thessaly contained the menacing
Pheraean power, and withal the finest cavalry in
Europe next to his own.[2]

He seems to have tried his strength first on certain

<hr />

[1] Cf. Diod. xvi. 34, with Dem. *in Arist.* 183.

[2] Cf. Justin, vii. 6. "Hinc Thessaliam non praedae cupiditate,
sed quod exercitui suo robur Thessalorum equitum adjungere
gestiebat, nihil minus quam bellum metuentem improvisus ex-
pugnat; unumque corpus equitum pedestriumque copiarum invicti
exercitus fecit."

of the Greek cities ; [1] but his Thracian allies took fright and called in Chares the Athenian. Philip eluded his fleet, and came back west to Methone, the one port of importance which Athens held still on the inner Macedonian sea. The imperial Republic was appealed to, but sent no help; Philip pressed the siege, and when his men had scaled the wall, took away their ladders and so forced them into the town.[2] The citizens — men, women, and children — were sent forth in the clothes they wore to find another home, and their city was razed to the ground; it had cost Philip an eye.[3]

It marks an era in Philip's life, this siege of a little port in Pieria, for it meant war open and declared with Athens. Amphipolis, indeed, had not been forgotten by the jealous Republic, but Philip could allege that for long it had not been an Athenian dependency *de facto*, and he made feint of debating still the question of exchange. Pydna and Potidaea had invited him of their own motion, and, though he took them, he did not keep them in his hands. Ancient states often hovered long between peace and war, inflicting and receiving minor injuries, tantamount

[1] Cf. *Olynth.* iii. 4. Abdera and Maronea, at any rate. Cf. Dem. *in Arist. l.c.* with Polyaen., iv. 2, 22.

[2] Polyaen. iv. 2, 15.

[3] Callisthenes (*ap. Stob.* vii. § 65) says the eye was shot out by one Aster, as Philip was marching to the siege of Olynthus; but Callisthenes seems to have confused the siege of Methone with the later operations against Chalcidice. Cf. Diod. xvi. 34 ; Strabo, p. 33 *a* ; Justin, vii. 6 ; Pliny, *Nat. Hist.* vii. 37 ; Plut. *Parallel.* ch. viii. ; and Suidas, *s.v.* Μεθώνη. The latter says that Aster was a Methonaean.

to *casus belli*, but sent no heralds. Philip knew well this practice and how to use it;[1] but Methone made nothing possible but open war; and the Athenians always looked back to that siege as a point of departure in the Macedonian's deliberate scheme to humble their country.

Nevertheless, in 353, Philip had no wish to humble Athens, except on his own coasts. Throughout life his rude nature hankered after the approval of the city which he called the "Theatre of Glory,"[2] and always he was more than half ashamed to use his brute broadsword against her wit. Athenians alone among his captives he freed unransomed, when the chance of war threw them into his hands; their land alone in Greece he neither entered himself nor allowed a single soldier to violate, even after Chaeronea. Had Athens not clung to her imperial relations with the coasts of Macedonia and Thrace, her orbit would never have disturbed that of Philip. It was the western ports which first embroiled the two; it was Halonnesus and the Chersonese which strained their newly made Peace; it was Athenian support of the cities on the sea of Marmora, which indirectly brought Philip down at last to Chaeronea. Neither his last acts nor his first can be justified by international right, as commonly understood; the attempt to acquit him by the laws of individual morality would be as futile as absurd. Let those that are without sin arraign by which code they will this architect of a nation.

[1] Cf. Dem. *Phil.* iv. 61.   [2] Plut. *Apophth. Phil.* 11.

It was late in that summer ere Philip could put
hand to his dearest project. The great knightly house
of Larissa had invited him to interfere in their quarrel
with the rival house of Pherae.[1] An intriguer could
wish no fairer field than Thessaly. One in name,
it was divided from end to end by the fatal feuds
of families. The great houses of Larissa, Pherae,
Crannon, Pharsalus, and Pelinna, idle and luxurious
feudal Barons with no overlord, rode and fought and
oppressed their serfs. They knew no voluntary
union ; but sometimes one house would so far increase
its power as to force submission or unequal alliance
on others, as the Aleuadae of Larissa had done in
time past, and to claim for its chief the title of *tagus*
of all Thessaly. More than twenty years before the
Larissan family sent their invitation to Macedonia,
a great Baron, one Jason, had arisen in Pherae — a
man of a genius unscrupulous and masterful as that
of Philip himself. This man, noting the success of
professional armies in Asia, used the revenues of his
cornlands and his port of Pagasae to buy soldiers of
fortune ; and ere he died, in the year after Leuctra,
lord of all the six thousand Thessalian knights,[2]

[1] Both Diodorus (xvi. 14) and Justin (vii. 6) possibly imply
that Philip made an expedition to help these Aleuadae of Larissa
earlier than 353. Demosthenes, however, reckons (*Phil.* iii. 25)
that up to 341 Philip had been marching about Greek soil for less
than thirteen years. I prefer to rate this explicit contemporary
statement above the very vague indications of the chroniclers ;
but it is quite possible that the *invitation* reached Philip earlier
than 353, but was put aside till it could conveniently be com-
plied with.

[2] See for Thessaly under Jason, the speech of Polydamas of
Pharsalus at Sparta in 374. Xen. *Hell.* vi. 1.

he could marshal with his mercenaries and allies the
most formidable force in Greece.   But by 353 he and
his sons had met tyrants' deaths.   A shadow of their
power alone survived at Pherae; and the Aleuadae
of Larissa had fair hope of tasting full vengeance
for the wrongs of twenty years, when Philip marched
south from Methone to gain a footing in Thessaly.

He appears to have underrated his foes, or over-
rated his friends.   The Pheraean Baron called up
seven thousand mercenaries from the spoilers of Delphi,
and against these Philip could make no head.   A second
check disheartened his men, and with much ado he
drew them back to Macedonia.   During the winter
he pressed the Thessalians to supply better support,
and when he came south again in the spring of 352
he was able to take the field with more than twenty
thousand foot and three thousand horse.   A host of
knights and mercenaries, superior to his own, was
awaiting him, and in the plain of Volo, Philip fought
his first great battle on Greek soil.   As champion
of outraged Apollo against the impious Phocian
hirelings, he exalted the superstitious confidence of
his soldiers by wreathing their helmets as for a
festival.   They charged with the fury of fanaticism :
the Phocian mercenaries and their leader Onomarchus,[1] stricken with panic, hardly awaited the onset
of the phalanx; and the Companion and Larissan
cavalry bore down on the Pheraeans until all broke
and fled together towards the sea.   An Athenian fleet
was standing in-shore, and those that had fled first

---

[1] Cf. Justin, viii. 2 ; and Paus. x. 2, 5.

stripped off their armour and waded out towards
the ships, but ere Onomarchus was out of his
depth he was killed by missiles. The victor crucified
the body, and put to death three thousand of his
prisoners, as sacrilegious men outside the pale of
international right.

The results of the Victory were grave indeed!
The Pheraean army had lost nearly half its numbers,
and its best ally. The Baron surrendered his city
without another blow, flying south of Thermopylae
with the last of his mercenaries; and his port of
Pagasae fell. The power which Jason founded had
received its death-blow, and it was for the Macedonian
now to be *tagus* of Thessaly.

Flushed with success, Philip conceived the idea of
pushing his pious championship of Apollo even to
Delphi. Perhaps already he craved for Hellenic
recognition; certainly he wished to secure Thessaly
on the south by breaking up the main Phocian force
and seizing the southern Gate. He was not, however,
to pass Thermopylae yet. News came up that it was
held by a strong force, not of Phocians, but Athenians. Chares had sent home word of Philip's project,
and the Republic that had been dashed too severely
by the disastrous result of the Social War to make
any serious effort to stay the Macedonian, started
at last from lethargy at the news that an army
greater than any since that of Xerxes' was making
for the pass. Philip had no idea of forcing his
passage against serious opposition. So he turned
back to Thessaly, and by the space of two years used

all his arts to make it his own. Nowhere, except at Pherae, whose last shadow of a tyrant he expelled in 351, did he cry *Vae victis!* He would be, forsooth, no more than *tagus*, with harbour-dues to recoup expenses, and the good will of free Thessaly for reward. He won the land "by wiles rather than by arms,"[1] fostering every weakening quarrel and supporting the masses against the Barons. To only one district, that of Magnesia and its port of Pagasae, did he lay imperial claim; for there his garrisons could command the harbour of Volo, matchless shelter for his own privateers, and dangerous inlet for those of his foes. Jason and his sons already had proved its value, and Philip's successors reckoned the fortress, which they built on its shore a mile from the modern town, to be one of the keys of Greece. It was largely this claim that so long delayed the settlement of Thessaly; protest upon protest was made by the Thessalians, and we find Parmenio engaged still in 346 in reducing one of the towns on the gulf.

The filaments of Philip's web stretched even to the long island of Euboea, whence Athenian influence could always threaten Thessaly. Gold and promises gathered a Macedonian party in Chalcis and Eretria, and fomented civil war. The opponents of Philip called upon Athens; but when Phocion, her general, arrived in 349, it was to find that Philip's gold had debauched even the leader of his own allies. Deserted on the field of Tamynae, he saved himself and his army, and chastised his betrayer; but the Athenians

---

[1] Polyaen. iv. 2. 19.

never recovered again all their prestige in Euboea.
Thenceforward tyrants ruled the cities in the interests
of Philip, or at best of themselves, and Athens felt
that she might be threatened at any moment from
vantage points whose possessors could turn both
Thermopylae and the passes of Cithaeron.

For half a dozen years after Pagasae we are
allowed no more than glimpses of Philip. His agents
appear in Greek towns,[1] and his privateers in Greek
waters; but of himself, so soon as he has left Thessaly, we hear only that he is on his own confines.[2] He
had set himself to finish that task which was but half
done when he marched into Thessaly, viz. the reduction
once for all of the western half of the Balkan peninsula. The northern Illyrians and Paeonians, and his
own Epirote kinsman, Arybbas, still professed independence.[3] The most part of the Greek coast towns, from
the Hebrus to the Axius, had yet to acknowledge Macedonian sway. Whenever the cloud lifts, we descry the
restless king warring far inland, now stricken with
sickness, now reported dead. At one moment he is
besieging Heraeonteichos by the Hebrus, at another
sweeping back through Geira to Stagira, Mecyberna
and Torone.[4] This much, at least, is certain — that,
the six years completed, Philip had only the east
of the Balkan peninsula to conquer, and hardly a

[1] Dem. *Phil.* i. 17, 41; *Olynth.* ii. 18; *De Pace*, 6; *F. L.* 10.
[2] *Phil.* i. 11.
[3] *Olynth.* i. 13. Cf. Plut. *Alex.* 2; *C. I. A.* ii. 115, which
proves that Arybbas, when beaten, sought refuge at Athens.
[4] *Olynth.* iii. 5; Diod. xvi. 52; Ael. *V. H.* xii. 54.

Thracian port west of Hebrus is reckoned thereafter independent of him. It was estimated that ere he came down to Olynthus in 349, he had suppressed the freedom of thirty-two Hellenic cities of Thrace;[1] and a later age interpreted as portents to Hellas the comets and earthquakes which marked the year 350.[2]

Philip, who had threatened Olynthus already three years before and driven her to compound her quarrel with Athens,[3] drew at last towards her walls in the spring of 349. The capital of Chalcidice, although not comparable to the greatest maritime cities of Ionia, Greece, or Sicily, could offer a resistance more serious and a prize more valuable than any port of Thrace, except Byzantium. She had risen to her dignity on the ruins of the first maritime empire of Athens, by forcing into an unwilling federation most of the towns on the trident peninsula,[4] and opposing herself consistently to the enfeebled leaders of the southern Hellenes. Sparta, indeed, at the zenith of her own power, had read her one rude lesson; but relying first on the Thracian tribes, and latterly on the Macedonian king himself,[5] Olynthus had persisted in asserting her headship; and the fitful efforts of Athenian admirals to re-establish their dominion in Thrace had gone far to unite her confederacy with her

---

[1] Callisth. fr. 42 ; Suid. *s. v.* Κάρανος.

[2] Pliny, *N. H.* ii. 27.

[3] *C. I. A.* ii. 105. Cf. Libanius, arg. to Olynthiac orations.

[4] See Xen. *Hell.* v. 211 ff, for a contemporary statement of the nature of her " federation."

[5] Dem. *in Aristocr.* 107.

in common resistance. To panhellenic sympathy, therefore, Olynthus had established no claim, nor indeed did she obtain it either before or after her fall. Only it chanced, as we shall see, that her interests were made the cry of a certain Athenian party, and that its leading spokesman saw fit to suppress her early record, to exaggerate both what she was and what she might have been, and to paint in vivid colours the dolorous impression caused by her catastrophe — a picture which the subsequent attitude of the Athenians towards the oppressor of Olynthus, and of the Peloponnesians towards Olynthian captives (to take the orator's own story) signally fails to support. In the trident Philip played his usual ruthless game. He broke into the confederate cities one by one, but, assuring Olynthus that he was not at war with herself,[1] contrived to convince her that he, her old ally, would hand over once more to her keeping the fractious members of her confederacy, chastened and subject as Potidaea seven years before. His spears moved stage by stage nearer the capital. The Olynthians suspected nothing, or lulled their suspicions ; when lo ! a Macedonian herald appeared at their gates, and throwing it in their teeth that they were sheltering two of his master's half-brothers, destined long ago to death at their kinsman's accession,[2] proclaimed his brutal ultimatum, that Macedonia was not wide enough for Olynthus and for Philip.[3] It was a bolt from the blue. No room

[1] See *Phil.* iii. 11.
[2] Justin, viii. 3.   [3] Dem. *Phil. l.c.*

was opened for grace, and the citizens could but shut their gates and look round the Hellenic world for help. One state only was there, independent of Persia and already embroiled with Philip, which possessed any considerable fleet. That state was Athens, and for the second time to Athens must Olynthus go.

The Olynthian envoys were received in the summer by the Athenian people, without, it seems, great enthusiasm — but they were heard. In the exhausted Republic an imperial policy had not been popular since the Social War, and now that there was trouble in Euboea, a majority of the citizens were disposed to accept the statements of Philip's agents that the Macedonian king's ambition was not directed against the Athenian state, which indeed, they protested, he held in high esteem. The loss of the Thracian mines however rankled in the soul of Demos, who had come to love free shows and to hate taxation as heartily as a Roman state-pensioner; and withal individual Athenians of position, like Roman nobles, foresaw in foreign commands very pretty opportunities for loot and blackmail. Therefore, rather perhaps because they did not love Olynthus than because they did, the Athenians acceded to the envoys' prayer so far as to despatch a half-piratical expedition of two thousand hired soldiers in thirty ships of war under their notorious *condottiere*, Chares. How this force conducted itself we may infer from Demosthenes' complaints in the second Olynthiac oration,[1] and also from the fact

[1] § 28; cf. *Phil.* i. 45.

that it appears to have done no sort of harm to
Philip. Chares was back in Athens by October;
and already, in response to a second appeal from
Olynthus, the still more notorious pirate Charidemus [1]
had taken eighteen Athenian ships of war, four
thousand light troops, and a small force of cavalry,
drafted from the Euboean army of Phocion,[2] and
gone off to Chalcidice ; where he raided the lands of
the Greek towns in Pallene and Bottiaea to the no
small satisfaction of himself and his men, but neither
to the serious hurt of Philip nor to the conspicuous
advantage of Olynthus. The latter, in fact, sent
presently to complain of these hireling hordes, but
only obtained early in 348 [3] the loan of Chares again,
followed this time by a citizen force of two thousand spears and three hundred horse, together with
seventeen ships of war. But we are not led to
suppose that any good result followed; Chares
returned probably ere the Olympic Truce was
proclaimed,[4] Philip not having been driven back
a single foot.

Already the lesser Chalcidic cities were under the
Macedonian's heel, and the Olynthian forces, after
two hard-fought but unsuccessful engagements,[5] were

[1] See Dem. *in Aristocratem, passim ;* and Theopompus, fr. 155.
[2] Dem. *in Mid.* p. 197.
[3] Such an interval before the third expedition is in itself
probable, and not at all inconsistent with the words of Philochorus
as quoted by Dionysius (*ad Amm.* 9). Holm (*Gr. Gesch.* iii.
ch. 17, p. 280) anticipates me in this view.
[4] Aesch. *F. L.* 12.
[5] Cf. Theopomp. fr. 155, for their partial success.

penned within their walls. Ancient sieges were slow
and painful if there was no traitor to open a
gate, and the besieged had access to the sea; and
Olynthus might have kept Philip without its walls
for long enough, had he depended on force alone.
The Macedonian, however, had his agents within the
gates as well as his pikes outside, and was working to
corrupt some leader of the aristocratic faction, which,
it seems, inspired the defence.[1] During the winter
the stalwart Apollonides came to be disgraced, and
traitors, Lasthenes and Euthycrates,[2] to be put in his
room, and from them the surrender was bought at
last in the early spring of 347. The aristocratic
knights were betrayed; the commons ceased to
resist; and more by fraud at the last than force
Philip found himself in Olynthus. He razed the
city to the ground, sold its citizens for slaves, after
the brutal Macedonian manner, which even his
hellenized son used, executed his two half-brothers,
and went off to Dium to give thanks at the great
festival of Macedonian Zeus[3] for the crowning mercy
of a united Macedonia.

Winter had set in when a herald appeared at the
court of Pella, announcing that an embassy was on its
way from Athens with overtures of peace. Philip had
still to realize two schemes in his earliest programme
of ambition. The eastern half of the Balkan peninsula remained to be subdued; and his supremacy

---

[1] *Phil.* iii. 56 ff.　　　　　　　[2] Dem. *Chers.* 40.

[3] Diod. xvi. 53.

must be established south of Thermopylae. He was meditating on the immediate prosecution of the first of these schemes, with its implied assault on Athenian interests in the Thracian Chersonese,[1] and on an aggressive movement in Euboea, designed, doubtless, to check the Attic privateers;[2] but the appearance of the Athenian herald induced him to postpone all this in favour of the second scheme. It was a singular opportunity. Athens, so devoutly desiring peace, might well let him pass Thermopylae without a battle; and for the rest he would answer himself with his diplomacy and his spears.

The Macedonian had been looming large in the Athenian sky these seven years past. Athens also, beyond question, had occupied no small place in the thoughts of the Macedonian. But it is a grave error in historical perspective to represent Philip as engaged consciously during all his reign in a great duel with Demosthenes. A right understanding either of that orator's position in Athens, or of the part played at this epoch by the Republic herself in the political arena of eastern Europe, will supply salutary correction. For fifty years past Athens had been hardly superior in naval strength to Rhodes, and for half that time distinctly inferior in military power to Thebes; and it is clear that Philip rated her capacity for offence hardly higher than that of Olynthus or Byzantium.

As a military power, Athens, never the equal even

---

[1] Aesch. *F. L.* 82. [2] Dem. *F. L.* 315.

of such little city-states as Sparta and Thebes, was
worth consideration now only in so far as she could
hire soldiers of fortune. For, like Venice in the
Middle Ages, she possessed but an insignificant
peasant class, the most part of her citizens being
townsmen of one town, engaged in commerce or sea-
going trade. The size of her army, therefore, would
depend directly on the measure of her revenues; and
these had sunk by 346 to a figure not more than
commensurate with her internal needs. Since the
Social War, the tribute paid annually to her by
other states had fallen to less than fifty talents; and
even that insignificant sum could not always be
realized. Internally, she seems to have been still
very wealthy; but since her citizens seldom or
never submitted to direct taxation, and had come,
with the spread of free thought and philosophic
scepticism, to be but lukewarm in voluntary bounty,
the State was scarcely tapping private capital at all.
Accordingly, we find that the forces which from time
to time Athens sends to Thrace or to Euboea are
hardly worthy of mention beside Philip's effective
armies, even had the Athenian bands been (as, indeed,
they were not!) properly paid and equipped, and
of assured loyalty to their mistress.

On the sea, Athens was hardly more formidable
than on land. For although she had still a larger
fleet than any single state in the Aegean, and
presently, under careful administration, brought the
tale of her ships up to three hundred (as the marble
navy records still bear witness), it is manifest that

she could neither put in commission any large
number of vessels at one time, nor keep such as she
did commission long on the sea. Men and money
were wanting to her fleet as to her army; and the
requisite ship-furniture was not in her arsenals.
There is no evidence that she ever had more than
fifty ships on active service after the Social War.
And, moreover, it must be pointed out that, although
it might be irksome to Philip not to have the command of the Aegean, that disability was not more fatal
to him than it proved two centuries later to Rome.
His was a land power resting on a continental basis,
and, in the main, independent of sea-going trade;
and even had Athens not had rivals on her own
element, such as Rhodes, Chios, Byzantium, and
Syracuse, the geographical position of Philip's realm
would have placed him beyond the reach of anything
but irritation from her admirals.

Weak as Athens was herself in offensive force, she
stood also practically alone. After the Social War
she never resumed an imperial position, nor was able
to count on the men or money of others. Her writ
ran only where her squatters had been planted,
in Lemnos, Imbros, Scyros, Samos, and the Thracian
Chersonese. On the cities of Thrace, and even on
Euboea (as the demands made by Callias in 342
suffice to prove), her hold was very weak, and only if
in a moment of common fear she came to be added
to some independent power, equal or superior to
herself, would she cease to be negligeable. That
moment came in 338; but even then she could not

outlast a single pitched battle, and fifteen years
later, after the Lamian War had flickered out,
Athens was forced to confess that she had not a
single army to put in the field.

As it had been given to Thucydides to exalt a
series of raids into a great national war, so the
transcendent oratory of Demosthenes has led historians
to invest his opposition to Philip with an importance
of which assuredly Philip was not aware. But since
Athens, through her letters and her art, takes a place
in universal history far above that due to her politics
or her arms, the historian to-day is bound to esteem
her by the former and not the latter standard.
She may be a weakling compared to Thebes, and a
pigmy beside Persia, but she has affected our world
so much more than either, that small events in her
history possess an interest far greater than the
great events of theirs. To ignore her, or even to
relegate her to lesser importance in relation to
Philip, is to forget that Philip himself, little as he
regarded her fleets or her armies, bowed himself
none the less to her culture as he bowed to the
arms of no other state. Consistently he modified
his policy and excused his actions, for fear of forfeit-
ing irretrievably her good will; and he looked to a
recognition by her as more to be desired and more
pregnant of advantage than twice a victory of
Chaeronea.

Therefore, every relation which Philip has with
Athens is worthy of more than ordinary note in his
biography, and it is no paradox to say that the

chance that we know so much of those relations, and so little of his intercourse with the Great King at Susa, and the princes of the Balkans and Albania with whom he was intriguing or warring all his life, implies no iniquity of fate. Certainly there is no more notable moment in his career, historically regarded, than this at which he became for the first time the theme of a supreme Athenian orator. He had been mentioned, indeed, as early as 355 by Isocrates, who, in a speech recommending peace with the confederate rebels of the Social War, assured the Athenians that the Macedonian king would not oppose their claim to Amphipolis;[1] and, in the same year, he was alluded to first by the great Demosthenes.[2] But it is not till after the battle of Pagasae that Philip inspired a whole oration.

It had been the policy of Athens for some years past not to intervene in foreign affairs. The ministerial majority, led by a few able men like Eubulus and Phocion, found the ground of their faith in the lesson of the Social War, in a depleted treasury, and in a just estimate of the present capacity of the over-politicized Athenian people; for practical support they relied on an idle populace and on a cultured landed class desirous only to possess its soul on its Attic estates. Opposed to these responsible statesmen was a fervid minority all for empire and for war, certain members of it being imbued with a genuine desire to arrest the slow decay of the state, more descrying in Opposition the road to political fame.

[1] *De Pace*, 22.　　　　　[2] *Lept.* 61.

Partly of one class and partly of the other was Demosthenes, now just thirty years of age, crying in season and out of season against the smug ministerial majority.[1]

In this year, 352, the foreign potentate most concerned with the traditional area of Athenian empire was Philip, and upon him accordingly the attention of the Opposition is concentrated. Therefore we are the richer for a series of speeches of surpassing merit as oratory, but neither convincing nor convinced. They were not productive, perhaps were not intended to be productive, of any result beyond that of bringing their author to the front of the political stage. There is the First Philippic, which impugns the slack military methods of the Ministry, and makes Philip's restless aggression occasion to call for a signal reversal of the ministerial peace policy. There is the speech for the Freedom of the Rhodians, spoken in 351, in which the orator lashes out, in passing,[2] at the official apathy about Philip's movements. There are the three Olynthiac orations, all delivered probably late in 349 (one perhaps early in 348) in the debates excited by the successive appeals of the Olynthians. This group of great orations is not to be taken too seriously. The orator knew very well that it was not among the practical possibilities of politics that the Olynthian quarrel should be taken up very strenuously, or the Sacred Fund, set apart for the providing of free shows, be voted for the war.

[1] Cf. De Pace, 6 ; Deinarch. in Dem. pp. 12, 102, 99 ; Plut. Dem.
[2] § 2.

Secure, therefore, in irresponsibility, he can flout the majority, and extol or depreciate Philip's power and character, according as the Ministry finds its excuse for inaction in contempt or fear of the foe. The three speeches have been placed in this sequence or in that, according as the necessities of Olynthus are pressed or ignored, as Philip bulks small or large, and as the recommendation of a financial expedient is tentative or precise.[1] But it is to be remarked that since the references in these orations to the Olynthian war are in the last degree meagre and vague, and those to Philip merely general, the Olynthiacs would possess for the historian only an academic interest, even did not the position of the speaker and the character of the action taken by the Ministry make it impossible to invest them with any responsibility for the Athenian expeditions.[2]

No sooner was Demosthenes on the road to recognition and office, than he rounded towards the policy of the majority, and was found among the ten envoys at Pella in the winter of 347. He was destined presently to revert to his former policy, thanks to circumstances beyond his own control, and to intensify it into that persistent Philippic Crusade which we associate with his name. In brief, it was the rare fortune of Demosthenes to be forced into consistency with himself; yet, nevertheless, there is no need to call him trimmer or opportunist. The young party-politician always must begin

[1] On such principles, II., I., III., must be the order.
[2] Cf., per contra, Ulpian, ad Dem. Olynth. I.

uncertainly; and if it be borne in mind that Demosthenes was not, as some have loved to represent him, a voice crying in the wilderness, but essentially and always a man of party, spokesman of one strong faction against another, we shall not degrade him to a political rogue,[1] any more than exalt him as political saint. His conduct of the embassies should make that last exaggeration impossible, although the conspicuous correspondence of his later action with the magnificent principles, that he enunciated so magnificently, set him as high as a politician has ever stood in a democratic state.

The reason of the herald's coming to Pella was on this wise. The Athenian people, seeing itself as far as ever from recovering the mines,[2] had left Olynthus to its fate a full year before; and now the destruction of its Chalcidic ally released it from its oaths of alliance and all lingering doubts. Already, in 349, Philip had been reported to desire peace, and latterly one Ctesiphon had brought a verbal message from him to the Athenians that he warred unwillingly against their city.[3] A motion even had been made in the Assembly at the end of 348, to invite Philip to make first move. Philip did not respond. It was hardly his part to come a-courting now! Therefore,

---

[1] "Malum virum accepimus" (Quintilian, xii. I. 14).

[2] That this was the sole object which aroused any public interest at Athens in the Olynthian war, is proved abundantly by all the authorities. The war with Philip is called consistently "for Amphipolis." Cf. especially, Libanius, arg. to Dem. *F. L.*

[3] Aesch. *F. L.* 13.

the first panic over, and their envoys recalled from the Greek states, the Athenian Ministry, hearing a renewal of Philip's expression of good will in the mouth of Aristodemus, an actor, put up one Philocrates to move for a commission to negotiate peace. Ten members were proposed — the mover himself and Ctesiphon, and six elderly colleagues, together with the two free lances, Demosthenes and Aeschines,[1] whose inclusion would muzzle the Opposition. This motion being agreed to, a herald was despatched, as we have seen; and late in the autumn the Commissioners crossed to Euboea, and journeyed overland up to Oreus, in order, doubtless, to avoid the privateers in the Aegean and the Thebans on the mainland. At Oreus they proposed to await their herald's return; but he not appearing, and the season being late, they took ship to the Bay of Pagasae, where Parmenio was beleaguering Halus, obtained his safe conduct, and so came in peace through his lines to Larissa, where at last the herald brought word that all was well. Philip was lying at Pella, and a few days later received them there with all honour.

This first audience, which the architect of the new order gave to the last brilliant spirits of the old, is one of the very few events of Philip's life that we can invest with circumstance. Aeschines, giving three years later an account of his acts to an Athenian jury, has left us a suggestion of the scene — the king

---

[1] These two were not on distinct sides of the house at this period. Cf. Aesch. F. L. 79, with Dem. F. L. 10, 11, 302, 310.

seated on his throne in the public assembly of his
vassals, and of those famous knights whom Demosthenes had disparaged as "no better than other
men ; "[1] standing before him a little group of unarmed
strangers with their sponsor and their herald, who
represented the crown of civilization in their time.
The older men first addressed the king, stating briefly
the griefs and proposals of their city, and made way
for the two young immortals, who behaved, however,
very much as mortals conscious of budding reputa-
tions. For we gather that they launched out into
lengthy harangues about the ancestors of the king
and of themselves, and the eternal laws of wrong and
right ; and the greater Immortal of the two forgot
his notes, and breaking down in mid-air, had to be
handled kindly by the "barbarian," and encouraged
to collect himself ; but all to no purpose. Thereupon
the herald bade the ambassadors withdraw out of the
presence ; and the Commission fell to wrangling about
the success or failure of this member and that, but
in the midst of the dispute came the king's men
to lead them back to the presence. And when
they were seated, Philip replied to them severally
with such courtesy and address that those masters
of debate knew not afterwards which to admire most,
his temper or his wit.[2] Thereafter he bade them to
a feast, and entreated them so well at his table
and always while they stayed at his court, that they
went back to Larissa vying in praise of him, but
agreed, nevertheless, when they should come to
Athens, to assume a more discreet reserve.

[1] *Olynth.* ii. 17.   [2] Aesch. *F. L.* 41 ff.

When the relative strength of the two powers is considered, and regard is had to the terms of the subsequent peace, it is evident that in all this matter Athens had done the kissing, and Philip but offered his cheek. And the mutual contradictions of the rival orators in the famous Embassy Speeches leave no room for doubt that the question of Amphipolis and the mines had not been insisted upon by the Commission, probably not advanced at all, for fear negotiations should miscarry from the very outset.[1]

Philip commissioned his herald to go to Athens with the envoys and bear a courteous letter, agreeing to a peace on the terms *uti possidetis*, with a guarantee that he would not attack the Chersonese, and adding, it seems, even a proposal of alliance. The Athenian Ministry asked no better terms, and received with all good will a few days later Philip's Commissioners, among whom were two destined to a wider fame. Parmenio, future lieutenant of Alexander in the conquest of Asia, and Antipater, the coming Regent of Europe, who was to return to Athens in very different case.

Meanwhile Philip himself did not rest on his oars. When the events soon to happen are considered, there can be little doubt that now or earlier he made secret overtures to the Phocians and to Thebes, and invited the deputations from those states which met him on his return to Pella. A man of Philip's clear

---

[1] Cf. Demosthenes' own view of the hopelessness of entertaining any idea of recovering Amphipolis, expressed long before this date (*Phil.* i. 12).

purpose leaves as little as may be to chance. But in
the interval he betook himself to the Hebrus, and
turned his hand to reducing an old foe, or old ally,
now leagued with Athens, the chieftain Kersobleptes,
whose dominions, lying very near to the Chersonese,
might be put out of Macedonian reach by the terms
of the peace, if not annexed before its ratification.
We know no details of this campaign ; we hear only
vaguely of the Macedonian armies as now on the coast
of Thrace, now on the Holy Mountain, which over-
looks the sea of Marmora, and in May Philip returns
to Pella with Kersobleptes at his chariot wheels.
There a crowd of envoys from the Greek States was
waiting, together with the Athenian Commission,
returned with full powers to ratify peace and alliance.

A biographer of Philip may resign with heartfelt
thankfulness to the historian of Greece the minute
examination of what had taken place at Athens ere
the Commission started again for Pella. And, indeed,
it may be questioned whether such history as can
be written from the forensic assertions of two rival
orators, each concerned to falsify his own and his
opponent's part in a negotiation which had come in
three years to stink in Athenian nostrils, does not
fill, as it is, too large a place in standard works, to
the wearying of the reader and the distortion of
perspective. The sum of events is this. The majority
of Athenians were plainly for peace at almost any
price, and both Aeschines and Demosthenes, then
stepping on to the threshold of office, went with the
majority. Certain difficulties arose from the fact that

the city had allies, who must be included, and that
the Macedonian Commission declined on Philip's behalf
to admit all of these to the Treaty. The Macedonians
gave way in the matter of Kersobleptes (a concession
which availed the Thracian not at all), but set their
faces as adamant against the Phocians, now impiously
holding Delphi and Thermopylae, and lying under
ban therefor. But the Athenian Ministry, in its
present mood, was not prepared to stand out for
Phocians any more than for Amphipolis, and having
put off its allies with vague assertions (for the allies,
it seems, did not wish to meet Philip so far beyond
halfway as the dominant partner), took the oaths on
the Macedonian terms. Philip's Commission, greatly
complimented, left for Pella, and the Athenian
envoys were reappointed and sent out again by way
of Euboea. Much was said afterwards about their
delays; they should have gone direct to Thrace and
by swearing Philip then and there, have saved many
towns; but evidently the Ministry had no mind to tax
Philip's forbearance, and had indeed bidden their Commission take the usual road, and wait at Pella till the
conqueror should be pleased to come back from Thrace.

Historians have laboured to account for this
humble attitude of Athens by laying stress on her
uneasiness for her citizens held captive since the
fall of Olynthus, on her hatred of Thebes, and on
the deception practised by Philip's agents. But,
surely, no further explanation is called for (if we look
at the acts of her responsible statesmen, Eubulus
or Phocion, and not only listen to the grandiose

utterances of Demosthenes) than her own consciousness that her effective forces had become, in 346,
feeble indeed compared to those of the Macedonian.

Never did Philip hold better cards than at Pella
in May, 346, and never better did he play his game.
Encamped about him in the plain of the Vardar was
such an army as united Greece could not excel; and
embassies from Athens, from Thebes, from the
Phocians, from the Thessalian synod, from Aetolia,
were bidding for his favour, each interpreting in
their own sense the purpose which alone he knew.
His whole soul was set on one great end — uncon-
ditional supremacy over the Hellenes — and he had the
most definite plan of action. First, he must secure
the command of the land route into central Greece;
second, he looked to obtain a recognized position in
the inner communion of the Hellenes; [1] and third,
he proposed to reduce the Greek states to an innocuous equality. In effect, he would seize and hold
Thermopylae; he would assume the double *rôle* of
champion of the Delphian Apollo and patron of
Athens; and he would crush the Phocian "Grand
Company," Sparta, and eventually Thebes.

The game must have been pretty playing for
Philip. It had leaked out that he was going to
march south; but whether to do more than help
Parmenio against Halus, the envoys were not agreed.
Collectively the Greek states, represented at Pella,
had suspicions of Philip's ultimate intentions;

---

[1] Cf. Dem. *De Pace*, 19, 22.

individually, they cherished immediate aims which he could advance. The one thing needful for the Macedonian was to keep doubt of his destination from becoming certainty till his goal was in sight, that he might arrive within touch of the venal Phocians in Thermopylae before any one could forestall his bid. It was easy to retain the Greek envoys, who knew well enough that their safe conduct through Thessaly depended on the king's advices to his lieutenant;[1] nor was it difficult, by giving secret pledges to their several enmities, to prevent their concerted action. The Athenians were talked to privily about the Thebans, the Thebans about the Phocians, the Phocians about the Thebans. Late in May, the peace with Athens being still unratified and no decisive answer having been given to anybody, Philip issued marching orders, and came through the pass of Tempe with all the envoys intriguing and backbiting in his train ; and so to Pherae, the scene of his triumph six years before. There he called a halt, as though to breathe before assaulting Halus. And at last in a *khan*, which stood on the great south road, over against a temple of the Twin Brothers, Philip swore a solemn oath to observe peace with the Athenians, and with their children's children. and put forward representatives of all his " allied " cities. from Epirus to Cardia in the Chersonese, to do the like. The final terms implied the abandonment of Amphipolis to Philip; the recognition that Cardia was his

---

[1] Needless here to listen to the eternal cry of bribery — the Athenian " Nous sommes trahis ! " (Dem. *Cor.* 32).

ally; the relinquishing of the great eastern islands, Rhodes, Chios, and Cos, to the satrap of Caria; and the acknowledgment of the right of the Byzantines to levy their own tolls in the Bosphorus. In effect, Athens accepted the fact that she was no longer imperial. Nevertheless, the ten Athenians received Philip's oaths and accepted a safe conduct, and, not a little relieved, took ship to Euboea, and came again to Athens early in June.

In time to come the Athenians were to repent that their envoys had accepted the oaths of Philip's allied towns by their proxies. They had bidden, said they, their Commission visit each several "allied" town in turn and judge its claim to be included or excluded; and the failure to obey led to wild accusations of venality and bad faith, culminating in one famous charge. But all that can be said nowadays is, that manifestly at the time of ratification the Athenians were too well pleased with peace at any cost to press such a point. And, indeed, it is difficult to see how better the envoys could have acted. If the master of so many battalions would not take oaths but at his own good time, who was to force him? And until he had taken them and given the envoys safe conduct, how should they go to the Thracian cities? At Pherae Philip was too strong and too nigh for the Athenians to be other than thankful to obtain full ratification of their peace without another day's delay. The cry about Cardia and against the Peace comes later in time, when the impunity which the Macedonian's ambition, not his fear, secured to Athens, while she lay at his mercy, had restored her assurance. For from first to last the Athenian ascribed to fear rather than to generosity any act of grace.

Whether Philip took Halus now or later, we know not ;[1] in any case it held out but little longer before being dismantled and given to the keeping of the Pharsalians. At any rate, it is clear that he delayed the shortest possible time before rounding Othrys, and confronting the eight or ten thousand mercenaries ranged under the Phocian banner at Thermopylae. A small Lacedaemonian force was with these, and a weak Athenian squadron watched events from Oreus. For the temper of the mercenaries was very doubtful ; their pay was in arrear, and their leader had quarrelled with the Phocian government.[2] Philip halted, and sent a herald into the Pass. Phalaecus, the *condottiere*, asked for time. He had envoys at Athens, and wished to know whether that city meant to support him. Should she not send help, his position would be scarcely tenable, with the Thebans in his rear, and the best army in Europe ready to assault his front. So the pickets of Phalaecus and Philip watched each other across the Asopus until the seventh day, or thereabouts, when the Phocian envoys returned to say that the Athenian assemblies were passing idle votes against Philip, and idle votes

---

[1] Demosthenes says (*F. L.* 36) that Philip had professed to detain the Athenian envoys, that they might mediate in the matter of Halus.

[2] Aesch. *F. L.* 132.

of sympathy with his opponents,[1] but plainly did
not intend to send a lance or contribute a drachma.
The Lacedaemonians decamped then and there ; the
Athenian fleet made no sign ; and three days later
Phalaecus had sold the Pass and the Phocian cause
to Philip, and marched his sacrilegious bravos into
the Peloponnese ; whence they betook themselves to
Elis, Crete, and Sicily, and as the Greeks loved to
believe, perished to a man miserably by the wrath
of Apollo.

Philip was within the gates of Greece. What would
he do ? For whom, against whom, would he be ? All
Greece waited, hoping somewhat fearing more, Athens
especially looking to her walls, and calling in her
country folk, though it was near the season of the
rural feast of Heracles. With masterly duplicity,
Philip held out the hand of frank fellowship to
Thebes,[2] who had been on the right side in the Sacred
War when Lacedaemon and Athens had been on the
wrong. The Boeotian cities, Orchomenus, Coronea,
and Corsiae, whilom allies of the Phocians, were handed
over to Theban mercies,[3] and Philip marched into the
mountains to avenge Apollo. Fire and sword went
through Phocis, as through no Greek state since Epaminondas had raided Laconia. Twenty-three cities
were dismantled, and broken up into open villages,[4]
a device learned from the great Theban, and after ten
years the Delphians were led back to their Delphi, and
put in possession of its spoiled and violated shrine.

[1] Dem. *F. L.* 50, 181. [2] Cf. Paus. x. 2, 5.
[3] Dem. *F. L.* 149. [4] Diod. xvi. 60.

The God who sat on the navel of Hellas acknowledged his new champion through the mouth of his Prophetess. The ancient and venerated union of the Amphictyons elected him by acclamation to the empty seat of the Phocians, receiving him thus into the innermost circle of the Hellenes. And in the character of the greatest Hellene of them all he sat in the Pythian chair of presidency that autumn, and gave the bay-leaf crowns to the victors at the games. With the noise of him all Greece was filled, even as the brain of that half-witted Arcadian, who, arrested at Delphi, cried that he was running and would run still, until he came to a people that knew not Philip.[1]

For the six years or more that follow, Philip's life alas! is withdrawn, except at rare intervals, from our knowledge. Alas, indeed! for these are the years in which his men-at-arms marched, the first foreigners since history had begun, into the Peloponnese, and he himself besieged and took cities on the Adriatic, and led his spearmen up to, or even beyond, the Danube; years, too, in which his final ambition took shape, "for it was coming to be his desire to be designated Captain-General of Hellas, and to wage the War against the Persian."[2] To such a purpose did the old Isocrates incite him now,[3] fired in the evening of his long life with a vision of a panhellenic Union, in which the petty quarrels

[1] Theopomp. fr. 235.   [2] Diod. xvi. 60.
[3] His Letter to Philip was written about 345.

of cities, which had made history during all his
days, would be forgotten. Years, finally, in which
the father began to educate the son to be not
less a warrior and more a Hellene than himself, little
thinking how entirely the execution of the great
project, with which his own soul was filled, was to
fall with all its glory to the boy.

It seems that Philip himself went back to his
capital to spend the winter of 346–345,[1] leaving
garrisons in Phocis and Thermopylae,[2] and orders to
his lieutenants to watch Thebes and obtain a footing
in Euboea, disposed already in his favour; and that
in the spring of 345 he sent out agents and troops to
secure to himself almost all the states of Greece,
except Attica. Everywhere his game was to divide, a
policy which he may have learned from Epaminondas.
Thessaly, so apt to be united by a powerful Baron,
was split in four, and Councils of Ten, acting for
Philip, and paying to him the revenues of the land,[3]
replaced the baronial rule in the cities. Euboea was
won over with the single doubtful exception of Chalcis,
and Macedonian garrisons were placed in Porthmus
and Oreus,[4] the points of entrance and departure on
the north road from Attica, which the embassies were
used to follow. In the previous autumn the king
seems to have gone to Thebes, to be received as a
gracious benefactor, where twenty years before he

---

[1] Diod. xvi. 60.

[2] Dem. *Ad Ep. Phil.* 4, says that Philip garrisoned Nicaea,
near Thermopylae.

[3] *Phil.* ii. 22; iii. 26, 33.

[4] Dem. *Phil.* iii. 12. 57, 58; *F. L.* 219.

had lived in exile. In 345, however, the most part of Philip's intrigue and coercion was exercised within the Isthmus to the breaking-up of the traditional supremacy of Sparta, against whom he could allege that she had ranged herself in Thermopylae with the violators of Delphi. But, although compelled now by superior force to swallow peace with Argos,[1] and to see Arcadia set up again,[2] and to resign Messene,[3] Sparta never submitted herself altogether, but in years to come alone of all the Greeks refused to serve under Philip's banner against Persia, and broke out against his son, so soon as he was gone into Asia. Furthermore we hear now of Philip's agents in Elis as the first cause of intestine dissensions in all its cities and of faction fights and massacres;[4] and also that he projected the seizure of Megara.

Athens herself, however, Philip did not touch.[5] Determined as he was to end her claims to imperial dominion on the coasts which he conceived to be his own, he respected nevertheless the soil of Attica more than if it had been holy ground. And not only so, but by letter after letter, and envoy after envoy, he tried to soothe the fears of the city and heal her wounded feelings. First he sent her two invitations

---

[1] Paus. ii. 20. 1 ; vii. 11. 2 ; Dem. *F. L.* 260.

[2] Paus. viii. 7. 4, 27, 10.

[3] Dem. *Phil.* ii. 13, 20, 26, and arg.

[4] Dem. *F. L.* 260, 294 : *Phil.* iii. 27 ; Paus. iv. 28, 4.

[5] There is a loose rhetorical passage in *Phil.* ii. 36, which might imply that Philip made a descent on the Attic coast; but we may be sure that, if a fact, we should have heard of it again and again.

to participate in the pious task of vindicating
Apollo;[1] then, taking no umbrage that she did not
comply, he communicated his own success in a third
letter, with many expressions of good will.[2]   All the
Athenians taken at Olynthus returned unransomed to
their country, — and indeed Philip prided himself on
taking no money for an Athenian.   Furthermore by
the mouths of his agents he promised constantly that
Athens should reap no small advantage from the
Peace she had made;[3] and doubtless he promised
sincerely, and withal fulfilled his word, as it seemed
to him, by crushing her old foes in Greece, and
exalting her as the one inviolate Queen of civilization.   Lastly, most signal act of all, some time
in 344, when master of all Greece beside, Philip
sent one, Python, to plead against the evil things
said constantly of him in Athens, and to bid for the
good will it seemed so hard to win, by proposing to
amend the Peace in those clauses which had vexed
the Athenians most.   And all this labour of conciliation, is it to be referred to no nobler an instinct
than fear?   It can scarcely be thought to spring from
that in 346, but what are we to say in 338, when
point for point it was taken up again after Chaeronea?

Rather to Philip's honour let it be recorded, as to
the honour of any warrior-statesman, that sword in
hand he paid homage to the arts of peace.   And not
less be it recorded to the honour of Athens, that she
did not accept his homage.   For ever since her third

---

[1] Dem. *F. L.* 51.   [2] Dem. *F. L.* 36.

[3] Dem. *Halonn.* 33.

Embassy had broken up on its way north, hearing that Philip was already within Thermopylae, she had protested against this great armament that paraded Greece, sparing only herself with an intolerable sufferance. Chafing at Philip's reception among the Amphictyons, she would have disowned even the Treaty she had sworn, had Demosthenes not intervened.[1] Checked in this act of folly, she was fain to console herself with decreeing exile against the chief authors of the Peace, and with harbouring all men disaffected to Philip, and with applauding Demosthenes when he flouted Philip's envoys, and with proposing preposterous amendments to the Treaty, and with sending Diopithes and a fleet to the Chersonese to sail as near to war as he might in time of peace. Now is the time when Demosthenes emerges finally from his uncertain youth, and, winning the ear of the citizens, adopts a strong policy to be maintained more or less till the day of his death. No longer is he " unstable in his ways, incapable of constancy to one policy or to one party," as Theopompus said of him in one of those vigorous sentences,[2] which show how much we have lost in losing the " Philippica."

It is easy to sit in judgment now on this policy of Demosthenes, easy to prove that resistance to Philip was worse than useless, and that Athens had not the internal resources to enable her to assume again an imperial position. She lost, maybe, the full favour of the master of her fate, and she should

---

[1] *De Pace*, 13.   [2] Fr. 106.

have been urged to take a less selfish and more
panhellenic view of the great king, who only aspired
to lead united Hellas against her ancient foe!
Demosthenes was unjust, improvident, blind to the
lesson of his age — be it so! Cicero too was blind
when he opposed Caesar and supported Octavian. The
greatest statesmen have been just as blind in every
age of change. But just as individual character gains
more by fighting out a battle than by a cunning
surrender, so the character of a people purges itself
in strenuous resistance of base elements that would
increase perilously, did it subordinate wholly its
choleric emotions to its pure reason. And inas-
much as this is so, the sympathy which has always
gone out to the leaders of forlorn hopes, and to
those who butt against stone walls, and to those
who will not take quarter, can be justified of its
unreason. And, moreover, it may well be doubted
if the tradition of Attic letters and art, with which
the Hellenistic age began, would have been near so
vivid without this last flash of Athenian freedom.
In any case, there would have been no such en-
samples of style and Atticism as the second, third,
and fourth Philippics, the speeches on the Chersonese,
the Embassy, and the Crown.

After 346, there was to be no more fruitless
epideictic oratory. Demosthenes and his party were
terribly in earnest, and by their deeds, as much as by
their words, laid up the store of hate which Philip
bequeathed to Alexander. Now Demosthenes is
making a tour of the Peloponnese, in the vain hope of

detaching the Arcadians and the rest from Philip; now at Athens he is urging the Messenian envoys to disobey Macedonian orders and stand by Sparta; but once more in vain. Then his partisan Timarchus moves that it be penal to supply Philip with munitions of war; and when the king sends his envoys to protest against all this covert hostility, Demosthenes retorts with the second of his Philippics, a masterpiece of invective against this sacker of cities, who cried peace where there was no peace, and suborned a great party to aid " in putting all the world under his feet."

With the winter Philip was gone north again, and so far as we know, came south of Thermopylae neither in 344 nor in five succeeding years. He was in Ambracia and Epirus, perhaps, too, in the western isles. He conducted a campaign against the races of the north, practising the Persian policy of transferring wholesale populations from mountain to plain, and plain to mountain, the better to break tribal traditions;[1] and coming down to Cardia, he made the Athenian farmers in the Chersonese shake in their shoes, and send urgent appeals to Piraeus. Of his direct dealings with Greece, if indeed he had many in these years, we know only his disputes with Athens about Potidaea and in the matter of Halonnesus, a wretched rock north of Euboea, which had become a nest of pirates, and been smoked out by a Macedonian admiral. Whereupon the neighbouring Peparethians, pirates also no doubt, settled on it, '

[1] Justin, viii. 5, referring obviously to Paeonia.

but were ousted promptly, and their own island was raided. In which matter no one outside would have concerned themselves, had it not chanced that Athens, conceiving herself to have a lien on both Halonnesus and Peparethus, took occasion to revive a dispute as to the *uti possidetis* clause in the treaty of 346.

The said clause had not proved efficacious in the sense intended by the Athenian Ministry of the time; for in addition to the difficulty about the Thracian cities, taken by Philip in the interval between the proposal and the conclusion of the Peace, there were on the one hand, many Greek cities, such as the Elean colonies in Ambracia, independent of either party to the treaty, and open, therefore, to subsequent absorption by Philip, to the prejudice of Athens; and, on the other, certain cities and islands existed which Athens considered to be in her own "empire," but for so many years had neither occupied nor done anything to protect, that her claim was scarcely to be maintained. Halonnesus was just such a case. Philip asserted, with some show of equity, that the Athenian right to that island had lapsed, but, for the sake of peace and quietness, he offered now to "present" it to Athens. The Ministry of the Republic stipulated, however, that it be understood clearly that Philip "restored" the island — a quarrel about words, or, as it happens in the Greek speech, about syllables, which raised the whole issue. Thereupon Hegesippus was sent up to Pella in 343, to press on Philip certain comprehensive amendments to the original Peace, designed to cover this case and those of all Hellenic cities not defined clearly in 346. He was instructed to propose that: (1) the phrase *uti possidetis* be amended to a declaration that each party do retain his *lawful* property; (2) all Greeks — being not parties, and still independent — be recognized as independent, and guaranteed by both parties; (3) Philip do restore the Thracian cities, taken after his envoys had accepted the treaty in March, 346. These amendments had all been proposed to, and received in silence by, Python and his fellow Macedonian envoys at Athens in the previous year; and it pleased the Athenians, therefore, to assume that Philip had accepted them in principle.

The king, however, irritated by the attitude of Athens, brusquely removed any such illusions from Hegesippus' mind. Amendment number one he rejected flatly; it was designed to cover a claim for the cession of Amphipolis and Potidaea, and other places which he, Philip, had held these ten years. To number two he made no demur: there was nothing in Greece worth speaking of still absolutely independent of himself, and the proposed clause seems not to have been framed to be retrospective. On number three he offered to accept the arbitration of some umpire mutually acceptable. No such umpire, however, was to be found, and the whole negotiation led to nothing but recriminations, encroachments, and reprisals which culminated three years later in rupture. During the irritation caused by Hegesippus' subsequent report at Athens, the famous charge of treason

in the First Embassy, in 346, was preferred at last by
Demosthenes against Aeschines in terms very trucu-
lent and hostile to Philip; but partly because all
men knew that Demosthenes as ambassador had
acted largely in sympathy with the man he was now
accusing after three years; partly because it was never
approved that a man should turn upon his colleague,
however greatly they had differed; partly perhaps
also because the Ministerial Centre were not prepared
to associate themselves altogether with utterances so
provocative to Philip, the case resulted in acquittal
and the enriching of literature with two incomparable
forensic harangues.

For the moment the restless Macedonian was not
concerned with Greece. He had reverted to his
great project, postponed five years before, of conquering the western shores of the Black Sea, and
the northern coasts of the sea of Marmora, and all
inland up to the Danube. To effect this purpose
he must break the back of the Odrysian Thracians
in Roumelia, of the Triballi in Bulgaria, and the
"Scythians" in the Dobrudscha, and be acknowledged suzerain by the great Propontic Greek
colonies, Byzantium, Perinthus, and Selymbria. That
done, and the Hellespont watched from Cardia, he
would have all the corn trade in his own hands,[1] the
food of Greece at his mercy, and the way to Asia
open.

His army was mobilized in the spring of 342,
and he went off to the north. The disappearance of

[1] Dem. *Cor.* 87.

contemporary chronicles has reduced our knowledge
of this great military venture to almost nothing, and
historians have been led to ignore [1] almost entirely an
expedition comparable to nothing in antiquity since
Darius' famous march to Scythia, and a worthy prelude to the conquest of Asia. We know that Philip
and his army were out for ten months at least, and,
spending the winter in the field,[2] endured, leader
and follower alike, grievous hardships by storm, sickness, and war.[3] But we hear nothing more precise
until the spring of 341, when they had returned
across the Balkans to the upper waters of the Hebrus,
and were warring with the Odrysian tribes.[4] In
Roumelia it was reported that the Athenian Diopithes,
sent out to reinforce the colonists of the Chersonesus,
had assaulted Cardia and raided inland Thrace.
Whereupon Philip detached a force for the relief of
Cardia and the chastising of the Athenian. Nevertheless, it was not to be war yet with the Republic,
for, when taxed, she disowned her admiral,[5] who
indeed was little better than a blackmailing buccaneer
with unpaid pirates at his orders.

But all this year a belief gathered strength that
Philip was about to rob Athens of the Chersonese,
and then speedily of her own liberty. Demosthenes
gives that opinion utterance in a speech boldly justi-
fying Diopithes, and in the third and greatest of his

---

[1] Possible allusions to this expedition are to be found in
Frontinus, ii. 8. 14, and Strabo, p. 320.

[2] *Chers.* 14.   [3] *Chers.* 35.   [4] *Chers.* Arg. 3.

[5] See *Chers.* 28.

Philippics, wherein he demands that all this latent bickering and underground trifling be exchanged for brute war, open and declared, cost what it may; and in a last Philippic, often ascribed to another orator, but "Demosthenic" from end to end, wherein the Athenians are warned that Philip in Thrace and the Chersonese is only preliminary to Philip in Athens, and that every drachma and every spear the city can muster must be used in war against him, who makes pretension, forsooth, to enlist the Greeks against another barbarian king who is far less their enemy. Two overt acts, moreover, were perpetrated by the Athenian Ministry, under Demosthenes' guidance, which Philip could not view with equanimity. Firstly, they formed a kind of anti-Macedonian League among some of the smaller states of Greece,[1] and chiefly won over to it Euboea, by sending Phocion to help its cities to expel Philip's partisans and to range themselves under Callias of Chalcis, and by promising to recognize the entire autonomy of the island for the future. Secondly, they sent envoys up to the Great King in Susa, to warn him of Philip's panhellenic project, and induce him to assist Philip's enemies. To counteract the first of these hostile moves and the depredations of Callias and Athenian volunteers,[2] Philip himself made a rapid journey, it seems, to Thessaly[3] in 341, leaving

---

[1] The rebuilding of the long walls of Megara by Phocion must have taken place at this period (Plut. *Phoc.* 15) as a sequel to long intrigues prosecuted there by agents of Philip *v.* agents of Athens. Cf.

[2] Aesch. *Ctes.* 83. [3] *Phil.* iii. 12; iv. 9.

his army in eastern Thrace ; and in order to reproach
the Athenians for their intrigue with Persia, and for
many covert acts of enmity, he despatched a long
epistle to be read in the Assembly. But still it was
not war.

The forbearance, however, of the Macedonian, his
reference of disputed points to arbitration, and his
abstention from the Chersonese, served him with the
Athenian Ministry as conciliation usually serves with
an oriental government. In short it emboldened the
Republic to take matters into her own hands. She
had encouraged the Thracian chieftains already in
the summer of 341 ;[1] now she went further, and sent
Demosthenes to Byzantium to urge the guardians
of the Bosphorus to break off relations with Philip,
close their gates on the land side, and hold out.

Byzantium, like Olynthus, had been for many
years no friend to Athens. She had shared with the
eastern islands and the cities of Asia and Thrace that
intense dislike of Athenian imperial pretensions,
which found violent vent both after Sparta's triumph
in 404, and again in the "Social War." If entire
autonomy was not to be attained, any barbarian
supporter — the Great King, the Carian viceroy, the
Thracian princes, even the Macedonian himself — was
preferred to the aggressive Ionian Republic, which
demanded so much and gave so little. But now
Athens was too weak to pretend to be more than an
ally, and Philip had become the more dangerous foe
to freedom. So the Byzantines listened to the

[1] *Ep. Phil.* 8. ff.

voice of Demosthenes, and persuaded Perinthus and
Selymbria to listen likewise; and almost at the same
moment the Macedonian army in its winter quarters
learned that the Propontic cities had declared against
them, and that the Athenians had solemnly removed
their pillar graven with the terms of the peace and
alliance of 346.

Demosthenes throughout the year 341 speaks of
Philip so constantly as moving on Byzantium, that
we must understand the Macedonian army to have
spent all that summer, autumn, and perhaps winter
in eastern Thrace, reducing the dominions of the
chieftains Teres, Sitalces, and Kersobleptes, to complete submission.   There seems to have been a sturdy
resistance, and in consequence a settlement more
drastic than it was Philip's wont to impose.   Not
only were the Thracian lands compelled henceforward
to pay him tithe, but he founded military colonies
here and there in all the region, continuing a policy
inaugurated by himself at Philippi, and destined to
be developed signally by his son and his successors
in Asia, Egypt, and Greece.   Of two among his new
cities we know no more than the names, Bine and
Philippopolis; but a third is said to have been a
punishment-colony, founded as a sink for two thousand
bad characters, and named Poneropolis, "city of bad
men." [1]   In the early spring of 340 the settlement

---

[1] Theopomp. fr. 122.   Plutarch, Pliny, and Suidas repeat the
statement, no doubt, from this passage.   Cf. Strabo calls it Calybe
(p. 320).

of Thrace was accomplished; and gathering up a siege-train, the like of which had not been seen in Europe, Philip marched his great army[1] down to the sea of Marmora, and sat down before Perinthus.

The siege which ensued must have been very famous in antiquity for Diodorus to have admitted so detailed an account into his Universal Chronicle. It marked, in fact, an epoch in military history, for in it was first applied on a large scale the scientific method of assault by simultaneous sap, bombardment, and storm, with which the operations of Alexander at Tyre and Gaza, of Demetrius at Rhodes, and of the Romans at Syracuse were soon to make the world familiar.[2] Clumsy devices as the rams and catapults and movable storming-towers may seem to modern science, and hugely laborious as were the works needed to bring them into action — the isthmus, for instance, built through deep water at Tyre, the mounds about the walls of Gaza, the valley filled with stones and trees below the Rock of Chorienes — such expedients were the only ones by which natural citadels could be reduced. In the Propontic cities, it seems, Philip could find no " Macedonizing" traitors or not enough; at hand was the sea, on which no blockade was ever quite effective in the day of small sailing craft. An Athenian admiral, Chares, was hanging off the Chersonese, and Philip, in order to get his own fleet through the Dardanelles

---

[1] Justin, ix. 1, alludes to its great size. Diodorus says he had 30,000 men before Perinthus alone.

[2] Cf. Frontin. iii. 9. 8, for Philip's methods.

at all, had to make a raid into the peninsula, and
seize the ports from which privateers were issuing.[1]
Even when the Macedonian admiral was safe in
the sea of Marmora, he was unable to prevent
the Byzantines throwing supplies continually into
Perinthus, or the Persian satrap of the southern
shore from running large convoys of provisions,
munitions of war, and men-at-arms.[2] For the Great
King at Susa had taken in earnest the Athenian
warning, and despatched the most imperative orders
to his governors in Anatolia to aid and abet the
foes of the Macedonian.

Perinthus was extraordinarily strong, being perched
on a precipitous hill rising at the end of a narrow
neck, a furlong out at sea; and as in so many
picturesque cities of the Levant at this day, its
lofty houses huddled one on the other, round the
rock "as in a theatre."[3] With sap and rams and
huge wooden towers rising a hundred and twenty
feet on their wheels, Philip was not long in breach-
ing and clearing the lines of defence across the
isthmus; but meanwhile the besieged had built an
inner curtain, and the assault was all to begin again.
The Macedonian projectiles cleared this second wall,
but the Perinthians returned to the defence, and,
well supplied with missiles, wore down the first stress
of Philip's assault. The king changed his tactics,
and divided his great army into successive storming
parties, keeping the besieged without rest night or
day. Piece by piece the inner lines were reduced

[1] Justin, xi. 1.   [2] Diod. xvi. 75.   [3] Diod. l.c.

to ruin, and their defenders to despair. At last they gave way, and the Macedonians rushed in, but only to be checked immediately at the lowest tier of houses, linked together by barricades. Of such ramparts there were as many as there were streets. The siege had lasted already far into the summer, and thanks to the Byzantines, the besieged were as well supplied as ever.

Philip tried a diversion. Drawing off a picked force, he vanished to the eastward, fell suddenly on Selymbria,[1] and presently appeared before Byzantium itself ere the citizens could call in their forces from Perinthus. The chief magistrate, one Leon, a student of peripatetic philosophy, and destined to be the historian of this siege, came out to parley. The Macedonian king in a merry mood said that, being smitten with love for the fair city, he did but come to her gates to sue for favours. "But these are not lovers' lutes," cried the Byzantine, looking round at the pikeheads, and went in again forthwith.[2] Philip himself led the assault with sap and storm.[3] The place was neither naturally so strong as Perinthus, nor so well fortified, and its citizens were but just equal to manning the great length of the wall. The Macedonian fleet hovered round the sea-front,

[1] Although this assault is mentioned only in the probably spurious documents inserted in the Speech *de Corona*, I feel no doubt it occurred. The name would hardly appear in those documents without suggestion from some authority; and, geographically, such an assault was almost inevitable on a march from Perinthus to Byzantium.

[2] Suid. *s. v.* Λέων ; and Philostr. jun.. *De Soph*. i.

[3] Hesych. Miles. *Orig. Const.* 26.

and raided up the Bosphorus, and into the Black Sea.
But the Byzantine resistance was obstinate, and just
strong enough; the defenders attempted no sortie,
but were content to hold the wall in the hope
that time would come to their aid. The crisis came
on a moonless night of wind and rain in the early
winter of 339. The storming party was already at
the wall when, it is said, the dogs of the city gave
an alarm, and the defenders, rushing to their posts,
saw by the light of a falling meteor in the northern
sky the nature of their peril.[1] The surprise had
failed, the storming party fell back, and the citizens
raised a statue to Hecate the Torch-bearer, and in
her honour struck coins bearing her emblem, the
crescent moon, which Byzantium has bequeathed to
Constantinople, and Islam borrowed all over the
world. Thenceforward the tide turned against the
besieger. His efforts to seduce Leon were not successful. The wall was repaired and heightened with
tombstones, like that of Athens of old. The Athenian
Chares, having got through the Hellespont, fortified
a headland over against the Princes' Islands, and
helped the Byzantines to rout Philip's fleet;[2] but
his wife dying, he sailed away, to be replaced by a
better man, the famous Phocion, with whom Athens
sent the best fleet she had commissioned since the
battle of Naxos. The Carian satrap brought up

---

[1] This tale, told in most detail by Hesychius Milesius, 27, is
alluded to by Steph. Byz. *s.v.* Βόσπορος; and by Eustathius,
ad Dionys. Perieg. 143.

[2] Hesych. Miles. 27, 28.

ships of the Chians and Rhodians, and it was reported that a fresh Persian force had been thrown into Thrace.[1] All Hellas seemed to be arming, and it was high time to go. The Macedonian fleet seems to have been blocked in the Black Sea by the Athenians who held the Bosphorus. Philip is said to have written a fictitious letter to Antipater in Macedonia, saying that Thrace had risen and his case was desperate. It was contrived that this should fall into the hands of Phocion, who withdrew to the Chersonese, leaving the strait open. The next problem was how to pass the Dardanelles, now closed by an allied squadron, but Philip, making preliminary proposals of peace, threw the enemy off his guard, and once more saved the most of his fleet.[2] His land forces were drawn off, the Chersonese was evacuated, and the Macedonian retired to ruminate on the most signal reverse that he had experienced in twenty years.

To Byzantium and the satraps he proposed peace ; with Athens he persisted in not accepting war ; and he proceeded to spend the rest of the year as far from Greece as might be, in prosecuting a raid up to the distant region where reigned Ateas the Scythian.[3] Partly, perhaps, he wished to remove from his soldiers' minds the memory of failure ; partly he desired plunder ; partly too he had a personal score

[1] Arr. ii. 14. Cf. Dem. ad Ep. Phil. 5.
[2] Frontin. i. 4. 10. Cf. Plut. Phoc. 14, for the loss of some Macedonian vessels.
[3] Strabo, p. 307; Justin, ix. 2.

to pay, for this Ateas a year before had invited his help against the Istrians, making offer even to the succession of his kingdom. Philip in response had detached a force, but Ateas' danger was passed before the Macedonians arrived, and he dismissed them scornfully with neither pay nor rations, excusing himself on the score of the leanness of his land. Therefore Philip was moving northward now, amusing himself by sending on messages in his own grim vein of irony. He had pledged himself, he said, during the siege of Byzantium, to set up a statue to Heracles at the Danube mouth. "Then," replied the Scythian, "send the statue to me." "But it must be guaranteed inviolable," said the Macedonian, and marched on. "If thou settest it up against my will," retorted Ateas, "it shall be overthrown and melted down for arrow-heads." For which reply the Scythian paid with twenty thousand of his women and boys, flocks and herds, and twenty thousand mares, taken by the victor to multiply on the Emathian plains. But in the Balkans the Triballian tribesmen fell on the retiring column, and having chanced to wound Philip sorely in the thigh, succeeded in driving off amid the confusion much of the spoil. And the king returned to Pella as winter drew on, with mortification threatening his leg to add to the many afflictions — the broken collar bone, the blinded eye, the gangrened arm — that he had endured already in the chase of glory.

This year, 339, claims a peculiar place in universal

history, as that in which the figure of the great
Alexander appears first upon its stage. He had
received his baptism of blood, if we may believe
Justin,[1] before the walls of Perinthus, and now being
turned sixteen, he was sent back to take the seals of
Regency from Antipater. And in such capacity it
fell to him to do three things of which tradition[2]
took note — to lead his first army against an Illyrian
rising, to found his first city,[3] and to receive a party
of envoys sent by the Great King of Persia,[4] doubtless
in response to Philip's proposal of peace. The
retailers of anecdote loved to record that the invader-
to-be gravely and narrowly questioned the Asiatics
on roads and marches, and the strength of the Great
King's armies, to their no small wonder. Nor is it
altogether incredible that even at sixteen Alexander
had a definite ambition of Asiatic conquest, which
issued in a little envy of his father, as Plutarch states.
His later career, at least, shows him a miracle of precocious development, destroyer of Thebes at twenty-
one, master of Babylon at twenty-five, dying worn
and aged at thirty-three with the world at his feet.
The blood of Philip flowed in his veins, mixed with
the strain of that savage witch, whom alone he feared

---

[1] ix. 1. But Justin states his age wrongly. He was barely
sixteen.

[2] Cf. Ps. Callisth. i. 23.

[3] Curt. viii. 1 ; Plut. *Alex.* 9 ; cf. Steph. Byz., whose *third*
Alexandria (Θράκης) this is. It was among the tribe of Mardi,
i.e. in the upper Strymon valley. Nothing certain is known as
to its precise representative in modern times.

[4] Plut. *Alex.* 5.

in later days and his successors feared after him; he
was bred in the boisterous court of Pella, his father
being always at the wars, and himself with his
singular beauty the centre of feudal idolatry : was
he not bound to become very early headstrong, self-
assured, self-centred ?

The famous story of his boyhood, how he mastered
and rode the wild horse Bucephalus, is worth repeat-
ing from Plutarch, for the picture it affords of father
and son at this time. A Thessalian appeared at the
court of Pella offering to sell for thirteen talents a
magnificent horse. Philip coveted the beast, and,
with his son, his courtiers, and his grooms, went
down in the evening into the plain below the city
to try him : but he could not be mounted, hardly
handled even, and at last the king, disgusted with
his fractiousness, ordered the vendor to lead him
away. Upon this the young prince, who had been
watching the trials with a fine scorn, interposed with
broad hints, which Philip for some time ignored,
annoyed with his forwardness, but was forced at last
to reprove, telling the speaker sharply not to set
himself up against his elders. The boy, however, was
not abashed, but offered to stake the price of the
horse on the trial. Without more ado he wheeled
the wild beast's head to the sun, having noted that
he was shying at his own shadow. Then, having led
him a little about the meadow, soothing and stroking
him, he slipped stealthily his upper garment and
vaulted gently on Bucephalus' back. The horse
started, but Alexander sat quiet, feeling his mouth,

and presently put him into a gentle canter, increasing
the pace gradually with voice and heel until he was
heading into the open country at full speed. The
gallop was soon over. No southern horse ever lasts
fully extended, and it was a very tame Bucephalus
that the prince rode back at last triumphant into the
meadow. The crowd cheered; the king, overwrought
by his excitement and fears, fell weeping, and kissed
Alexander on the forehead, crying, " Boy, find thee
a kingdom for thyself, for Macedonia is too strait
for thee and me!"

Plutarch says, no doubt truly, that it was on
account of this early development of a temper to be
governed only by a precocious reason, that Philip sent
now for the great Aristotle from Atarneus to take in
hand the boy of fifteen, making thereby a conjunction
of immortal names which has set rhetoricians vapour-
ing, fabulists romancing, and poets singing ever since.

Through the winter Philip nursed his wound until,
big with fate, the spring of 338 came in. Early in
March a herald came to Pella bearing a request from
the Holy Synod of the Amphictyons, that the king
would be pleased to use his army to coerce on their
behalf a contumacious town near Delphi. Philip
needed little pressing; it was always to his mind to
head a Hellenic league; he had work of his own to
do in Greece, and the memory of Perinthus and
Byzantium to efface. The word went through his
camp for active service, and that with all speed.

The appearance of this herald was so opportune, and

the sequel of his message so momentous, that many historians have credited Philip with having invited his invitation. Admitted that habitually the Macedonian left little to chance; admitted that the artifice was quite in his vein; admitted that two-thirds of the Holy Synod were his dependents; admitted that, having done much violence to Hellenic feeling on the Propontis, and proposed lately a general peace, he may have thought it expedient not to move south without the sanction of a formal invitation, master of the Gates and lord of many battalions though he was—all these things being admitted, nevertheless, neither does any ancient authority state that he had foreknowledge of the herald's coming, nor do the antecedent facts point that way. The Amphictyonic quarrel, which resulted in Philip being invited, and need be noticed only in so far as it bears on him, had been on foot for at least a year; and it is not to be disputed that great efforts had been made by the Holy Synod to settle it without calling in the Macedonian. He was invited only in the last resort, the Thebans being friends of the guilty Amphissa, the Athenians having decreed the withdrawal of their forces from the venture, and the Amphictyonic *condottiere* having been handled severely when the greater states ceased to support him. It is quite possible that Philip long had contemplated an expedition to the south; but as he kept his own conscience, no one in Greece probably knew the fact then, and no one can prove it now. In any case, it seems distinctly not proven that either himself or his paid agents cooked

up the Amphissian quarrel, or led it to an issue
favourable to his own ambition. It is generally more
true that a great man uses than that he makes his
opportunities.

Thessaly was Philip's own, and Thermopylae was
held by his garrison. Without let or hindrance,
therefore, his army marched south to Nicaea in May.
Here was the situation. The object of his march
was Amphissa, a town of sturdy mountaineers, north-
west of Delphi. The Amphissians had been called
to account in one of those superstitious panics,
which, like the excitement after the affair of the
Hermae at Athens, proceed from the most primitive
motives, and require no subtle explanation ; in brief,
it was demanded of these mountaineers that they
should desist from an old standing occupation of
certain sacred domain land of Apollo. But they had
declined to obey the Holy Synod, and for a year
had resisted its resort to force. To arrive within
striking distance of them, Philip must lead his army
round the end of Oeta into Phocis and the basin
of the Cephissus and, when he should turn up into
the defiles of Parnassus, he would leave on his left
flank Thebes, which had supported Amphissa all
through its revolt, and was strong enough to cut
his communications with Thermopylae. The hostility
to himself in Greece was now, as he well knew,
greater than in 346, and since his failure on the
Bosphorus, the fear was less.

His first measures, therefore, were directed to the
safeguarding of his flank and communications. The

Theban garrison, to which he had handed Nicaea eight years before,[1] was bidden retire, and Philip established Thessalians to guard in their place the southern mouth of the Pass.[2] Then, pursuing his way into Phocis, he reached the ruins of Elatea, where his path towards Amphissa forked west from the great south road which traversed the Copaic plain to Thebes. Since 346 the site had been untenanted, for Elatea was one of the towns whose inhabitants had been punished in that year by being distributed into villages. Here Philip called a halt, and prepared to establish a fortified camp. At the same time he seems to have sent an embassy southwards to Thebes, to persuade the city to detach itself from Amphissa and act with himself.

Here is an event which has been misrepresented both in ancient and modern times, perhaps more than anything in history. The fortification of Elatea by Philip was manifestly the reasonable precaution of a prudent general. If it menaced any city, that city was Thebes. The site of Elatea lies more than sixty miles by any practicable road from the nearest point of the Attic frontier, and at least ninety from Athens. The whole Copaic plain, the Theban territory, and the range of Cithaeron intervene. There was absolutely no ground, in 338, except Demosthenes' unsupported word, for the belief that Philip was entrenching Elatea as a menace to Athens. There is absolutely no other ground for the same belief being held now. But in spite of the geographical absurdity, in spite

---

[1] Dem. ad Phil. ep. 4.   [2] Aesch. Ctes. 140.

of the positive denial given by Philip's subsequent
action, the suggestion, for which a great orator in
the interests of a policy succeeded in obtaining
credence two thousand years ago, has been accepted
absolutely ever since !

Word came to Athens one day towards sundown,
that Philip was fortifying Elatea.   The news caused
great excitement, for the city considered herself at
this particular moment to be still at war with the
Macedonian, and always was agitated by the passing
of Thermopylae.   Furthermore, with the self-conscious vanity of a great people, the Athenian, like
the Briton, habitually relates to himself every event
that happens in his world.   Doubtless on that spring
evening, season of chatter and intercourse in all the
East, there was much discussion of the news, and
an Assembly was summoned for next morning at
sunrise, no abnormal hour at shadeless Athens in
April.   Here, however, was an obvious opportunity
for the War Party.   Thebes, hostile to Philip's errand
in any case, having taken already the same side in
the matter of Amphissa as Athens, might reasonably
be expected to regard a fortified Elatea as a menace,
and to ally herself with Athens ; and with her help
Ministers could hope reasonably for a vigorous prosecution of their policy, and a prosperous issue, the great
success of the previous year at Byzantium being considered.   Philip once beaten decisively, the restoration
of the Athenian Empire would follow in due course.

There was no vote needed for war, for war had
been the city's nominal relation to Philip these two

years past ; but in the interests of vigorous action by
land, and of alliance with the unpopular Thebans, it
was necessary to arouse the citizens to a sense of private
peril. Demosthenes undertook this task, and with all
his eloquence coloured Philip's design, declared Elatea
to be but a stage on the road to Attica, and pointed
out the nakedness of the frontier should the Thebans
take sides with the Macedonian. The case seemed
clear as daylight; the citizens shouted for action;
and while the levies were being called out, Demosthenes himself undertook to conduct an embassy to
Thebes and sue for the Theban alliance.

In the Cadmeian city he found Philip's envoys,[1]
newly come from Elatea. For what passed then and
there we have the worst authority in the world, the
statements of two contradictory pamphleteers, who
published years afterwards, in the guise of orations,
apologies for their own conduct in this matter.
Demosthenes[2] is the less precise; he relates that the
Thebans first heard Philip's legates and their urgent
request that Thebes would join their master in war
on Athens, or at least give him passage to Attica;
but the effect so produced was swept away from the
Bocotarchs' mind as soon as himself, Demosthenes,
appeared. Aeschines[3] says that at the first audience
Demosthenes was received coldly, and the Bocotarchs

---

[1] Marsyas, fr. ap. *Plut., Dem.* 18.

[2] *De Cor.* 211 ff.

[3] *Ctes.* 149 ff. There is a doubt whether his description
really refers to this first embassy of Demosthenes to Thebes, or
to another just before Chaeronea. On the whole, I adhere to the
view in the text.

sent notice to the Athenian force, already on the move, not to enter Theban territory. Demosthenes, however, at a second audience demanded if not alliance, at least free passage for the Athenian army; and, at last, by persistent working on the fears of the Thebans, and promising that his own city should take only second place in the field and pay two-thirds of the cost of the war, the orator persuaded the Boeotarchs to swear alliance.

The end at least is certain. Thebes concluded a league for offence and defence with Athens, and received the forces of the latter within her walls; and the two took the field against Philip with a larger and a finer army than had been drawn from Greek cities for many a year. The larger Peloponnesian states, threatened or cajoled by Philip,[1] stood aloof, waiting the event, Arcadia, perhaps, as Aeschines said afterwards, only for want of funds;[2] but certain of the smaller, Achaea, Corinth, and Megara, with the islands of Corcyra, Leucas, and Euboea, joined the allies; and Byzantium promised to see to the safety of the corn ships.

One point only in these preliminary matters calls for more remark. Demosthenes states, and he alone, that Philip declared through his envoys from Elatea that his march was directed against Athens. When his entire abstention from any forward movement towards Attica, and his refusal to violate a foot of Athenian territory after Chaeronea, are recalled, it seems most improbable that his private purpose

[1] *Cor.* 218.   [2] *Ctes.* 240. Cf. Paus. viii. 27. 10.

was ever anything of the kind; but that he should
have said so to the Thebans is far from dissonant
with his character, or with the usual methods of
diplomacy; and that his envoys, confronted with
Demosthenes, bid against the latter on the spur of
the moment with such a statement is most credible.
The fact itself, indeed, is more worthy of credit than
the authority for it.

Word of the new alliance was brought to Elatea
by the returning envoys. Philip indited a letter of
bitter reproach to the Athenians, and anxious missives
of encouragement to the Peloponnese, but proceeded
none the less on his road to Amphissa.[1] The allies,
if we are to believe Polyaenus,[2] threw a force into the
passes of Parnassus, but by his old device of leaving
a sham despatch in the enemy's path, the Macedonian
got through. Amphissa had been reinforced strongly
by Athenian hired troops,[3] and a desultory campaign
seems to have been waged for some weeks on the
slopes above the Corinthian Gulf[4] and the hills
bordering Boeotia. The allies gained two small
successes,[5] of which they made the most, but by

---

[1] Plutarch (*Dem.* 18) inverts the order of these events; but I
agree with Holm and Hoffman (schol. Dem. ii. 5, 44) in dis-
regarding his sequence.

[2] iv. 2, 8.

[3] Aesch. *Ctes.* 146.

[4] The surprise of Naupactus (Theopomp. fr. 46) seems to
belong to this war.

[5] One of these skirmishes is alluded to by Demosthenes (who
alone has recorded them) as ἡ χειμερινή (*Cor.* 216). This term
must mean the "Battle of the Storm;" but the translation of it
as "Battle of the Winter" has led to the absurd supposition that

August they had fallen back on the great south road, and concentrated all their forces at the crossing of the Cephissus in the plain before Chaeronea.

On the 7th of the Athenian month Metageitnion — in early August or early September (how Metageitnion fell in 338 is doubtful) — one of the decisive issues of the world's history was fought out. On the one side stood the miscellaneous array, half mercenary, half civic, of the last imperial Greek city-states; on the other was ranged the first great army of a national power. Tried by any standard, Chaeronea ranks as a great battle. The Macedonian came down from Elatea with thirty thousand of the best infantry, and two thousand of the best cavalry in the world. The allied army is stated variously to have been more and less than his,[1] and probably was about equal in numbers.[2] The Theban horse and light troops, if we may judge from their condition three years later,[3] ranked hardly inferior to the Macedonian ; but the Greek army was hampered by a dual command, Theban and Athenian, and we gather that it was not too harmonious in face of the foe; for

Philip spent a whole winter, spring, and most of a summer, ranging about Amphissa, and to a general distortion of the chronology, 340–338. Grote, for instance, tries to include the end of the siege of Byzantium, a last campaign in the Chersonese, the march up to Scythia, the return through the Triballian country, the march through the Gates, the fortification of Elatea, and the marshalling of the allies, all in the one year 339 !

[1] Cf. Diod. xvi. 85, with Justin, ix. 3.

[2] We gather from Aesch. Ctes. 146, that the larger part of the Athenian mercenary force was shut up still in Amphissa.

[3] Arr. i. 7.

there were some who would have fallen in with
Philip's proffered terms rather than fight. The
gods were not for the Greeks; portents and inauspicious omens ushered in the fatal morning.

We know too little, alas! of what happened on
that memorable summer day, to fight the battle o'er
again. No surviving author of antiquity has described
it. By inference only can we set out even the
skeleton of the battle array : on the Macedonian
side, the Thessalian and allied cavalry to the right;
in the centre the phalanx, mercenaries to right,
Macedonians to left, behind a bristling hedge of
spear points; on the left probably the Guards and
Philip himself; and, flanking these and the whole
array, the matchless feudal " Companion " cavalry, led
to-day by no less a captain than Alexander. In the
adverse array, facing the Companions and the Macedonian left centre, was the Theban phalanx, with
the Sacred Band in its centre front; on the left
ranked the Athenian brigades and mercenaries, and
the Achaean [1] and other allies, probably out-flanking
Philip's right. On either wing, and ranging before
the battle-line in the faulty Greek manner, were
targeteers and cavalry, the last used only to skirmish
and pursue.

Allusions and anecdotes which survive imply that
the fight was stubborn and long drawn out, Philip
keeping back his decisive charge until the unseasoned
levies opposed to him should begin to tire.[2] The

[1] Paus. vii. 6. 5.
[2] Polyaen. iv. 2. 7 ; Frontin. ii. 19.

heavy Theban phalanx wore itself out slowly against the mobile veteran formation of Macedonian spearmen; the Athenians with better fortune broke the allies and mercenaries on Philip's left, and rushed on, shouting "To Macedonia!" "These men know little of winning!" grimly remarked the king, and threw his phalanx into the fatal gap which now had opened[1] between Athenians and Thebans. It seems that the latter proved the harder to break, and gave way only to Philip's heaviest blow — a flank charge by the Companions, led by Alexander;[2] but not before there had been one perilous moment when Philip, owing, it is said, to a sudden quarrel in his own phalanx between the Macedonian and the mercenary spearmen, the former perhaps jeering at the latter for having been broken by the Athenian onset, was struck down and hardly saved by his son. For which service,[3] and for such credit as he claimed for the charge which decided that day, Alexander was never forgiven wholly by his father. It was the end. The Greek line gave way along its whole length, the Theban leader fell, the Sacred Band died in its ranks, lovers and loved, the Athenians ran, Demosthenes with the rest, and the supreme effort of Greece was spent.

The Athenians lost three thousand men, killed or taken; the Thebans mourned their general, and probably not less of the rank and file than their allies. Pursuit seems not to have been pressed far, for it

[1] Polyaen. iv. 2. 2.   [2] Plut. *Alex.* 9.   [3] Curt. viii. 1, 23, 24.

was from Lebadea[1] that heralds came the same
evening to supplicate the victor to give up the
dead. There is a tale, strangely characteristic of
Philip, told by more than one authority[2] about this
night at Chaeronea. The suppliant heralds were
bidden to wait — one authority says their request
was refused — and Philip himself made meanwhile
a great feast with his captains. It was such an
orgy as his soul delighted in, with many a light o'
love, and music and dancing; and in the grey dawn
he reeled out mad drunk through his camp and on
to the corpse-strewn field, shouting songs of tipsy
triumph, and jeering at the Athenians and their
runaway Demosthenes. But among his huddling
prisoners stood forth an Athenian orator, one
Demades, a man of incisive speech, as many anecdotes attest, and he faced Philip unabashed, "King,
when Fate has cast thee for Agamemnon, art not
ashamed to play Thersites?" And something
in the gibe, perhaps because it reminded him
of that world of culture to which he had bid so
long and so doubtfully for acceptance, some dim
conviction of a shameful inferiority, penetrated
to the fuddled sense of Philip. The impetuous
captain tore off his garlands and trod them under-
foot with the winecups and flutes and licentious
emblems of his crew, and ordering Demades to be
loosed, went away humbled and ashamed.

[1] Plut. *Vit.* x. Orat. p. 849.
[2] Cf. Theopomp. fr. 262, with Diod. xvi. 87, Plut. *Dem.* 20,
and Sext. Empir. *Adv. Gram.* p. 281.

Certainly afterwards he comported himself towards one part of his beaten foes with a forbearing and, as it were, an apologetic temper[1] that is all the more conspicuous by contrast with the measure that he meted out to Thebes. That city, into which the Macedonians presently marched, was made to feel all the bitterness of defeat. Her headship of the Boeotian towns was stripped from her for ever, and Orchomenus and Plataea were encouraged to rise again on the north and the south.[2] And not only this, but her own civic autonomy was destroyed, her leaders being proscribed or banished, and their lands seized for the king; and, while a Macedonian garrison was installed in the Cadmeia,[3] a body of three hundred men, formerly exiled for adherence to Macedonian interests, was put in office in the lower city to work their will on the lives and goods of the citizens.[4] Thus did Philip remove the last obstacle to his sway in northern Hellas, paying the city which had taught him war and cost him most the rude compliment of a treatment more brutal than any great state of Greece had experienced since the Persian War.

But to Athens, his consistent foe, who now was cowering desperately behind her walls newly repaired with gravestones and the trunks of trees — to Athens, who had proposed even to enfranchise her aliens and free her slaves, and had sent round to the remnant of

---

[1] Cf. Justin, ix. 4; Diod. xvi. 87; Polyb. v. 10, xvii. 14.
[2] Paus. ix. 1. 8, 37, 8.
[3] Paus. ix. 1. 8; and Arr. i. 7.   [4] Cf. Justin, ix. 4.

her allies to beg men and money for a last stand, he "behaved so in victory that none might feel him victor."[1] Not only did he restore freely the Athenian dead — he had made the Thebans pay a ransom — but all his two thousand Athenian prisoners. Furthermore, he sent back Aeschines[2] and other envoys who had come to him, and with them Demades, to assure the terrified citizens not only of peace but his alliance, and he gave withal a signal pledge of good faith by allotting to the Republic of the spoil of Thebes the oft-disputed border town, Oropus. No Macedonian soldier was permitted to violate Attic soil, but in order to ratify the peace, Philip sent to Athens personages no less than Antipater, his Regent, and his own famous son, who saw then, for the first time so far as we know, those most glorious works of a civilization which it was to be given to him, more than to any Athenian, to spread to the ends of the earth.

It was an extraordinary attitude for the master of irresistible legions to assume in the moment of decisive victory. From a military point of view Philip had nothing to fear, and next to nothing to gain, from Athens. The Republic had now no allies worth mentioning that had not been crushed equally with herself at Chaeronea, except the Propontic cities, with whom her tie of friendship was very loose. She had ships, but never could commission two large fleets at a time; and her army had almost ceased to exist. A few triremes and a small

---

[1] Justin, *l. c.*   [2] Dem. *de Cor.* 282.

force of cavalry were all Philip could expect her to contribute to the alliance with himself.[1] Demosthenes, after abandoning the idea of a last desperate struggle behind the walls, to furthering which he had given his voice, his money, and his official service, never credited his city with any further power of resistance. In his funeral oration over the dead of Chaeronea,[2] and in his continued capacity as Minister,[3] he contented himself with mourning over lost greatness, and with devoting his energies to lightening the public poverty.[4]

Philip's attitude, however, was no other than the logical consequence of all his previous conduct towards the Athenian city. While he could not brook her rival empire,[5] he hankered after her approval of his own, and confessed an inferiority which no arms could adjust. And now that she was at his feet, he could confer so great a favour that — man of no delicate susceptibilities as he was — he thought she might be won. Needless to say, he only seemed to succeed. Her adhesion to his panhellenic League against the Persian was only compelled, as not he, but his son lived to know. But nevertheless in spite of his failure, there must be conceded to him a certain enlightenment in the conception of this policy, and a certain rude nobility in the execution; and, at the least, Philip may claim to rank with

[1] Plut. *Phoc.* 17.
[2] See *Cor.* 285–288; Aesch. *Ctes.* 152; Plut. *Dem.* 21.
[3] Plut. *Dem. l.c.*   [4] Aesch. *Ctes.* 159.
[5] Cf. Paus. i. 25. 3.

Sulla, who like him warred on Athens, and like
him spared her when at his mercy in hope to
find grace in her eyes, regarding not her weakness,
but "the weight and repute"[1] that once had
been hers.

The twelvemonth after Chaeronea was spent by the
Macedonian King in smoothing the last obstacles in
his way to what had been growing during the past
decade to be the crowning ambition of his life. He
was become at last lord of the Hellenes *de facto;* he
would be acknowledged Captain-General of Hellenism
de jure. Now that Thebes was crushed and Athens
bound by treaty, there was no doubt of his being
acknowledged Captain, except by the Peloponnesian
states, which had been neither for him nor against
him at Chaeronea. So, having secured Corinth, he
displayed his spearmen in the spring and summer of
337 within the Isthmus. The most part of the states
bowed low: Elis, a friend of old, added a new monument to the Altis, the round *Philippeion,* and set up
therein chryselephantine statues of the conqueror, his
progenitors, and his kin — the first of many Macedonian effigies destined soon to stand in Athens and
Olympia;[2] but Sparta, a little exalted perhaps in the
day of her hereditary foe's humiliation, would have
none of the new Crusade. Philip had to make a
demonstration in the Eurotus valley, in the course of
which a party of his men were handled roughly near

---

[1] Diod. xvi. 8.
[2] See Paus. v. 20. 10; i. 9. 4; vi. 11. 1.

Gythium;[1] but raid her fields and sack her towns as he might, Sparta would not acknowledge him. To his demand for Laconian citizenship, she retorted quite in her old manner, that at least he could not prevent the Spartans dying for their country;[2] and Philip was fain at last to content himself with cutting her territory down to the point at which she would become innocuous, but beyond which he might have outraged Hellenic sentiment, and with obtaining his recognition by the states of Hellas with one dissentient voice.

His ambition was satisfied formally about a twelvemonth after Chaeronea. Delegates from all the states, except Sparta, came to meet him at the Isthmus. We do not know what arguments he may have proffered at the Congress; we hear that he spoke at length about the Crusade against the Persian, and aroused some expression of enthusiasm, to which doubtless the presence of his army without the walls lent a certain warmth. No one in those latter days felt strongly on the Panhellenic Question, or was bitter against the Great King of Susa, whose *darics* alone, not his men-at-arms, were to be expected in Europe; but many of the Greeks, doubtless, were not averse to the restless Macedonian departing for Asia. From one motive or another the delegates were content to acclaim Philip Captain-General, and to promise the spearmen, cavalry, and ships which he asked each state to provide, that his venture might

---

[1] Frontin. iv. 5. 12.
[2] Paus. iii. 24. 6 ; v. 4. 9.

assume a panhellenic character. If their fellow-
citizens grumbled privately, the returned delegates
reminded them that they could hardly have done
less for the master of so many legions. To Philip
it mattered little if the panhellenic movement was
factitious now; a successful campaign in Asia would
go far to give it reality, and common danger and
common triumph would unite his Macedonians and
their Greek allies. In 337 he had probably no such
Asiatic Empire in view, as that which later his son
conceived; he was possessed rather with an idea of
nation-making at home, to which end the mere
warring with a common enemy would conduce more
than the sack of the latter's towns, or the loot of
his camps.

The word given for a twelvemonth from that
time, Philip left Greece, well pleased to gather up
his forces for the great adventure which should
crown all previous successes, and set the seal on
his nation and his fame. He had a great army to
equip and supply, and all that winter the arsenal
of Pella[1] must have rung to the sound of his
arming. By the spring of 336 his host was ready,
and making two divisions, he despatched the lesser
in advance under Parmenio, with Amyntas and
Attalus for lieutenant-generals, to hold the passage
of the Dardanelles, and secure the Greek cities on
the farther shore against his own coming with the
second division and the allied army of Greeks. The
total of the Grand Army we do not know. Justin

---

[1] Cf. Strabo, p. 752; Livy, xlii. 51.

gives an absurd aggregate of two hundred thousand
foot and fifteen thousand horse for the Greek con-
tingent alone. Alexander, however, began his venture
two years later with not more than forty thousand
men; and at no higher figure is it probable that
Philip's national Macedonian force should be estimated.
But there remains to be added the auxiliary host of
Greeks, who would have been used rather to garrison
towns and keep open communications than to accompany the seasoned troops into the heart of the
Persian Empire.

Philip put off his own march to the autumn, for
he had his house to set in order. His family affairs
had been going ill these two years past. Himself
being always in the field,[1] and consorting now with
this woman, now with that,[2] it is small wonder if
his Jezebel of a Queen did not keep in the paths of
strict virtue. A votary of the Cabiric mysteries
before marriage was open to more than suspicion,
and Philip was rumoured always to have doubted
his own paternity of Alexander. The legends of
the serpent seen with Olympias, and the seal set
thereafter on her womb; her affectation of divine
relations,[3] and that worldwide story of her seduction
by an Egyptian astrologer, are so many popular
improvements on the contemporary scandal which
the Macedonian, Attalus, blurted when he prayed

---

[1] Cf. Ps. Callisth., i. 4.

[2] Ἀεὶ κατὰ πόλεμον ἐγάμει, says the contemporary Satyrus
(fragm. ap. Athenæ. xiii. p. 557B).

[3] See Plut. Alex. 2, 3, etc.

tipsily for a legitimate heir to the throne of
Philip, and received Alexander's drinking-cup in his
face.[1]

The relations between father and son had long
left much to be desired. Seeing, however, that
Alexander was made Regent in 339, and led
the Companions at Chaeronea in 338, we may
infer that mutual jealousy had not led to an outbreak before that battle. The open rupture came,
it seems, in 337, after Philip's return from the
Congress of Corinth. He had fallen in love with
a Macedonian lady,[2] niece of his general Attalus;
and she, more ambitious than the dancing-girls[3] and
the like who had yielded to the king's embraces,
worked upon his growing distaste for his wife, until
she induced him to prefer a definite charge of in-
fidelity against Olympias and to wed herself. The
Epirote, bidden, like a woman of the harem, to cover
her face, departed raging to her brother, and presently
her son came to an issue with his father. During
the feast at the new nuptials, as a sequel to a brawl
with Attalus, alluded to already, Philip drew his
sword, and made for Alexander in drunken fury;
but stumbling over the fallen cups, he suffered himself to be pacified by his officers, while Alexander,
gibing at the man who would cross to Asia, but
could not pass from couch to couch, betook himself

---

[1] Plut. *Alex.* 9.

[2] *Cleopatra*, acce   to Plut. *Alex.* 9; Justin, ix. 7; Paus.
viii. 77; Aelian, *V.*   xiii. 36; Diod. xvi. 91. But *Eurydice*,
Arr. iii. 6.

[3] *E.g.* the Larrissean who bore him Philip Arrhidæus.

to Epirus, and having seen his mother safe,. went up into Lyncestis.[1]

Philip, however, coming to himself, invited his son to return; but presently he fell out with the youth again, not this time for a fault, but through a misunderstanding. For it seems that Pixodarus, satrap of Caria, wishing to stand well with the coming invader, sent to negotiate a marriage between his eldest daughter and a natural son of Philip, Arrhidaeus, begotten of a Thessalian dancing-girl. Upon this Olympias, convinced that by hook or by crook her own boy was to be robbed of his succession to the throne, had Alexander persuaded that this was too brilliant a match for his bastard half-brother; for the Carian satrap was at that time the wealthiest of princes, and almost a king in his own right. Accordingly Alexander despatched a Corinthian friend to Caria, to tell the satrap that he, the legitimate heir, was willing; whereat the Carian, who had not dared to look so high, was mightily gratified. But Philip, hearing of the plot, took one of Alexander's intimates aside, when the boy himself was out of the way, and expressed his high displeasure that his heir should have deigned to propose alliance with a Carian subject of the Persian King, and a barbarian to boot. And he followed up his reproof with stringent punishment of the Corinthian, go-between, and decrees of exile against four intin es of his son, who, he believed, were suborn by Olympias to

---

[1] Plut. *Alex.* 9. The Romance (. Callisth. i. 21) has a picturesque exaggeration of this historical scene.

poison the mind of the boy.[1] Among these last were some marked for fame in different ways : Harpalus, who would rebel against and rob Alexander at Babylon ; and Ptolemy, destined to be the historian of the Conquest of Asia, and himself a king.

Such was not a state of affairs that Philip cared to leave in and about Macedonia on the eve of a long absence, and he proposed therefore to render harmless his divorced queen by detaching her powerful brother. Accordingly he offered to the latter a formal reconciliation and the hand of Alexander's sister. The overture was accepted, and Philip determined to make of the wedding a magnificent demonstration of the unity of his panhellenic Empire. In pressing terms he invited representatives of the states of Hellas and all notable Greeks to repair in the autumn to Aegae, the old capital of his kingdom. The great actors of Greece were invited to attend and perform the classic dramas ; games were projected on an Olympian scale, and shows and banquets ordered, even to the entire depletion of the royal exchequer. No matter! Was not all the gold of Asia about to flow into the coffers of Macedon ?

A few days[2] before the opening of the festival, the new queen was delivered of a boy. Here at last was an heir of undoubted legitimacy. We are not told that Philip ever proposed actually to dispossess Alexander in favour of the little Caranus, as the baby was named; but Olympias, watching from among the Lyncestians, jumped to a conclusion,

---

[1] Arr. iii. 6; and Plut. *Alex.* 10.   [2] Diod. xvii. 2.

and warning her adherents of Alexander's peril, coun-
selled speedy action of the most desperate kind.
Whether she admitted her son to the plot or no the
world has never agreed, and probably never will agree.
The measures that Alexander took afterwards, and
the terms in which he spoke of his father, tell neither
for nor against his guilt. That subsequently he should
have put out of the way not only the accomplices of
his father's assassin, but also his own rivals, the baby
Caranus, and the queen's uncle and brother, is only
what an oriental monarch does as matter of course.
But we are bound to remember how little love was
lost between father and son, and how much Alexander
desired that Asia should be left for himself to
conquer.[1]

The great day of the marriage feast arrived. A vast
crowd of sight-seers had thronged into the theatre
before daybreak,[2] and at sunrise a procession entered
with superb effigies of the twelve Olympian gods,
and of Philip himself, thirteenth. Men recalled
afterwards that this public apotheosis was itself the
most signal of omens, and interpreted too late a
cloud of portents, how the prophetess of Delphi had
replied to Philip's demand for an auspicious oracle
ere he should attack Persia, with a vague hexameter,
which signifies, being interpreted, — "The bull is
garlanded ; his end draws on ; the sacrificer stands
ready."[3] Again, had not the Athenian herald,
offering a crown of honour the day before, stated
solemnly that his city would give up to justice any

---

[1] Plut. *Alex.* 5.   [2] Diod. xvi. 92.   [3] Paus. viii. 7. 6.

man who attacked the king? and did not Neoptolemus, the great Athenian player, recite at the royal
banquet overnight an apostrophe to Death ?

But no one that morning thought of oracles or
omens, only of the king's entry, now at every moment
expected. The royal procession approached at last,
and halting a moment, Philip bade his nobles and high
guests precede him, and his guards stand back, that
he himself might be the more conspicuous entering
the theatre in his white robe, hero acclaimed equally
by Macedonians and by Greeks. The leaders entered
the building ; the rearguard hung back obediently,
and Philip stepped forward alone under the gateway.
In that instant a man sprang from the lateral corri-
dor, thrust a short Celtic blade between the ribs of
the king, and rushed off as his victim fell. In the
wild confusion that arose, the assassin came near
getting clear away, for he had friends and swift
horses ready ; but his sandal caught in a vine-stock,
and pursuers were on him before he could rise. They
pulled him to his feet, and pierced him through and
through with their spears.[1]

Philip was found to be dead. Who was first cause
of his murder, there is no doubt. Seek the woman,
slighted, and cast off! The assassin was a mere tool,
one Pausanias, an Orestian favourite, ill-treated it
seems by Philip, and unable to obtain redress for a
degrading insult put upon him by the new queen's
uncle, but not a man of such calibre as would

[1] Diod. xvi. 94.

avenge himself unsupported. His hysterical, half-feminine rancour was remarked by the disaffected party, itself reinforced, for aught we know, by Greek sympathy or Persian gold,[1] and the Celtic sword was put by others into his hands.

So perished the maker of Macedon, at a moment and in a manner which make his death the most dramatic in history. In the prime of his life — he was only forty-six — at the supreme crisis of his fame, on the eve of the greatest enterprise of arms the world had seen, he having steered the ship of his ambition through breakers and rocks to the open sea, — to fall at the whisper of a woman and by the hand of an androgyne!

For all that, it may be said of Philip that perhaps he died none too soon. The great work of his life was accomplished. Macedonia was already a nation, and, as Phocion warned the exulting Athenians,[2] by the death of its creator, the army of Chaeronea lost no more than one man. Further-more, the work which was to follow was not for Philip to do. The expansion of the Greeks into a new nationality, blending with and absorbing the barbarians around them, could be effected only by a leader of a personality more magnetic and a genius more universal than his; and the conquest of Asia from the Hellespont to the Punjab would demand a

[1] Arr. ii. 14.
[2] Cf., for their attitude, Arr. i. 10; Aesch. *Ctes.* 77; Plut. *Dem.* 22.

master in civil organization as well as a master
in war.

For while the creative military genius of Philip
ranks with the very first in the history of arms, and
he added to his magnificent excellences of person a
certain statesmanlike breadth and insight and foresight, which have been equalled seldom, he was in
some respects not a great man of civic affairs. To the
bitter end he understood but very imperfectly the arts
of peace. He could conquer, but usually he was
embarrassed by his conquest. Often in the record of
his life we have to note that his work must be done
twice, even thrice over. Thessaly, for example, was
organized into due subjection only after years of
desultory fighting and intriguing; in Euboea Philip
never wholly succeeded at all. There is a certain crude
and tentative character about his dealings with the
Greeks, and with Athens especially, which his son
never would have displayed, never indeed did display. Those all-powerful bonds of trade, that astute
balancing of nationalities, that subtle use of religious
influences, which made every province that Alexander
left behind him as much his as if he had spent all
his life in organizing it alone, — these things were
hardly dreamed of by his father. Philip could have
marched, no doubt, to the confines of India equally
with his son, but all behind him would have been
swelling up like the belly of that wineskin, on
whose corner a Brahman trod to demonstrate to
Alexander the futility of conquest. It was well for
Philip, and it is very well for the world, that it was

not by him that the West was to be led against the
East. "Europe had borne," indeed, "no such man,
take him for all in all, as the son of Amyntas;"[1] —
until she bore Amyntas' grandson!

Of Philip's conscious constructive work in Macedon
we have spoken already. History will never deny
him the credit of having made there a Nation and a
Power. But it were idle to ignore that posterity has
always overbalanced its praise by bitter censure for
what he did in Hellas.

The interest of the modern world in Philip, and
his place in universal history, depend after all most
on his relation to Greek civilization. Therefore we
must examine, in conclusion, the indictment so often
repeated, that the Macedonian destroyed Hellenic
liberty, and the measure of the wrong he did to
civilization, if that indictment be true. And since
Athens contained always the quintessence of Hellenism, and in this century had come to gather more
and more to herself all great Hellenes, wheresoever
born, let the inquiry be narrowed to her polity; and
the charge, on which Philip shall stand arraigned, will
be this — that, Athens still possessing all the elements
and conditions of vigorous life, with promises yet
unredeemed, and much still to be developed in her
for whose full flower mankind would have been the
better, he, Philip, did so restrict her imperial scope,
and oppress her liberal aspirations, as to cause grave
hurt to civilization. The charge implies, it will be

_____
[1] Theopomp. fr. 27 ; Suid. *s.v.* παράπαν.
10

noted, two **assertions of fact**: first (which is matter
of knowledge), that Athens was vigorous up to
Philip's day; second (which is matter rather of
opinion), that the continued vigour of her civic life
was still the most precious condition of human
progress.

The comparison of the life of states to the life
of the individual is something more than a mere
analogy. Organized in a polity, individuals have a
corporate intellect and corporate emotions, corporate
morality and corporate vices; and, associated, they
display a corporate development from youth to manhood and manhood to age. The youth of the Athenian
polity lies in the centuries before the Persian War.
From that fiery trial the city emerged into manhood.
Can it be that a century later she was falling already
into sere senility?

The most ardent advocate of Athenian liberty
has not denied that early in the fourth century the
Athenian polity was showing signs of exhaustion.
The slackness of its political life during that period
is attested too well, and confessed too universally, to
need demonstration. The orators have depicted for
us even to satiety the figure of the too intellectual over-
politicized Athenian, who is the later type of Demos.
We know so familiarly that loafer in the market-place
and on the hill of Assembly, averse equally to
personal service and to direct taxation for the weal
of his city; who was little better than an out-pauper
with his constant cry, *panem et circenses*, having
replaced the unreasoned belief of his forefathers that

the individual exists for the state, by a reasoned conviction that the state exists to support and amuse the individual. That his city should have a circle of tributary dependencies whose contributions would pay for mercenaries to fight and row in his stead, for ships to secure his corn supply,[1] and for free shows in his theatre and his stadium, was a consummation which he contented himself with desiring devoutly. He would neither fight nor pay for its accomplishment, and with his idle criticism, his spoiled temper, his love of litigation, and his ceaseless talk he so hampered his own executive[2] that it could carry out no imperial policy, and the few men of action left in the city hastened to reside beyond his reach.[3]

As a matter of fact (and this consideration is very germane to the issue) during this period Athens had no truly imperial position at all, not even a hegemonic one, for which it might be claimed that it ennobled leader or led. Her First Empire, so soon as, having ceased to be a militant League against Persia, it lost its first justification, had assumed another under the reasoned direction of Pericles. The imperial Republic, keeping her tributaries entirely under her control, was to elevate them with herself into a splendid organism, representative of the best in Hellenism as against all the world. Obligations

---

[1] For the importance of this supply, cf. *Hell.* v. 1, 28; 4. 61; and Dem. *Cor.* 87.

[2] Cf. *Phil.* i. 46, 47.

[3] Theopomp. fr. 117; Nep. *Chabr.* 3.

which could not be enforced upon her were to be acquitted of her own free will more fully than her subjects could have dreamed. Hence that largeness of ideal, and especially that exalted sense of obligation, which characterize the policy of Athens in the fifth century and are reflected in her literature and her art. The citizen has an ambition transcending mere civic life; the calls upon him keep him alert and active; his ruder energies find worthy vent, and his sense of demi-godlike superiority to his kind renders him incapable of what is sordid and small. In this way the First Empire justified itself awhile to the leader herself, and may perhaps find justification also at the bar of history, notwithstanding that the led for their part in no way identified themselves with, nor even acquiesced in, this ideal of their leader.

But the Second Empire, falsely so-called, that is the revived League of 378, must be judged less favourably by history. The incompatibility of the Periclean ideal with weak human nature had come to be proved before Pericles' own death by protest after protest from the "allies," followed by actual revolt. The very loftiness of the leader caused her to be hated with such a hatred as has been meted out to few imperial cities; and the constantly increasing coercion which she had to practise towards her dependencies throughout the closing decades of the century went far to neutralize any ennobling effect of her imperial position. Athens stood, at the opening of the fourth century, amid the ruins of her First Empire, disillusioned, her demi-godlike state past for ever, herself tumbled rudely to a lower level of obligation and ideal.

Therefore, when, after the conclusion of a series of free commercial alliances and the reconstitution of her own means of offence and defence, Athens succeeded, a generation later, in imposing her headship once more on above seventy cities, she did so under conditions which precluded this restored " Empire " from having any ennobling or elevating effect even on herself. The Second League was formed by the coercion of a single victorious fleet, and had a host of foes both within and without. In the original articles of association, which have been preserved to us on the official marble,[1] Athens abandons by implication all the imperial rights which in her first Empire she had assumed in virtue of her own demi godhead. This League the Republic forms, not for her own aggrandisement, but in the interest of the continued existence of herself, equally with that of the smallest signatory. She admits that she has no right to use the lands of the allies for her own benefit, or to try their citizens by her laws. They, for their part, agree to send deputies and contributions to her for convenience' sake, being obviously jealous of her headship, and prepared to dissociate on the slightest sign of her assertion. With hardly anything in common but jealousy, such a League did not need a Philip to break it up, and as a matter of fact it had dissolved by no act or devising of his, before ever he laid a finger on Athenian possessions.

[1] *C. I. A.* ii. 17.

Thereafter Athens in the fourth century had a number of uncertain, free allies, but no subject empire really under her own control, except those tracts in Samos, and on the northern shore of the Dardanelles, which were held, in contravention of her sworn assurance, by bodies of armed colonists, together with the unimportant islands of Lemnos, Imbros, and Scyros, and, for a brief period and very doubtfully, Euboea — and these few she effectually could neither protect nor coerce.

Small wonder that Imperialism, when not recalled as a glorious memory of an earlier age, connoted little to the orators and historians of the fourth century but piratical raiding and the levying of blackmail, truckling to the Barbarian,[1] complaints and protests from islands and cities, mercenary expeditions, and shifty evasions of sworn treaties. So far from ennobling, it reminded of decadence of prestige abroad, and was associated with failure of political morality at home.

It is contended, however, that in this first half of the fourth century there was merely an eddy in the stream of Athenian progress; that the polity of Athens was not really old, only exhausted for the moment by mighty effort, and about to have risen again, a giantess refreshed. Now a state no more than an individual can put on its youth again, but not less than an individual it may hasten its age. While the pulse beats at fever heat, both an individual and a state live many years in one. The

[1] Cf. Aesch. *Ctes.* 238 ; *Dem. Phil.* iv. 31.

Athenians, who had started manhood under the tremendous stimulus of a general belief that they were a chosen people, continued to live at the highest pressure under the guidance of Pericles and Periclean ideas for more than two generations. It was the existence of a huge slave population, of course, that made it possible for the privileged citizen body to cultivate exclusively its intellectual and physical perfection. It was the quick Ionian wit of its members that inclined them to the life political. The ephebic training gave every young citizen the same ambitions and the same tastes, and Periclean state-socialism took from them all concern for old age. Thus not merely a leisured minority, but the whole body of citizens, was able to lead for two-thirds of a century a life more intense than has fallen to the lot of any class in history; and the Athenian state passed through the experience of three centuries at least in that one, working out a more complete evolution in politics, in art, and in letters, than many another people has developed in a millennium.

Beginning the century as an aristocratic state, Athens ended it as a democracy developed to the last degree that that form of polity, as understood by Greek publicists, would admit. There was no reserve, nothing still to come in the next age, no large proletariate, for example, whose gradual emancipation might initiate fresh phases of vigour. The proletariate of Athens was all servile, and reckoned outside the polity. Henceforward there is no further constitutional development to be remarked in Athens, but merely abuse of what has been developed already, as obligation ceased to be felt and self-indulgence increased. The orator system, for instance, is no new feature, merely an inevitable exaggeration of an old one. When Athens was aristocratic, but not imperial, we hear most of her Archons; with the rise of her empire the Generals come to the front; with its fall, and the disappearance of the aristocracy, the Talkers preside over the State. Alexander demanded the surrender not of generals, but orators. Demosthenes himself was a symptom of democracy in decay.

If we turn from politics to art and literature, we note the same complete evolution. Sculpture has passed in a century from archaism to the birth of mannerism with Praxiteles. All writers on the subject recognize a pause in the fourth century. The artist in marble or bronze has no more to learn, no new world to conquer; his art has come down to earth, and is henceforward to be imitative or reforming only. The case is not otherwise with literature. The Epos is fixed finally; prose style culminates in Isocrates; Euripides has developed the Drama to the last point of humanism which the peculiar conditions of the Greek stage would admit, and presently with Menander it is to cease to be scenic and to become literary.

Furthermore, let two things be remarked in Athenian literature which, more than anything else, argue that the Athenian polity was aging, and not enduring a mere passing reaction. It has been remarked often

that towards the end of the fifth century the tone
of Athenian writers becomes distinctly anti-imperial.
Thucydides, Aristophanes, Euripides, Plato, are none
of them for the Empire. All condemn in their
several ways the imperial idea, although, as certainly
as our own giants in letters of the Elizabethan and
Victorian ages, those great Athenians owed their
own intellectual eminence to the imperial position
of the society in which they moved. The explanation is not far to seek. The intellectual activity,
which the empire stimulated, had led, on the one
hand, to a dawning sense of a circle of obligation,
with which Empire was not consistent, on the other,
to ideals of human happiness not necessarily political.
The Athenian had become conscious, and a race, once
it has reasoned about its own existence, has left its
demi-god state behind for ever, and is no longer
"chosen." The heyday of life vanishes with the
birth of reflection.

Secondly, it is surely significant that poets, both
of the first and second order, should cease from
Athens as the fourth century advanced. For a
nation to confine its artistic effort in literature to
the study of assonance and hiatus in prose, and
that mainly *ad captandum* in the shallow style
of the orator, implies surely that the evening of
creative power has set in. That there should have
come to be a demand for elaborate harangues, smelling
of the lamp, was a sign of political decadence; that
the literary class should have supplied almost nothing
else, is proof that the decadence extended to art.

Philip obtrudes himself on this Athenian stage when decadence is no longer a tendency but an established fact; when democracy has passed into mobrule, and opportunists, like Eubulus,[1] are at the helm of state. The Macedonian was responsible not for the predominance of such opportunists, but merely, like Sparta of old, for the line they elected to take. He appears also when there exists no longer at Athens generals even of the type of Chabrias or Timotheus,[2] but in their stead *condottieri* and respectable corporals like Phocion; when no poet has been seen since Euripides, prose has reached its last expression in the orator, and artists are passing into imitative artisans. So far as we can see, there loomed before the Athenian, in the middle of the fourth century, no future except to develop exaggeration, refinement, mannerism, and imitation in the small round of in-bred city life, and to pass away at last, monstrous or decayed.

The sum of this whole matter may be set down thus. Had Macedon never arisen, the city of Athens probably would not have been very different at the end of the fourth century from what actually she came to be; and Philip may be acquitted at once of having done, even indirectly, any grave hurt to civilization by his action towards her. Nay more — and now we face the assertion that the continued vigour of the civic existence of Athens, had it been

---

[1] Theopomp. fr. 96. Cf. Aesch. *Ctes.* 25 ; Dein. *in Dem.* p. 102, 99.

[2] Nep. *Chabr.* 3.

possible for it to be sustained, would have been the
most precious condition of human progress — Philip,
by hastening the decadence of the Greek city-state,
did the Greek race in particular, and all mankind in
general, no small service. Needless to say, no such
service was in his thoughts. Needless to say, it was
not he that first set going, or he that conducted to its
height, the overflow of Hellas. The banks had been
leaking obscurely for a half century past. Mercenaries, trading colonists, favourites of kings, and barbarian chieftains, had been learning to forget their
civic allegiance in wider spheres of energy; and
Cyrus the Younger, Agesilaus, Jason of Pherae, had
all done their part to awake dim consciousness in the
Hellene that it lay but with himself to possess the
world. But it needed a mightier arm than theirs
to break down altogether the barriers which con-
fined the citizen to his city. Philip may be said
to have cut decisively the dykes, Alexander to have
guided and controlled the flood.

This is not the place — another may be found
more suitable — to portray the Greek of the coming
age, called so justly the Hellenistic; for the expansion of Hellas reached, of course, its full limits only
under the successors of Philip's son. But as it was
Philip who, at least, made that expansion possible, it
is but just to link his name loosely with those great
benefits which were to accrue to Hellenism and the
world in the new era. Briefly, the Hellene, being
cut as by a pruner from the aged stem of his polity,
began an independent development in a new soil,

with new juices to feed upon and a new sky opened overhead. No longer bound by the tyranny of corporate evolution to refine on the already too refined, and to follow the grooves which decline to corporate death, his individual genius could enter on a new progress. Born and trained to a higher grade of political capacity than members of any other contemporary race, he applied to all communities into which he came higher and more universal principles of government than they had known hitherto; and in the new field those principles took a new and larger scope than in his own little polity of old. His mind having been exercised through thought and the application of thought, he could apply it to any science or condition of life, and accordingly everywhere he instituted an advance on what had preceded him. But removed from the hothouse atmosphere of his parent polity, his genius takes now a more practical aspect. It turns to applied science rather than the pure theoretic, to decorative and domestic art, to application of literary form and finish, to the presentation of useful knowledge, to treating, in short, art as made for man rather than man as made for art. Aristotle, Euclid, Eratosthenes, and Ptolemy the geographer are more genuine products of this new era than Apollonius, Callimachus, or Theocritus; the artistic culinary implements of Pompeii express it more aptly than the Sidon sarcophagi, the Pergamum frieze, or the Laocoon. The Greek went out to be the leaven of a world, which had not forgotten art and theory, but was no longer to live by art and theory alone.

It was remarked long ago that the modern world has taken no political institution consciously or directly from Athens, that is to say, in letters and in art the Athenian is not our immediate forefather. For if it is true that all the roads of civilization lead back to Greece, equally it is true that they run for vastly the greater part of their course not through Greece. But none the less all along those roads, down to the gate of modern times, the Greek is conducting us always, himself the spirit of progression. Had no Philip nor such rude giant driven him forth from the frontiers of his little state, our present debt to Hellas had been little greater than can be contracted by conscious archaists in political science, in letters, and in art. But Philip it was that forced the Hellene into the open sea, and therefore, if it be that " nothing moves in the world which is not Greek in origin," it is owed to no man more than the Macedonian. And surely if the great dead still may note the course of progress, in which once they played a part, a reconciliation must have been sealed long ago in the Elysian Fields between Demosthenes and his " barbarian of Pella."

PORTRAIT BUST OF ALEXANDER
Tivoli Herm in the Louvre

ALEXANDER

THE bloody mantle of a murdered king has dropped seldom so uneasily as upon the shoulders of Alexander. His legitimacy had been impugned by his father. The party that looked to him was not dominant at court. A dispossessed uncle and a half-brother were at hand to claim his succession. His mother had contrived certainly, and he himself was suspected to have been privy to, the cruel catastrophe that had just befallen.

It can have been with no too sanguine hopes that the boy allowed friends and flatterers to buckle his corslet and lead him to claim Philip's throne. A few minutes earlier the butchered king had been borne back to his palace. The streets on that October morning, all in gala trappings for the interrupted feast, were probably as empty now as the fatal Theatre; for it was the doubtful hour after a great crime, when an oriental crowd runs instinctively to cover. Presently, however, what might not the assembled nobles and burghers attempt? What would be the policy of that brilliant gathering of Envoys Extraordinary? What last and most, was

likely to be the mood of the great Army of Asia,
marshalled in the Vardar plain?

In the event this concurrent presence of ambassadors and soldiers in the first critical hours saved
Alexander. Ere another's standard could be raised,
he had had time to appeal in person to his father's
allies, and to all sections of his father's army.
The representatives of the former in the presence
of the latter would have assured any heir of their
loyalty perhaps with equal effusion; and honestly
and promptly the army declared for the hero of
Chaeronea. Olympias had counted on memories
of that great day, and Alexander appealing now
with beauty and youth for his allies, did not appeal
in vain.

We can call up his image more distinctly than
that of his father; for Plutarch, who had seen portraits by Lysippus and read contemporary memoirs
now lost, has left a descriptive chapter, to be compared with such copies of the Lysippean type as survive, and with countless idealized heads on medals and
in marble. In all antiquity Alexander was famous for
beauty of face, not quite of the then accepted type,
but fuller featured and more ardent. Plutarch reports
that his skin was singularly fair and clear, and though
in stature not above the ordinary, he had the frame
and aspect of an Olympic athlete. His father, indeed,
once proposed that he should enter the lists for
the great foot-race, but the haughty boy would not
compete with less than his social peers. Further we
are told that habitually his head was inclined a little

PORTRAIT BUST OF ALEXANDER
in the British Museum

towards the left shoulder, more probably in an unconscious pose than through malformation or disease,[1]
and that large and liquid but fiery eyes[2] arrested
attention most in his face. In a copy of a portrait bust, brought from Alexandria to our national
collection, the spectator does remark indeed the
character of the eyes, deep sunk beneath brows extraordinarily prominent, and shaded by very full lids,
which fold over on themselves, the whole giving a
singular impression of amplitude and life. Not less
remarkable, however, are the mouth and chin, both
sensuous, and inspiring insistent suspicion whether
the Macedonian conqueror can indeed have been so
indifferent to the lusts of the flesh as the ancients
agreed to believe.

This bust in the opinion of some critics[3] is a too
emphatic copy, and less faithful than the Tivoli
herm of the Louvre ; others[4] question if it represent
a portrait at all. But in the matter of the mouth
there is no need to take cover behind such doubts ;
the tradition of antiquity and the sculptor are both

[1] Torticollis, or atrophy of the right side. *Vide* extracts from
a paper by A. Déchambre, quoted in *Rev. Arch.* Ser. i. ix.
p. 422. The learned doctor in his *résumé* (p. 433) says,
" L'antique connu sous le nom d'hermès d'Alexandre représente
un personnage atteint d'un torticolis par raccourcissement du
muscle sterno-mastoidien droit."

[2] Cf. Plut. *Pomp.* 2.

[3] *E. g.* Th. Reinach, in his discussion of the Alexander-heads on
the Sidon sarcophagus (*Une Nécropole royale*, etc., text, p. 293).
Cf. frontispiece to this volume.

[4] *E. g.* F. Koepp (*Ueber das Bildniss Alexanders des Grossen*,
Berlin, 1892).

to be justified. For two things about Alexander must be borne in mind. On the one hand, he had no characteristic more salient than an inordinate pride of self which stepped in whenever his emotion threatened to break from control. He owed that pride to many causes — equally to the very plenitude of his powers, and to the circumstances of an early life, spent in bitter quarrel with his natural guardian, and in the premature independence which such relations in a feudal state induce. Exalted by the admonishment of a great tutor, the boy had been also early invested with command, and exposed to every intoxication of flattery. By one of these influences or another, Alexander had manifestly been brought, ere he reached manhood, to regard, as many men not professedly moral have regarded, sexual surrender as to be withstood always and everywhere. Those impulses which threaten most absolute dominion over self, he dreaded most; and in the sequel, largely through the strenuous part for which he was cast during all his life, he succeeded in keeping them under, as few ascetics have done. He who had refused angrily to marry and leave an heir before he set out for Asia, begot only two children of his body, the second, Roxana's boy, after four fruitless years of wedlock; and since death interposed early between his will and its inevitable decay, he has remained a pattern of continence to the ages, the most signal example perhaps in history of the subjection of the flesh to inordinate pride!

On the other hand, his nature was neither cold

nor passionless. The flame burned fiercely enough in Alexander, little issue though it found in the love of women. The most beautiful of these he affected to regard as " soulless dolls,"[1] but none the less he gloried in wine and song and feasting, like his father before him.[2] And even if we did not know his record so intimately, we might assume that no nature coldly intellectual could display the half of Alexander's recklessness ; no man not essentially emotional would risk so much for ideas ; no one not frankly passionate had attached a great host to himself by a bond which held for seven years through sands and snows, and survived at the Sutlej and at Opis. But we do not depend alone on inference. Was there not in Alexander's life at least one emotional friendship, a friendship of that type which, based obscurely on passion, in certain natures passes the love of women ? Perhaps he consciously directed the imperious current of his emotion into that channel to avoid all risk of sexual slavery ; but even so, if we believe Plutarch[3] and the consent of antiquity, Alexander stands absolved of all suspicion of sin ; and we must count him not worse than the best of the race and school of Plato in the age before the idealization of woman.

The prince, called thus suddenly to Philip's seat, had enjoyed no common education. The nature inborn in any son of Olympias (Aeacid though she was) would be rather that of an Albanian

[1] Plut. *Alex*. 21. [2] Cf. Athen. x. 45. [3] *Alex*. 22.

chieftain than a Greek citizen; and if indeed Alexander sprang too from Philip's loins, he would be also on that side but a rude Hellene. On this proud mountain stock, however, had been grafted, by Philip's example and the precepts of his tutors, all the most exclusive sentiment of a Greek. Confident heir of a new-made order, cradled in the late-invented militarism, and imbued almost at his father's knee with the idea that whoso disposed of the forces of Macedon could dispose also of the earth, Alexander had been subjected to all exalting influences, and those untempered by parental control worthy the name. By inevitable consequence, in a latitude of early maturity, he was become full man ere he ascended his father's throne — a man who for years had been forming most definite ambitions, and, in measuring his personal powers against those of all the leading spirits of his sphere, had rated himself their equal or their better. He would know and do what no man else had known or done. "Not rightly," he wrote to Aristotle, "hast thou published the doctrines that thou taughtest to me by word of mouth, for why should the rest of the world be even as I?" To himself he seemed to be the "god in mankind," with no straiter limitations, no gentler code of right, than a demi-god of Homer's world. There are many stories of the boy's precocious self-assertion. Like a potentate of our own day, educated under influences not dissimilar, who maybe has modelled himself a little on the Macedonian, Alexander believed in royal roads to knowledge. He

would grasp the innermost mysteries of philosophy
before he had learned well its rudiments; he thought
to have penetrated the *arcana* of medicine, and
gravely lectured his most venerable physicians. But
the ready smile fades in wonder, that, seeing who
this prince was, and how brought up — seeing that
his interests ranged from the conquest of the world
to the collection of specimens — seeing withal that
his follies were committed all before men — nevertheless such tales should be so few !

So we are confronted, from the very outset, by a
most masterful and conscious character, self-reliant
to a fault, little hampered by restraints of constitution
or family, but disciplined somewhat in Philip's hard
school of arms. Add a most brilliant, precocious
intellect, given the widest scope by contact for three
years with the mind of Aristotle and deeply tinged
with the romantic side of Hellenic culture ; add the
frame and constitution of an Olympic victor, and,
again, the beauty of a Praxitelean god. Alexander's
physical excellences attracted those whom his intellectual force might have daunted or repelled; and
the two together endowed him with a personal
magnetism which seems to have been felt equally
by the subtlest Greek and the rudest barbarian in
his service. On a far greater scale than Alcibiades,
Alexander was born to do the most good or the
most harm to all his world.

What nature of inheritance devolved on this
leader of men ? A professional army of probably

not less than 60,000 men of all arms was absolutely ready to his hand, mobilized at the moment of his accession. That force was in a state of perfect discipline and efficiency, having received the last touches of its maker; and no soldiery in the world could compare with it for purposes of offence. The Macedonian navy, however, was but a small, neglected force, hardly adequate for coast defence, and inferior to fleets which several Greek and Asiatic cities severally could put on the sea at short notice.

In territorial possession the boy received absolutely what still we call Macedonia, with the most part of Roumelia, bounded west by the Albanian watershed and north by the Balkan chains; but the Black Sea slope was part savage and half-subdued,[1] part friendly but independent, under Byzantium.[2] Absolutely also he was lord of Thessaly. The completeness of sub-jection to Macedonian rule is shown best in all this region by the fact that it has left no coinage of this period but that issued by the royal mints of Macedon.

The remainder of the Balkan peninsula lay also in dependence more or less complete. Greece south of Thermopylae was kept in check by military occupa-tion, the Gates themselves, the Theban citadel, Chalcis the key of Euboea and Attica, and the Corinthian

---

[1] These Thracians are still called αὐτόνομοι in Alexander's reign (Arr. i. 1).

[2] Which city sent ships to help Alexander in his Thracian campaign (Arr. i. 3).

approach to the Peloponnese, being held ' strongly
with royal troops. But the cities continued to coin
their own money,[1] and to be regarded nominally as subject allies of the Macedonian king, a condition which
they detested and would repudiate as soon as might
be. Epirus remained an ally without being subject ;
and all round the outer circle of the west and north
the highland tribes of Albania, Montenegro, Servia,
and Bulgaria were in an ill-defined tributary position
towards Macedon, which called for rude correction
from time to time; for Philip's latest operations in
those Balkan regions had not contributed much to a
definite settlement. Finally, Macedonian troops were
at this moment in possession of the farther shore of
the Dardanelles, and a little of the inner land of Asia.

It was a somewhat thorny heritage of Empire. No
part of it was quite sound, not even the core, which
it had been Philip's life-work to expand and assure.
Through him indeed it was become loyal enough to
the Macedonian crown, but not by any means was
it so certainly attached to the person of the new
king. The old trouble with the Feudatories was not
quite past and done with : Alexander had to proceed
at first with extreme caution in dealing, for example, with Lyncestians ;[2] and the arch Lyncestian

---

[1] The value of the numismatic test may be illustrated by the
change which supervenes in Athens and the Peloponnese after the disastrous end of the Lamian War in 322. Their independent coinage
becomes thenceforward as non-existent as that of Thessaly.

[2] Certain of whose chiefs fought on the Persian side in Asia,
e. g. Neoptolemus at Halicarnassus, and Amyntas at Issus; and
Polemon fled to the foe at a later period, but returned to allegiance.

conspirator could not be put to death until years after his guilt was established.[1] Still more dangerous seemed certain of those who, having been foremost in Philip's councils, knew that his elder son perhaps would not, had the father lived longer, have been his designated successor.

Eager to realize the legacy of his father's hopes, the son had first to secure the inheritance of his father's deeds. Alexander's seat in Europe was none too sure. Greece, agitated by Demosthenes, showed a most uncertain mood;[2] the Balkan tribesmen were openly defiant. To neutralizing these foes within and without the first year and a half of the new reign had to be devoted, and in that brief but strenuous schooling in peril and patience the exuberant boy sensibly matured. Most notable is it, how these two preliminary campaigns in Europe display already the assertive personality of the future conqueror. Alexander has a perfect machine left ready to his hand, but its mechanical perfection induces in him no mechanical habit; even thus early he quickens it with all the fire of his own spirit. When at the outset the Thessalians bid him wait without their closed door of Tempe, convention would have enjoined

---

[1] Cf. Arr. i. 25, with Curt. vii. 15, and Justin, xi. 2.

[2] The state of Greece at this crisis is well set forth by B. Niese, *Geschichte der griech. und makedon. Staaten*, etc. (i. pp. 53 ff.). In fact, this passage and another on the condition of Greece and the West generally during Alexander's last years (p. 161 ff.) are the best in Niese's too summary and too little critical work (1893).

the assault or the purchase of what had long been
held to be the one practicable pass. But the new
Captain, without a moment's hesitation, turns to
the impracticable route, and succeeds. His spearmen are bidden cut steps along the sea-face of Ossa,[1]
and get through where goats hardly had passed
before. For result, the rising insolence of the peninsula abjectly collapsed, and not a murmur was heard
except from Sparta, when the boy came down to
Corinth to claim the proud prerogatives of his father.
And for further result, a year later, only the reported
death of this stripling of twenty, at whom Demosthenes had been jeering so lately, emboldened tortured
Thebes to raise the standard of revolt. Warning of
the dreadful phalanx did not dash the spirit of the
rebels, for they were told it was led by Antipater, or
by some namesake of Alexander. Then lo! the boy
himself was without the walls. Just as he found
himself with his army at the moment that the ill
news came to Lake Ochrida, unreinforced, careless of
his communications and his supplies, he had made
straight for the nearest gap in the frontier range,
and in fourteen days was seated over against the
Cadmeia. There was one sortie, and a tough tussle
in the streets with the stiff-backed Theban burghers,
and not another sword was unsheathed in Greece for
five years.

In the previous Balkan campaign, too, the ἀριστεῖα
had been not less Alexander's, half reckless barbarian
that he was, half heir of the highest civilization in

[1] Polyaenus, iv. 3. 23.

his age, and always source and spring of action. He demanded and obtained from his soldiers the prowess of single champions. In the very first engagement they must break up their close, confident formation, and, crouching under their shields, let Triballian waggons hurtle over their bodies down the Balkan slopes.[1] They were ferried in a single night across the greatest river in their world, to demonstrate in a land absolutely unreconnoitred. The most complicated movements of the parade-ground had to be executed calmly in an open valley, for the psychologic value of the spectacle upon the watching ambuscades which beset flank and rear. And already we find Alexander obeyed implicitly by professional soldiery, doubtless not a little because he was the bombastic young athlete, darling of rude men, who dropped the generalissimo whenever there was a wild charge to be headed, who risked himself and the flower of his force across the Danube, simply that he might say he had crossed it, and prodigally spent health and strength in being first in every forced march, first through every doubtful ford, and first into every fenced city. A measure of self-conscious display was added to impulse, for Alexander was but twenty-one; and there are well-known tales of his frank disappointment if his audience remained unmoved. But whether when Diogenes grimly tells him, would-be Lord Bountiful, to stand away from his sunlight, or when certain hairy Kelts, to whose thews the boy's soul had

[1] Polyaenus, iv. 3. 11.

warmed, refuse in the true Scots spirit the shadow of a compliment to all his fishing, Alexander has always enough conviction or enough nobility to keep his temper and his dignity. And, indeed, the very frankness of the boy's self-assertion, inspiring still a kindly sentiment for him in this fair spring of his year, reveals the secret of his extraordinary personal magnetism. However conscious the pose, however deliberate the action, there remained in Alexander to the end so much of an exuberant child of nature, who used all his powers recklessly for all they were worth, that custom never staled the enthusiasm he so openly sought.

A year and a half passed by, and by the time that the young Captain was ready for the great venture in whose inception his father had died, and whereof himself had dreamed long, the noise of him and the fear had spread from the Danube to the southernmost isles of the Greek sea. He was become to the mass of his Macedonians a Hero who could do no wrong; but this idolatry was not enough for his ambition, and he was bent on winning a like throne in the hearts of the Greeks. Even as Philip, so Alexander, piqued by the precious exclusiveness of Athens, paid involuntary homage to her pre-eminence in a world more universal than his own; but more than his father, for he had had the better Hellenic training, he would make appeal to her literary and artistic sense, sparing the house of Pindar, sleeping head on Homer, and proclaiming in an open letter to

Aristotle, that he set the great achievements of pure intellect above all feats of arms. A romantic vein having led him in this first bloom of his youth to set up the Homeric Hero as his life's ideal, the title of Captain-General of Hellas, which seemed to lift its holder to an Agamemnonic pinnacle, was taken probably by Alexander at the first much more seriously than by Philip.

The boy could not, however, have been possessed of the intelligence which was his, had he supposed the Greeks, least of all the Athenians, to be with him heart and soul. The reception which the news of his father's death had met with south of Olympus, the obstruction offered to his own first entry into Thessaly, the revolt of Thebes, and the sympathy shown to her beyond Cithaeron, had supplied warnings patent to a duller man than Alexander. And, indeed, it was clearly to conciliate a hostile spirit of which he was uneasily conscious, that he began by making not only appeal to Athenian culture, but the same sort of gracious concession to Athenian political pride that his father had fancied would be grateful. Like Philip, Alexander never violated Attic soil; like Philip, when he had to arraign certain statesmen for words or deeds hostile to himself, he ostentatiously left the convicted in the hands of the sovereign Athenian people. Unlike Philip, however, he seems not to have believed that such favours could avail alone, but to have relied for ultimate success rather on his own personality, on his physical beauty, on his intellectual culture, and on the

Homeric spectacle he was about to display of a new Achilles gone to Asia. Ruined Thebes he hoped thus would be forgotten,[1] thus the enthusiastic applause of the Academy be won, thus that he might make of his present Empire and his future conquest one Hellenic unity, himself acclaimed by free conviction the one worthy prince of the whole.

Behold, then, a very sanguine and large-hearted youth, somewhat conscious and greedy of recognition and applause, bid adieu to his mother on the Macedonian border in early spring of 334, and march off with forty thousand men-at-arms and his hopes for the Dardanelles. Those " hopes " which, after giving away almost all his substance with a quixotic indifference to money and luxuries which remained characteristic to the end, Alexander had said, laughing, would pass the straits alone of all his treasures, were already full-fledged. He proposed nothing short of complete dispossession of the great Darius in favour of himself, Captain-General of Hellas, in short, the establishment of his own panhellenic Empire in the room of the Persian.

It might be superfluous to emphasize this so obvious ambition of the young Alexander, were it not that there is hardly a commentator or a critic but has forgotten it by the time the Conqueror is come to Issus. Thenceforward special reasons are sought and supplied with a wealth of perverse ingenuity for almost every forward movement. From Egypt to

[1] Plut. *Alex.* 13.

the Euphrates, from Persepolis to the Caspian, from the Caspian to the Sir Daria, from Balkh to India, Alexander is said to be forced by this particular consideration of policy, or that fresh goad of masterful fate. In truth, however, the motive influence was always one and simple. From the first Alexander looked to reach no goal, and indeed reached none, either at Memphis, or at Arbela, or at Babylon, or at Persepolis, or in the little gorge where Darius lay dead, so long as any tiara but his own was erect in the Persian Empire, or a single satrapy had failed to acknowledge his sway. And such a plan of campaign was, beyond a doubt, what contemporary Greeks understood by the due wreaking of the revenge of Hellas. That the campaign of Vengeance should be merely demonstrative, to be relinquished when the Palace of Xerxes was burned, or his successor had been done to death — that one should vanquish but not possess the lands of the vanquished — this was neither contemporary theory, nor likely to be contemporary practice. At least no such conception was present to the minds of those who saw, some with grief, some with joy, but all with surprise, Alexander burn at Persepolis what they recognized was now become his own.

We are not called upon to find a fresh motive for progress west of the Indus. The simple scheme of dispossessing the one rival Emperor in his world and possessing in his room, had been Philip's last absorbing idea; it had become that of the boy Alexander even before his father's death; it continued to be his when king. From the very first in Asia Alexander assumed the position of the Persian, replacing the latter's satraps with his own, continuing the old system of administration, with, at first, special indulgence for Greek cities,[1] accepting even Persian officials if proved loyal to their new Great King; and every province, witness Egypt in chief, was organized as a possession for ever. The Macedonian put his own purpose nakedly enough in replying to Darius' overtures before Arbela,[2] that he required all the king's lands, not any part: "I, Alexander, consider the whole of thy treasure, and the whole of thy land, to be mine." How can this be misconceived? The Conqueror did not march on a bee-line to Susa, but he was making thither not less but more surely, because from Side, from Issus, from Arbela he turned off the main track to fix his footing so surely that no one after him ruled in the western empire of Persia but on western lines before the Hegira.

Ultimately, as will be seen in the sequel, the Conqueror's ideal came to transcend these primary limits, and the conquest of Persia was forgotten in the conquest of the Earth. Equally, but much earlier, the outward sanction which the Conqueror

---

[1] Cf. his letter to the people of Smyrna, the record of which is preserved in an inscription (*C. I. G.* 3137, ll. 100 ff.) ; also similar privileges granted to Priene (*B. M. inscr.*, iii., No. 400).

[2] On the authenticity of these letters to Darius, see Pridik, *De Al. Magni epistularum commercio*, pp. 39 ff. That learned scholar accepts them as at least embodying genuine matter. Niese accepts them also, but without criticism.

had sought at first for his conquest was forgotten
also. Partly it had become meaningless in the face
of facts; partly it was needed no longer. What
survived through all change was the single human
desire, which was actuating Alexander on the hither
shore of the Dardanelles, and would be prepon-
derating on his death-bed, the desire, namely, of
acquisition. Trite as it may seem, this needs saying
again. Alexander, like Philip, was but a man of his
age and race — an age and race whose greatest thinker
laid it down for law that Hellene was justified absolutely in enslaving barbarian. No more subtle moral
rule claimed the attention of a Hellenic conqueror in
Asia at that day, than the right of the stronger.
The world was that Hellene's oyster whose sword
could lift the shell.

Why Philip wished to be first and foremost a
Hellene has been discussed in the former essay. All
the motives which actuated him were but stronger
in Alexander. Both wished to rest on a unified base
wider than Macedonia, both to conquer and hold a
vast Empire beside. Both — for they were Hellenes
by birth and training — believed that the second
element to be incorporated with the Macedonian,
both in the base and in the conquest, was the Hellenic; but Alexander understood the better how to
deal with it. One cannot be too fearful of crediting a youth who makes history with a consciousness
in advance of his epoch, or beyond his years. To
claim for Alexander that he conceived the regeneration
of the world by the Hellene is sheerly absurd; to

suppose that thus early he foresaw altogether even what Hellenes would effect for his own selfish end of Empire, is to rank him with the Prophets. But to say that he had learned from his father's and his own experience that a base on which Hellene and Macedonian would fuse firmly together must be outside the traditional home of either; that the Hellene would prove of even greater service in the holding of Empire than in the conquering thereof; and that with a view to both these considerations the Hellene's commercial interest must be appealed to, and his commercial aptitudes utilized — this is only to place Aristotle's pupil early in his precocious life among the more enlightened minds of his own day.

Alexander came, then, in this April of 334, to the shore of the Dardanelles, with an ambition to possess all Persia as already he possessed all Greece. He was captain of the Hellenes, full of faith in the Hellenic nationality, and most desirous, in the interests of security as well as of sentiment, that enforced obedience might give place through the gods and himself to some such willing recognition of his own preeminence as Pericles had enjoyed awhile at Athens. His mood was of the most exalted and romantic; he crossed and landed with the strictest Heroic usage, solemnly visited Ilium, and went through a whole archaistic masque as another Achilles.[1] And when

---

[1] He even returned after Granicus, and promoted the squalid village to be a free city by way of thanksgiving (Strabo, p. 593); and it is probably the ruin of this New Ilium that Schliemann

a few days later he found himself for the first time
face to face with his foe, scorning, as a Hero might,
all counsels of caution, he charged forthwith with
a rush of horsemen through the stream of Granicus,
himself seeking and fighting single combats as before
windy Troy. The spoil was dedicated as a solemn
firstfruits to the gods of the Greeks, and in formal
terms Alexander decreed annihilation to those dastard
Hellenes who were found opposing in arms the Captain-
General of their race.

Scarce two months later at Miletus Alexander again
had at his mercy a body of Greeks, equally guilty;
he allowed them to surrender on terms, and took
them into his service. It is a small matter, but
a straw on the stream of events. What had happened since the " Cavalry Battle," to ease the conscience of the Captain-General? In effect enough
to make Miletus a point clearly marked in the
passing of the enthusiastic boy into the calculating
man of affairs. For those two months had proved
to demonstration nothing less than that the maritime
states of Hellas, those that alone greatly mattered,
were in their hearts not for Alexander, but for his
enemies. The larger islands, Rhodes, Chios, and
Lesbos, and nearly all the lesser, kept open ports

found in the uppermost layer at Hissarlik (cf. Schuchhardt,
Schliemann's Excavations, pp. 79 ff. ; and *C. I. G.* 3595 for its
increase under the Diadochi). It was not a foundation to serve any
purposes of commerce or strategy; for Antigonus was under the
necessity of creating hard by a new city for those ends, namely that
Alexandria of the Troad, which became well known in subsequent
centuries.

to the Persian admirals, and the city of Athens had been at no pains to disguise her sympathies. Her continental position and twenty of her ships, held as hostages by the Macedonian, made her warn Pharnabazus off the Piraeus; but openly she sat within her walls watching for the first Macedonian reverse, and indeed had sent already, or was about to send soon, an envoy direct to Darius.

In brief, Alexander had failed entirely to carry Athens with him on the wind of his enthusiasm. He had failed, partly because some of her best spirit survived still, refusing to be comforted for the loss of Empire ; partly because she had outlived her heroic period. At that stage of her conscious intellectualism, when oratory and philosophy had become popular diversions, an exuberant Homeric champion struck no true note of admiration. There was felt in Athens no longer any enthusiasm for crusades, and at best but a languid interest in the physical excellences of a youth who assumed the Hero and dared kings to battle. She was perhaps, to tell truth, a little wearied with him, and needed only encouragement by an active agitator to express her feelings in open hostility.

Therefore, at Miletus, the first sanguine hour of Alexander's life has closed, and on the wreck of his exuberant illusions begins to rise a sterner purpose. Greece must be coerced if she will not be courted. Her command of the seas shall be broken by the capture of the coasts of the Levant, and her people be bent willy nilly to do panhellenic work. For

Alexander knew that, even in spite of themselves, they would do it for him. And therefore, not having resigned all hope that they might be brought some day to see with him eye to eye, he retained, and put forward still the style and title of Captain-General. In face of present hostility, however, it was no longer worth while to maintain an offensive fleet; and, accordingly, he issued now his much canvassed decision to "burn his boats" and leave himself stranded in Asia.

It has not always been understood how inevitably that decision followed on the revelation that had been made. The sea was the element of the Greek. No fleet that, as yet, Alexander could requisition would make head for a moment against the squadrons of Persia and the Hellenic powers, should these combine. Furthermore, like most self-reliant men, Alexander was never easy about operations not conducted under his immediate eye. He could not be on the sea and the land at once; furthermore, he had never contemplated, when he equipped his own small squadron, that it would remain always small; and therefore, now that the expected reinforcements were accruing rather to the fleets of the foe than to himself, the Macedonian had no choice but to disband his few ships, become too precarious hostages to fortune.

This early disillusionment, though it cooled the boy's spirit all too soon, and when pressed home by much future trouble with Greeks, embittered him not a little, and forced him in the end to adopt a policy

alien to modern sympathy, was in certain ways
salutary. The remembrance of it, and futile regrets
that recurred from time to time all through his life,
served for his *memento mori*, a constant check on
the confident animalism of his physical nature. Had
Alexander never experienced anything less stimu-
lating than the favour and applause amid which he
started for Asia, his splendid mental powers might
have been exercised but little. Nature had framed
him for a great warrior; necessity made of him a
great organizer of peace; and it may be said that
Greek hostility did at least as much as Greek precept
to give him the claim that is his to have been more
than conqueror.

The check that he had experienced on the sea
turned Alexander's eyes wholly to that element for
two years. The campaigns of the last half of 334,
of 333, and of 332 had all for their objective the
littoral of the Levant. Alexander took little trouble
except with the coast districts, and little account of
the Persian armies but as incidental checks. After
traversing Lycia and Pamphylia with much thorough-
ness, and marching and counter-marching for some
weeks along the coasts of the latter, when at last
he turned inland the conqueror stayed not to
organize, hardly even to conquer, but was content
to sweep clear a road up to some point which
would be convenient for his reinforcements and
command a practicable route to the south-eastern
coasts. Gordium, where in the valley of the

Sakkaria a natural route from the Sea of Marmora
— in part now the line of a railway — meets the
track of the royal Anatolian highway of antiquity,
was such a point; and accordingly Alexander came
thither in the spring of 333. Thence he set forth
again in early summer, without visiting any part of
the Black Sea littoral, content with a formal submission made by the Paphlagonians ere he left
Ancyra. All the rest of the work to be done in
Asia Minor was left to satraps, and after two years
the Cappadocians were able still to join Darius at
Arbela.

The Macedonian had reason enough to hold in
slight esteem the peoples of the Anatolian plateau,
and to despise the foreigner who so long had claimed
sovereignty over them, but, holding their lands by
neither a military[1] nor a civil organization worth
the name, has left hardly a memorial of his two
centuries of. empire! Alexander's attitude, however,
implied not so much contempt for the inner land, as
anxiety for the coast; and for the coast he went
again hot and hard, covering in a day and a night,
we are told, not less than sixty-two miles, and thereby
succeeded in swooping on the Cilician Gates before the
Viceroy of Cilicia had begun to think seriously of
reinforcing his pickets in the pass. How much time
and trouble the unsparing Captain must have saved
by that forced march may, perhaps, be estimated, if
we recall that until Ibrahim Pasha, little more than
a half-century ago, blasted the rocks in the famous

[1] See Niese, *op. cit.* p. 66.

defile, every camel had to be unloaded before it could pass.

Spent by long noons and sleepless nights, Alexander brought his army, in the fearful heat of a Cilician August, to the sea-level, having descended three thousand feet in about three days. Small wonder that then and there he caught the Cilician fever![1] — the which mischance gave him, indeed, a notable opportunity of knitting more tightly the bonds of affection between himself and his immediate circle at a moment when murmurs, provoked by recent labours and his own exuberance, were beginning to be heard, but it lost a precious month. Let it not be supposed, however, that it was Issus that immediately was delayed. The settlement of an important maritime province came first in Alexander's mind. Darius was camped all the while no farther away than the plain of Sinjerli beyond Amanus; but his rival found time to visit Soli twice, and to raid the hillmen of the Tracheia district, ere going leisurely enough to meet the Persian by the indirect way of Mallus.

It is only the dazzling appeal that pitched battles make to the imagination which gives Granicus and Issus their bulk in Alexander's history. The first of those battles had been really a small affair, always regarded by contemporaries as a cavalry skirmish. It was not more comparable in respect of difficulties overcome or important result to the

---

[1] The famous bath in the Cydnus is more likely to have been aggravation than cause of that malady — a foolish attempt to alleviate the first flush of heat.

subsequent sieges of such cities as Halicarnassus, than was the fight at Issus to the siege of Tyre. Alexander himself wasted not a day's pursuit on either of the Persian Grand Armies which he met west of Euphrates. He found them in his path, dealt a smashing blow, and left them to break up as they might, himself in each case continuing on his way irrespective of theirs. There was hardly more respect shown to the defeated army of Issus than to the Pisidian hillmen.

That Issus, however, proved so light a matter to Alexander, was due, it is well known, to a particular mistake of the enemy. Had Darius stayed where he was encamped at first, Alexander must, in the interests of his own base and communications, have gone to find him, and been faced by a problem hardly less serious than ultimately he was to meet east of Tigris — how, in fact, with a very small force effectually to cut up an immense host, deployed where it could bring its overwhelming weight of flesh to bear. Partly, no doubt, because he expected such a task, Alexander took so much time to make Cilicia his, having little expectation that Darius would do anything so suicidal as move his unwieldy army through the mountains. The news that after all this clumsy host had deserted its chosen ground, and was to be met not even in the open Aleian plain, but in the cramped defiles of Issus, seemed to Alexander too good to be true; and on its confirmation, he turned back — and no wonder! — hot-foot and exulting, careless that his communications had been cut, careless that he was trapped, knowing

that the very stars in their courses would fight his
battle. We must admire the skill and force with which
he proceeded to follow up his advantage on the field,
himself always in the front, inspiring the vital movement and securing the event against any possible
mischance; but let it be remembered at the same
time that, from the very first, he was playing the
winning game, and we shall confine our admiration
to the degree and the manner in which he knew how
to win.

Certain consequents of Issus, however, are of more
importance to Alexander's individual history than
the battle itself; for through it, in two ways, illu-
mination came to him, and a distinct change in
his personal attitude ensues. In the first place, not
only had he been placed by the capture of Darius'
baggage in possession of much correspondence between
the Great King and Hellenic states, but also, for
the first time, he had seized in flagrant fault the
persons of Hellenic envoys sent up to the Persian.
These springs of irritation fell to be added to all
that had been happening for a year past in Greece,
to the crusade preached by Agis of Sparta, to the
militant speeches of the anti-Macedonian orators at
Athens,[1] and to the unequal struggle of his friends
in the islands with the ubiquitous Persian admirals.
In the second place, the final proof thus furnished, that
he could never hope to enjoy to the full the Periclean
form of kingship, coincided with the first revelation

---

[1] Demosthenes and Hyperides, in the summer of 333. *Vide*
Droysen, p. 242.

of the possibilities of another form. "This, it seems," said Alexander, as he gazed on the state and luxury of Darius' tent after the battle, "it is to be a King!" And, although he would have no commerce with Darius' harem — a continence due as much to temperament as to chivalry — and remained contemptuous of luxury,[1] it was not for nothing that, having become possessed of a large slice of wealth by Parmenio's capture of Damascus, he learned now what wealth could buy. Alexander's simplicity before this epoch had been the unconscious habit of his race; hereafter it will be conscious policy. He has eaten of the fruit of the Tree, and with growing consciousness begins inevitable hardening. We detect the process presently in the tone and tenor of his letters to Darius, in his arbitrary attitude towards his prisoners and the vengeance meted out to Tyre and to Gaza;[2] but best in more private matters, so far as we may know them. The famous scene in the tent of the captive queens at Issus is perhaps the last glimpse afforded in Alexander's life of that unreflective chivalry which had induced him, a month or two before, to take his chance of death by poison rather than show suspicion of a friend.

He was not, indeed, solely responsible for the change. Some of his followers had eaten also of the same fruit, and taken the greater harm; for shortly

---

[1] Cf. e. g. Plut. *Alex.* 57 ; Polyaen. iv. 3. 10.

[2] The story of the punishment of Batis, the brave defender of Gaza (found in Curt. iv. 6, and Dion. Hal. *de Comp. Verb.* pp. 123–125), is not to be set lightly aside for an utterly incredible cruelty, as Droysen pretends.

after Issus the first whispers of treason were breathed by Philotas to his mistress. Therefore, never again could Alexander afford so well to take chances as they came, never again to give without receiving directly the value of his gift. The illusions of boyhood had melted at Miletus, the hopes of youth have begun to fade at Issus. Alexander at Tyre is removed by two stages of growth from Alexander at Troy. He has become already older than his years, a man harder and more reflective, seeing farther and deeper than is congruous with his age of twenty-four: and after another year of most strenuous effort (for the capture of Tyre remains the greatest of his triumphs over natural difficulties and obstinate resistance), when the coasts of the Levant had become wholly his, and he was come down to the Mareotic shore, we find him founding his greatest Alexandria with the calculation and the providence of a mature man.

It was once the fashion to endow Alexander the Founder with more than human foreknowledge of the future of his foundations; now, by reaction, we are asked to deny him design. Alexandria in Egypt, it is said, was no better than a lucky accident. The new foundation was meant at most to be an improved Naucratis, at once emporium for Greek traders to Egypt, and garrisoned post of observation on the Nile valley. Circumstances, in no way foreseen by the Founder, made a cosmopolitan city of what had been at first a mere Greek harbour in Egypt.

Needless to say, many circumstances of which

Alexander had not foreknowledge, still less had control, did combine indeed to raise Alexandria in two generations after its birth to the rank of second, if not first, city in the Mediterranean, and undisputed first in the Levant. The Founder did not foresee the Indian and Arabian trade which would come in by way of Coptos and the Nile, much as half-consciously he did later to open a route for that trade. The Founder did not foresee the influx into his city of an obscure race of Semitic traders, risen from the ashes of their Phoenician cousins, — the Jews, of whose cosmopolitan expansion the ruin of Tyre and the rise of Alexandria are jointly the first cause. The Founder did not foresee into what wise hands Egypt was to fall at his own death, and how she, and Alexandria within her, would grow at the expense of the rest of his distracted Empire. The Founder did not foresee that Hellenism would follow his own footsteps so far abroad, that its centre would shift to a great city of Egypt and a great city of Syria.

Certain things, however, were not hidden in the womb of the Future. It must have been patent to a meaner intelligence than Alexander's, that the great trading area of the Levant was for the moment without focus. Tyre lay an utter wreck, and the other Phoenician cities, never in recent centuries of great account beside her, had been stripped lately of such fleets as they had. It might have been patent to less than Alexander, that, if Greeks were to seize this favourable occasion, it must be done by settling at a point not already occupied ; and that, if Greeks and

Macedonians were to coalesce into a Hellenistic nation, there was no land on the eastern Mediterranean left so open to mixed colonization as the Egyptian. Racial fusions, be it observed, were quite within the scope of the political foresight of Alexander's day. Greek colonies for three centuries had supplied an object lesson in the feasibility of such fusions and the rapid gathering of strength which ensued upon them. To plant rival sections of one race on a new soil, in the sure hope that their old dissensions would be forgotten, was not much beyond what had been the notorious policy of many Greek lawgivers and of the Apolline priests. In the event, Alexandria in Egypt did become the scene of just such a fusion, and remained the capital of the resultant Hellenistic nationality.

Did Alexander, however, consciously found it for nation-making? He founded it, assuredly, for some special reason or other, as he had created his first Alexandria to guard the defiles north and south of the bay of Iskenderun. He selected for the second the one possible site on the Egyptian coast[1] for a great port, as all previous and later experience has gone to prove. For the new harbour must lie outside the reach of the Nilotic silt; therefore not on the Delta coast-line. It must be sheltered from the west,

---

[1] A great authority on Ptolemaic Egypt has recently called this fact in question. Surely a moment's consideration of the peculiar conditions of a Delta coast, and a glance at the Admiralty charts of this particular Delta littoral, leave no doubt, even to one who has not surveyed the district with his own eyes (see Mahaffy, *Empire of the Ptolemies*, p. 11).

the prevailing wind in the Levant; therefore no point on the exposed shore trending north-east from Pelusium would serve. It must be, lastly, within reach of sweet Nile water; therefore it could hardly be placed farther west than Rhacotis. The site now chosen was eminently defensible, having Lake Mareotis in the rear; and the tradition of history has ascribed unanimously to Alexander a personal share in, and solicitude for, the inaugurating of this Egyptian city, of which no mention is made in connection with any other of his foundations. And reasonably; for Egypt beyond a doubt held a peculiar place in Alexander's affections, as the land of the particular God by whom he secretly fancied himself to have been begotten.

Alexander, then, may be assumed to have intended his Alexandria in Egypt to be an important harbour; but important to what end? As the key of Egypt? Yet he kept his main garrison always at Memphis. As a gate whereby Greek trade of the old type might enter the Nile valley? For that alone a new foundation was scarcely needed; Naucratis had existed long, and long continued to exist. But to gather in a wider commerce? If that end be allowed, then it must follow that Alexandria was created as a direct consequence of the ruin of Tyre, and was intended to be a new focus for the Levant: and even if Alexander did not consciously create a new capital to concentrate a new mixed nationality — though such a purpose was neither beyond the scope of his intelligence, nor anything but consonant with his general policy — the fact will stand that consciously he created a new local capital for commerce.[1] And, surely, to do that is to open the door to so many possibilities of expansion, that the Founder of such a city, if it prosper, may claim credit for the greatness and wealth which have followed on his action.

The conception thus ascribed to Alexander is no way incredible on circumstantial evidence. For, first, such commercial aims in colonization had been in the Greek air for centuries, and Alexander would have been perfectly familiar with them, even had he not sat at the feet of the greatest of Greek economists : and, second, in his subsequent career the Founder of Alexandria will give ample proof that he was indeed familiar with economic questions, and had a vivid interest and belief in the influence of commerce. His instructions to Nearchus before he left the Indus; his removal of the obstructions in the Tigris water-way;[2] his proposal to create a second Phoenicia on the shore of the Persian Gulf[3] — these are instances of a single-minded commercial purpose, which conditioned also, but less directly, many other enterprises, the explorations, for example, of the Caspian, the Persian Gulf, and the Indus, and probably the foundation of all the Eastern colonies,

---

[1] Cf. *Econ.* ii. 33, for the reflection of a contemporary view of the Founder's purpose (whether by Aristotle or another). Even Niese admits that Alexandria was intended " den Verkehr mit Griechenland und Makedonien zu vermitteln und eine sichere Verbindung Ägyptens mit diesen Ländern zu gewähren " (p. 85).

[2] Strabo, p. 740 ; Arrian, vii. 7.

[3] Arr. vii. 19.

whose representatives survive still as ganglia in Asia's nerve system of caravan roads. Hereby we are ascribing to Alexander no prophetic view of the regeneration of Asia or the mission of the Hellene, indeed no altruistic motive at all. His was simply a highly enlightened selfishness, which, having conquered by the sword, knew it could possess in permanence only by fostering the influences of peace. To Alexander commerce and Hellenism were means not ends, means indeed far from clearly grasped or understood; but in so far as he did grasp and understand them, his is the glory to all time of having applied on a great scale for whatever end the greatest influences for peace in the world of his day.

If any further proof were needed that we have to reckon already with an advanced student of statecraft in the Founder of Alexandria, it can be supplied by the organization which he imposed in this same winter on the whole province of Egypt. We are allowed to see only its skeleton, and to detect little more than its singularity — a singularity which proves that, however he may have learned them, Alexander certainly knew those unique difficulties which Egypt presents to foreign occupation. With marsh at one end and tropics at the other, eight hundred miles of deserts on its either flank, and itself nowhere more than thirty miles in breadth, the Nile valley has called always for a peculiar scheme of government. Arrian is probably right in saying that the Macedonian system, with its lack of an all-powerful supreme official, its three nationalities set

one against the other, and its counteracting civil and
military powers, anticipated in some ways the Roman.
For if Augustus, who indeed was a professed disciple
of Alexander, had needed a model for the imperial
settlement of the Nile valley, he would have looked,
not to any Ptolemaic king who had ruled Egypt
from within, but to the first western emperor who
had held it as a foreign possession.

But this precocious Founder and craftsman in
politics has not forsworn yet all the dreams of his
youth. Between creating a city and organizing a
province, he is capable of the romantic folly of the
expedition to the oracle of Ammon.

What can be said certainly of this folly? Hardly
more than that indeed Alexander went to the
Ammon Temple. He can have made no general
announcement either of what he asked its priests or
of what they replied.[1] For the rest, the record of
this expedition is shrouded in inconsistency and myth.
As Arrian's two best authorities[2] insisted on distinct
routes for Alexander's return from the Oasis, we may

[1] Cf. Arrian, iii. 4 *ad fin.*, and Plutarch's quotation (*Alex.* 27)
from Alexander's letter to his mother, speaking of the "*secret*
answers which he will tell on his return to *her alone.*"

[2] On Arrian's authorities for the Anabasis, and indeed on the
whole subject of the *Quellen*, see Fränkel's monumental work
(Breslau, 1883), and lesser and more recent inquiries by R. Peters-
dorff, *Eine neue Hauptquelle des Q. Curtius*, etc. (Hanover, 1884);
E. Pridik, *De A. M. epistularum commercio* (1893); and A.
Zumetikos, *De A. Olympiadisque epist. fontibus et reliquiis* (1894).
Niese devotes a section to the subject, but hardly attempts
criticism.

infer with some confidence that neither chronicler
accompanied him. And with almost equal confidence
it can be maintained that the expedition was a small
affair that assumed little importance at the time, but
came to be subject of general gossip at some later
period, when recollection of the facts was confused
and vague. Whether Alexander, when he started
along the coast from Mareotis, was making indeed
for Ammon, or not rather for Cyrene — even this
must remain uncertain; for his historians dismiss
with a mere mention the submission of the greatest
Greek colony in Africa, which was made to him on
his way.[1] How did those Cyrenian envoys come so
aptly to Paraetonium? Their city must have been
summoned to surrender, or have been fearful of an
attack. Paraetonium, be it remarked, lies a good
deal further west than the usual point at which a
caravan leaves the coast and strikes across the desert
to the oasis of Siwah; and indeed had Alexander had
merely Siwah for objective, his natural road had lain
not by the north at all, but through the Fayum.

Let the conjecture, then, be hazarded for what it
is worth, that if indeed a large force went with the
king to Paraetonium, on receipt of the Cyrenian
submission the most part of it was sent back;
and Alexander seized the occasion to fulfil an old
ambition by going to Siwah. He struck inland
with a small party, such as alone can traverse
so much waterless desert; and since no chronicler of

---

[1] Diod. xvii. 49. Arrian omits, but Curtius (iv. 7. 9) confirms
Diodorus.

his acts was included in his following, the Alexander of history melts into the Iskender of romance until such time as he reaches Memphis again.

The obvious purpose of Alexander, as Pharaoh, was to pay a visit of ceremony to his official Father, Amen. His added secret object was to ask a particular question as to his own carnal origin. All tradition agrees on this last point. Likely enough, Olympias had worked on a mind already full of romantic Homeric ideas. His father had publicly called him bastard. Was he, then, after all, like one of the Heroes, god-begotten on a mortal woman? It is not impossible that, in this matter, Alexander was doing no more than the behest of his mother; for he himself mostly made scant account of oracles and divinations, unless they chanced to agree with a policy preconceived. As a boy, he had treated cavalierly even the Pythia. As a man, he refused to listen when a soothsayer forbade his venture across the Sir Daria; he committed palpable fraud with the auspices to save his dignity at the Sutlej; and replied with scornful sarcasm to the last warnings of the prophets of Bel. Why, however, Alexander chose to ask his question of Amen of the Oases rather than of Amen of the mother-shrine at Karnak must remain doubtful until we learn more of the religious connections between Egypt and Europe at this period.[1]

---

[1] Prof. G. Maspéro, in a recent article (*Comment A. le G. devint dieu en Égypte*, in the *Annuaire de l'École pratique des Hautes Études*, 1897), explains Alexander's choice of Siwah simply by the

None of the authorities, however, on whom Arrian relied, knew what passed in the Holy of Holies. Later gossip was better informed — not impossibly by report of Alexander's own loose talk with intimate friends. It is certain, at least, that publicly and officially Alexander remained son of Philip[1] till his death, and found no greater inconsistency in asserting his private belief that Ammon had indeed begotten him, than Queen Hatasu or Amenhotep III., being children respectively of Thothmes I. and Thothmes IV., found in depicting on their temple walls at Der el Bahari and Luxor a legend of their miraculous begetting by Amen.

Certain historians, however, have laboured to elevate Alexander's expedition to Siwah into the familiarity of the Greeks with the god of the Oases, as compared with their ignorance of Thebes. This does not, however, go far enough. Why in the first instance was Ammon of Siwah so familiar to Greek legend? For the rest, Prof. Maspéro's learned and ingenious article is a most welcome contribution to this question. The author, as an Egyptologist, examines the ritual observed on these ceremonial visits of Pharaohs to their Father, Amen; and from his point of view he reaches much the same conclusion as to the significance of Alexander's visit as is expressed above, namely, that no exceptional public policy was involved. At most the new Pharaoh was legitimized for Egypt by a dogma of miraculous conception, like Queen Hatasu, Amenhotep III., and later, Caesarion. Prof. Maspéro's explanation of the euhemeristic genesis of the Nectanebo myth agrees with my own, published in January, 1896, in the *Eng. Hist. Review*.

[1] Cf. his letters to Darius and to the Athenians (Plut. *Alex.* 28), and also Arr. ii. 5; iii. 3; iv. 8; vi. 3, in all of which passages reference is made to his Heraclid descent, of course through Philip.

inception of a great policy. The king, say they, about
to proceed to the East, and already desirous of exaltation above his Macedonians and Greeks, deliberately
assumed divine character as son of Amen. Mis-
placed ingenuity! Every king of Egypt had been
son of Amen since the growth of Thebes. The last
Nectanebo, as well as the first Ptolemy, bear the
title on their inscriptions equally with Alexander.
In Egypt sonship to Amen was so far from being
an exception, that it could not be escaped by a
Pharaoh. Outside Egypt it was useless. Who,
beyond Pelusium, worshipped Amen, or, beyond
Euphrates, even knew his name?

Furthermore, evidence lacks wholly for the divine
style, least of all with any express statement of sonship to Ammon, being used officially by Alexander; or
for such "divine honours" as Persians paid or Greeks
decreed being rendered as to the son of the Egyptian
god. The men of the East prostrated themselves
to Alexander as to all their princes; and when the
Macedonian demanded the same adoration from men
of the West, it was not as son of Ammon, but as
Emperor, that there might be no invidious distinction
among his subjects.

Moreover, with respect to this matter two things
must be distinguished sharply, which usually are
confused:[1] a claim, however publicly made, by

---

[1] I did not keep them distinct myself in an article written in part
as an undergraduate, and published in the *Eng. Hist. Review*, April,
1887. J. P. Mahaffy confuses them also in his criticism of that
article in *Problems of Greek History*, p. 165 ff.

Alexander to be of divine parentage is one thing; the
institution by him of any cult of himself is wholly
another. In Greek mythology, it should be borne
in mind, the first of these things did not involve
the second. Neither was Achilles worshipped in the
Greek camp, nor Aeneas in the Trojan, because they
had goddesses to their mothers. Alexander himself,
although his Macedonian royalty and the manner of
his life led him to assert personality in a manner
foreign to Greek civic usage, and even to give his
name to cities, appears to have introduced no effigy
of himself on to his coinage. In his lifetime we never
hear of his temples, altars, groves or games, such as
not a generation later were dedicated to the living
Demetrius. Greek adulation suggested the paying
of divine honours to Alexander more than once,
but the supposed prompting of these by an Imperial
Decree rests on an inference so indirect from a
statement historically so worthless that one can only
wonder how it has found a place in the creed of
a responsible historian.[1]

There is, in short, hardly any question of public
policy involved. Alexander went to Siwah purposing
little more than to test a romantic belief which he
owed to Homer, and in diverse ways to both his
parents; and ever afterwards he hugged to himself
the belief that the Egyptian Zeus was not only his

---

[1] Practically it rests only on a passage in Aelian, *V. H.* ii. 19.
See my article quoted *supra*, in which I have given every shred of
evidence. Grote, at any rate, little as he loves Alexander, omits the
whole question of the Decree as not worth serious discussion.

official but his fleshly father. In moments of confidence and moments of exaltation, such as became
more frequent as his imperial position developed,
there can be no doubt that he made a boast of
this divine origin, and thereby gave a handle to
malcontents, and maybe some difficulty to himself
in junctures when it was expedient to make appeal
to his dynastic feudal position. It was a foolish
fancy, no doubt, incompatible with the more advanced
thought of his time, but quite consistent with the
belief of older fashion that gods were really existent
in human form with human passions.

This much may be granted; but it cannot be
conceded by historical truth that Alexander seated
himself even in imagination on Olympus, as *praesens
deus*. He never pretended that his veins distilled
ichor, claimed supernatural powers,[1] or affected to be
fed by the smoke of altar fires. Had he cherished
such delusions or made such pretensions, his earthly
success had never been attained. His wildest imagination did no more than set him among the half-divine
Heroes: his sober reason claimed that he was godlike
man, one of those noblest mortals who in a peculiar
sense are sons of the common Father.[2]

And with this let us leave an incident possessed
of no great import nor grave result, and unworthy
of much attention, were it not that in such affairs
as this — by his sick-bed at Tarsus, or in the Queens'
tent at Issus — we get a passing glimpse of Alexander
in an atmosphere less artificial than that of the

_____
[1] Cf. Plut. *Alex.* 17.   [2] Plut. *Alex.* 27.

Council chamber, and for once not obscured by the dust and blood of the battle-field.

In Egypt Alexander had received tidings that his admirals had triumphed on the Aegean, where, since the fall of Phoenicia, they had been able to take the offensive. The submission of Cyrene had completed their conquest, and the rising walls of Alexandria were to assure the enjoyment of its fruit. With the sea went one half of the Persian realm : it remained to win the other half. To accomplish this second part of his primary scheme, Alexander marched out of Egypt in the spring of 331. He assured himself, in passing, of the complete humility of Tyre — caution significant in the Founder of Alexandria ! — and reached the Euphrates late in July. Neither there, nor in rounding the head of the Mesopotamian Desert, nor during the five days that his army was ferrying itself painfully over Tigris, was he opposed seriously. The Persian outposts fell back so weakly from every point of vantage, that it seems as if their commander, Mazaeus, had begun already to serve the new master, for whom afterwards long and faithfully he governed Babylon.

The Great King was waiting beyond Tigris, on the threshold of the inner half of his realm. He lay at a point where great roads come together, those from farther Asia through Hamadan and Tabriz, that from Babylon and the Gulf, those from the Armenian gorges of the Tigris, and from the West by the way Alexander himself had marched. It is this concurrence that gives importance still to Mosul, and determined in the dawn of history the site of Nineveh. But already, in this year 331, Nineveh was a forgotten ruin, and the great battle which decided the fate of the East, though fought almost within sight of the famous Assyrian mounds, has taken its popular name, not from the once imperial city nor from the nearest village, but from Arbela, an obscure local capital situate sixty miles away: and "of Arbela," in defiance of geographical purists, this battle will be to the end of time.

A glance at Arrian's list of the Persian array will show how much more formidable that host must have been on its own chosen ground, than any that Alexander hitherto had encountered. Grouped round a nucleus of Greek veteran swashbucklers more numerous than all the Macedonian force, were the picked guerilla fighters of the warlike East, all in enormous strength : — masses of those nomads of Turkestan, accustomed to fight in hordes, who were hereafter to give Alexander much trouble ; Pathans and hillmen from Chitral and Khond and all the range of Hindu Kush against whom four years later the Macedonians would have to fight every mile of their way ; wild mountaineers of southern Persis, Lars and Lurs and Kurds and Bedawin from the Mesopotamian and Arabian wastes. Decisive defeat alone would find out their want of a real principle of cohesion : undefeated they were most formidable. For even had the host contained elements less warlike,

its mere weight brought to bear in an open plain, the
sheer butcher's work that must be done to break it
up, caused it to present a terribly difficult problem in
the days of direct charging and hand-to-hand battle.
The gravity of his danger did not escape Alexander.
The dare-devil youth, who had rushed across Granicus
and turned hot-foot and jubilant to meet his pursuers
in the defile of Issus, is seen now displaying the
caution of a veteran. With Tigris and Euphrates
behind him, mountain and desert hemming him in,
he must win outright, or be trampled in retreat
under the hoofs of a cloud of horsemen.

The preliminaries of this most famous fight of
antiquity display the Captain at his best. Most
cautiously he moved four marches along the Babylon
road, and having met and driven in the first scouting
parties of the foe, called a halt, to collect information,
rest his army, purge away all non-combatants, and
fortify a camp. He could afford to take his time.
A host, such as that opposed to him, neither would
nor could be moved at short notice. At the second
watch of the fourth night his columns, selected and
stiffened, set out again, having some eight miles to
cover, and hoping to be within touch of an unready
foe at dawn. But from the top of the last range
of hills the Persian army was perceived in the plain
of Gaugamela, ordered already in line of battle.
Alexander once more gave the order to bivouac : for
he was in a very strong position, and might well
wait yet another day to study the ground and the
dispositions of the mighty host below. Thus the last

daylight of September passed away, the Macedonians
resting for the most part, the Persians nervously
standing to their arms ; and as the night falls Plutarch,
with a rare graphic touch, sketches on his canvas the
great plain kindling to the horizon with myriad barbarian fires, and the flare of the torches carried before
the Great King as he passed restlessly up and down
his lines. The hum of the immense multitude rose
to the Macedonian posts on the hill-tops, and old
Parmenio, mindful of many fights, gazed over the
limitless vista of fires, and listened to the confused
roar that came down the night wind. How could
the little army behind him overcome in equal fight
by day that swarming host? It seemed madness
to await the morning light, and he turned to the
royal tent to urge a night attack, the counsel of
despair. The king cut short his argument with a curt
reply, that must have astonished the veteran student
of strategy, " Alexander will steal no victories ! "

Not a moment for theatrical phrases, it might be
said ! but indeed no moment is adapted better for
them than the eve of a battle, and no audience will
be so responsive as an army waiting the signal to
attack. Moreover, sound policy was expressed in this
phrase, as Arrian, commander of Roman frontier
legions, perceived. For the iron Macedonian discipline
would have counted but little in a night attack, and
the practised soldier have been almost on a par with
the brigand. A victory half won in the dark might
well have been followed by a rally at dawn, and the
weary Macedonian army would have found itself still

opposed by scarcely diminished myriads. And even were final and complete victory granted, its moral effect under such circumstances would be so little as by no means to ensure the breaking up of Darius' host. In sober reason, it was better that the attack on such odds should be delivered with every resource of the parade ground, the General being able to discern the critical moments over all the field ; and that victory, wherever declaring itself, should be victory patent to all.

The argument with his Marshal and the decision forced upon him seem to have cleared Alexander's mind. Dawn found him sleeping. Uneasy generals gathered about his tent ; surely the fight was to be that day, and yet even the signal for the army to breakfast had not been given ! The Marshal bade the bugle sound the call ; but the king still slept on, and Parmenio, having called him repeatedly by name without success, ventured at last to awake him with his hand. " How is it," protested the Marshal, " that thou, who so often surprisest the watch, canst sleep on such a morning as this ? " " I have followed Darius up and down through all Asia," said Alexander, " and shall I not sleep now when he is given into my hand ? "

Of the great battle, which has made the first day of October an anniversary famous for all time, a civilian had best say little more than that its course justified all Alexander's previous caution, and that never did the Grand Army owe more to the man who had given them their military training, and to his son who led them now. Far out-flanked, at one time almost surrounded, cut off for three parts of the day from their only support, the entrenched camp, they remained steady as on the parade ground by the Vardar. No battle in antiquity is described so fully as this of Arbela, and historians have not known which most to admire, the confidence of the western army, or the skill with which it was directed; the discipline which opened the ranks to let scythed chariots thunder harmlessly through, or the temper with which the left wing, cut off and ridden over, recovered itself before help came.

There is a story told by Curtius of the awful night that followed, when a rout of half a million men went roaring through the dust to the Zab, which, if true, shows how the spirit of dare-deviltry was latent always in the cool calculator of chances. It is said that, the fever of that chase seizing him, Alexander himself rode fast and far into the night, and turning back at last with only a remnant of his staff was confronted by a large body of the flying foe. The barbarians saw their chance, and bore down upon the Conqueror. But Alexander, taking up the Homeric part, spurred at the leader, and having struck him down engaged with fury the next man and the next. The barbarians rode ten to one, but Victory herself seemed to sit on the Macedonian's helm. The fugitives wavered, Alexander and his band pressed their advantage, and their foes turned and fled once more into the dark.

Darius got clear away to the eastward through

Zagros, and so to Hamadan ; his vast army dispersed to its deserts and hills at the four winds of heaven. Both king and army were ignored by the Conqueror as absolutely as after Issus : for Alexander for his part kept on straight to the south, pursuing his predominant purpose to assume methodically and in permanence the Persian lands. Babylon, which had nearly proved a Capua, but for his prompt action — action not to be forgotten when, mindful of Hannibal, we estimate the issue of the struggle between Rome and the Macedonian that was never fought — Susa, Persepolis, the southern capitals with their stores of bullion, were swept into the net, and almost a year elapsed ere Alexander troubled himself again about the Great King.

Indeed, as a single expression, the Persian Empire had ceased to exist. Alexander never met again an imperial army. For the future his affair was to be with the levies of irresponsible satraps or frontier kings, and the half-independent hillmen and nomads. The campaigns of the rest of his life are, in fact, precisely such as the Persian kings had always had to wage from time to time for the holding of their outlying provinces or the securing of their communications. And he himself seems to have understood that this was to be ; for in the camp outside Babylon he made changes, for the first time, in the organization of the military machine he had inherited ; in fact, he took there first steps towards multiplying units in the interest of detachment and mobility, and towards that denationalization which gradually he would promote in his eastern campaigns. Later events gave to his aims an extension and scope not as yet conceived; but in the obscure allusions of Arrian and Curtius we may espy at Babylon in 331 the birth of ideas which were in fair way to be realized in 323 at Babylon again.

There was, however, more involved than a military idea. The little cloud was rising no bigger than a man's hand. Alexander's position towards the different elements in his army and realm had been from the first ambiguous. He was officially both King of Macedon and Federal Captain-General of the Hellenes; but neither the habitual attitude of his Macedonians towards his Greeks, nor of his Greeks towards his Macedonians, was consistent with the relation in which each stood to the General. Alexander had started for Asia with good hope that the ambiguity would disappear as by common service and common interest a single Hellenistic nation was evolved, over which he himself would reign as freely accepted sovereign. The attitude of the Hellenes in Greece had raised, as we have seen, a first difficulty; the attitude of the elder Macedonians was now raising a second. The party which Parmenio led had no panhellenic ideals. They would have had Alexander even as Philip and his forefathers had been — feudal king of the Macedonians. conqueror of the Greeks if he would, and of the Persians if he could. Their chief had urged acceptance of Darius' terms after Issus, seeing no larger question involved than acquisition of territory, and fearful that further conquest might shift the centre from Macedon. "I would accept, were I Alexander," said the old Marshal. "And I, if I were Parmenio," replied the King, well knowing how radically their points of view diverged, and why.[1] For there had been many mutterings among the Macedonians, as we are to learn hereafter; and an actual outbreak with the Greeks took place, it is said, on the field of Issus.

Alexander, indeed, had no idea of remaining Macedonian King. His ambition demanded a much more catholic position; and his sympathy, unlike Philip's, was not really with his ruder subjects.[2] For these reasons he had begun the advance as Captain of all the Hellenes; but the adhesion of the wider nationality was so little spontaneous, wherever military duty and the magnetism of his own presence did not have effect, that the title soon proved to be little worth. Now at Babylon a dignity, still more catholic, in which Macedonian kingship and Hellenic hegemony would alike be absorbed, was beginning to loom in his mental vision.[3] Always as he advanced,[4]

[1] Diodorus (xvii. 39) tells us that Alexander suppressed the actual letter of Darius when it came up for consideration in the council of the generals, and read a letter much less equitable. If true, this action shows conclusively that Alexander well knew his own aims and those of the Macedonians to differ, and that he feared the too sudden enlightenment of his vassals.

[2] Cf. Plut. *Alex.* 28; and the story of the Clitus tragedy, narrated below, p. 231.

[3] Cf. Plut. *Alex.* 47, for the sympathy which young Macedonia showed to this idea.

[4] For, as Talboys Wheeler excellently says (*Hist. of India*, iii. p. 153), Alexander was, like ourselves, of "the true Aryan or political type of conqueror, which identifies itself with the empire it conquers."

he widened his pantheon to receive successively Melkarth, and Amen, Jehovah,[1] and Bel; and more and more readily he accepted natives of the East to rule in his newly won cities and provinces. In a word, Alexander was passing already, scarce knowing it, from King to Emperor.[2]

The same opposition which had forced Alexander to the inception of this change, when redoubled and unified by the change itself, forced him, as we shall see, to develop his new position far more completely than at first he had contemplated. For since it compelled him to rely on all sorts and conditions of his subjects, it led to the breaking down of national privilege, and the inevitable widening of his own ideal. Indeed, quite as much as, if not more than, congenital lust of acquisition, opposition may be said to have led him in the end to that oecumenic scheme which began to take visible shape a year from this, and had absorbed his whole ambition ere his death.[3]

For the moment, however, the change worked

[1] On the often-debated question of Alexander's visit to Jerusalem, see Niese, *op. cit.* p. 83.

[2] Not merely to *Great King*, in the Persian sense. This cannot be too much insisted upon. Alexander never proposed to put Persians in a position of superior privilege, but of equality only; and he obviously intended, in pursuance of a distinct policy, that a non-Persian capital, Babylon, should be his own centre of empire. (See Strabo, p. 731.)

[3] The last despatches which Alexander gave Craterus to convey to Antipater, and which were opened in Cilicia on the news of the Emperor's death, are said to have contained a plan for transporting European peoples into Asia, and Asiatic into Europe (Diod. xviii. 4).

inwardly more than outwardly. If the Macedonian King has almost ceased to be, the Captain-General of Hellas is, by consequence, all the more conspicuous in this year. It is the year of the famous burning of Persepolis, with all its formal parade of restoring the spoil of Xerxes, and its orgy of the vengeance of Hellas, who spoke not inappropriately in these decadent days by the beautiful courtesan who led the rout. It is the year also of the surrender of Darius, Greeks at the Caspian, and of the Greek envoys who had fled with the Great King, to whom, for the last recorded time, Alexander solemnly proclaimed his Hellenic mission. But that mission was coming to be believed in neither by leader nor by led; and in the valleys of Afghanistan it dropped, scarce remarked, out of mind, the quicker, perhaps, for the news of the revolt of Agis and the treason trials of Prophthasia, but long doomed to disappear.

The southern provinces and the treasure cities of the Eastern Empire had all fallen to Alexander in six months after Arbela, at no greater cost than a little hill-fighting. The north, however, as he knew well, was no way disposed to follow tamely the fortunes of the south. The Great King himself was still in his northern capital of Ecbatana with tiara erect; the great Viceroys of the East had not deserted his cause; and about him stayed still the nucleus of a formidable army. So long as these things were so, the Conqueror had realized his original scheme no more than his later dreams.

Alexander took up the offensive again from Persepolis in April, when the snows had vanished from the passes. At starting he seems to have thought that Darius would stand and fight near Hamadan.[1] That illusion was soon to be dispelled. There was treachery in the Persian Court, and the northern nomads had not responded a second time to the war-summons of their King. At a point three days south of Hamadan news reached the Macedonian army that Darius had gathered up his few thousands of men, evacuated his last capital, and gone north-east for the passes which lead to Meshed.

The vast treasure left in Ecbatana compelled Alexander to proceed thither instead of cutting across to the Teheran road; but he was determined, none the less, to pursue and to capture at all costs the person of Darius. For as previously he seems to have thought that another victory would secure the submission of the north-east, so now he took on the hope that the capture of the King's person would spare him the march into Bactria. News, however, came presently to Ecbatana that modified all his plans. Darius had been degraded to a mere puppet by the great Viceroys of the north-east, who were his keepers and proposed to be independent of his fate. In the interests of his own legitimate establishment on the Persian throne, it was still desirable for Alexander to possess himself of the person of its last Achaemenid occupant, and it was

[1] According to Curtius' authority (v. 8. 2), such indeed had been Darius' original intention.

more than possible that, should the stiff-backed Viceroys be captured with the King, after all their provinces would make peaceful submission. Such speedy success, however, could not be reckoned upon, and Alexander felt that now he must lay plans openly for a long eastern march.

First and foremost came reorganization. In view of the probable duration of the coming campaign, its certain hardships, and the necessity, if the eastern provinces were to be more than overrun, of planting and peopling colonies far out of sight of the West, the feudal and political character of a large part of the Grand Army must be swamped as far as possible in the professional element. The character best adapted to the work that lay before the expeditionary force, was that of a Grand Company, owning no obligation but a common tie of devotion to its general, his venture, and his star. The Macedonians would be retained, for to follow the King was their simple feudal duty. The professional part of the Philippian army, even if not Macedonian by birth, could be relied on to stay by the standards, for it knew no other trade half so lucrative. But to all the allied political contingents, especially the Greek, which had been sent by their cities to assist a Crusade for which neither they themselves nor their Captain-General felt unmixed enthusiasm, there must now be offered a choice between retiring from further service or re-enlisting simply as soldiers of fortune. The most part at once took their dismissal, their pay, and a regal gratuity, and set out for

the sea. But "not a few," we are told, volunteered to become Alexander's men absolutely, whether
from love of adventure, or of prize-money, or of
the person of the conqueror himself; and of their
mind will be henceforward nearly all Alexander's
Grand Army. Its complexion is so professional that
many of its veterans seem to have retained little
or no desire to return to the West. The old
Body Guard, for example, were still selling their
services as the "Silver Shields" to this king and
that in Asia long after Alexander had been laid in
Memphis.

Thus openly did Alexander prepare in Ecbatana
for long campaigns of conquest. But still he had
hope of saving much time and toil by overtaking
Darius and his party before they reached the desert
of Khorasan : and as soon as might be he started in
pursuit with the pick of the expeditionary force. It
is a strange chapter in history, this grim, stern chase
of king by king in the heart of Asia — from Hamadan to Rhagae on the confines of Teheran,[1] and from
Rhagae to the defiles on the borders of the desert.
At the entrance to those defiles, in the midst of a halt
to collect supplies, news arrived that the miserable

---

[1] Plutarch (*Alex.* 42, *pace* Niese, *op. cit.* p. 100) cannot include
only the march to Rhagae in his eleven days, for the distance between
Hamadan and Teheran is not above the half of what he states ; and
we have no reason to suppose that either Alexander's rate of marching between those points, or the nature of the country traversed,
entailed any special hardship. Plutarch evidently speaks of the
whole march, up to the capture of Darius, and has got his distance
right, his time wrong.

treachery ahead had reached its crisis. Darius was become actually a bound prisoner in the hands of his Viceroys, and the faithful Greek mercenaries, who had remained by him to the last, were gone north through the Elburz chain. Forthwith Alexander, without waiting for the return of his foraging parties, took all his cavalry and the most athletic of his footmen, and pressed forward all a night and half a day. A few hours' rest were followed by a second night of marching, and at dawn the column reached a deserted camp of the fugitives. Here further news was obtained that the Viceroys meant to give up their King, if pressed by the pursuit. It was no time for rest, and at nightfall Alexander was again in his saddle, and careless that men fell out and horses foundered, " still he drove on," until at high noon he found himself in a village not twenty-four hours behind his quarry. The Viceroys, however, were reported here to intend a forced march in the coming night; and Alexander's column had almost spent its effort. Was there no short way? The villagers knew of a path more direct than the main road, but it was without water. The King, without hesitation, unhorsed his weaker troopers, mounted the sturdiest of his footmen, and at dusk led up the short cut at a trot.[1] Fifty miles were covered in that night, and as dawn broke, lo! the fugitives were just ahead, straggling over the road, weary

---

[1] See Curzon, *Persia*, i. pp. 293 ff., on the Sirdara Pass; and for a lengthy discussion of all the ancient authorities, Th. Zolling, *A. des G. Feldzug in Central Asien*, pp. 93 ff.

and some unarmed.[1] There was a wild panic and stampede : a few rallied for a stand, but it was very brief. The captive King was bidden by his jailors to leave his waggon and mount a horse ; but he refused obstinately, and the sorry tragedy reached its catastrophe with a vengeful sword-thrust, and the clatter of flying hoofs. The last scene is singularly pathetic as Curtius finds it in authorities now lost.[2] The driver of the King's waggon had fled with the Viceroys, and the mules, feeling the reins on their backs, wandered off the road, in quest of water, and dragged the dying man to a pool in a little lateral gorge. There a Macedonian rider found him, and mercifully gave him to drink ; and with words of gratitude on his lips, the gentle prince, of whom as man no one has said an ill word, but few will venture a good one as king, breathed his last. The rhetorical historians and the poets of the East have loved to imagine that Alexander found " Dara" still breathing, and received from his lips a legacy of empire and edifying moralities on the vanity of greatness ; but more sober chroniclers record that the Conqueror came up only after the end, and with some natural impulse of emotion covered the poor body with his cloak.

Fortune, it has been remarked by many critics,

---

[1] An added motive for Alexander's haste was the fear of giving the Persians time to destroy supplies. Cf. Polyaenus, iv. 3. 18, for the similar motive for rapid pursuit after Arbela.

[2] I agree with Niese, that the earlier part of Curtius' dramatic narrative of the Flight is not to be taken au pied de la lettre ; but rather because he has antedated things than because he has related incidents that never occurred.

never served Alexander better than when it delivered into his hand Darius already dead. The Macedonian, say they, obtained the inheritance of the Persian without either the odious obligation of putting him to death, or the equally odious and more dangerous necessity of dragging an ex-king captive at his chariot wheels. Alexander himself, however, seems to have felt more chagrin than relief. So far as there was odium abroad, it fell as justly on him who had hounded the Great King to a miserable end, as on those who, pleading dire necessity, actually killed him. As a rule, on the occasion of a dynastic change in the East, the execution of a king dethroned does not follow immediately on his fall. For a time he may serve many ends of his conqueror; and in such a captive position a man of so weak a character as Darius might have been of no small advantage to his jailor. Furthermore it must be borne in mind that Alexander already had in his hands a wife and daughter, held very dear by the fallen prince, and far from ill-disposed to their captor, through whose influence and agency the Macedonian might easily have been legitimized with something like the open consent of the fallen king, and might have used this consent to compel obedience from the eastern Viceroys. The grief, which all authorities report that Alexander displayed on seeing the dead Persian, sprang in the main, we are glad to believe, from a generous impulse of remorse; but it may well have been embittered by the reflection that a fearful chase through three midsummer days and four nights had resulted in no greater gain than this poor corpse. The real holders of all that Alexander had not won already for himself before he began the pursuit had made good their escape. Having made this point for the occasion his winning-post, the Macedonian had spent his last effort to reach it. His track was strewn with his horses and his men ; his heavy columns were lagging far in the rear; and, after all, what could he do but lap the royal mummy in boughs, as still is a practice in Asia, and having sent it forward to the tombs of its House in Persis, go back slowly by the road he had come ?

Nevertheless, although the death of Darius did not constitute in itself a decisive moment, historians have been right in regarding the summer in which it took place as cardinal in Alexander's career ; for it was then that first it became clear to all men that there was presently to be neither King of Macedon nor Captain-General of Hellas, nor Great King of Persia, but an Emperor of Europe and Asia. The little cloud of Babylon was swelling over all the sky. It is the turn of Alexander's year.

He had transformed his army at Ecbatana, and by the time he reached the Caspian the new character of his following was beginning to react inevitably on himself. All the remainder of this year, 330, in which Alexander begins in patient earnest the advance into the Far East, overrunning Mazenderan, and thence following the great Indian road until winter overtakes him in Seistan, a shadow is spreading over the glory of his early days. There is no decay of his own powers, for much that he will do hereafter is not more inferior to the exploits of his former years than the days of July to those of June. Nay, rather, his genius will rise to the greater occasions that present themselves. But as his soldiery become less responsible and more servile, so the Captain exalts himself, obtruding always more and more the garish aspect of his personality; until we begin to lose sight of anything but his single figure looming larger and sombre against the lurid sky of his evening.

The disorder within may be known by the sore that breaks outwardly. An ulcer was spreading among the Macedonian members of the Grand Army. Till now, as every point in advance had brought gain of a rich land, or a fair city, or a mighty treasure, all ranks of the vassals had been buoyed up in toil and peril by hope presently to possess their souls in wealth. But hope of return had become hope indefinitely deferred: their king's ideal was growing manifestly above and beyond their own; and they felt that daily their privilege became less, as the privilege of others became more.

In particular, certain of the prouder Macedonian vassals of the elder school had begun to foresee with bitterness their effacement in the colossal shadow of Alexander, many cherishing in secret the memory of Philip, first and last a Macedonian, who had made so much of his native nobility, and now was spoken of lightly by the son he had not loved. Parmenio, once Philip's right hand-man in war, represented to this party the heroic age, and, whether he wished it or no, was looked to as chief. But he was old and not assertive of himself, and the habit of feudalism lay heavy upon him;[1] and therefore it was upon his son Philotas that there fell the active lead in this discontent. Philotas seems to have been a man of little restraint and a rude manner, who, holding high office, ran riot in private speech against the royal boy, who, he said, owed everything to him and to his father. Certain of his words had been brought by a Greek girl to Alexander's ears in Egypt before the close of the year 332;[2] but partly from trust in Parmenio, partly, no doubt, for fear of exasperating a strong section of his Macedonians, the King contented himself with observing in secret, in the hope that common service in the Advance about to be resumed would gradually eliminate the malcontent spirit. Before long, however, having fancied himself to have been supported but indifferently by Parmenio's command at Arbela, he was moved to adopt a more decided policy, and to keep the old Marshal behind the main advance in positions where he could be checked by commanders of a fidelity more assured.

The murmurs grew loud on the Caspian shore; for, having purged his Grand Army of all but volunteers, friends, and vassals, Alexander was

---

[1] Plutarch quotes from Callisthenes that Parmenio inwardly regarded anything but kindly Alexander's growing power, ambition, and surroundings of ceremony (*Alex.* 33).

[2] We have this on the best authority. *Vide* Arr. iii. 26.

venturing to assume something of the dress and style of an Asiatic, and the aloofness of an Emperor.[1] The hint was not lost on either Macedonians or Greeks; did it not imply that the Grand Army was no longer of the West, but become definitively of the East? Throughout a long halt at Zadracarta, and the subsequent march towards Seistan, disaffection gathered strength, and a certain party, which covertly imputed all its personal woes to the King, spoke in secret of poison and daggers. But there can have been little combination in conspiracy, for the story goes that matters came quite fortuitously to a head at Prophthasia during the winter of 330,[2] through none other than Philotas being made privy, all unexpecting and involuntary, to the vapourings of a nobody. The same idle words presently reached Alexander's ears also, but not, as they should have done, from the lips of Parmenio's son. Philotas may or may not have been guilty of sympathy with the vapourer; at any rate, he had let the matter drift, and the King, waiting for some pretext to strike a decisive blow at the malcontent party, chose to assume his guilt. Alexander was in a stronger position in this far land than in Egypt, for the mass of his army had fallen into an absolute dependence on his

---

[1] Cf. Plut. *Phoc.* 17, for his omission henceforth of the usual courteous greeting to his correspondents. The fact of the Median royal dress, etc., is beyond question, though it seems to have been assumed only on certain festal or religious occasions; *e. g.* at Maracanda, Bactra, Susa, and Opis. Turgid lies are told about it by such as Ephippus of Olynthus (*ap. Athen.* p. 537 E.).

[2] See Appendix for the chronology of the next three years.

life. Philotas was arrested at once, and haled before
the general feudal assembly; but such evidence, as
was adduced there and then, established criminal
negligence, hardly more. An adjournment was proclaimed, and in the night Hephaestion wrested in
the torture-chamber a confession from the son, which
included the father's name. That evidence was more
than enough for such a Court; the faithful vassals,
transported with rage, acted both as judges and
executioners, *Macedonum more,* and in twelve days
three swift dromedaries bore back, across the plains
of Khorasan, the death-warrant of Parmenio.[1] The
Lyncestian Alexander, who, at first a suspected
friend, had for four years been a prisoner of state,
was dragged forth also and put to death — a warning
to all his tribesmen;[2] and subsequently four or five
intimates of Philotas were put on their trial; but
Alexander had been warned to accept easy satisfaction,[3] and the most part were dismissed scot-free.

It was a grievous necessity, which has been
regarded often enough as judicial murder. But if
the ulcer of discontent was in the Army -- and there
seems no doubt that it had been spreading there these
two years — Alexander had little choice, in view of the
tremendous needs and risks of warfare, but to cut —

[1] Strabo, p. 724. The ordinary rate of travelling was thirty to
forty days to Ecbatana.

[2] Diod. xvii. 80; and Curtius, vii. 1. 6.

[3] According to Curtius' authorities, there was much grumbling
after Philotas' death (vii. 2. 10), and Alexander had to make a
punishment battalion (cf. Diod. xvii. 80). Also the garrison of
Ecbatana came very near open mutiny in sympathy for Parmenio.

and he cut strongly. Regicide was not spoken of
again in the camp, except by one little group nursing
a private grievance of the moment; and to secure
this immunity Alexander, after all, had taken means,
the moral responsibility for which is not more than
rests on any general who decimates a mutinous
company. Let whoso sits in the seat of judgment
on this matter remember that he has not one-tenth
of the evidence that was before the Emperor; and
that he is revising the acts not of a civil, but a
martial court.

At the same time, while we recognize dire necessity
in this matter, we would not maintain that the discontent of the great vassals was causeless, or indeed
anything but reasonable. The loss of privilege is a
very bitter fruit, whose taste long remains in the
mouth. They would have been more or less than
men had they swallowed and smiled! And, moreover, the sun of their feudal system no longer shone
as graciously as of old. The enthusiastic boy who
had led them out of Macedon was dragging them
inexorably into far deserts and sky-kissing hills,
as an irritable and uncertain despot, flaming into
dangerous passion and collapsing into as dangerous
remorse. His many hurts had not been suffered for
nothing — the stroke on the neck and head in the
Balkans, the fever at Tarsus, the stab in the thigh at
Issus, the almost fatal bolt-wound at Gaza. Every
change in a character such as Alexander's makes for
intensification; insensibility to pain becomes positive
cruelty, impetuosity grows to foolhardiness, and

diplomacy to deceit. The man who had wept over
the corpse of Darius made presently so brutalizing
an exhibition of a regicide at Balkh as to shock his
greatest eulogists; the cool deliberator of Arbela
is become the almost suicide of Mooltan; he who
never refused quarter to surrendered foes, stains
his record on the Swat with a massacre of men on
parole.[1]

Fortunately, whatever the decay of his character,
neither was Alexander's mental force nor was the absolute devotion of the rank and file to his person abated.
He had studied to ripen that goodwill of the soldiery,
which had been won ere he came to the throne, into
something little less than worship, by arts which
sympathy with fighting men enabled Philip's son to
apply with rare success. By magnificent funerals and
posthumous honours to those who fell in battle, by
huge gratuities when money was flush,[2] by personal
recognition and fellowship in all things,[3] by voluntary
concessions such as the despatch of the married men
from Halicarnassus to spend winter with their wives,

---

[1] Diod. xvii. 84. Alexander's act is condemned especially by
Plutarch.

[2] E. g. one talent to each horseman, and ten minae to each foot-
soldier, discharged at Ecbatana in 330; six minae to each Macedonian horseman, five to each allied horseman, two to foot-soldiers,
at Babylon in 331 (Diod. xvii. 63).

[3] A story is told by two authorities (Curt. viii. 4. 15, and
Frontinus, iv. 6. 3) of Alexander restoring a frost-bitten soldier by
seating him on his own seat by the fire. Cf. the well-known
story of the draught of water in the desert (infra, p. 253); the
debt-paying at Susa; and Alexander's sacrifice of his own super-
fluities in order to obtain destruction of those of his men (Plut.
Alex. 57; cf. also 41).

by the confidence with which he drank the perilous cup at Tarsus, — by these and many other means Alexander bound his men's interests to his. Add such enthusiasm as beauty, daring, and pre-eminent powers will breed, and the dependence of men lost in a strange land ; and perhaps we shall cease to wonder at that marvellous temper which Alexander's army shows, even in its most mutinous moods, when it is accepting in sorrowful silence his taunts at the Hyphasis, or uttering heart-broken protests at Opis. Many armies have made a massacre to avenge a general's wound, as the Macedonians did in Chitral ; and many, in similar plight, might equal the wild joy of the phalanx at Mooltan, when its single hope came back from the gates of death. But how many veterans, who had mutinied against a particular decree, have accepted the same a few days later, unmodified in a single point, as the time-expired men accepted their dismissal at Opis?

Nothing short of such devotion will account for the readiness with which the Army followed whither their Captain, leaving Seistan in the spring of 329, was about to go — into the snow-blocked ranges between Candahar and Cabul in midwinter ; through Hindu Kush and over the deserts of Turkestan in midsummer ; up and down huge foothills of the Himalaya, which European armies hardly can penetrate even now ; across the Punjab in the Rains ; and finally into that land of Gedrosia, which later Moslem conquerors regarded as a fit resort for the souls of the damned. Nothing short of such devotion will

explain the acquiescence of so many in the sentences
of exile which were pronounced whenever there was
planted one of those military trading colonies, of
which we know so little but the fact of their foundation. How large they were; built upon what
plan, Greek or Oriental; endowed with what com-
munal government — who can say?[1] We are told
only that at this point or that the "geographical
eye" of the Emperor sees that a city "would become
great and prosperous among men," and inexorably
he details men-at-arms to build its walls, and a draft
of his Macedonians or Greeks, the least fit for further
marching, to form an official class and a garrison
among a proletariate of camp followers and natives.
The Europeans were not too willing. When Alexander came back through Hindu Kush in 327 by
way of his yearling city of Alexandria *ad Paropamisum*, he found it in a very unsatisfactory state.
Two or three years later some three thousand colonists
of the north country shook the dust of their exile
off their feet, while over twenty thousand, after the
Emperor's death, set out from the same region for
the west.[2]

[1] Diodorus (xvii. 83) does indeed tell us that a town at the foot
of Hindu Kush was peopled at the first with seven thousand natives,
and three thousand camp followers and volunteers; but with that
our knowledge begins and ends.

[2] See Curt. ix. 7. 1, and Diod. xvii. 99, xviii. 7, for the circumstances of these movements, which seem to have led to the breaking
off of Bactria from the rest of the empire even while Alexander was
alive. The number of Greeks — stated even as high as forty thousand — is to be accounted for by the very numerous colonies and
garrisons in Bactria, and a large infusion of camp followers.

This development of Alexander's colonial policy is the most interesting feature of the eastern campaigns. Out of the sixteen Alexandrias enumerated by Stephen of Byzantium which can be referred with probability to the son of Philip, not less than eleven are to be placed east of Persis, whilst in the north-east alone we are told by other authorities that Alexander founded at least eight cities.[1] Such

---

[1] Justin states that there were *twelve* colonies in the north-east (xii. 5); Strabo *eight* (p. 517), while Curtius mentions *six* in and about Margiana alone (vii. 10. 15). We know of only two individually — Alexandria ἐσχάτη, on the Sir Daria, near Khojend (Arr. iv. 4. 1; and Pliny, *N. H.* vi. 16), and Alexandria κατὰ Βάκτρα (Steph. Byz.), which seems to have been a foundation on the northern slopes of Hindu Kush, designed to watch the direct passes from Cabul (cf. the old reading of Pliny, *N. H.* vi. 23). But Hephaestion's commission, τὰς ἐν τῇ Σογδιανῇ πόλεις συνοικίζειν (Arr. iv. 16. 3), implies a larger number; and the high figures given (*e. g.* by Diod. xviii. 7) for the total of the subsequent mutineers supports the statement of Strabo, and even that of Justin. Pliny (*N. H.* vi. 16) explicitly states that Alexander founded a colony also in the oasis of *Margiane, i. e.* Merv; which was destroyed by the Turkmans, and then reconstituted by Antiochus. This deliberate assertion has been much called in question, simply because it is hard to see how or when Alexander himself can have gone to Merv. But it is quite unnecessary to assume that no Alexandrian colony was founded without Alexander's presence. There are definite instances to the contrary, *e. g.* in Sogdiana itself Hephaestion was sent out to plant colonies (Arr. iv. 16. 3), and Leonnatus had a similar mission in Beluchistan (Pliny, *N. H.* vi. 23). *A priori* it is most probable that Alexander would have taken pains to secure the most direct road from the west to his Sogdian province, and the colony may very well have been founded by an expedition sent from Balkh in 328 (possibly that referred to by Curtius as going to the *urbs Margiana*, round which six colonies were planted, vii. 10. 15: Curtius would in that case be wrong in representing that Alexander himself led the expedition; but such a mistake is very natural to a careless

development, however, was in practice rather than theory. Whereas in the west of the new empire city life existed already full grown, and new centres needed to be created only at certain important key-positions, Alexander found such organizations almost non-existent in the basins of the Oxus and the Indus, and was forced to create them new in the interests of imperial unification. In districts open to nomad raids and hill brigandage, communication and commerce cannot be maintained without strong cities not far apart; and we may credit Alexander with some inkling at least of what Imperial Rome afterwards understood so clearly, that nothing settles rude and wandering tribes like open markets and the introduction of an attractive apparatus of civilization.[1] It may be recalled that it was in the west only that Rome, when her time came, had such work as this to do; for the east, thanks to Alexander, and to successors working on Alexander's ideas, was organized already as she would have wished to have it. It was the chief glory of the Delphian Apollo that he fostered the birth of cities; and to all time it will be the chief glory of Alexander that not only did he

chronicler of a single hero's deeds). Or the city might have owed its origin to the generals who marched up to Balkh with reinforcements in December, 328. The Hellenistic sites in these remote regions are not satisfactorily identified yet, but their number and size are attested by the large finds of Graeco-Bactrian antiquities, which have found their way to India and Russia in recent years. On F. v. Schwarz's book on Turkestan, see Appendix, p. 299.

[1] See Arr. Ind. 40, for Alexander's policy in the hill-country of Persis.

select a unique site in familiar Egypt, but on the
unknown map of Central Asia¹ chose situations
for great cities so wisely that their importance
survives to this day with little change of locality
in Herat, Farrah, Candahar, Ghazni, Cabul, and
Khojend!²

As the Conqueror moves east and north from

¹ Unfortunately we are left very much in the dark as to the
amount of information which Alexander or his father may have
possessed before setting out to conquer the East. Xenophon and
traditions of the Ten Thousand would serve for the road up to
Babylon. Plutarch, moreover, tells a story of the conqueror as a
boy closely questioning as to roads and distances a Persian embassy sent to his father. Route-notes of returned Greek envoys
may have been collected, giving indications as far as Ecbatana.
But Alexander's surprise, expressed some years later than this,
that envoys from Europe should be able to reach him more quickly
in Media by way of the Black Sea than by the way of Asia Minor
or Phoenicia, does not imply much idea of the lie of the land.
Similarly his delusions about the Caspian, about the country
beyond the Jaxartes, and about the identity of the Indus with
the Nile, and his ignorance of the outflow of the Five Rivers,
show complete fog as to the Eastern map. The capture of the
Persian Records must have put him in possession of official information as to distances between centres of administration, ere he
went north-east, and he seems to have had with himself a body of
men — the "Bematistae" — who concerned themselves with routes;
but whether to lay out a line of march beforehand, or only to measure it as it was being traversed, we do not know. At least they
recorded the distances covered. Alexander had also engineers with
him, but mainly for siege purposes. Another obscure point is his
commissariat, if indeed he had any. The facts recorded of his
Gedrosian march make it appear as if the army was expected to live
on what it could collect day by day. Out of the large number of
Greek camp followers, however, from whom Alexander largely peopled his eastern colonies, there may have been many sutlers and
vendors of provision.

² See Appendix, p. 297.

Seistan, the scene grows, with the man, more tremendous. The Hindu Kush interposes its stupendous
wall, the Desert spreads its deathly sands, and the
mighty stream of Oxus rolls across his path ; but
all are vain. The mere distances that Alexander
covers in this vast region of Central Asia excite our
interest, rather than the driving of Turkman hordes
into the desert, and incessant fighting among hill
forts ; and even the chain of cities which he created
to far Khojend, and the provincial organization which
after three campaigns he imposed from Balkh to
Samarcand,[1] remain so unknown to us by anything
but the fact of their long survival, that they fail to
divert attention from the personality of their creator,
forcing his tireless way even to the Sir Daria, the
uttermost limit of the Persian Empire, and, in his
belief, of Asia. For beyond it he found Scythians
whom he thought to be Scythians of Europe, and a
little farther on saw in fancy the girdle of the whole
world, Homer's Stream of Ocean, of which he had
been told the Caspian was but a bay. Presently
would end, thought he, ἡ οἰκουμένη, the world of
human life, beyond which could lie only the region
behind the sun, such a land of spirits and demons
as afterwards the Greeks credited him with having
explored — so far out of their ken lay the steppes
of Turkestan and the plains of the Punjab !

---

[1] That he did create such an organization might be inferred
indirectly from the fact of the subsequent kingdom's existence;
but the summoning of the Hyparchs to council in 328 (Arr. iv. 1),
supplies direct evidence.

No sooner, however, was Alexander at this limit of earth than the land rose behind him, and he was forced to reconquer. With a rapidity and energy which he never excelled, but a severity harsher than his earlier wont, he inflicted, ere summer ended, a signal chastisement on the northern strongholds, and then, partly in bravado, and partly to assure the rising walls of a new city, destined to become Khojend, he threw himself across even the Sir Daria itself, and rode for a day against the astounded nomads of the Mogul Dagh, contracting by foul water a dysenteric flux, from which he was hard put to it to recover.

Almost a whole year, however, had to be spent in desultory campaigns before the back of the revolt was broken finally. With vast deserts to west, and the huge gorges leading eastward to the Roof of the World, Sogdiana and Bactria offered too many refuges to rebel chieftains to be brought under at the first attempt. The western wastes, after one serious reverse — the worst that ever befell Alexander's forces (he himself was not present) — were cleared readily enough, and cruel revenge was taken on the fertile valley of the Saravshan ; but the hill forts of the east occupied all an autumn and spring, and taxed every resource of the Macedonian's ingenuity and all the discipline and dash of his men-at-arms. It was not till the summer of 327 that the Emperor was ready to repass the Hindu Kush ; and so obstinate had been the resistance, and so apt did the hill country appear for fresh revolt, that he was prompted to seek the first of his two political marriages. Roxana, daughter of one of the greatest of the hill chiefs, was selected by the conqueror, and we are told much of his enslavement to her beauty;[1] but it should be noted that we hear no more of the Queen for the rest of Alexander's campaigns, and that she conceived no child by him until a few months before his death.

Through the cloud of expeditions and sieges and official acts one lurid gleam falls in the Bactrian year full upon the man. The Emperor was lying in Samarcand at the late winter season, in the interval between his second campaign in the north-west and that to come in the east, having just succeeded in retrieving finally the grievous mishap his lieutenants had met with in the past summer. It seems that in consequence of that event there had arisen some odious comparison of the Macedonian marshals with their ever-victorious King,[2] and that Alexander by reason of his triumph and of much feasting was more than ever disposed to override prejudices of race. Especially it fell out, at a great banquet given to all sorts and conditions on the Festival of the Dioscuri, that the court rhymers made invidious capital of the disaster, and the talk at table chancing on the Immortal Twins, whose day it was, certain Greek soldiers of fortune pointed in tipsy flattery to the coincidence

---

[1] *E.g.* by Curtius, viii. 4. 25. His further statement — that the Macedonians regarded the alliance with much disfavour — is more credible.

[2] Plut. *Alex.* 50.

of the birth of the so-called sons of Tyndareus
with that of Alexander; for both, said they, were
fathered on a mortal, who were really children of
Zeus, and how much greater was the conqueror
of Asia than those sackers of Aphidnae! A little
leaked out also in direct disparagement of Philip.
Alexander, far gone in wine, smiled on the talk;
but a knot of his elder Macedonians took it ill,
reviving memories of the elder king; and at last
Clitus, emboldened by the privilege of a foster-brother,
took up cudgels for the old Maker of Macedon, crying
shame on the decriers of the king whose men had
opened Asia. Alexander, to his honour, took the
implied rebuke quietly enough, but Clitus was fool
enough, or drunk enough, to point it with a direct
personal sting. The insulted Emperor threw an
angry warning across to his foster-brother, but only to
receive in the teeth an outrageous gibe at his Median
dress and would-be imperial state. He sprang to his
feet, but restraining himself a moment, bade his
Greeks note what barbarians were these Macedonians
after all! Clitus, not to be browbeaten, thanked God
devoutly he at least was none of the slaves! It
was too much. Alexander snatched a missile, and
leaping the table felt for his dagger; but it had been
withdrawn privily from his side, and in the confusion,
while he called in wild Macedonian speech for his
body-guard, friends hustled Clitus protesting from
the banquet. The ill-starred man, however, broke
away, and rushing back to another door. drew
aside the hangings and shouted an insulting line of

Euripides down the hall. Alexander turned to the voice, and seizing a weapon hurled it at the falling curtain, and behind it his foster-brother went down in the agony of death.

From wild wrath to the repentance of a madman a nature like Alexander's passes in a flash. Rushing to the fallen man, the Emperor drew out the fatal lance, and tried to throw himself on its point.[1] But the great officers seized his wrists, and ordering the corpse to be withdrawn hastily, attended their lord to his chamber; where for three days and nights the exalted and overwrought spirit passed through the darkest valley of self-abasement, till specious platitudes of kismet and predestination began to soothe, and a sophistic Greek infused a baleful balm, reminding the successor of Darius that emperors stand above obligation and above law.

So Alexander came to his confident self again. But the sorry tragedy had left a mark, and seems to have prompted the Emperor to make a more strenuous attempt at Balkh in the following spring to break down invidious distinctions of nationality, and obliterate Macedonian privilege. Not only the Macedonians, however, but the Greeks as well, proved mighty stiff-necked about paying homage in the eastern manner by prostration; and a lesson, rude but effective, was read to Alexander by the discovery of a second plot against his life, hatched indeed from the trivial grief of a Page, but fostered, it appears, by those of more

---

[1] I see no reason to doubt this attempt at suicide. It was the received tradition in antiquity (cf. Cicero, *Tusc. Disp.* iv. 37).

weight who had fallen out of favour in the recent matter of the homage.

A strangely significant picture this, that the meagre chroniclers throw into relief — this inheritor of a European throne in his Persian robes, perfumed and tiaraed, with a motley company drawn from half Asia and half Europe, listening in Samarcand to Greek song and Greek talk! How far and fast had the world moved since Marathon! Greeks were fraternizing now with Persians, both at their ease; only the Macedonians sat glowering and constrained, masterful, stiff-necked Northerners that they were. They might well feel uneasy! Their native speech had become so rare at the court of their King that a word of command, shouted in it, rang on unwonted ears like a tocsin. And what a strange position among all these is Alexander's! — he drinking rose-crowned among his captains, knowing that he is using them, each and all, as means to an end which they comprehend not, and, comprehending, would not accept. With one section of his following, the Macedonian — that, by custom, most attached to his person — he is out of all sympathy. With a second, the Greek, he is for the moment in accord, but the greater one day will be its undeceiving. With the third, the Oriental, this Homeric paladin is on terms at all only by stifling the prejudices of his education and all recollection of his first ideals. Insensibly and inevitably his fortune has lifted him out of the plane of all contemporary men, and it will raise him ever higher and higher on his pinnacle of isolation, until his nerves begin to crack and his head to swim. /

For also all ties of private sympathy were falling fast away from him. His mother, alone of all his nearer kin, had been anything to him in his youth, and the wild harridan had come near estranging herself altogether in this seven years' absence by the dangerous discord that she fostered in Europe. " A heavy rent is this I pay for my nine months," groaned her son, on hearing from Antipater of some fresh outrage; but he clung, nevertheless, to her memory — he had little else to cling to; and even though he forbade her to touch public affairs, he allowed her tears to weigh against all his Viceroy's griefs. Had not his foster-brother, too, fallen by his hand? and did not he bear hardly less heavy on his soul the deaths of many others near and dear, who had fallen in his wars? Of his earliest intimates and comrades in exile, Ptolemy, Erigyius, and Nearchus were with him still; but Harpalus, who had played him false already, and would betray his trust once more, was left behind in Babylon. The other strong attachment of his boyhood, that to his great tutor, had been strained by long absence and gradual divergence of ideas. Aristotle had now resided for long in Athens; and from that centre of Hellenic exclusiveness he came to speak and write less and less kindly of his royal pupil who would obliterate the heaven-ordained privilege of Hellenes. Those of Aristotle's school who had accompanied Alexander had been most consistent opponents of his imperial ideal, and latterly Callisthenes, their best and bravest spirit, accused of complicity in the Page's plot, had paid with his life for representing too well his master in philosophy. Philotas and Parmenio, Clitus and Callisthenes, head a grievous death-roll, which after the Indian campaigns fills apace. Many of the names written thereon in the last years of Alexander are doubtless those of men, cruel and rapacious, who indeed had misused their office ; but also many, doubtless, fell victims to their inability to grasp an ideal grown too wide, or were placed in a mere semblance of fault by the suspicion with which fear had begun to cloud the mind of their sovereign.

The spring of 327 was far spent ere Alexander moved south from Balkh, and, marching back over Hindu Kush, came down to his city founded eighteen months before. The last labour of his Herculean doom lay before him as he entered the Indian satrapy. In the Persian imperial scheme India lay rather west than east of the Indus, and signified the basin of the Cabul River, and as much of the Indus Valley as the Great King could hold tributary. But the limits of his assumed Persian inheritance were becoming too strait for Alexander. Had he not given warning of a scheme of Empire more universal when he asked, at sight of the Caspian, if that was not a part of the girdling Ocean Stream, and when he questioned the Scythians of Tashkend about Europe? Soon the oecumenic ideal will develop apace. Ocean seems the only true limit of empire. Where, then,

is its Stream on the east? As the army pushes
forward, it recedes. The Indus proves after all not
to be the Nile,[1] and a still greater river is reported
to flow beyond its tributaries. Let that, however,
be crossed, and Ocean could not but be near; and
therefore sore indeed was the constraint put on the
Captain by the refusal of his army to leave the
Punjab. Foiled on one side, the sanguine man
turned south to seek the Stream again, and having
arrived at a tidal sea put his whole soul into such
an expedition as would prove that there, at least,
his work was done. No Greek conceived of anything but fairy-land beyond a tidal ocean. As the
Pillars of Hercules were notoriously the limit on the
West, so this beach of the Indus Delta, on which
Alexander's ships were left suddenly aground, could
seem nothing else than an uttermost edge of earth.
From this moment, therefore, was born Alexander's
last and most vast project of rounding off the
world south, west, and north, with a fleet and army
proceeding through Africa to Europe, which two
continents he seems, following his favourite Homer,
to have pictured as shallow half-moons, their chords
resting on the interposed Mediterranean Sea.

The hillmen on the northern streams of the Cabul
basin gave Alexander, as they have given every
invader since his time, some very tough fighting; and

---

[1] For this strange, passing delusion of Alexander's, we have
the authority of Arrian (vi. 1) and Strabo (p. 707). Both seem to
derive from one source — Alexander's letters to Olympias.

the late autumn and early winter were spent by a
Macedonian column in the upper valleys of Khond,
Kafiristan, and Chitral, chasing agile foes from rock
to rock, and taking innumerable walled villages, the
larger of which, such as a certain Massaga on the
Swat, cost short but formal sieges. The year 326 was
well begun ere the Emperor could come down to the
Indus, having captured the last and strongest hold,
situated on the great river itself; and he found ready
the material for a floating bridge, prepared by his
main body, which had come direct from Cabul by the
Khyber Pass.

That wild land of the north-west, however, was not
really subjugated. Alexander himself had to go back
to Dir and deal another blow ere he left the Indus.
His lieutenants in the following year were still raiding
and fighting, and a year later still his Viceroy was
murdered as prelude to a general revolt, in which, after
the great Captain's death, most part of Afghanistan
and Khelat slipped again out of Macedonian hands.[1]
But at this moment Alexander had not patience
to tarry among hill forts, and with the first of the
spring had ferried his Grand Army across the Indus,
and was marching into the north of the Punjab.

A local *rajah* of the Indus Valley had made terms
with the western invader, but the main levy of the
warrior peasantry of the upper country was waiting
in arms behind the Jhelum. In all Asia Alexander
had not been brought to face a problem more grave
than now. For he had come, hardly knowing it, to

[1] Strabo, p. 698.

the threshold of a new world, and into conflict with an unknown civilization, as stable and cohesive as his own. It was no group of robber chieftains that waited beyond the river, but the able prince of a great and warlike empire;[1] no accumulation of gregarious nomads, but a disciplined force possessing all his arms, and one that he had not—a corps of war-elephants. At Arbela there had been a weak spot at the heart of the foe, and most loose attachment of his members. At the Hydaspes the enemy's force was uniform, disciplined, confident, and marshalled on its own ground. The torrential rains and heavy heat of a clime utterly unlike anything in their experience were beginning to tell on Alexander's men : and if an issue was to be come to at all, passage must first be forced across a river wider than the Tigris —the first great river, indeed, which had been held in force against the Macedonians.

All the world knows how Alexander triumphed. The battle of the Hydaspes, won after long de-moralizing delay, takes established rank among the most brilliant operations of ancient warcraft. The strategy which distracted the attention of the foe till a river half a mile wide had been all but crossed on a black night of storm, is only equalled by the supreme audacity of the venture. The confidence of the Grand Army is never more amazing

---

[1] See Talboys Wheeler (*op. cit.*) on the ancient Kshatriya Empire of the Punjab. He quotes from Ferishta how the great King " P'hoor" marched to the frontier of India to oppose Alexander.

than here at Hydaspes, and, as always in strenuous
action, the Captain himself is seen at his best. His
imperious soul was fulfilled now only in most intense
excitement, for it had come to be with him as with
the Spartan, that he "went to ruin in the day of
peace." In the dust and stress of battle the heroic
side of Alexander's character at once appears. In
instant sympathy with his own men, and generous
to those of his foe, tireless, fearless, swift to decide
and swift to act, he is hardly ever at fault, and never
weak. So he remains the one general of history
who won all his battles.

From the Jhelum to the Chenab, the Chenab to the
Ravi, and the Ravi to the Sutlej, the Grand Army,
swelled now with Afghans and Punjabis, marched
without serious opposition, save at one stockade of the
Cathaeans near Amritsar; and princes even of Cash-
mere sent to propitiate the new Conqueror. Ganges
itself was said to flow but twelve marches distant
through rich cities and fat lands. Alexander gave the
word to bridge and pass the last of the Five Rivers.

But the western soldiers faced about. The awful
climate [1] had forced on a crisis. Eight years ago
many had looked last on wife and child and home.
There was not a regiment but had been decimated
since it marched out at the first, and no survivor
who kept a whole skin. Turn they would, and reap
some reward in life for so long labour. [2]

---

[1] See Strabo, p. 691.

[2] These are, of course, the members of the original Grand
Army led by Alexander across the Dardanelles, though all the

Here is, perhaps, the most singular mutiny in history. There seems to have been neither heat nor anger, but simply the dogged determination of weary men. The unanimity was absolute, and the mortified Emperor might beg, demand, decree — no mutineer yielded a step to pity or to fear. The spirit of the whole Army is represented admirably by the speech that Arrian puts into the mouth of Coenus. There is the true note of weariness, the old spearmen's sense of the injustice of hope so long deferred, their sore sickness for home, and, through all, an uneasy fear lest they offend beyond pardon the idol of all their hearts, and the one man who could lead them back.

For three days Alexander waited, gloomy as Achilles in his tent; but the camp lay in silence unbroken. The Captain knew the sign, and bowed

rest joined in this mutiny. A large part of the Army of India, however, must have been composed of men of shorter service, for during the past eight years a great many reinforcements had marched up and been drafted into the ranks; e. g. 3,650 of all arms joined at Gordium in 333 (Callisthenes, ap. Polyb. xii. 19. 2, raises this reinforcement to 5,800 men); 4,000 Greeks at Sidon in 332; 900 Greeks and Thracians in Egypt early in 331; 15,000 men at Susa late in the same year; 1,500 of Darius' Greek mercenaries in Hyrcania in 330; 6,000 Indians at Nysa, at the Indus, and at Taxila in 327–326. Diodorus adds 30,000 Greek mercenaries incorporated at the Hydaspes. To counterbalance these, which are probably only a part of the fresh drafts, we must subtract an indefinite number who took their discharge at Ecbatana, the large garrisons and colonizing drafts left here and there, and the losses by battle or sickness. But on the whole the Grand Army increased very largely as it went on. Arrian tells us, in the *Indica* (19), that it had reached a total of 120,000 men on its return to the Hydaspes. Niese has a good passage (p. 158) on the changes effected during the Eastern march.

his stubborn head.[1]   He decreed a solemn taking
of omens, as though bent still on passing the river,
but the gods kindly took on themselves to give the
veto. The word went forth for return, and the
veterans gave vent to their pent-up emotion in
weeping and shouting and crowding about Alexander's tent to tender humble gratitude and humbly
to pray for pardon.

Twelve altars rose above the Sutlej to the gods of
the Greeks, and long were fed by the *rajahs* of this
region ;[2] and there, at the end of the world, was held
the last of those Olympic contests by which the
Emperor, throughout his Indian march, sought to
inspirit his men to resist the Rains.   Exotic, indeed,
these contests must have seemed — expressions of a
sanguine civilization, that exalted the flesh, in a far
contemplative land, where bliss is impersonal Nirvana
through the flesh mortified.   Exotic indeed, and
therefore India, when Alexander left her, was still
what she had been when he came.   For not only was
she too vast and too old to learn in the summer of
one year, but the superiority of the newly imported
civilization was not sufficiently obvious to weigh
against all in it that was uncongenial.   As a great
French eulogist of Alexander[3] most justly says : " Ce
qui manqua à Alexandre ce fut de porter à l'Asie
une religion plus pure et plus lumineuse que les rêves

[1] If we can trust Diodorus' authorities, Alexander had several
motives for compliance ; indeed, it was hardly possible to have
kept the field much longer in any case.

[2] Plut. *Alex.* 62.

[3] Lamartine, at the end of his *Vie d'Alexandre*.

de l'Olympe, qui ne valaient pas les rêves des mages ou les mystères pleins de divinité de l'Inde." The Hellene was baffled by the difficulty that still confronts even those who would introduce the creed of Christ to Brahmans. The advance that he proposed in theory and practice was too delicate to induce change in minds already habituated to a high and congenial philosophy, and by reason of race and clime little prone to move. In vain the drama of Athens [1] was exhibited by Alexander to Indian eyes, in vain her nude athletes wrestled and her four-horse chariots raced. These things but passed as a midday dream through the ecstatic brain of a *fakir*; and those fifteen Brahmans on the Lower Indus who refused to be impressed by the Conqueror and took his messenger scornfully to task, as one who, compared to themselves, grovelled in the flesh, spoke finally for the whole cultured class of India — a class shallow, vainglorious, prone to evade by quibble the obligation to know, and able to be degraded, but neither wishing nor able to be raised by western methods to western ideals.[2]

Therefore, although some personal memories survived as to Chandragupta, the adventurer-sultan of

[1] On the question of the performance of the *Ajen* on the Hydaspes, see Droysen, i. p. 639, note, and Niese, *op. cit.* p. 156. The latter gives ample reasons for continuing to believe that India was the scene.

[2] The Greeks, for their part, seem to have been greatly impressed with the Brahmans. The apocryphal and romantic literature connecting Alexander with them and their King, Dandamis, is very large.

Patali-putra, who, as a boy, had seen the Conqueror,[1]
Alexander's name is said not to appear in Sanskrit
literature;[2] and he faded slowly from Indian tradition,
until the wave of Islam brought him back on its crest,
transfigured as *D'hulkarnein,* the "two-horned," the
Prophet.

The Return was not to follow the line of the
Advance further westward than the Jhelum. Two
months before, ere Alexander had left the two cities
that he had founded at the scene of his triumph over
Porus, he had issued orders that such of his soldiers
and camp-followers as were natives of the Levantine
coasts should prepare a river flotilla. For he had
learned from native report that the Four Rivers
flowed into the Indus, and that the united stream
could not be the Nile, for it ran presently into a sea.
Was that sea not part of Ocean Stream? He would
descend the water-way, opening out and securing his
new Indian province as he went; and thereafter there
would remain no more to be done on the southern
edge of the world.

The flotilla was ready, and the leisurely voyage
begun, by November of 326. The most part of the
army marched still by land, meeting the fleet at
successive points; and as soon as the Levantine boat-
men settled down to an understanding of such new
navigation, all went smoothly enough. Too smoothly,
perhaps, for Alexander's unquiet spirit, for all the
while he was raiding on this side and that, without

---

[1] Plut. *Alex.* 62.   [2] Max Müller, *India,* p. 274.

much ostensible provocation, unless it were that the tribes refused to bring down supplies. Such warfare by the wayside, with its little of definite purpose, and its absence of permanent results, might well be ignored, were it not that in its course occurred the most famous, the most foolish, and not the least characteristic of the exploits of Alexander's autumnal years.

The affair befell in a certain city of the southern Punjab, probably hard by where now stands Mooltan. The streets were already in the hands of the Macedonian column, but the mud walls of the citadel held out still. The attacking Guards had no siege-train, nor, it appears, more than two ladders; and the scaling parties seem to have been hanging back until more and better means of ascent should be procured. Alexander, however, seldom could wait. Seizing a ladder from its bearers, he reared it with his own hands against the wall, and crouching under his shield, climbed, followed by two esquires, while by the second ladder a sturdy veteran also reached the battlement. The defenders of the wall fell back from close quarters with the glittering figure of the Emperor; but bolts and stones rained about him from the nearest towers and the rising ground within. The Guards saw from below that their Captain was in imminent danger, and began to swarm pell-mell up the two ladders; but these, being probably only such as could be requisitioned from houses of the town, collapsed under the rush, and left the attack for the moment paralyzed. Alexander could hardly remain where he was, unsupported and a mark for all missiles. Another man would have dropped back again on his own side of the wall; but the dare-devil madness was awake in Philip's son, and, with scarce a moment's hesitation, he took a flying leap, the light gleaming on his ringing arms, full into the fort, and by a miracle found his feet. His three followers, for a few instants, hung back from the leap, and meanwhile Alexander, who had set his back against the outer wall, kept the astonished Indians at bay with stones and play of sword. But when the three Macedonians had scrambled down to join their Captain, and no one else appeared, the enemy took heart. The veteran man-at-arms was first to fall, shot in the face; the esquires covered Alexander as best they could; but a stone fell with stunning force on his helm, and before he could recover his guard, an arrow struck right through corselet and breast-bone to the lung. The stricken man faced the foe a few moments longer, then reeled and fell; and his shield-bearers stepped across the body for a last stand. But the Guards without the wall had been finding methods of despair, and by one way or another — by hoisting themselves on other men's shoulders, by driving pegs into the hard mud — here and there they gained the battlements, and with shouts of rage leaped down within the wall. The Indians drew back; a gate was forced; and the furious spearmen hewed their way through the fort until not a soul — man, woman, child — was left alive.

Alexander had come to himself, and demanded to have the barbed head cut out of his chest. This was done — some say by a Coan leech, others by the rude surgery of Perdiccas' sword — and in the flux of blood that followed, the Emperor fell again insensible. A report that he was dead flew round the main camp on the Chenab. But Alexander was not to die yet, and after some days, hearing that the worst news was gaining general credit, and grave disorders threatened, he demanded to be conveyed by boat down to the flotilla. As his bark approached, the whole army crowded to the shore, believing it to bring their Emperor's corpse; but ordering the curtain about his bed to be drawn aside, Alexander stretched out a hand towards the bank, and a wild shout went up from the host. Not content with this demonstration of life, he refused, on landing, to enter the litter prepared, but had himself lifted on to a horse, and so rode painfully to his tent, the scarred veterans casting flowers in his path and fighting with one another for a touch of his hand or his knee, or of just the hem of his garment.

Friends were found to tell Alexander the candid truth — that such Homeric championship was no part of the duty of a general, and least of one on whom the lives of an army depended so absolutely. But he liked best the old Boeotian pikeman, who said, in his rustic dialect, that his Captain had played the man, for in this world it is ever a law, "Take no pain, get no gain!"

Many were the days of slow convalescence ere

again the Emperor could embark, and by easy stages reach the main stream of Indus, where he decreed the founding of two cities near the point of confluence; for so he hoped to cover the great western road up the Bolan Pass, by which the larger part of the army would be bidden presently to march to Persis. Thence the flotilla dropped down to its goal, the apex of the Delta, as it was then, some miles south-east of Haiderabad,[1] and there it was docked at the deserted town of Pattala.

There was brief repose for the army, but not for its Captain. The fever of unrest had burned into his inmost soul, and, grown familiar now with ever-lengthening vistas of empire, he would accept nothing less than all the earth. His oecumenic scheme was developed fully, and henceforth would condition all his acts. First and last, Ocean was in his thoughts. Already the voyage of Nearchus was planned, the ships were collected, and the first wells dug to the eastward; and the Emperor had paid in person his solemn homage to the great World-Stream, having sailed down both outflows of Indus and a mile or two out on to the broad bosom of the deep. The main part of the Grand Army was departed already for the Bolan Pass, and, simply for the fleet's sake, a small picked force that remained was destined to follow its unsparing Captain into the hideous land of Gedrosia — he knew well how hideous![2]

---

[1] General Haig (*Indus Delta*, p. 18) places Pattala thirty-five miles south-east of Haiderabad.

[2] See Arr. vi. 24; Strabo, p. 722.

The famous ocean voyage, which the bosom friend
of Alexander's early years now volunteered to lead,
is the most curious incident in all the Conquest.
The Emperor showed a preliminary solicitude for its
equipment, a poignant anxiety for its fate, and an
exuberant joy at its safe arrival in the Persian Gulf,
which are not to be explained simply by the danger
to which he believed himself to be exposing friends
and followers. These dangers no doubt he magnified
as much as did Nearchus himself. Demon-haunted
Ocean, with its tremendous cataclysms, possessed
once a horror for the sailors of inland seas which
now can hardly be realized, even in the light of such
recitals as Arrian's account of this voyage; and, as
has been said already, Alexander had too little confidence in the ability of others to carry through critical enterprises without his own personal presence.

Nevertheless, so unique a display of nervousness
and emotion by a nature case-hardened as that of
Alexander had come to be must have drawn from
deeper sources than those of the moment or occasion.
The interests which Alexander believed to be involved
in the success of Nearchus' voyage were for him
paramount. Not only would the arrival of the fleet
in the Persian Gulf prove that the limit of earth
had been reached indeed, but also that there was
an open Ocean-way by which the different extremi-
ties of a world-empire could be joined. It may be
said with truth that Alexander was actuated by
both commercial and geographical motives. He had
commerce distinctly in view when he explored both

mouths of the Indus, and established docks in the lagoons on the eastern arm; and he proposed directly to enlarge the bounds of knowledge when he enjoined Nearchus to take careful note of all he might pass by land or sea.[1] But always there was an ulterior aim, the better securing of the permanence of his own empire. And with this in view he seems to have been possessed, in his latter years, by the idea of opening water communications. Few have had better reason than Alexander to know how slow, how costly, and how wasteful is transit by land; and after eight years spent in marching across a continent, it is small wonder that he looked about for a better way. Much of his later time was spent on the water. He was more than seven months on the Indian streams; he took ship again on the Karun River, and made his way from its mouth up the Shatt-el-Arab and the Tigris; and last of all we find him exploring the water-ways about Babylon.

Therefore Alexander endured more and spent more to ensure the success of this voyage of Nearchus than in all eight years of conquest. Starting nearly a month ahead of the fleet, he made direct for the Purali River, and thereafter, with a small detachment, followed the waterless coast-line, digging wells against the arrival of the sailors.[2] And not only temporary but permanent provision was made in the sorry Beluchi land; for after the usual raids *in terrorem*, a colony was planted on the last outskirts of cultivation,

[1] Arr. vii. 20.
[2] See Haig, *op. cit.* App. E., on this march.

surely in the least desirable locality ever favoured by
a Greek founder![1] The reason for the existence of
such a city, and indeed for any expedition into this
region, is to be sought in no other consideration than
the interests of the sea route round its coasts. Most
sparsely inhabited by unwarlike peoples, so poor as to
yield the scantiest food for those few, cut off by the
Gedrosian Desert from affording any reasonable route
to the West, Beluchistan might have been left un-
visited more fitly than many outlying districts which
Alexander had passed by — the north of Asia Minor,
for instance, the hills of Kurdistan and Armenia,
or the oases of Merv and of Khiva. In all the
Mekran Alexander met no foes, hardly even a human
being, founded no cities, and annexed no territory.
He did no more than devote himself and the lives of
his men to making provision for Nearchus. Parties
were sent down from time to time into the ghastly
littoral " to see what harbours there were existing, to
dig wells, to establish markets or stake out anchor-
ages, to prepare all, in short, for the passage of the
fleet." The explorers go down and find no living
souls but half-human fish-eaters, and returning, are
bidden by the Emperor to take all the corn that he
has been able to scrape from the upper country, and

---

[1] There seem$ to have been *two* colonies planted in Beluchistan,
not only this, alluded to in the text, founded by Leonnatus (Pliny,
N. H. vi. 23; Arr. vi. 28, 5), but also one founded by Hephaestion just west of the Purali (Arr., vi. 21. 5; and Steph. Byz.
s.v. Oritæ). Pliny indeed (*l.c.*) indicates a third — "Arbis oppi-
dum" — founded by Nearchus, but probably it was not more than
a temporary factory.

cache it here and there on the coast. The convoy itself, however, is presently so famished that it dares to break the imperial seals and eat a little of the corn ; and Alexander has no choice but to pass the heinous offence in silence.

The story of the Macedonian march through the Gedrosian Desert is like nothing so much as a feverish dream.[1] The miserable column ploughed its way, worn, famished, and parched, over an ocean of powdery hillocks into which feet sank " as in mud or untrod snow-drifts." [2] The animals laboured even more grievously than the men, and uncertainty where water would at last be found was the worst of all their miseries. The marches dragged far into the night after all a day, and far into the day after all a night.[3] Soon the men begin to kill and cut up privily the horses and mules, telling their officers that the beasts have dropped of themselves ; and though the deceit is patent, Alexander must go grimly on. There are not beasts left to carry the weak, and the waggon-loads of sick have long been abandoned in the sand. Men drop out, and die horribly, writhing as in the throes of cramp. If one falls asleep in a long night march, his comrade lets him lie, for each man thinks only of himself ; and when at last water is found, the pool is quickly fouled

---

[1] Cf. Arrian (vi. 23 ff.) with Strabo (p. 722). Neither author is given to rhetoric.

[2] Arr. vi. 24.

[3] Strabo reports that as much as seventy-five miles had to be covered on one occasion between water and water !

with swollen corpses.[1] Alexander seems to have done all in human power to lighten the awful trial, himself scouting for water and riding farthest and longest, or leading the march on foot; and if the famous story that he rejected a draught, brought to him in a helmet, be true (and if indeed it happened here, and not in the pursuit of Darius), it shows that there was not only heroism in the captain, but courage still in the men. On the sixtieth day after leaving his latest colony[2] Alexander dragged a sorry remnant into the land of the living, two-thirds, it is said, of his original force being left behind in the hell into which he had led them ; and the final halt was called late in December of 325, at a pleasant spot inland some five days' journey from the mouth of the Shur River.

Ill news met the Emperor. Craterus arrived indeed in safety with the main army, having marched by the Bolan road to the Helmund Valley, and come thence across the plains of Kirman, and great was the joy of reunion ; but with him came also evidence of much rottenness in the central provinces of the empire. Several governors had made uneasy haste to meet Alexander; and not only they, but a crowd of suppliants, anxious to report deeds of viceroys and generals done in the years of his

[1] To this march must be referred the story in Polyaenus (iv. 3. 28), that Alexander once prevented his army breaking its ranks by declaring a river to be poisonous.

[2] Mr. Curzon says (*Persia*, ii. p. 234) that from Alexander in 325 B.C. to the year 1809 A.D., no European is recorded to have penetrated into the interior of the Mekran.

absence. The chief crimes alleged seem to have had a political and religious colour, namely, violation and robbery of temples and tombs, especially in the holy places of Persis.[1] We are told no more than that in many cases Alexander held guilt to be proved, and had governors degraded or executed; which severity pleased mightily the Persians, and instilled a wholesome terror into those in authority throughout the empire. We could wish, however, to have had more information as to the motives and nature of the proved acts; for that this sacrilegious form of robbery should have prevailed exclusively, where so many other forms were possible, and mainly in Persis and Media, is strongly suggestive of an organized policy on the part of the Macedonians left in those provinces, to counteract by insult and spoliation Alexander's favour to Persians at the front. It is said that successive rumours of the Emperor's death in India and in Gedrosia had reached the central provinces; and these may have unchained there those national hatreds which Alexander had almost effaced from the Grand Army.

Grave as were these troubles, they seem to have weighed on Alexander less heavily than the absence of news from Nearchus; and no messenger ever brought him tidings more welcome than a local official from the Gulf, who appeared in the camp one

---

[1] The violation of the Tomb of Cyrus is the capital instance, and Strabo's emphatic statement about it (p. 730) really goes farther to confirm than to refute the accusation against the satrap; it certainly supports the theory that the crime was political.

day, saying he had seen the fleet. In hot haste
messengers posted along various roads to summon
Nearchus inland; but when days passed and no
confirmation of the news came in, despair took possession of Alexander. The first messenger, however,
had spoken truly enough, and, as Arrian pictures it,
giving momentary play to the Greek in himself, a
few mariners, weather-beaten out of all recognition,
the sea-salt stiff in their hair, and their faces bleached
by long sea vigils, were brought at last to the camp,
where none knew them at first sight, and so into
Alexander's presence. The Emperor came forward to
meet them, and, falling on the neck of the admiral,
fell a-weeping for the crews of which he supposed
them to survive alone. Whereupon Nearchus made
haste to announce that all his ships were safe and
sound in port, and Alexander wept the more for joy,
and swore a great oath that he would rather hear
that news than be hailed conqueror of Asia from sea
to sea!

The story that Nearchus had to tell must have
fallen upon Alexander's curious ear like the tales
brought back by seamen of Magellan. And even as
we hear it now, shorn of almost every grace, and
become hardly more than a catalogue of the daily
runs, even so, in the meagre narration of a Roman
officer, it retains a certain odour of salt and mystery
of the unknown sea. We are shown the nervous
crews, hardly reassured by the thought that their
Emperor, having put in command one of his dearest
friends, cannot expect them indeed to perish, creeping

out of the Indus estuary and beating up the coast to north-west, having made an inauspicious start before their time for fear of the Indians, who had become insolent and aggressive since the departure of the Army.[1] Then for four and twenty days they are forced to await the lulling of a head monsoon, but at last they can beat out again and hug noon by noon along the shore, pushing timidly between islands and the coast for fear of the swell of open ocean. They seem to have been equipped with little or no appliance for storing water, and, like the land army, to have been expected to live entirely on what they could find on their way. Once they shipped as much as ten days' provision, but soon fell into dearth and distress again, having aboard no standby, it seems, of dried flesh, or biscuit, or grain. Therefore they had to land continually, and indeed they suffered sorely if the sea was kept for long together, for the boats were cranky, needing frequently to be overhauled, and most of the sailors no better than sheer landsmen, worn out as much by the swell of the great deep as by their ceaseless fears. Arrian interrupts his catalogue at rare intervals to give a picture of some shore adventure. At one point half-naked savages rushed to the water's edge brandishing heavy lances with fire-hardened points, and the ships, like the typical pirate schooner with its brass guns, threw bolts and stones from engines on their decks, and under such cover the lighter armed and more active swam to the shallows, and there forming, charged

---

[1] Strabo, p. 721.

up the beach. But at other points the natives bring
down kindly enough their poor gifts of fish and
meats and fruits of the earth, only to be tricked on
one occasion by Nearchus with such sorry perfidy as
our navigators used often enough in the South Seas.
For, gaining entrance in all amity to a stockade, the
admiral shut the gates and held the fence till search
had been made from house to house for grain. Very
little was found after all, for the wretched Ichthyo-
phagi used powdered flesh of fish for their flour, and
even the sheep ate sea things, and tasted like sea-bird
meat; and we may hope that Nearchus and his
buccaneers went back a little shamefaced to their
ships. A comic scene of panic is caused by a school
of blowing whales; but Nearchus, taking heart and
ordering his men to shout the war-cry and his
trumpets to sound, puts his own ship at a spouting
monster, who astonished — and no wonder! — dives
incontinent and, coming up again astern, spouts
as before; and all the sailors breathe again and
hail Nearchus as their only saviour. Thus in much
distress for grain and all kinds of food, the fleet
reached at last the mouth of the Persian Gulf, and
came near making across, on the advice of Onesicritus,
to Ras Mussendom, which loomed high on their left
hand. In which event they would have wandered
down the coasts of Oman and Muscat, and probably
have perished miserably without seeing the Army
again. But fortunately Nearchus insisted that the
letter of his commission enjoined him to explore all
the coast-line, gulf and bay alike, and so they kept

17

on, hugging the right-hand shore, and about the
eightieth day since first loosing from the Indus bank
brought up in a harbour hard by Bunder Abbas.
There they went ashore to build a stockade and to
recruit, and certain of them, all unsuspecting, lighted
on a man dressed as a Greek and speaking the Greek
tongue; and they fell on his neck, and asked how
he came into that strange land. But behold, he
was one of the Army, and the Emperor himself
was distant but five days' journey in the upper
country. Whereupon Nearchus and Archias took a
few followers and made inland for the camp, as
already has been narrated.

This voyage, thought so marvellous a feat, is no
more than the short steam run from Karachi to
Bunder Abbas;[1] and, in fact, it added little enough
to the knowledge which the Army itself had bought
so dearly by the land march. But as Columbus for
the Spanish and Portuguese navigators, so Nearchus
for the Greek, swept away by this venture a barrier
of superstitious imaginings more awful than all the
storms of the deep. Like that mysterious island
at the mouth of the Persian Gulf, on which no
man could land and live, till Nearchus showed it
to be not different from any other land, so the
Ocean had been proved at last to be essentially a
sea like any other familiar sea, vexed, indeed, with
greater heavings, running with a mightier surf on
its coasts, and subject to wider change of tide, but

---

[1] The eastern portion of it is treated with special local knowledge by Gen. Haig. (*op. cit.*, pp. 10 ff. and App. F.).

devoid as the waters of Greece of demoniac whirlpools
and magnetic rocks and man-eating sirens and worse
terrors without name passing the wit of man to avoid.
To Alexander in particular the voyage seemed to
make certain much that had been most doubtful
before. The problem how he should conquer the
other half of the earth now appeared shorn of half its
difficulty. For surely he might sail on westwards
where Nearchus had shown the way. Henceforth
there need be but few of those heartbreaking marches
of the earlier conquest, which year by year led farther
from the base and ended in despair and mutiny; for
the sea would afford a main road, always open.[1]
Accordingly Alexander's last months were all devoted
to preparing for a great expedition by way of Ocean.
Ships were to be brought in sections from the
Phoenician ports to the Euphrates, put together on
the river, and navigated down to Babylon. Scouting vessels were sent out to determine the projection
of Arabia; and the waterways from the Gulf to the
huge dock projected at the capital, were explored
and rendered navigable.

It has been a commonplace of historians to depict
Alexander as emerging a madman from Gedrosia;

[1] He had not emancipated himself, however, from the necessity
of having an accompanying land force (cf. Arr. vii. 25). But
the ships were evidently to be the main vehicle of the advance,
and would be invaluable for the transport of a proper siege train,
the conveyance of which by land had been all along one of
Alexander's most insuperable difficulties. Cf. Diod. xvii. 22, for
the retention of a few ships in 334, probably to serve a like
purpose.

and, indeed, he might well have been no less, seeing that the horrors of that march, in which he had spared himself no more than of old, followed within a few months on the terrible wound at Mooltan ; seeing, further, that that hurt was preceded by three others in the Afghan hills; that in Turkestan the fibula of his leg had been broken, and he had all but died of dysentery ; while all these strains have to be added to a list already long enough when the advance to the Far East was begun ! [1]

None the less, if he is to be judged by his acts, Alexander was never in fuller possession of bodily and mental vigour than in his last two years. He displayed, indeed, exuberances and passions exaggerated to the point of disease, but never was more clear and tenacious of purpose, or more astute and bold in adopting and adapting means. The half world he had won already had to be ordered and made secure, and, that done, in pursuance of a scheme long formed he meant to march to win the other half. But bitter experience had shown, that a second time neither might he leave national divisions unreconciled behind him, nor could he dare to start with a simple national army. The task, therefore, to which he set himself, in the years 324 and 323, was the fusion of nationalities alike in the official and military classes. He found it necessary both to destroy and construct. First he must purge the officials of their stiff-necked nationalists — that he effected by judicial process in Carmania and Persis ; and he must clear the army of

---

[1] *Supra*, p. 222.

the stiff-necked veterans—this he did at Opis. Second, it behoved to import into both services, as far as possible, an element ready fused. This object was attained, for better or for worse, by the Susian orgy of intermarriage, and by drafting Orientals into all ranks of the army. Incidentally to the main issue Alexander contrived to remodel his own court, to reform the tactical structure of his army, to distribute his offensive strength between land and sea, to institute relations with western courts, and to neutralize the ever-pressing danger of Greek jealousy. A full two-years' record, it must be allowed, even for a sane man!

It will be objected, however, that neither tenacity in the pursuit of an aim, nor extreme astuteness in the choice of means, are inconsistent with mania. The true test is the nature of the aim. Waiving the tenable position that the scale of Alexander's provision and preparation is too vast to be consistent with anything like madness as usually understood, let us be content to consider simply this final aim, which has been called mad, the aim, in short, of world-empire. Must we deem it mad, because no sane person at the time could have conceived its accomplishment? As the map of the world was pictured in the fourth century before our era, Alexander would imagine that he had not more left to win than already was his. Both on the Sir Daria and the Sutlej he saw reason to believe that the limit of earth was so near as, in the one case, to render further advance unnecessary, in the other, to necessitate perhaps a single additional campaign. Recall that he was now not much more than thirty-one years of age; that with the exception of a few outlying provinces, his conquests had not proved difficult to hold together, while he believed himself to have established a new and quicker route for his main advance, and an ever-open road of communication. As the scheme of the second conquest would have been projected on such a chart as could have been set out at Babylon in 323, how would it have appeared manifestly impossible? Others beside Alexander, and later than he, saw no impossibility in the accomplishment of his last programme, or Livy would not have had to maintain that Rome could have held her own against even the Macedonian.[1]

But if the sane contemporary would have believed the scheme not impossible, could he sanely have held its accomplishment justified by the laws of God or man? Here we enter on the question of historical right and wrong, a slippery matter, wherein the ethics of a later age are most apt to be substituted for the ethics of contemporaries. The right of the stronger to take and hold was as much morality as a Macedonian king could be expected to practise; and for the very highest international ethics of the time we need look no further than that famous statement made by Alexander's own tutor concerning Hellenes and barbarians in the opening of his treatise on Politic. Aristotle at least, who there laid it down that the higher civilization has

[1] ix. 17.

right absolute to enslave the lower, would not have
condemned on moral grounds Alexander's scheme.

On the ground, however, that that scheme was not
conceived in the interests of Hellenism unalloyed, the
great thinker might have condemned it, probably as
he did condemn much that Alexander had done. But
to such a judgment posterity must make reply that,
in the expansion of Hellas, contaminated Hellenism
was soon proved to go farther and effect more than
Hellenism pure. Aristotle, living in an epoch of
transition a life secluded from affairs, was more prone
to look back and less able to see forward in such
an inquiry, than those who had been engaged, with
however little understanding, in planting the Hellene
in new soils. And, indeed, if Alexander were conscious that a question of morality was involved in
conquest at all, he might well have held all the
right to be on his own side, and yet, as the ethics
of his age stood, and as have stood the ethics of
many ages subsequent to his, have been absolutely
sane.

If we look to the means which Alexander adopted
in his last months to advance his great aim, we
perceive that in conception he anticipated the cardinal
cause of the provincial success of the Roman Empire.
For he saw that universal conquests could not be
accomplished, still less retained, with the strength
of a single mother-people, but that the one half
the world must be enlisted to conquer and hold the
other half. Had he lived to subdue North Africa,
we may be sure that Moors and Numidians would

have been found fighting under his banners in Spain and Gaul, and Spaniards and Gauls in Italy. His mixed army of Europeans and Asiatics, organized in Babylon in the spring of 323, was no more than the predecessor of those Gaulish and German legions which brought Emperors to Rome.

When the historian finds Alexander punishing with drastic severity Viceroys of his own race whom he believed, wrongly or rightly, to have outraged alien faiths and extorted provincial money, his thought will pass on to Tiberius and the *quinquennium Neronis*. When he sees Persians and Bactrians set high in a Macedonian empire, he thinks of Trajan the Spaniard, Elagabalus the Syrian, Maximin the Goth, and Philip the Arabian. The so-called Epigoni — those Oriental youths trained in the Macedonian manner, who were brought to Susa to be enrolled — recall the heirs of client kings, educated perforce in the Eternal City, and those children of the camps, who were the backbone of the legionary system. Only when we come to assist at the famous marriage festival whereat Alexander and all his captains formally took to themselves wives of the Orientals, and prizes and remission of debts were promised to such of the rank and file as would follow that example and beget citizens of the united empire, do we lose sight of Rome. Nothing so artificial ever entered into the policy of the most cosmopolitan of the Italian emperors.[1]

---

[1] Alexander's project of forcing races to exchange habitats (mentioned already in note to p. 209) should be recalled here, although it was never carried out. Grote regards it as a new and

The Roman universal empire, however, was a system independent of the life of an individual ; the Macedonian empire, as yet, but an expression of the genius of one man. The distinction is too obvious to need precision. What the cosmopolitan emperors of Rome inherited crystallized through unconscious centuries, Alexander had received fluid from his father. Did we know more details of the forty years of Augustus, we might find actions not less artificial than the Susian nuptials, although whereas the first Roman Emperor had ready to his hand the work of the last Dictator and all two centuries of senatorial system, the Macedonian had to start, like a Scipio, with just a military system and a hardly welded nation. Alexander, it may be, showed himself in this matter the young man in a hurry. But, be it not forgotten, he had to conquer young or conquer not at all, for only in full physical vigour could he hope to endure such labours as he was projecting for himself ; and further, that haste largely spells success in the subduing of low civilizations. Rapid action is apt to be dubbed hurry or decision, as it fails or succeeds. Alexander had not the deliberate Western to deal with, but quick, adaptable Hellenes, who, as all know who are familiar with them now in Asia and Africa, rapidly form with Oriental civilizations an amalgam marvellously last-

monstrous conception, abhorrent to the humane world. But surely such tribe-transportation had long been a Persian usage ? Philip himself had practised it in Paeonia (Justin, viii. 5 ; see *Philip*, p. 103), and it is part of our own habitual policy on the north-west frontier of our Indian Empire.

ing. We are considering for the moment, not the advantage of this amalgam, but the mode of its formation and its chances of permanence ; and in this connection it is enough to remind critics that a "mixed" empire, with an Asiatic centre, successively Seleucid, Parthian, and Persian, survived Alexander's death by fully a thousand years.

The mutiny of the Army, which the concentration of so much artificial action into a few months induced presently at Opis, can make no difference to a judgment of Alexander's policy by results, for, so far as we can see, that mutiny left no mark. The Emperor deviated not one whit from his purpose ; the Army continued loyal as before. The time-expired men went home ; those designated for further service remained with the colours, and a year later displayed more conspicuous devotion than ever to their dying Captain. The ebullition had but left the Empire stronger, as the casting out of humours by an unsightly eruption leaves the body.

Late in 324 Alexander passed from the southern Residences to his northern capital, making, in a sort, an imperial progress through the heart of the Empire, to appease recent griefs and promote future unity ; and at Ecbatana there fell upon him, as a stunning blow, the loss of Hephaestion. It followed close on the second treason and final flight of another of the few intimates of his boyhood, Harpalus, whilom Treasurer of the Empire, who, conscious of vast peculations and most unbridled life, vanished from

Babylon as his master approached from the East, and
fled to make a chapter of history in the last days
of free Athens. And now Hephaestion, too, was gone,
the congenial enthusiastic nature which had been so
much more to Alexander than Ptolemy's sagacity or
Nearchus' careful courage, the friend, more than a
friend, and closer than a brother, who alone awoke
a gentler emotion in the breast of the lonely Conqueror. For there come, alike in discouragement and
exaltation, to all men, however strong of body or
brain, moments of craving, in which the soul gropes
blindly for another soul ; and the most strong, if he
owns this need most rarely, feels it most imperious.
The blood of Olympias ran hotly in the veins of her
son beneath that crust with which ambition and its
fulfilment had overlaid him. In all things passionate,
he passionately craved sympathy, and all the masterful yearnings of his soul had been satisfied first and
only by Hephaestion. The rest of the world had
dwindled beneath his feet; and lo! now in a
moment he was left in such a solitude as has
seldom been the doom even of kings. All the
savage in Alexander was unchained : he passed
from paroxysm to paroxysm of emotion, at one
moment abased in utter despair, at another seeking
to fulfil his soul in strenuous cruelty. The last
resources of extravagance were exhausted in sending
the dear ghost worthily to the world below, and such
a monument arose as only kings can raise to the
one human being with whom they have been able
to lay aside the king.

Little by little time assuaged the pain, and his great scheme of coming conquest resumed its mastery over Alexander's mind. He set out for Babylon very early in the new year, and not inopportunely encountered on his road a group of envoys, despatched by many peoples of Africa and Europe who had caught the fast-spread news that the Conqueror of the East was coming to the West. The Ethiopian kingdom of Meröe, the great Republic of Carthage, many races of Spain and southern Gaul, and certain peoples of central and southern Italy, sent to spy the way of the wind. Envoys from the rising Republic of Rome, however, did not accompany the other Italians;[1] and this fact suggests that among the objects of the latter was the securing, if possible, a future friend against the menacing growth of the former.

The sight of the men of the West would seem to have revived all Alexander's interest in his oecumenic dream; for we hear that he sent an officer back to explore the Caspian, and find its opening into the girdle Stream.[2] And his spirit so far recovered that

---

[1] Can any one maintain the contrary now, in face of the express statement of so well read a Greek as Arrian, a Roman official of Hadrian's time, that all the Latin and all the decent Greek authorities omitted mention of any Roman embassy (see Arr. vii. 15)? The earlier letter of Alexander to the Romans *in re* the Illyrian pirates (Strabo, p. 232), has also been often called in question, *e. g.* by Grote, Westermann, etc.; but Thirlwall, Niebuhr, and Schäfer accepted it.

[2] According to Strabo's authorities (p. 509), Alexander seems to have supposed the Caspian to communicate with the Sea of Azov, and both with the Ocean.

he made sport of certain solemn words of the priests of Bel who came out to deter him from entering their city of Babylon "There are prophets good and prophets bad," laughed the Emperor, quoting Euripides; "the best guesser is the best seer." For he knew that these priests had peculiar reasons for not desiring his presence in Babylon, where he might be expected to make inquiry into certain trust-funds of the god. Nevertheless, he was rendered somewhat uneasy by the persistence of the prophets of evil, and would have gladly given way to their super-stitions so far as to enter his capital with face to the rising, not the setting sun; but finding that he could not take an army through the western marshes, in the end he came in by the east.

Alexander's intention was to start for Arabia late in the coming summer, and Babylon was already a scene of tense activity. Embassies from the leading states of Greece were waiting to assure their over-lord that the civic governments had accepted his imperial decree,[1] promulgated at the late Olympic festival, that they should amnesty and receive back their several political exiles, and thus divide their houses against themselves. The ships, ordered in sections from Phoenicia, had arrived; along the quays of Euphrates others were in building, while a myriad crew had begun to excavate a basin to hold a thousand hulls.

---

[1] Their compliance, as a matter of fact, left a good deal to be desired. Cf. Diod. xviii. 8, and inscriptions and authorities quoted in Droysen.

Cruisers sailed out at once to explore the Persian Gulf and bring back word of Arabia. But in the event they could only report that the peninsula would take more time to circumnavigate than Alexander had imagined; for the boldest skipper had gone no farther than the coast of Oman. Meanwhile the Emperor was waiting for his lieutenants to bring down from Persis the picked Asiatics whom he proposed to draft into his Army of the West, and he took occasion of the delay to explore the waterways on the west of the main stream of Euphrates, which creep through a wild tract of reedy marsh, full of ruinous tombs of long-forgotten kings. Especially he proposed to see the so-called *Pallacopas*, a canal which acted as a huge culvert to draw off the spring inundations into the marshes. The cutting and closing of its slimy embankments had given annual trouble in default of proper sluices, and Alexander now selected a spot for a main water-gate, and left instructions to his engineers to execute a great work for the better regulation of the outflow in the coming summer.

He returned to Babylon with the spring, to find twenty thousand picked Asiatics arrived, and he set himself to draft them into the ranks of the Grand Army on a new system, probably thought out long before. His primary object being half-political, he required that the Asiatic element should be fused entirely with his Macedonians and Greeks. This could not be effected to any real purpose by simply arming and drilling the new recruits like the rest, and letting them rank in distinct brigades. Rather it was necessary to incorporate them in the Macedonian regiments themselves. This policy, however, entailed a further military change of the most signal sort. The Oriental recruits were not adapted for ordinary phalanx fighting; to make them adopt inordinately long pikes, heavy body-armour and close order, was to make inferior heavy files of men who had superior capacity for light warfare. Alexander was probably not averse on any grounds to a radical modification of the old phalanx formation, which even his father had never valued very highly. The son, so far as we can follow in singularly deficient authorities his successive efforts at reorganization, had been inspired in every military change by a desire to promote greater capacity for division and, by consequence, greater ease of movement. For some years he had been using but seldom the old close formation — even in pitched battle at the Hydaspes his pikemen seem to have attacked in open order [1] — and now that he had a steadfast nucleus of veterans, he proposed to throw the compact phalanx overboard. The basis of the new disposition was to be the file of sixteen. In this only the three leaders and the rear-rank man were to be Macedonian pikemen; the core, ranged twelve deep in open order, was, throughout the fighting line, to be composed of Asiatic archers and throwers of missiles. We are told no further details, but we

---

[1] Cf. a statement of Frontinus (i. 3. 1), that Alexander always fought in *line* (*i. e.* not in the regular column formation of the phalanx), if his army appeared eager for the fray.

may be sure that the general idea implied that the light files should sally forth to attack, and retire, when charged, behind the triple wall of pike-heads. Fate ordained that the new organization should never be used in the field by its inventor; but it is obvious that, had he himself survived to discipline and direct it, a new infantry array would have come into being as much superior in mobility to the old Macedonian and Theban formations as the latter in their day had been to the Spartan. For, if for no other reason, when three-fourths of each file, which formerly could only back up the front ranks by its weight or fill the places of the slain, was employed in active operations of offence and defence, the whole force was become vastly more effective.

We have said that its inventor never used this new disposition; and there is no evidence that any one else adopted it. Certainly in European Macedonia the older formation held the day until its glaring defects were found out by the Roman legionaries. The reason is no doubt that no one in that age could have fought with Alexander's new phalanx except Alexander. He had left it untried, and probably largely untrained; and since it is a commonplace of strategy that a mobile force manœuvring in many units, while vastly more effective, if well handled, than a compact force of few units, is fraught with the greater danger if disordered, this new mixed phalanx demanded, after its inventor's death, first a further organizer, and second a great leader. Alexander left behind him many capable marshals, but certainly not one heaven-born genius in war.

The drafting seems to have been superintended by Alexander in person, for a story, told by a good authority, has survived, concerning an omen that occurred when the king had been sitting through a long day, seeing to the incorporation of the Asiatics. Feeling athirst, he rose, and left his throne empty for a few moments, during which some crazy creature, such as begs in Eastern streets, wandered, no one observing, towards the royal chair, and sat himself down. The eunuchs, moved by some occult superstition, dared not drag him away, but beat their breasts for a calamity to come ; and although Alexander had the man seized and examined under torture, yet he said nothing more than that he had done this thing he knew not why, the spirit moving him.

It was already summer. The Army of the West was organized, dock and ships were ready, and captains and full crews had been allotted to each vessel. The Emperor had fixed the 19th of the current month for the start of the division, which was to follow the fleet along the coast, and the 20th for his own departure for the Gulf. It was now the 14th, and nothing remained except the final sacrificial ceremonies and festivals of adieu. Huge Babylon thronged in that brilliant May with the officers and men of the great Expedition, and with embassies and countless officials, sent up even from Antipater's vice-royalty of Europe to wish the Emperor good speed.

From this point the Court Diary narrates the catastrophe, and a historian had best imitate the admirable simplicity with which its entries have been reproduced by both Arrian and Plutarch, the latter expressing a noble sense that no rhetoric or dramatic setting can enhance the pathos of the story. On the 15th a great feast was given to the Grand Army,[1] at the expense of the Emperor, who presided in person. He would have retired thence to bed, but a Thessalian officer, one Medius, who seems to have succeeded in some way to the privileges of Hephaestion, prayed him to honour a parting revel. Alexander consented, and stayed through the night. The next evening he honoured Medius again, and once more sat long over the wine. Towards dawn he rose from table, bathed, and breakfasted, but feeling somewhat feverish, ate but little before lying down to sleep. He woke after a few hours in a high fever, but insisted none the less on offering the daily sacrifice, and talking with the generals over details of the Expedition, decreed to start in three days' time. Thereafter he had himself carried to a cool garden-house beyond the river; but the fever did not abate for the change, and he had to put off the setting-forth of the Expedition first by one day, and then definitely to the 23rd. On the 21st and 22nd he convened the generals again, to remind them that all must be ready; but he was now very ill, and, needless to say, on the 23rd no corps moved from Babylon. The Emperor, none the less, talked still in half-delirium

[1] Or to the crews of the fleet only? (Plut. *Alex.* 75).

of the start, and on the morrow, taking a fancy
that the commanders must stay nearer to him, had
himself carried back to the great Palace in the
city, where they could wait in the ante-chambers;
but when they came into his presence he could not
utter a word. For two days and nights the fever
raged still more fiercely, and on the 27th[1] a clamour
rose in the ranks of the Grand Army that the
Emperor was already dead, and the generals were
hiding the fact. Veterans gathered thick about the
palace gates, demanding admission to the death-
chamber, until, for fear of mutiny, the chamberlains
were forced to admit them in Indian file : and so the
old spearmen of the Asian Conquest passed in a last
review before their Captain, but he " could not speak,
and only touched the right hand of each, and raised
his head a little, and signed with his eyes." That
night certain of the marshals kept vigil in the fane
of Serapis, seeking a sign that they should convey
the Emperor, as a last hope, to the presence of the
god. But a voice from the night bade them let him
be, and towards sundown of the 28th Alexander died.[2]

We are told that deep silence fell upon the great city
and camp of Babylon for four days and four nights,
each man looking helplessly to his helpless neighbour;

---

[1] Plutarch, using also the royal journal, puts this event a day
earlier, and leaves about thirty-six hours between the vigil of the
marshals in the temple and the end.

[2] The symptoms and cause of this malady have been treated,
though somewhat cursorily, by E. Littré (*Sur la maladie d'A.
le G.* Paris, 1842) : the doctor decides positively against poison.
Without this expert opinion, the question would be even less easy to

and thereafter, the embalmed body lay other thirty days while there was being decided the first tussle of that funeral contest, which, grimly foretold by the dying Emperor, would shake his empire from sea to sea. The great Expedition of conquest never started ; the Grand Army never fought again under one leader ; the Empire never owned a second single

decide than that other, which arises from Alexander's death — Did he leave any will, or depute any successor to his empire? A death-bed partition of the world by him was a favourite fancy of romanticists and rhetoricians; we find it as early as the First Book of Maccabees (i. 6) — "He parted his kingdom among them, while he was yet alive ; " — and it reappears in all versions and derivatives of the Romance cycle. But against it we have the weighty negative evidence of the better historians, who repeat nothing but his whisper, "τῷ κρατίστῳ," — "to the best man." In fact, by the time Alexander could realize that he was in danger he had become almost incapable of speech and half-delirious; and it should be noted that the Army acted after his death as if entirely unguided by any word of their dead Captain. His last despatches, opened by Craterus in Cilicia, seem to have been in no sense testamentary.

As to the poison question, circumstantial evidence would leave the decision very doubtful. On the one hand, we have Plutarch's statement that no hint of it was heard for six years, until Olympias found she could use it as a charge against Cassander ; and the further fact that, whatever fears Antipater and Cassander might have entertained, they were about to be left in peace for many years while the Emperor was conquering the West. On the other hand, it must be said that suspicion of poison attaches so inevitably to a royal death-bed in the East, that it is almost incredible that nothing should have been said in this case for six years, unless it was the interest of some one in power to suppress what was a well-known fact. Alexander's recent developments of imperial impartiality supplied motive enough to unmitigated Macedonians like Antipater and his son ; and the accounts of the poisoning, though conflicting, are precise enough. On the whole, we may fall back with thankfulness, though without entire conviction, on the expert decision of the question.

Emperor; the destinies of the West were left to be settled by Carthage and by Rome. But although nothing that Alexander left unfinished at his death was done by another as he himself would have done it, very little that, indeed, he had done was ever undone. No part of the vast area, that he had traversed this side the Indus, was governed for many centuries but by an administration western in origin or in type. Greece never recovered an independent voice to recall her sons from their mission in the ends of the earth, and Hellenisticism grew steadily out of Hellenism. Alexander's own principle and model of colonization, the general scheme of his provincial organization, the channels into which half-unconsciously he had directed trade, his types and standards of currency, and the military system of his father and himself, held good until, and even beyond, the coming of Rome. He did more than any single man to break down that proud division of the world into few Greeks and myriad barbarians, which had stimulated the seed of civilization, but was become a cramping and suffocating influence on the grown plant. He did more than any single man up to his day to make one part of the world known to the other, and, unconsciously enough, so to widen the application of his great tutor's principle of social organization, that little more than three centuries later a Church became possible which contained Jews, Greeks, and Latins, "Parthians, and Medes, and Elamites, and the dwellers in Mesopotamia."

The personal figure of Alexander has never suffered

eclipse. Because his empire in no part, but the
Indian, reverted to what it had been before him, he
himself put on instant immortality as the political
god of his legacy of kingdoms from the Oxus to
the Nile. For many generations idealized portraits
stamped on coins kept his individuality in mind over
well-nigh all the world. The Seleucid Empire, the
Ptolemaic kingdom of Egypt, and the original realm
of Macedon maintained a worship of him as the
genius of Hellenistic rule. Groves and games, altars
and images [1] took his name, and he seems to have
been promoted definitely, even by the Senate of
Rome, to a thirteenth throne in the august circle
of Olympus. The organizer of that greater empire,
which absorbed nearly all that Alexander had won,
and under whose system in a sense we live still, set
him up as chief of his gods. Augustus not only
paid to Alexander divine honours, and used his
effigy as the imperial signet, but imitated, we are
told, the knitting of the brows which was habitual to
the Macedonian, and that famous inclination of his
beautiful head towards the left shoulder, which the
Marshals and Successors had affected, and we hear
of as a fashion still in the time of Severus.[2]

This cult of a Hellenistic Genius supplied a model
for the establishment of the universal worship of the

---

[1] See, *e.g.* Strabo, p. 644 (Clazomenæ); Amm. Marcell. 22. 8
(Borysthenes); Clem. Alex. *Coh. ad Gent.* p. 211. A. ed. Migne
(Alexandria); Chrysost. vol. xi. p. 240 (Antioch).

[2] See Clem. Alex. *l.c.*; Cyril, *c. Julian.* vi. p. 205; Chrysost.
In Ep. 2 *ad Cor. Hom.* 26, p. 580; Suet. *Aug.* 18, 50; Aurel.
Vict. *Epit.* xxi. 4, p. 211; Themist. *Orat.* 13, p. 175, B.

Genius of Roman Empire. But, unlike Augustus, Alexander the man was never lost in an impersonal system. He had been so pre-eminent above his followers in almost all his powers, he had done so much of his work with his own hand, and exalted so conspicuously his own personality always and everywhere, that in tradition and legend his individuality could not die. Him the Parsees curse still as the destroyer of their sacred books at Persepolis; he, as *Iskender D'hulkarnein*, or *el Junani*, " the Ionian," is reverenced still as mythic founder of nearly every old city from the Euphrates to the frontier of China. The making of his myth began early. At the very first the mere possession of his body had been accounted the best of all title-deeds in the scarcely established order of things; and the dispute for its possession, the gorgeous funeral train which after the lapse of a year set out with it for Damascus, the beauty of the sarcophagus, in which it was conveyed to Memphis, and the splendour of its ultimate installation in Alexandria, were hardly less notorious than the living man had been. And if Alexandria ascribed the birth of its fame to Alexander, Alexander in turn has owed much of his own undying memory to Alexandria. For whereas the tombs of Roman Emperors rose outside a capital which had seen centuries of greatness before them, and rulers as conspicuous since their day, Alexander lay in the heart of a city he had himself created, and in which he was the first and only Emperor. The two main streets of the town met and crossed before his mausoleum. Round about it, in reverent subordination, were laid the generations of the royal dead of Egypt. The façade of the Museum, focus of Hellenic culture, and resort of the civilized world, faced across to his sepulchre. No god displaced Alexander there. Emperors of Rome, who came to his city, Augustus and Severus, made pilgrimage first to his tomb, and paid homage to his embalmed corpse ;[1] and still at this day, after a dozen centuries of decline, and three generations of rapid renewing, the holiest place in Alexandria is believed to conceal Alexander's grave.

Nor is this all. Long after Clement could point in fervid exultation to the ruined tomb of the city-god, whose mortality had been proved at Babylon, even after Islam had swept over all his empire, Alexander was still growing in name and fame. The ubiquitous traditions of his actual words and deeds, the local identifications of him with older folk-heroes, which cropped up presently over all the western East, and most in Hellenistic Egypt, were collected from time to time, and made the basis of popular tales ; and at last, probably about the third century of our era, all were crystallized into a single work of romance, which in a thousand years passed into more men's ears, and became the spring and basis of more literature, than any record of true history. The Greek Romance, whose earliest form has come down to us under a false name of the historian Callisthenes, strings on a tangled thread of

[1] Suet. *Aug.* 18 ; Dio. lxxv. 13.

ALEXANDER OF EPIRUS H
T

Alexander's real words and acts a fascinating broidery of those marvels and moralities which are the common heritage of half the world. From the Greek it has passed to Latin, to Syriac, to Ethiopic, to Arabic, to Hebrew, to Samaritan, to Armenian, to Persian; from the Latin to early English, to French, to German, to Italian, even to Scandinavian. Through this universal cycle Alexander took on new immortality as the evidence of his actual works on earth grew fainter. Islam itself adopted him among her Prophets, and carried his forgotten fame back into India. A world that he himself never saw, on the Ganges[1] and the Blue Nile, in Britain and in Provence, became familiar with his name; until his romance ended by ousting his history from Byzantine chroniclers, and still, by a curious irony, engrosses most the attention of scholars.[2]

Independently, however, of all myth or romance, Alexander has been received into the small circle of

---

[1] See especially Spiegel, *Die Alexandersage bei den Orientalen*, and chap. 6 of the fifth book of the same author's monumental *Eranische Alterthumskunde*.

[2] Within a very few years, we have had elaborate works produced in England by Dr. Wallis Budge on the Syriac and Ethiopic versions. The early French, the early English, and texts of the Latin versions, have been published in a generation which has seen no critical edition of Arrian or Plutarch. Articles and inaugural dissertations on this subject succeed one another in Germany, and recently Th. Reinach has published a fragment of a new Greek version (*Revue des Études Grecques*, 1892, p. 306). Indeed, to obtain the reward of public interest for a real addition to knowledge, a scholar could not do better now than re-edit the original pseudo-Callisthenes, disentangling its skeins, arriving through the versions at its earliest form, and showing

the Great. The proud title is his not as conscious apostle of light any more than as " gurges ille miseriarum atque atrocissimus turbo totius Orientis," [1] but because, having the greatest powers, he set up the greatest aims consistent with his day, and pursued them greatly. Philip lives hardly outside the world of scholars. The son is still a master to all masters in war, and his type has been chosen by Art for the Hero. Judge how we may his intentions and his acts, this at least cannot be doubted, that since so much that he said and did, and so much that is credited to him, has passed into the common thought and speech of mankind, saint or sinner, devil or god, Alexander is among the Immortals.

what amount of real tradition and genuine folk-lore it embodies: and he will find considerable help in the recently published work of R. Raabe ('Ιστορία 'Αλεξάνδρου. Leipz. 1896), who has rendered the Mechitarist text of the very early Armenian version back into Greek.

[1] Orosius, *Hist.* iii. 7.

ALEXANDER HAMILTON
From a Medal — Original in France

APPENDIX

On Questions of Chronology in Alexander's Reign

SINCE the accepted schedule of Greek chronology was drawn
out, mainly by Ideler and Clinton, there have not been
wanting scholars to call the foundations of the whole system
in question; and we may yet be asked to renounce even
those cardinal dates which, calculated on certain eclipses,
have served for starting and correcting points. Whenever
that revolution takes place the reigns of Philip and Alexander
no doubt will have to be moved back or forward *en bloc*.
But since those wholesale processes can hardly make any
difference to the actual consecution of events, and since,
relatively to one another, the items of the careers of both
kings will maintain their position, for the present we may
leave the larger question alone and make inquiry only into
the relative dating of certain events in the reign of Alexander,
which have been subject of controversy [1] or need to be discussed. These fall into two divisions :—

(A.) The cardinal dates of Alexander's Birth, Accession,
and Death.

[1] The works to which I shall refer directly or indirectly most often are
Ideler, *Ueber das Todesjahr A. des G.* (Abhandl. d. Berlin. Akad., 1820),
and *Handb. d. math. und techn. Chronologie;* Droysen, *Hellenismus*, vol.
i., Fr. tr., app. vi.; Clinton, *Fasti Hellenici*, vol. ii.; Unger in I. v. Müller's
Handb. der klass. Alterthums-Wissenschaft, pp. 773 ff. ; Schrader, *De
Alexandri M. vitae tempore* (Bonn, 1889); Kohn, *Ephemerides rerum
ab Alexandro M. in partibus orientis gestarum* (Bonn, 1890); and the
histories of Thirlwall, Grote, A. Holm, and B. Niese.

(B.) The disposition of events within those *termini*, more especially during those parts of the years 330–327 which the Grand Army spent between the Caspian and the Indus.

A.

On the cardinal dates I do not differ materially from the resultant of the views of Unger and Schrader, accepted in essence by Kuhn, and based largely on an observation concerning the Olympic periods communicated by H. Nissen to the *Rheinisches Museum* in 1885 (vol. xl. pp. 350 ff.); and I should not discuss those dates here at all if it were not that the latest views are not very well known or accessible, and that the second matter, viz. the disposition of events between the cardinal points (*v. infra*, B.), can hardly be expounded clearly except in sequence to a preliminary statement of the *termini*.

There can be no serious question as to the total duration of either Alexander's life or his reign. These are stated by Arrian (vii. 28) on the express authority of Aristobulus, the most trustworthy contemporary and companion of the Emperor, as

> LIFE . . . . 32 years, 8 months.
> REIGN . . . . . . 12 years, 8 months.

By consequence, Alexander must have been just about 20 years of age at his Accession, as indeed he is explicitly stated to have been by Arrian (i. 1) and Plutarch (*Alex.* 11).

It is to be noted, before we pass on, that the month-numeral in this passage of Arrian is the less possibly erroneous, since it is repeated — καὶ τοὺς ὀκτὼ μῆνας — and since Diodorus, the only other surviving authority (except Eusebius,[1] whose numerals are both corrupt and contradictory) who attempts precision, varies only by one month (xvii. 117).[2]

---

[1] Like Clement of Alexandria, who quotes from Eratosthenes, Eusebius in one passage gives a round number of *twelve* years, and divides it into equal halves by the death of Darius.

[2] The fact that only *eight* years are assigned to Alexander's reign *in Egypt* cannot be made much use of in the absence of certainty as to the

Within what precise yearly and monthly points, however, do these periods of Alexander's life and reign lie ? It is obvious that any one of these three cardinal points, if certainly ascertained, will serve to fix the others.

Fortunately, though there are no eclipses to help us, two of the points can be connected with that great standby of chronologists of antiquity — the Olympic Games. Plutarch, in a well-known synchronistic passage (*Alex*. 3), and again in *Consol. ad Apoll.* 6 (if that treatise be Plutarch's), mentions that Philip received at the same time, under the walls of Potidaea, news of the birth of his son, of a successful battle in Illyria against the northern hillmen, and of the victory of his team at Olympia. There is no reason to question the main fact of this synchronism, for Greek memory was tenacious of nothing so much as Olympic records. The three announcements may be taken to have arrived near enough to one another for the new-born babe, as Schrader acutely observes, to be reputed ever afterwards " The child of two victories. "

The *year* of birth, therefore, being a multiple of four, can be no other than 356, unless the whole system of Greek chronology, as at present accepted, is to be thrown overboard. For in 360 Philip was hardly yet seated on his throne ; in 352 he was certainly not besieging Potidaea. Furthermore, we know that Eratosthenes fixed Philip's murder to Olympiad cxi. 1, *i. e.* 336–335, at which time Alexander was about twenty years of age. Any one of the surviving express statements of Eratosthenes is held rightly to be weighty evidence, and for all practical purposes we may safely follow it, and, counting back twenty years, fix 356 as the year of Alexander's birth.

The *month* raises the more difficult question. According

date from which that computation starts — whether, in fact, from Alexander's first entry into the country, or his coming to Memphis, or his foundation of Alexandria, or his second coming to Memphis, when he settled the system of government. The actual entry into Egypt may have been made any time from October (Unger, *Chron. des Manetho*) to December, 332.

to Aristobulus' statement, we must reckon thirty-two years
and eight months to Alexander's death. Now there are some
independent grounds for believing that the Emperor died not
before the summer of the year. There is a not very sure
allusion in Quintus Curtius (x. 10. 31) to the heat prevailing
at the time; there is a more sound argument to be deduced
from the fact that whereas Alexander was still in or about
Hamadan in winter-time (for the snows lay deep in the
Cossaean mountains during his campaign there), he had still
to accomplish the march to Babylon and there to do great
works of reorganization and preparation, which were completed ere his death. But even more consideration is to
be attached to a probability that Alexander, about to sail
by way of the Persian Gulf into the Indian Ocean, must
have taken the *monsoons* into account. Two years earlier
he had based his calculations for Nearchus' voyage upon the
seasons of those winds, and since that voyage he must have
become still better informed of them and more convinced
of their influence. He would time his start so as at least
to avoid the *south-west monsoon*, if not immediately to get
the benefit of the *north-east monsoon* on emerging from the
Gulf, and as the latter wind begins to blow in November,[1] if we
make the most liberal allowance possible for the voyage down
the Shatt-el-Arab, with all the initial delays concomitant with
so large an expedition, and for the coasting voyage and
conquest of the littoral of Arabia on the west of the Gulf
as far as Ras Mussendom, we can hardly set the projected
start farther back than the very end of May.

If Aristobulus' eight odd months are reckoned backwards
from such a date, we find ourselves in the early autumn, and
must place Alexander's birthday in October. How will this
month accord, however, with the coincidence of his birth
and the Olympic Games? The latter usually have been

---

[1] See a valuable note in General Haig's *Indus Delta* (1894), p. 16.
The *south-west monsoon*, according to General Haig, ceases in September,
so that Alexander might have timed himself to start west during the
interval of calm. See *infra*, p. 294.

supposed to have opened with the first full moon after the summer solstice,[1] and the gap between the news of an Olympic victory in July reaching Philip (a matter of a week at most), and October is rather wide even for a Greek synchronist. In an article published in 1885,[2] however, H. Nissen drew attention to certain *scholia* on Pindar (*Ol.* iii. 35, 33) which do not square with the received view as to the month-date of the Olympic Games; and from the statements in these *scholia* he derived an Olympic cycle, in accordance with which the festival opened on dates varying over a period of two months, and in this particular year 356 began as late as September 27. This calculation, which was made without reference to any controversy concerning Alexander's life, has been adopted in principle by later inquirers,[3] and, in fact, it tallies so singularly with the necessities of Alexander's case, as well as with other points in Greek history,[4] that, personally, I have no hesitation in accepting it and fixing Alexander's birth early in October, 356.

On this reckoning, Alexander's Accession must have taken place about the same month in 336. The actual date should be placed rather earlier than later, as time has to be allowed for a military demonstration in Greece before the winter.

Alexander's Death must be dated to June, 323,[5] considerably less than a year after the Olympic festival of 324, at which (βραχεῖ χρόνῳ πρότερον τῆς τελευτῆς, Diod. xviii. 8) his

---

[1] *E. g.* by the latest historian, B. Niese, to judge by the date he assigns to Alexander's birth (*Geschichte*, p. 51). Clinton's dates are of course all based on this belief, and it forces him to add two months to Aristobulus' statement of the duration of Alexander's reign. See also A. Mommsen, *Ueber die Zeit der Olympien*, 1891, pp. 80 ff.

[2] *Cit. supra.*

[3] *E.g.* Schrader and Kohn, *opp. cit. supra.* Unger has doubts, but quotes.

[4] Cf. Nissen's article.

[5] = June 13th, according to German chronologists (Unger, Kohn), while the birthday = October 3rd. But Schrader is surely right in abstaining from such precise dating, which can only rest on the unsound month-computations of ancient chroniclers, *e. g.* the pseudo-Callisthenes! (Unger.) The old views about the death-date are to be found in Ideler, *Todesjahr*, etc.

Decree concerning political exiles was promulgated. This dating makes it possible and probable that the Greek embassies which came to Alexander on his road towards and arrival at Babylon, were concerned with that Decree.

B.

It will be observed that I have taken no account of precise statements by Plutarch or others as to the actual Attic or Macedonian months in which any of the events discussed above took place; and, following Droysen in his criticism of Ideler (*l.c.*),[1] I should recommend a like reserve as to all the month-dates given for intermediate events by Arrian,[2] or Plutarch.[3] The grounds of such reserve are, that (*a*) those recorded in the *Macedonian* calendar cannot be fixed at present with any adequate certainty on the extremely scanty and conflicting *data* which we have as to that calendar, its synchronisms and its adjustments, in the period of Alexander — *data* which acquire no greater precision by comparison with another most dubious system, the Egyptian of Ptolemaic times (see Unger, *op. cit.* p. 776); (*b*) those month-dates that are recorded in terms of the *Attic* calendar have been converted from the Macedonian on a system or systems which are unknown to us, and, in face of the utter inconsistency of, *e. g.* Plutarch's adjustments (*v.* Droysen, *l.c.*), they cannot be relied on for a moment. There is also one doubtful month-date given in the *Julian* calendar by Justin[4] (= Trogus Pompeius), viz. *mense Junio*, for Alexander's death. This, though probably correct, we will ignore likewise and on the same grounds, the more readily

[1] Cf. also Kohn, *op. cit.* pp. 6 ff. But Niese uses the month-dates freely.

[2] *Anab.* ii. 11, Issus ; 24, fall of Tyre ; iii. 7, passage of Euphrates ; 15, Arbela ; 22, death of Darius ; v. 19, battle of Hydaspes ; *Ind.* 21, start of Nearchus.

[3] *Alex.* 16, Granicus ; *Camill.* 19, Arbela.

[4] xii. 16. The synchronistic passage in Ælian (*V. H.* ii. 25) is not worthy of serious consideration.

since the reading of the manuscripts is subject to the variants *mensem unum* and *mense uno.*

I will venture, therefore, in dealing with events in Alexander's life between the fixed *termini*, to proceed rather upon a Thucydidean system of summers and winters, checked by certain definite records of the duration of particular enterprises. We have one astronomical fixed date in the first half of Alexander's reign, namely, the *lunar eclipse* which preceded by a few days the battle of Arbela. This has been calculated for the night of September 20–21, 331.[1] Plutarch states that the camps were pitched in sight of each other for the first time on the eleventh day after that eclipse; and thus we arrive with sufficient certainty at October 1st as the date of the actual battle.

Neither before Arbela nor after it until the death of Darius, is there any serious question of chronology. The last-named event took place in the course of the year succeeding Arbela, and it can be calculated within very narrow limits of error from the fixed date of that battle. We have to allow for —

March to Babylon, at least 40 days[2]		
Halt in Babylon . . . 34 "	(Curt. v. 1 ; Just. xi. 14)[3]	
March to Susa . . . . 20 "	(Arr. iii. 16)	
Stay in Susa . . . . *x* "		

---

[1] Doubts have been raised about these eclipse computations ; but I am assured by astronomers that they are practically subject to no doubt. This particular eclipse is the first in history for which we have recorded observations in more than one place. See G. Hofman, *Sonnen- und Mondfinsternisse,* p. 28 ; Oppolzer, *Canon der Finsternisse,* p. 338 ; and Ideler, *Handbuch der Chronologie,* i. 347.

[2] Murray's *Guidebook to Asiatic Turkey* (new ed. 1895) gives eighty-two hours from Mosul to Baghdad, and sixteen from Baghdad to Babylon. This is equivalent to about three hundred miles. To march this distance, about thirty days are necessary, and ten more must be added for halts, crossing of Tigris, etc.

[3] Q. Curtius may be used where rhetoric and romance do not come in. The remarkable coincidence of his work with Justin's Epitome suggests that Trogus Pompeius himself, rather than Greek chroniclers, is the foundation of Curtius' history.

March to Persepolis . .	30	days [1]	
Stay in Persis	120	"	(Plut. Alex. 27) [2]
March to Ecbatana . .	12 + x	"	(Arr. iii. 19)
Stay in Ecbatana . . .	x	"	
March to Rhagae . . .	11	"	(Arr. iii. 20)
Stay in Rhagae . . .	5	"	(Arr. iii. 20)
Last stages of the pursuit	5	"	(Arr. iii. 21)

Total 277 + x days.

The death of Darius, therefore, took place near Shahrud, about the three hundredth day after Arbela, i. e. *at the very end of July or beginning of August*, 330. This, as it happens, coincides, according to received computation, with Arrian's statement (iii. 22) that the month of the murder was the Attic *Hecatombaeon*.

Alexander gave up further pursuit of the satraps, and returned to pick up his stragglers and heavy column somewhere near Semnun. The events, therefore, of Alexander's latter years have to be fitted in time and place between two points fixed chronologically and geographically : —

Early August, 330. Semnun.
Early June, 323. Babylon.

The period within these limits is portioned out less satisfactorily and with less certainty than the first half of Alexander's reign, largely because the scene of action was for the most part geographically so little known to his chroniclers. [3] In considering this period, we must call in geography to help chronology, and chronology to help geography.

---

[1] It is to be borne in mind that Alexander was interfered with on this march, first by the Uxians, secondly, and more seriously, by Ariobarzanes. The distance is about 4,200 stades. Curtius (v. 4. 18) states that Persis was already under deep snow.

[2] Curtius (v. 6. 21) gives details of a winter campaign in the hills of Persis, lasting thirty days. This fact is confirmed by Arr. *Ind.* 40.

[3] Perhaps also because the most learned and orderly of the contemporary chronicles, that of Callisthenes, ended with Darius' death, or shortly after that event. The author was put in chains in Bactria early in 327, and executed not long afterwards.

Sure results cannot be hoped for where the site of hardly a single town mentioned by the chroniclers is known beyond question, and before really satisfactory study can be made of the subject the exploring scholar must go through Central Asia. In the mean time we can perhaps show what is possible or what impossible, and the boundaries of our ignorance.

We are often left in so much uncertainty about the exact line of Alexander's marches in the far East, and so seldom are told the duration of his halts,[1] that it would be perfectly futile to attempt to calculate his progress by the method employed above to determine the date of the death of Darius. But in the course of these years we have certain facts recorded as to times and seasons, which, proceeding from actual observation of eye-witnesses,[2] may be set forth and used as a base, although one far from assured : —

(*a.*) Alexander marched through the Paropamisadae ὑπὸ πλειάδος δύσιν, hills and passes being blocked with snow. He kept the high range of Hindu Kush on his left hand, and wintered below the mountains, having India to his right hand, and built a city. Thence he crossed the chain, and in fifteen days from his winter quarters reached Adrapsa in Bactria (Strabo, pp. 724–5).

(*b.*) When Alexander was on the Jaxartes (Sir Daria) it was high summer. The watercourse at Cyropolis was dry (Arr. iv. 3), and terrible heat was experienced during the raid across the river (ibid. iv. 4).

(*c.*) The army left the Paropamisadae μετὰ δυσμὰς πληιάδων, and was in Khond and Chitral in winter time (Aristobulus, *ap. Strabon.* p. 691).

(*d.*) The Indus was crossed obviously when not in flood, *i.e.* before spring was far advanced.

---

[1] I am obliged to ignore Curtius in this connection, since he never gives his authorities. Not but what he often enough squares with facts, as F. v. Schwarz sufficiently shows (*A. d. G. Feldzüge in Turkestan, passim.*)

[2] *Ex hypothesi* I ignore the few month-dates that are given us ; *v. supra.*

(*c.*) The army " went down " into India at the beginning
of spring (Aristobulus, *l.c.*).

(*f.*) Rains began after the army left Taxila (Aristobul.
l.c.).   The *Jhelum* is represented as running 1200 yards
broad when the army reached it, ἦν γὰρ ὥρα ἔτους ᾗ
μετὰ τροπὰς μάλιστα ἐν θέρει τρέπεται ὁ ἥλιος (*Arr.*
v. 9).

(*g.*) Some section of the army was encamped near the
bank of the *Chenab* κατὰ θερινὰς τροπάς (Nearchus, *ap.*
Strab. p. 692).

(*h.*) The rains continued all along the march to the *Sutlej*
and back to the Jhelum, with etesian winds (= south-
west monsoon) (Aristobul. *l.c.*).

(*i.*) The flotilla started down the Jhelum, πρὸ δύσεως
πλημάδος οὐ πολλαῖς ἡμέραις, and in fine weather.   It
arrived in the district of Pattala, περὶ κυνὸς ἐπιτολήν,
after ten months' voyage.[1]   It had experienced no rainy
weather, but the Indus was in full flood.   The summer
monsoons were still blowing out at sea (Aristobul. *l.c.*).

(*j.*) Nearchus, one month after Alexander had left for
Oritis, started κατὰ πλειάδος ἐπιτολὴν ἑσπερίαν, the monsoons not yet being favourable (Nearchus, *ap. Strabon.*
p. 721).   In the end he had to lie to for twenty-four
days in the interval between the summer and winter
monsoons (Arr. *Ind.* 21).

(*k.*) The voyage of Nearchus took, as nearly as can be
calculated from the itinerary in Arrian's *Indica, eighty*
days in all, up to Harmozia on the Persian Gulf, near
which place Alexander had arrived already.

(*l.*) Alexander's Decree for the Amnesty of Exiles was read
at an Olympic festival ; this must fall in late summer, 324.
The Decree must have been despatched from Asia at
least four months before.   It seems probable, therefore,
that Alexander was back in the west of his empire

---

[1] Five months, Pliny, *N. H.* vi. 60, and seven months, Plut. *Alex.* 66.
Perhaps Plutarch is reckoning time of actual sailing only, exclusive of halts.

by April, 324. (Diod. xviii. 8; Dinarch. *in Dem.* 100. 28.)

(*m.*) When Alexander was raiding the Cossaean hillmen near Ecbatana, there was much snow. He had celebrated the Dionysia before this at Ecbatana. If this festival corresponded to the Athenian usage, as is probable, it must have been held in October.

(*n.*) When Alexander was in the marshes near Babylon, inspecting the *Pallacopas* canal, it would seem as though the early spring floods were over, and he was in a position to see the damage they had done.

If these *data* are taken as check-points, it will be observed that three years are satisfactorily accounted for. From point (*c*), when the army is in the Cabul basin, to point (*l*), when it is in Persis or Susiana, there is no serious gap. At the period of the setting of the Pleiads (middle of November) in a certain year, Alexander was still near Cabul;[1] in the succeeding months of winter he prosecuted his Khond and Chitral campaign, and crossed the Indus in very early spring of the following year, before the high snows had melted. He left Taxila just as the rains began (*i. e.* in April), and was on the Jhelum when that river was already considerably swollen, as is the case in May. There a delay ensued owing to the difficulty of forcing the passage against Porus, and the actual battle of the Hydaspes was not fought till about midsummer. The distance from the Jhelum to the bank of the Chenab is so small (hardly above forty miles on this line) that there is really no difficulty about points (*f*) and (*g*), allowance being made for a little laxity in statements

---

[1] Four or five months seems a long time for Alexander to have delayed in the Cabul district. But it must be remembered that not only had he to reconstitute *Alexandria ad Caucasum* (Arr. iv. 22. 5), but, apparently, to found or refound several other cities (cf. Diod. xvii. 83, and Pliny, *N. H.* vi. 23, 92). Among the latter was probably the original Cabul itself. *Ortospana*, now renamed *Nicæa*. Among new foundations were perhaps Pliny's *Cartana* and *Cadrusi*, and Stephen of Byzantium's 5th Alexandria, ἐν τῇ Ὀπιανῇ κατὰ τὴν Ἰνδικήν, which General Cunningham would identify with the modern Afghan village of *Opian*.

made (as Droysen acutely remarks) merely to explain the rise of the rivers, not to fix dates. The forward march to the Sutlej and the return to the Jhelum would fall easily within the latter Rains. After a halt to prepare for the voyage, the start of the river flotilla took place a few days before the setting of the Pleiads (*i.e.* early in November). The final docking of the fleet at the apex of the Delta of the Indus was at the flood time, about the rising of the dog star and during the prevalence of the monsoons at sea. This period suits well enough with August. Nearchus started about the evening rising of the Pleiads in the interval between the monsoons.[1] According to the calculations of Förster, given by Droysen (p. 794), the Pleiads rose at the Indus mouth in this year on October 12th. I cannot agree with Droysen that merely *conventional* mean risings and settings of the Pleiads are intended in these astronomical quotations from Alexander's generals. These statements are far more likely to be based on actual observations recorded at the time by Aristobulus and Nearchus, and good for the particular latitudes and longitudes in which the observers happened to be. In countries where the seasons were very different to those of their home, the strangers would naturally have turned for guidance to familiar stars and have observed their risings and settings precisely enough. The winter monsoons begin to blow ordinarily in the Indian Ocean in November.

---

[1] There is a difficulty here. Gen. Haig (note *cit.* p. 286) who knows Sindh well, says, "The violence of the south-west monsoon is past by the middle of August, and a month later the wind drops almost entirely." The period at which, according to the reckoning given above, Nearchus started, is invariably the calmest in the whole year. Yet twenty-four days' continuous gales were experienced. If Aristobulus' statement as to the duration of the river voyage (*ten* months), and the astronomical coincidences, are not to be rejected, these storms must be set down as an extraordinary occurrence. If the astronomical coincidences are thrown overboard, then we might reckon with Plutarch the voyage at *seven* months, bring Alexander to Pattala in June, and date the start of Nearchus to July, and his arrival in the Persian Gulf to October. The chronology of the rest of the three years would hardly be affected in any case.

The reckoning deduced from the *Indica*[1] brings Nearchus to Harmozia about the New Year, and Alexander to Persis and Susiana easily enough by the middle of spring.

As Alexander came south through Hindu Kush after a spring campaign in Bactria, we can date his passage to the summer of a certain year, and thence until full spring or summer three years later his movements can be traced sufficiently well both in time and place.

Indeed there is not much more doubt for the remainder of the time up to Alexander's death. The Emperor went northwards in the late summer, marched up to Ecbatana in fifty days,[2] and spent autumn and early winter there, raiding the Cossaean hillmen after Hephaestion's death. He came to Babylon early in the succeeding year, 323, and died in June.

Therefore we can now reckon back from the *fixed date, June*, 323, without interruption through four years, and establish the fact that *Alexander recrossed Hindu Kush in the summer of 327.*

There remain three years reckoned back to the end of July, 330, within which fall the conquest of Hyrcania (Mazenderan), the march through Khorasan, northern Seistan, and Afghanistan, to the passes of Hindu Kush above Cabul; the passage of that great range; the advance to Balkh, thence to the Oxus, and thence to the Sir Daria; the protracted conquest of all Turkestan south thereof, and the return to the neighbourhood of Cabul.

In this period, if we omit, for the moment, all reference to Arrian, Diodorus, or Curtius, we have for chronological guides only the statement of Aristobulus, quoted by Strabo, that part of the Afghan march was made about November, and the inference about the season at which the army was on the Sir Daria, quoted above on p. 291 (*a.*) (*b.*).

Chronologists have agreed to fix the arrival of Alexander

---

1 See Vincent, *Voyage of Nearchus*, p. 340 and previous.
2 Diod. xvii. 110.

at Hindu Kush to December, 330, have brought him to
the Sir Daria in the summer of 329, and have allowed the
balance of that year, all the year succeeding, and the following spring of 327, for the conquest of Turkestan.[1]

There is, however, a most grave objection to this disposition
of events, and one of which not nearly enough account has
been taken. The distance from Zadracarta (near Sari, on the
Caspian littoral), where Alexander resumed his advance after
overrunning Mazenderan, to the foot of Hindu Kush north
of Cabul by way of northern Seistan and Candahar, *is at
least* 1300 *miles.* The stages by the great caravan route are
in round numbers as follows : —

Sari to Shahrud	at least	100	miles
Shahrud to Meshed	over	300	"
Meshed to Herat	about	220	"
Herat to Candahar by the great road[2] . .	about	330	"
Candahar to Hindu Kush north of Cabul .	about	350	"

1300 miles

Now the death of Darius cannot have taken place before
the very end of July, 330 (" *non ante X Aug.,* " Kohn, *op. cit.*
p. 9). After that event Alexander retraced some stages of
his route, collected his forces, crossed the Elburz chain, over-
ran all Mazenderan, apparently pushing westwards towards
Resht, and finally halted for fifteen days at Zadracarta. It is
hardly conceivable therefore that he can have resumed the
main Advance before the beginning of October at the very
earliest. How, then, can he have been in the " land of the
Paropamisadae," *i.e.* at nearest, the mountains between
Candahar and Cabul, by any part of November of that same
year? The thing becomes even more impossible when we
recall that, after leaving Meshed, he went some way on the
direct road to Balkh before being recalled to Aria by news

---

[1] Such is still Niese's view in 1893 (*Geschichte,* p. 113).
[2] Alexander almost certainly did not take a direct route, but deflected considerably to the south into northern Seistan.

of its revolt; that he fought a short campaign there and prosecuted a siege of Artacoana; that he founded a great colony near Herat; that he made a halt among the "Evergetae," according to one authority (Curtius) of not less than sixty days, and that there, or wherever "Prophthasia" may have been, the whole affair of the Treason Trials was transacted; that he founded three more great colonies in the region of Candahar;[1] and finally that he had a most difficult

[1] Cf. the statement as to Alexander's eastern foundations made on p. 228. That statement is intended to imply nothing more precise than that Alexander founded cities in the *districts* in which certain important modern towns now stand. It is not implied that Herat, Farrah, Candahar, Ghazni, Cabul, or Khojend, are placed actually on Alexandrian foundations, for there is, as yet, not a tittle of evidence to prove that. But the East is prone *stare super antiquas vias*, and the natural conditions which direct the course of roads remain the same. These take the same easy valleys and passes and make for the same oases now as of old, and their points of bifurcation will not vary greatly. For example, there can be practically no question that Darius fled eastwards along a great road, which had long been in existence, and that the same conditions, the Elburz Range and the deserts, keep the same track still in use as the main highway: Teheran has but succeeded to Rhagae, Meshed to Susia. Similarly, as Alexander was advancing at first from Meshed by a great route to Balkh, which skirts south of the deserts of Merv, so, on hearing of the defection of Aria, he turned south to Herat, and thereafter followed the already existing high-road to India. This, in Sultan Baber's time, led from Khorasan "by way of Candahar," and was "a straight, level road, not going through any hill-passes" (*Memoirs*, Eng. tr. Leyden and Erskine, p. 140); and the main caravan route is still the same at this day. It runs south from Herat, skirts the north of Seistan, passing Farrah to Candahar, and thence turns north-eastward to Ghazni and Cabul. In the record of Alexander's march over this line, we hear of the foundation of five colonies at least.

(i.) Of the first — *Alexandria of the Arians* — we are told by Pliny (*N. H.* vi. 17. 23) that it was situated on the River Arius and in the road to India, and by Strabo (p. 723) that it was the point of bifurcation for the direct road to Ortospana (Cabul) and the ordinary route to Drangiana (Seistan). This last fact tells so strongly for the site, or at least district, of HERAT, that, added to the very probable identification of the names *Arius* and *Heri-rud*, it amounts almost to certainty; and we need not invoke the doubtful aid of modern local tradition, which, indeed, ascribes almost every old town east of Euphrates, as far as the Chinese border, to Alexander. The new Alexandria cannot have been far removed from the old Artacoana,

country to traverse between Candahar and Cabul! A year rather than three months is required for a march of 1300 miles with such delays and under such conditions.

and was, perhaps, founded in the same district to fulfil the same function towards caravan trade, and to be a check on the native capital.

A statement of Ammianus, however (xxiii. 6. 39), that this colony was connected by water with the Caspian, and only fifteen hundred stades distant from that sea, raises a question. The *Heri-rud* now loses itself in the sands at least two hundred miles before the Caspian Sea, and Herat is about thrice fifteen hundred stades from the nearest point of the latter's coast. The great changes of course, to which rivers in this region are notoriously subject (*e. g.* the Oxus, now debouching in the Aral Sea, once flowed to the Caspian), might be taken to obviate the first difficulty, and an easy corruption of numerals to explain the second. But I suspect that really Ammianus is confounding a distinct city with the better known Herat foundation, and that his Alexandria was situated, perhaps, on the River Ochus (Atrek?). In Roman times, and, indeed, down to our own day, the geography of the remote Khorasan region was very little known, and confusions are the rule. Another *Alexandria* or *Alexandropolis* is referred to by Pliny (*N. H.* vi. 25), and marked on the Peutinger Table much nearer the Caspian than Herat, and in the region of *Nicaea*, which seems, from Strabo's account (p. 511), to have been on the edge of the northern desert and in the basin of the Ochus. I would suggest that this Alexandria was somewhere about Kushan, and on the Atrek, and that it is confounded by Ammianus with Alexandria of the Arians.

(ii.) The double authority of the author of the treatise *De Fort. Alexandri* (5) and of Stephen of Byzantium (*s. v.* Φράδα) represents *Prophthasia* as a foundation, or rather re-foundation, of Alexander's. The latter, in mentioning that its earlier name was Φράδα, seems to imply that that name survived the re-foundation; and, if that be so, it is most tempting to look for it still in FARRAH of Seistan. Such reversions to earlier native names are characteristic of Asia from the Indus to the Aegean. The only difficulty (for Alexander certainly passed by or near Farrah) lies in statements as to the distance of Prophthasia from Alexandria of the Arians. The ancient authorities (Pliny and Strabo, quoting Eratosthenes) represent these cities to have been a little less than two hundred miles apart. From Herat to Farrah is about a hundred and fifty miles. The ancient reckoning seems to have been made, however, from Alexander's march, and is therefore subject to an error of excess. In any case, Prophthasia is in Seistan; and partly in the north of that region, partly, perhaps, farther south in the Helmund valley, I should place Alexander's wintering 330–329. (On Seistan, in mediaeval times, see Sharaf-al-din 'Ali Yazdi's History of Timur, in the English translation (1723) of Peter de la Croix's version, ch. 43, ff. In modern times Gen.

Compared to this march the distances traversed by
Alexander north of Hindu Kush are nothing. From the

Goldsmid has described its remains in *Journ. of R. G. S.*, 1874, p.
167 ff.).

(iii.) The Afghan colonies are a most difficult problem, to which I can
contribute nothing beyond what is set forth by Droysen (vol. ii. App. iii.
pp. 674 ff.). It may be there are *three* foundations to be placed in the
Candahar region; it may be only *two*, for Isidorus' first *Alexandria*, near
"*Sigal*, the royal city of the Sakae," is, perhaps, no other than a western
name for Phrada-Prophthasia in northern Seistan.

In the Cabul region there was one very famous foundation — *Alexandria
ad Paropamisum* — which seems to have come to be widely known in
the East as *Alessada*, capital of the *Yona*, or Ionians, and to have
been "missionized" by Asoka. We know it to have been situated at the
foot of Hindu Kush (Arr. iii. 28. 4; iv. 22. 5; Diod. xvii. 83; Curt. vii.
3, 23), and to have been some distance north of Ortospana (Cabul) (Pliny,
N. H. vi. 17). It was not, however, the only foundation or re-foundation in this region (*vide* note, p. 293); nor is there one site only in the
Cabul district where Hellenistic remains have been found. Alexander
evidently attached great importance to the southern keys of the seven gates
through Hindu Kush (cf. *Memoirs of Baber*, Eng. tr. pp. 139 ff.), and
occupied several points, not only Beghram and Charikar or Opian,
but the Bala Hissar as well. Which of the many ancient sites in this
region represent which of Alexander's foundations, and, indeed, which
represent Hellenistic towns at all, we have yet to learn. A material
advance in knowledge can be made only through careful exploration by
some one thoroughly conversant with Hellenistic remains. Nothing proves
this more conclusively than F. von Schwarz's book on Alexander in
Turkestan, already quoted. The author has travelled all over Trans-
oxiana, but, owing to his want of archaeological knowledge, or concealment
of it, he fails to satisfy us about a single site. His work is useful for
roads, passes, and distances, but fixes no points. Nor is any service
rendered by mere multiplication and complication of conjectures by those
who have not visited the sites themselves. Droysen has collected the
data of ancient authorities; Wilson (*Ariana Antiqua*, ch. iii.) and Cunningham (*Ancient Geog. of India*, pp. 16 ff.) have said as much as can
be said usefully about the modern sites by those who are not Hellenistic
experts. We can only sit down and wait for changes in the political
frontiers of Asia and for the exploring scholar.

It seems, however, not too much to assert even now that all the great
road-centres from Herat to Hindu Kush by way of the Helmund valley
and Candahar, were appropriated by Alexander. We have fair evidence
for the fact of his colonizing the districts of Herat and Farrah, and
even better evidence for that of Cabul. Between these points we have
to fit in two cities at least, in all reasonable probability situated on

main chain to Balkh, and thence to the limit of the Advance, is not more than 400 miles in all, and it must be noted that the subsequent Sogdian campaigns were fought within an area much less extensive, *i.e.* in just the country between the Oxus and the Saravshan River. There is nothing in those campaigns, as recorded by Arrian or Curtius, to necessitate an allowance of longer time than a spring, a summer, an autumn, and a spring.

Let us suggest, therefore, that the Advance to the Hindu Kush occupied, not three months, but *fourteen or fifteen*, and that the Army came through the " land of the Paropamisadae " in November, 329; further that it reached the Sir Daria in the early summer of 328, spent the rest of that summer, the autumn, and part of the winter in crushing the Revolt, and the spring of 327 in subduing the last of the hill fortresses — where lies the difficulty? Not in Strabo, of course, nor in the induction drawn above as to the season of the advance to the Sir Daria; but in objections derived not only from statements of Arrian, but from his silence.

To take the last objection first. If a winter halt was made anywhere on the Advance to Cabul, Arrian gives no indication of it. The force of this objection, however, is almost wholly discounted by the fact that *no more does Arrian mention the winter halt at the foot of Hindu Kush.* The fact of that halt we learn simply from Strabo. Arrian, for his part, implies quite as clearly that the Advance was continuous from Zadracarta to the Sir Daria, as from Zadracarta to Hindu Kush.

The other objection is the more serious. Arrian (*Anab.* iv. 1 ff.), after relating the advance from Balkh to Maracanda and the Sir Daria, the suppression of the first Revolt, the demonstration across the Sir Daria, the disaster to the Macedonian square in the desert, and Alexander's vindictive campaign against Spitamenes, brings the Emperor back over

the great road, which has not changed ; and there arises a strong presumption that their sites are represented with little change by CANDAHAR and KELAT-I-GHILZAI, or GHAZNI.

the Oxus to *Zariaspa*, where " he remained, ἔστε παρελθεῖν
τὸ ἀκμαῖον τοῦ χειμῶνος " (c. 7). Here occurred the punishment of Bessus, the death of Clitus, and a visit from a
Scythian embassy. Thereafter Arrian relates (but without
mentioning the coming of spring, as more usually is his
custom) that Alexander recrossed the Oxus, and prosecuted
a second campaign in Sogdiana, again visiting Maracanda;
but he gives almost no details at all, filling up chapter 17
with an account of a diversion made by Spitamenes in the
rear ; and in chapter 18 he states that the victorious marshal
rejoined his Emperor at Nautaca, where the main army was
reposing, ὅτι περὶ ἀκμαῖον τοῦ χειμῶνος ἦν. Presently on
the approach of spring — ἅμα τῷ ἦρι ὑποφαίνοντι — Alexander
moved from Nautaca, conducted a hill campaign against the
rock fortresses which still held out, married Roxana, recrossed
the Oxus to Balkh, where occurred the affairs of the
Prostration and the Pages' conspiracy, and towards the end
of spring — ἐξήκοντος ἤδη τοῦ ἦρος — marched south for the
Hindu Kush and India.

Now all the last part of this narration refers beyond doubt
to the spring of 327, and it should be observed, in order that
the small size of the area of operations may be realized, how
much is done there in a period unquestionably not longer
than three months. Does the earlier part of the narration,
however, up to the halt at Nautaca, refer to *one* year or to *two ?*
It has been usually inferred that two years are meant,
and that the winters alluded to in connection with Zariaspa
and Nautaca are distinct seasons.

It will be remarked, however, by every reader of Arrian,
that in that case their author, for some not obvious reason,
has dealt most perfunctorily with the second of the two
years. Alexander's own operations during the long period
of a twelvemonth occupy but a few lines at the opening
of chapter 16, and a few words in the middle of chapter 17,
and are related absolutely without detail. The rest of these
two chapters is devoted to contemporaneous operations of
marshals in command of other columns or of garrisons. If

Arrian really intended to convey the idea that this is the
history of a whole year, he has dealt with it as he deals, in
the *Anabasis*, with the history of no other year before or
after. In short, he leaves 328 without further comment
than a brief account of not important operations, prosecuted
over an area less than 200 miles by 150.

Curtius (vii. 4 ff.), the only other ancient authority we
have for the details of this period (for there is a *lacuna* in
the manuscripts of Diodorus covering the whole Bactrian
expedition), relates the incidents of the first march to the
Sir Daria, of the Revolt, etc., substantially as Arrian does;
and also, like Arrian, he brings Alexander back again over
the Oxus, but to Bactra, not Zariaspa.[1] There Bessus is
punished; but we hear nothing of Clitus yet, nor of the
Scythian embassy; and, without any indication of a long halt,
we are told that the Army, having received reinforcements,
took the field again, and in four days was back at the Oxus.
A campaign against hill-forts and the like in Sogdiana
follows; and Alexander, after visiting Bazira, comes to
Maracanda, and there, at last, occurs the Clitus affair. The
halt there is represented as but short (not much above fifteen
days), and Hephaestion is sent back across the Oxus *com-*
meatus in hiemem paraturum; but Alexander himself retired
no further than Nautaca. Here he spent two months and
tertio mense ex hibernis movit exercitum (cap. 4). A campaign
against hill-forts, the affairs of the Prostration and the Pages,
and the advance to India follow in due course.

There are, in this account, certain additions to Arrian's
narrative, and two discrepancies with it, one grave, namely,
that with regard to the locality of the murder of Clitus. The
chief points, however, are confirmatory, and the main stream
of events is not inconsistent with Arrian's; but we gain a
clear impression that, while the halt after the first return to

---

[1] See, on the identity of these places, Droysen, ii. Fr. tr. p. 679.
F. von Schwarz (p. 65) maintains a contrary view. For him Zariaspa =
Tschardschui, on the road from Merv to Bokhara. But see note, *supra*,
p. 299.

Bactra was very brief, that at Nautaca involved a distinct wintering.

The heads of Diodorus' narrative (which survive in an index to his seventeenth book) serve to confirm Arrian and Curtius in their common statement that Alexander returned, after the first revolt, to the Bactrian bank of the Oxus. They further imply but a short halt there, and proceed to support Curtius with regard to Bazira (called Βάσιστοι) and his localization of the Clitus affair. Thereafter Alexander goes to Nautaca, and a campaign follows in a season of heavy snow, as is the case in Curtius' narrative. With the marriage of Roxana, and the march southwards to India, we reach the summer.

The sole serious chronological *crux*, then, in these authorities consists in Arrian's two distinct allusions to winter. When we remember, however, how small is the area of operations, and how long the winter of Turkestan, it seems far from impossible that *both allusions refer to the same winter.* The phrase, ἀκμαῖον τοῦ χειμῶνος, in both cases can easily enough mean, " full winter-time, " and be applied equally to December or to February. These two allusions, as we have seen, are not divided by any mention of *spring*, nor, indeed, by any account of protracted operations. All that is required by the words of Arrian and Curtius is that Alexander should have returned to Balkh about November of his first year in Turkestan, left it again in December, recrossed the Oxus, marched rapidly towards Bokhara, turned east to Samarcand, and finally come to a halt early in February at Nautaca (Karshi, or Shahrisab). Thence, intending himself to remain *two months* (Curt. *l.c.*), he seems to have despatched some part of his army under Coenus, to pass the remainder of the winter at Balkh (Arr. iv. 17), where Hephaestion had already prepared supplies (Curt. *l.c.*). Alexander resumed operations against the hill-forts early in April, and thereafter there is plenty of time for him to be in Balkh by the middle of May, and to start for the Hindu Kush again ere the end of that month.

On the one side, therefore, must be set a slight confusion or vagueness of terms in a not contemporary chronicler, due possibly to the failure of his best-ordered authority, Callisthenes; on the other, there is a most glaring geographical difficulty, not to be got over if we accept, on the one hand, the eclipse date for Arbela, on the other, Strabo's statement that a winter was passed just north of Cabul. I have myself no hesitation in bowing to the geographical difficulty, and *allowing fourteen months for the march from the Caspian to Cabul.*

Nor am I in this view without the positive support of an ancient chronologist. Diodorus, in the chapters which precede the *lacuna* in his seventeenth book, begins an Attic year after the murder of Darius (ch. 74) and ends it just as Alexander is about to enter the land of the Paropamisadae (ch. 82). This is to say, that in Diodorus' view the first winter after the Caspian had been left was spent in Drangiana, and not until the following *July* did the Army march northwards from Candahar. And this view I have little hesitation in maintaining to be absolutely correct. The place, where the winter of 330 was passed, was Seistan, and Curtius' sixty days among the Evergetae perhaps represent accurately enough the duration of the longest halt, that, namely, in the Helmund valley

The following table will serve to sum up the conclusions arrived at in this discussion : —

Alexander born	early October	356
" succeeds Philip	September or October	336
" wins Arbela	October 1st	331 .
" overtakes Darius	first days of August	330
" leaves Zadracarta	October	"
" halts for winter in Seistan	December	"
" resumes advance	spring	329
" reaches Candahar	summer	"
" reaches Cabul	November	"
" takes up winter-quarters at the foot of Hindu Kush	December	"
" passes Hindu Kush	early spring	328
" reaches Sir Daria	June	"

INDEX

THE END.

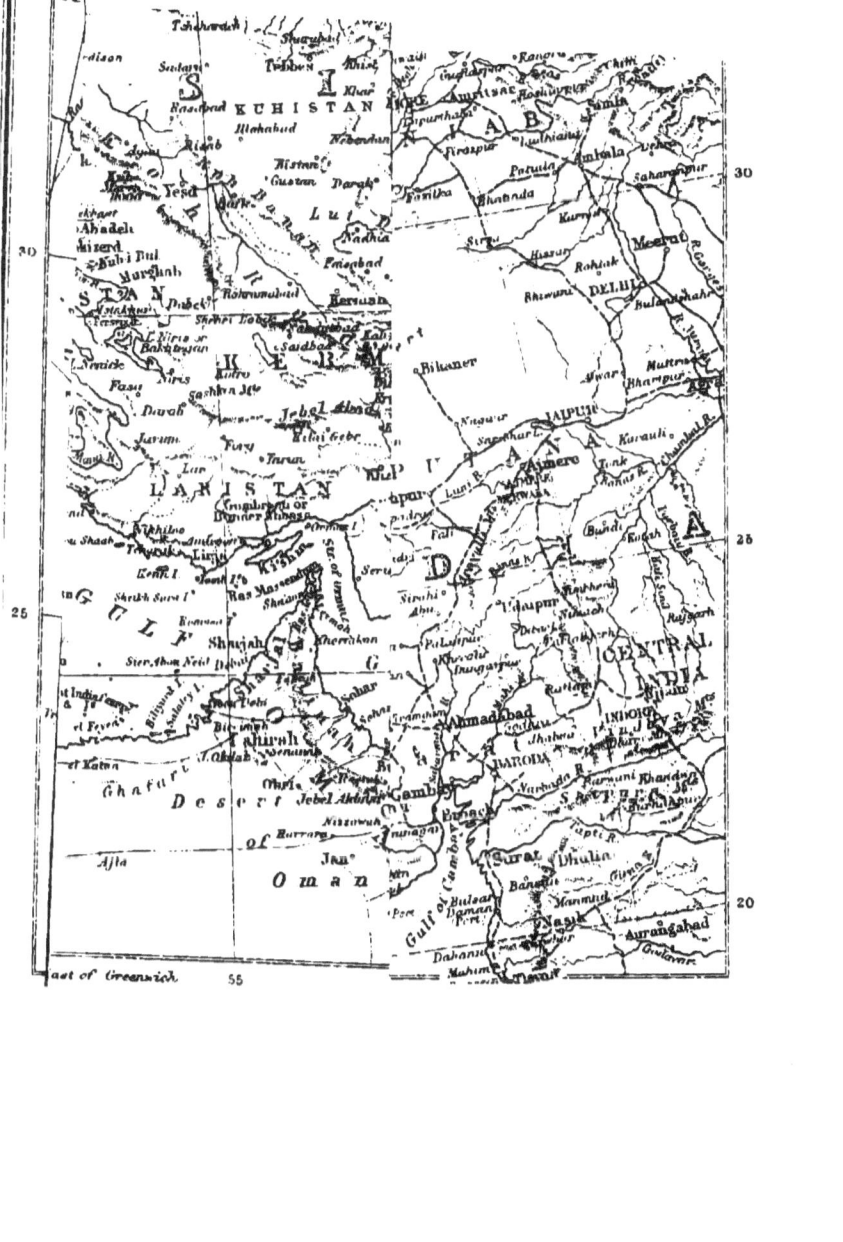